COINCIDENTAL EVIDENCE -

THE WATER KILLER STORY

A Novel by

Harold (Mernie) Budde

Copyright 2019 by Harold Merwin Budde Productions

Dear Becky,

Thank you for buying my book. I hope you enjoy it. Take care

Melissa Buckle

P.S. I always liked Amy better than you. ☺

All Rights Reserved

This book may not be reproduced or transmitted in any form without the written permission of the author and publisher. It is not legal to reproduce, duplicate, or transmit any part of this work in either electronic or printed format. Recording of this publication is expressly prohibited. For permission requests, email the publisher at :

HMBudde2012@gmail.com

Contents

Dedication
Prologue – 25 Years Ago
Chapter One – Present Day - 25 years later
Chapter Two
Chapter Three
Chapter Four
Chapter Five
Chapter Six
Chapter Seven
Chapter Eight
Chapter Nine
Chapter Ten

Chapter Eleven
Chapter Twelve
Chapter Thirteen
Chapter Fourteen
Chapter Fifteen
Chapter Sixteen
Chapter Seventeen
Chapter Eighteen
Chapter Nineteen
Chapter Twenty
Chapter Twenty-One
Chapter Twenty-Two
Chapter Twenty - Three
Chapter Twenty – Four
Chapter Twenty - Five
Chapter Twenty - Six
Chapter Twenty - Seven
Chapter Twenty-Eight
Chapter Twenty - Nine
Chapter Thirty – Chandler – 4:46 PM
Chapter Thirty – One – Bixby and Little - 4:47 PM
Chapter Thirty – Two – Abigail Granger – 5:14 PM
Chapter Thirty - Three – Bixby and Little – 5:19 PM
Chapter Thirty – Four - Chandler – 5:21 PM
Chapter Thirty – Five – Granger – 5:38 PM
Chapter Thirty – Six – Chandler – 5:43 PM
Chapter Thirty – Seven - Bixby and Little – 5:46 PM
Chapter Thirty-Eight – Chandler – 6:09 PM
Chapter Thirty – Nine - Bixby and Little – 6:43 PM
Chapter Forty – Elvin McCormack – 7:04 PM
Chapter Forty – One – Chandler – 8:13 PM
Chapter Forty – Two – Bixby and Little – 8:16 PM
Chapter Forty – Three – Chandler – 8:24 PM
Chapter Forty - Four
Chapter Forty – Five - Three Years Later
Chapter Forty-Six
Chapter Forty-Seven
Epilogue

Acknowledgements

DEDICATION

Over the years, many of my friends and colleagues have been euphemistically "let go" from their jobs, involuntarily parting ways from companies after many years of loyal service before they could leave on their own terms. Most of them were told of their impending departures during a meeting with someone similar to the character described in this work of fiction.

You probably thought that person was crazy to let you go. Turns out, you may have been right.

May all of you land exactly where you need to be, and never look back.

PROLOGUE – 25 YEARS AGO

My grandmother was sleeping, as she often did in the afternoon. She seemed very peaceful as I approached with a pillow from the side chair we kept in the room when we wanted to sit with her. My mom spent lots of nights in that chair, not intending to sleep through until morning, but often waking to daylight. The pillow helped her get as comfortable as possible in a chair never intended to be slept in.

Back then people did not have the advantage of being able to Google something to get a quick answer. The question of how long you have to smother someone with a pillow until they suffocate went unanswered. I figured five minutes, but I had no idea how long it really took before her afternoon nap became permanent sleep. After I knew she was no longer breathing, I returned the pillow to the chair and went to the living room to watch TV, waiting for my mom to get home.

I have killed many people in my lifetime. Many plus one if you count my grandmother. I guess she would count. I'm not sure why she wouldn't.

I'll start with my grandmother. I was fourteen at the time. She was 87 and fast approaching the end of her life. My mother went grocery shopping and forced me to stay home with her to keep an eye on her. I wanted to go to my friend's house and play video games, and she told me I needed to stay with my grandmother for a few hours while she went to the store. In retrospect, my mother got almost no time to herself, and her mother demanded so much of her. I'm sure the trip to the store was one of the only breaks she ever got anymore. Yeah, I could be a little selfish back then. But who wasn't as a teenager?

Being forced to stay home made me very angry, although I did not show it. Instead I just smiled my fake smile and nodded. No need for confrontation since I knew what I would be doing.

My grandmother had been lost in her own world for several years since my grandfather died. Her dementia had become so pronounced that she was losing control of even her basic bodily functions. My mother steadfastly refused to put her in a nursing home, and while my father worked at the post office, she stayed home to care for her mother. During the summer and after school, the responsibility fell to me when she needed to run errands. And, looking back, I am sure she needed at least one break once a day, and probably deserved far more.

Not that I cared when I was a teenager. I saw it as a punishment and I grew to see my grandmother as an unacceptable burden who was ruining my formative years. I could not hang out with my friends and be cool because of her, and for this I was resentful.

My mother would be gone for at least two hours. I made my way into what had once been my game room. Now it held a hospital bed, my grandmother, and all of her medications. It seemed like every surface in the room held a bottle of something she needed to take at various points throughout the day and night. Do not even get me started on the smell. My friends would not come to my house anymore of it.

I still have dreams about the sensation of watching her life slowly drain from her eyes. Even in her confused and addled state, I think she understood what was happening and thanked me for it. Her body seemed to resist just for an instant, then it relaxed and a calm came over her. I was the instrument that delivered her to a better place. For me, I was filled with an indescribable elation and a desire to do it again and again.

I heard the hum and vibration of the garage door opener as I watched whatever was cool for kids to watch back then. I did not rush out to help my mom with groceries as that would show that something was not right. Even at age fourteen I knew how to avoid raising suspicion.

"Craig, honey, can you help me with the groceries?"

"Just as soon as there's a commercial." We lacked the technology to pause television back then. How did we live?

"Now, honey. I have things that need to get in the freezer right away."

"Fine." I pushed myself off the couch with a heavy sigh to let her know just how much of an inconvenience it was to help her. This was in character and true to my usual ways.

"How is your grandmother?"

"Great, I think that new medication is really wiping her out though. She's been asleep the whole time you were gone. I checked on her like three times and she was sound asleep." I grabbed a bag of various cuts of beef and pork chops and headed to the basement freezer.

My mom sounded mildly perturbed. "If she sleeps all afternoon it will be hard to get her to sleep tonight. I need to wake her up." Inexplicably, she carried a bag of groceries down the hall with her to the bedroom on our main floor.

I was calmly putting the family size hamburger, carefully double-wrapped in the store plastic bags by my mom, into the chest freezer when I heard the sound of several cans hitting the floor. I ran upstairs and my mother was already in tears, realizing that her mother was gone.

My summer was much improved after that afternoon. I mean, the wake and the funeral were a drag, but then things got way better.

CHAPTER ONE – PRESENT DAY - 25 YEARS LATER

Working at home and trying to find a job starts out slowly. All of your friends and former colleagues are very enthusiastic about helping you "land" again. "Land" is code for getting a new job. I remember the first day of the rest of my life well. My former employer has graciously agreed to pay my full salary plus benefits for twelve months after they engaged in a reduction in force and a departmental restructuring. I know, the irony of the director who specializes in reduction of force implementations is himself the victim of a reduction in force. But, being paid to do nothing for up to a year seems like a dream come true for some people, and at the beginning, it seems like that to me as well. I mean, how hard can it be for a man of my skillset, engaging personality, and team player tendencies to land again?

I spend the first morning getting my office arranged. My wife Jennifer works as a senior marketer for a smaller company about 25 minutes from our house. She started working again when our youngest started school full time. Despite my reassurances that I will be working again soon, she worries all the time. She worries so the rest of us don't have to worry.

I love my wife. We have a good marriage with two daughters who make us proud. That statement will seem unlikely once you get to know more about me, but it is true. I have been told that I out-punted my coverage when the former Jennifer Sales agreed to marry me. And they are right. A beautiful and vivacious brunette with hazel eyes, she has been my soul mate for our 18 years of marriage. When she is not working, keeping the house in order, or getting the kids to their events on time, she is jogging on the treadmill or working out at the local facility. If she weighs more than the night we met at that dorm party our sophomore year I do not see it. I am within twenty pounds of my college weight, but hey, I was awfully skinny back then. One of my resolutions during my down time is to start a serious exercise regimen that includes increased biking and lifting weights again.

The way my severance agreement works is if I work again for my old company I will not collect any severance. If I work for another company, I will get paid by both, a concept known unofficially as "double dipping." I assure Jennifer over and over again that my intent is to double dip and show my former employer that they have done the wrong thing in letting me go. It will be the ultimate revenge; they pay me their full allotment of severance plus benefits while I make the same or more with another company.

My first pass at organizing the office complete, I now look at my computer. It is something we bought for the kids before everyone needed their own tablet and smartphone. Heavily used at first, it now sits in the extra bedroom on the main level and is getting close to becoming a conversation piece. As in, "Remember when this was the only way to access the internet?" I start out by deleting unnecessary programs and anything that detracts from my computer's new status as my 'find a new job' computer. I drop the toolbars and extensions because they cause the computer to run more slowly. I delete Facebook accounts, remove stored passwords, remove games

I have never heard of, and compress data to improve performance. I guess that makes me sound like I am some sort of computer geek, but in reality, I have just had to clean up after my girls as they rampaged through our electronics for many years. Call me a practical geek technician with his family as his only client.

I spend most of the morning modifying the computer to meet my new job searching needs. By most of the morning, I mean that I realize at about 10:30 AM that I need a snack, so I go to the kitchen to forage for something sweet, and then something salty. After eating, I return to the computer and continue to pare down the stuff clogging its memory, and then I get hungry again.

I am feeling a little sluggish after I eat the lasagna leftovers from three nights ago, so I grab a drink and take it with me to the office. I notice that my desk, really a table that used to be in our breakfast nook, is not yet organized to my standards and I start moving things around again. Why is there never a waste basket in the room? I go out to the garage and grab one that is too large, but will do for now. And, I grab a basket for recycling as well. I am very conscious about the environment. While in the garage, I realize that I have not put my tools away properly after a weekend project, so I spend a few moments putting them in order.

Before I realize what is happening, I hear the bus rolling down the street of our neighborhood. I turn my cell phone over and realize that it is close to 3 PM and my children will be in the house within seconds. Where has the day gone?

We have two daughters. Mallory is 15 and almost ready to take the driver's test and begin driving. She is tall for her age, and very thin, much like her mother. They share the same hair color and high cheekbones. Angela, almost 13, is average height with hair more like my dishwater blonde. Both girls have hazel eyes like Jennifer. The sisters have a fragile truce that allows them to coexist in the same house, but with teenage girls anything can cause a dust-up to occur.

Mallory hates that she and her sister have to ride the bus together every day. She keeps careful track of Craigslist ads and wants to pull over whenever she sees a car for sale on the side of the road. Jennifer and I tell her that we will add a third car if her grades stay up and she shows she needs the car for something other than avoiding riding the bus to school every day with her sister.

"With your dad not working," Jennifer tells her repeatedly, "we do not need a third car. That is just not a priority."

We have learned from friends that giving a teenager their own car gives them a new level of freedom on your dime, and that freedom must be metered out in small doses with strict supervision. Grades, once a priority, often slip while the family gas expense and insurance rates soar.

The girls, most days not speaking to one another, still manage to make a significant amount of noise, enough that I have to walk to the kitchen and ask them to quiet down. Angela is watching "Grey's Anatomy" on her tablet with the volume on high, and Mallory is texting furiously on her cell while talking. Normally, a sister is the last person another teenager sister will share with when something happens at school, but in a manner only understood by these two participants, they seem to communicate pretty well.

"Hey Dad, find a job yet?" Angela has always been very close with me, but I expect that to change as she gets older. Mallory will only put up with me until she gets her car. Until then, she remains angry at me that her friends get treated better than her and have their own cars all lined up when they pass their driving tests.

"Not today, honey. Got lots of stuff done, though." I hope she does not press the issue since I really have accomplished nothing tangible. "Please keep it down in here because I need to be able to focus. They say finding work is a full-time job, and I have a few more hours that I need to put in today."

Angela turns down the volume on her tablet while Mallory turns away and grabs a banana. The silence is restored as I make my way back to the office.

After sifting through my severance package materials from my former employer, and sadly realizing that they kept several people busy throughout the year creating some excellent content, it begins to dawn on me that my old company really does not want me back. After all I have done for them? I feel my ego beginning to deflate, and I experience a moment of anxiety. "Am I going to be out of work forever? Is 39 too old to move on and start over?" Thoughts race for a few moments, and I take a deep breath. Big obstacles must be encountered head on and in small, manageable pieces. And, that is exactly what I am going to do. Tomorrow.

I spend the rest of my first day straightening the drawers and the cabinets in my office. No more excuses – everything is set up exactly as I need it. I will encounter no more road blocks, there are no more reasons to be distracted. Tomorrow the job search begins in earnest. Bet your bottom dollar. Tomorrow.

When Jennifer gets home, she sorts through the mail and comes to the office to see me. I am busy on the computer poring over a job site. Before I heard the garage door open, of course, I was reading about musky fishing in Canada and researching whether someone new to the sport should borrow or rent equipment, or if it is best to buy it for themselves. I conclude that I need to buy equipment, but not top of the line, since my salary is only guaranteed for another twelve months. A boat, what kind of boat will I need? I hastily close that browser window and reopen my LinkedIn home page and wait for Jennifer to come in the office.

Jennifer kisses me on the cheek and I hug her somewhat awkwardly from my desk chair. Another thing I now realize is that I will need a more comfortable desk chair. The current one squeaks and my butt is numb from sitting in it all day.

"How was your first day of job searching?" she asks.

"It was great." I lie. "I set up my profiles on several job search sites, and I applied for three jobs."

"I hope you're keeping track of the jobs you apply for," she rubs my shoulder as she talks. My shoulders and neck are tense and respond to her massaging technique.

"Of course, I have a tracking spreadsheet." I mean, I intend to build a dandy spreadsheet. Right after I apply for those three jobs. Tomorrow.

"You know," she continues, ramping up the massaging efforts as she finds a knot in my right shoulder. "I have a friend at work whose husband lost his job. She says it took him three years to find something, and it was not in the same line of work. They had to sell their house and move in with her parents because he was unemployed for so long."

"I'm sure I will not take three years to find something," I reassure her. "I will be working by the end of the month. Two at the outside."

"But what if you don't find something?"

I often have found that the best way to handle situations like this is to change the subject. "I put the steaks in the refrigerator to defrost just like you asked. Want me to fire up the grill?"

Jennifer shrugs her shoulders in agreement and leaves the room. I do not need to hear about some dude who was out of work for three years and moved in with his in-laws. That's a kick in the gut I do not need right now.

Dinner that night is upbeat and engaging. Our family dinner tradition is to go around the table and each person tells something good about their day. While it may seem trite and banal, once we got started doing it, we all miss it when activities and work get in the way.

The next morning, I am up with everyone else. Jennifer left earlier for her workout at Lifetime Fitness while I get the girls off to school. Getting two teenage girls on the bus in the morning is not like TV. I do not make pancakes and fresh-squeezed orange juice and invite them down for a joyous family gathering before handing them lunch boxes and affectionately patting their heads as they stroll down the driveway to the waiting bus. Instead, it is like trying to wrestle with a crocodile that has you in its mouth.

A trip upstairs to knock on their doors, listening to groans and promises that they are already up and getting ready. Then, five minutes later, back upstairs to repeat the same process. When they finally do get out of bed, I have to walk in and see that they are indeed up and getting ready. Note for tomorrow, if I do not see them on their feet it means nothing. They each grab a snack bar and dash out the door, promising to eat something better when they get to school. I am too annoyed to disagree. If things get tighter around the house they will need to eat at home and not deplete their food accounts at school. For today, however, I am glad to have it quiet again.

Back in front of my older, slow computer again, reviewing my resume. I have always kept my resume up to date as I made my way through my career. I had a boss once tell me that you are always interviewing for your next job, which I took to mean always be on your best behavior and if someone expresses interest, be ready with a recent resume to present them.

Job search sites and the placement firms recommend having multiple versions of your resume prepared for different opportunities. If I want executive level Human Resources, I need a resume that makes it seem like I have a multitude of experience there. If it is more of a sales or marketing opportunity, some tweaks are in order. I start with what I consider to be my base, go-to resume and save it. I click to print it because I want to see what it looks like on paper. The printer makes a beeping sound that indicates that it is out of paper. Oh no, we're out of paper.

Several minutes of searching follow. No luck. I need a trip to the store for paper and some other office supplies since this office will be my temporary workplace for the foreseeable future.

When in the midst of a life-changing event, such as a gap in employment, it is important to build a support team. These are the people who can assist whenever something is needed within their purview. I can see someone helping me with my hair as I prepare for an important interview, a clothes consultant for the same, an exercise buddy to keep me moving, and an electronics/office supply person to keep the home office operational. Today I need the electronics/office supply person. Thus, a trip to Target or Wal-Mart for cheaper copy paper is economically sound but will not support my bigger need to build out my support team. I need to head to Staples for Max, Max Depot, or Home Depot for Office. I can never keep the names straight, but at least I should be able to find one relatively close to home.

CHAPTER TWO

It turns out that in this 'search and buy online' world that we now live in, office supply stores are not right around the corner anymore. When you have all the supplies you could ever need at work, you don't notice that your nearest store is now a 30-minute drive away on the border of Woodbury and Oakdale, two suburbs located east of St. Paul. That's OK, though, since it gets me out of the house after spending yesterday staring at my computer and getting little accomplished.

It's weird to drive on the freeway without a significant time crunch during the work week. You move along in traffic but you do not feel the urge to force your speed on others. Driving becomes, for me at least, a social experiment and not an annoyance that must be endured to reach a destination. Ahead I see a sign indicating road construction and the requirement that two lanes of traffic merge to one lane in less than a mile.

Minnesota has long been deemed a "Nice" state by other states. It means we citizens are polite and courteous in our interactions with others. This is especially true, I believe, in how we drive in construction zones. If traffic is needed to move to one lane due to road construction, we lemmings pull over immediately into the remaining lane and patiently wait our turn. This is how we all share the load and the inconvenience.

The Zipper Merge started with an advertising campaign by the State of Minnesota to change how drivers handled reductions in lanes during road construction, and to alleviate some of the frustration of long lines of stalled traffic. In order to best accommodate the volume of vehicles, both lanes need to be used until the last possible moment, and then each car in their respective lane moves move forward in a neat, alternating fashion. One car, each lane, combining together like the teeth of a zipper joining. It seems like a reasonable solution.

You could not ask for a better milieu to observe how the Zipper Merge plays out in reality. An angry driver pulls in front of the ending lane well before the electronic arrows signal its end and forces several cars to pull into the continuing lane early, backing up traffic even more. This is done amidst many horns honking repeatedly. In this case the driver is in a gray Toyota Camry. I would identify it further but what's the point? Every sedan made looks about the same, and gray is about as drab and unnoticeable as it gets. Maybe this guy's problem is that his life is so dreary that the only thing that makes it worthwhile is fixing the perceived rude behavior of fellow drivers attempting to Zipper Merge?

I took some psychology and sociology courses in college – wait, perhaps this is a second career I should consider? Because this traffic jam is now taking forever, I find myself plotting out the details of my future while cars slowly make their way to the continuing lane. No, let's return to the excitement playing out in front of me.

There is a Subaru Outback with Wisconsin plates that makes the most aggressive move yet. He decelerates fast in order to avoid running into the back of the Camry blocking the ending lane. He honks his horn aggressively and gestures angrily while yelling at his windshield. This lasts for a few seconds before the Subaru darts onto the shoulder and squeezes by the Camry and accelerates briefly before reaching the end of the lane. Foiled, the Camry driver moves farther left into the ending lane so that no one gets the bright idea that the shoulder can be used to get around his self-created roadblock.

The crisis in Zipper Merge compliance ends and traffic slowly makes its way over the bridge that is reduced to single lane traffic. Modern load leveling tactics that would reduce wait times in construction zones suffers a setback on this day.

Far faster than the traffic manipulation starts it is over, and the two lanes open up again. I get to a spot where traffic returns to normal and I accelerate with no cars in front of me. Time to let my Lexus sedan do its thing.

The Lexus represents a splurge after a particularly good annual management bonus. Depending on your position in upper management your decision to buy a new car with your annual bonus every spring can range from Chevrolet to Tesla, from practical to full-on mid-life crisis appeasement. My wife and I decided that since I drove farther to work I deserved a more comfortable car, while she would stick with the kid-mover SUV. Not that she loses too much comfort in a Honda Pilot, but at moments like these when I punch the accelerator, there is no doubt that my Lexus is the better car.

My car appreciates the chance to show off for me as I quickly go from very slow to very fast. Not 'State Troopers laying tack strips across the highway to flatten my tires' fast, but let's just say it felt good to be alive and driving a Lexus. I am the poster child for driving satisfaction.

It seems like a moment in time that will go on for hours, but it is really just a few seconds. The reverie is lost when the same Subaru Outback from before the construction zone pulls in front of me, slows down perceptibly, and starts tapping his brakes. How did he go from way ahead of me to behind me? Ah, the mysteries of traffic. I check my mirrors, signal, and start to pass him in the right lane. As soon as I do, he pulls in front of me again. I try to return to the left passing lane. He does the same. He will not allow me to pass him in either lane.

As my anger grows, his driver side window lowers and he puts his left arm out the window and gives me the finger. I have no idea why he is doing that. I avoided eye contact when he was angry at the Camry and he pulled around it on the shoulder. He now sticks his head out the window and glares at me while gesturing even more animatedly. I am not sure how he can stay in his lane and glare at me out of the window, but, somehow, he manages.

It dawns on me after he puts his head back inside the Outback that he thinks I am the Camry driver from before. The curse of the nondescript gray sedan bites me. I am not sure how to communicate to this nimrod that I easily paid twice as much for my Lexus as the Camry owner paid for his, and that he has exacted revenge on the wrong enemy. The moment of exhilaration has definitely passed.

Because we created distance between our cars and the others who made their way through the construction, I am able to keep an eye on the Outback. Who in this world deserves to be shamed by someone driving a Subaru? That's a short list for sure. Take another bite from your organic granola bar and shackle yourself to a maple, tree hugger. Don't shame the wrong people for breaching Zipper Merge protocol. Say, does that J Bar on the top of your car hold two kayaks? Groovy, dude.

My exit is approaching in another mile. I am emotionally drained from the recent excitement, and starting to refocus on my errands. But, then I see the Outback pulling off on the same exit ramp as mine. I start to run a mental checklist of typical Subaru destinations. Whole Foods, Trader Joe's, REI, Granolas-R-Us? Where is he headed? Toner and paper can wait – this is way too intriguing to let go just yet. I am now hoping that he will go to a place that carries the office supplies I need. Who needs to be loyal to a store when you can tail the jerk who flipped you off just a few moments ago?

Imagine my disappointment when he pulls into the Cub Foods parking lot, like the one place that does not carry what I need. Still curious and maybe realizing I have nothing but time these days, I also pull in and hang in the periphery as he parks. The Subaru makes its way to the part of the lot closest to the store. Mr. Outback pulls in and parks in a spot reserved for pregnant or new mothers. He jumps out of the car and heads into the store.

I stop my car and look on in horror and disbelief. Road rager and a parking lot cheater as well? Is there anything this guy won't do to irritate me? I formulate a plan of response.

The first thing I do is pull up behind the Subaru to get the license plate number. In today's world you take a picture of it on your smart phone and go to Google. There is probably an app that makes it even easier.

I begin to realize that it is time to take a deep breath and let this incident go. I need to complete my errand. Somewhat reluctantly, I turn the car around, drive out of the parking lot, and cross over at the light to the office supply store.

As I said, online shopping is slowly squeezing the life out of traditional stores like this office supply store. As an example, I offer the fact that I stand alone in the store that morning. Two cashiers do not even look up from whatever they are doing over by the checkout lanes. A third employee seems to be stacking and restacking something over to my right. I try not to judge, instead reminding myself that in a few short months I might be wearing a red vest with a name tag and also trying to look busy enough to avoid having to interact with customers. Just how far will the mighty fall?

"Good morning, sir. What can I help you find today?" The young woman exudes an energy that I have never possessed at any point in my life. Janelle, according to her name tag, seems beyond eager to please.

"I need high quality paper and toner cartridges for my HP printer," I reply.

"Well, you certainly came to the right place today, sir. Let me show you our paper first because that's closer to the front of the store. We have several big sales this week for our loyalty club members. Are you in our loyalty program? If not, we can take care of that at checkout. With these savings, it's a no-brainer."

Janelle seems a bit deflated when I let her know I am not currently a loyalty program member. "How do you look in the mirror in the morning knowing that you are not getting our weekly ads and flash sales sent directly to your email or to your smart phone, or even better, both?" That's not really what she says, but is probably what she's thinking.

I let her know that not too long ago someone did all of my printing and office supply shopping, so I am just now entering into the game. Janelle, bless her overly-exuberant heart, decides I need a primer on how paper is graded based on weight, thickness, and matte or gloss finish. To think I just wanted to pick up 500 sheets of paper suitable for printing my resumes and cover letters? What a dope I am. I can hardly wait to learn about toner cartridges. Three 500 sheet packages later, one high quality and two for everyday printing (buy one, get one 50% off with loyalty club enrollment), cheerfully carried by Janelle, and we are on our way to printer cartridges.

I am surprised that Janelle directs me to only the HP cartridges and I ask why. She explains that the fail rate of substitute toner cartridges is too high to recommend to customers. "We stand behind our store brands of course, but why go through the hassle of having to return one that the printer does not recognize when for a few dollars more you can get one that works for sure? You're a busy man with no time for that kind of aggravation." Hard to argue with the logic, especially with the 50% off of the second cartridge that I am certainly going to need for the amount of printing I will now be doing. I leave the store with everything I need as well as a new resource. Janelle is my electronics and office supplies teammate.

As I leave, Janelle assures me I will have no trouble finding another job because I am so smart and analytical. Based on the money I just spent I find that hard to believe. Based on the money I just saved as a new loyalty program member I figure she is probably right. I am being smart and analytical about how smart and analytical I am. That is high-level smart and analytical.

This is where it gets even more interesting. This young and attractive woman puts her cell phone number into my phone contacts using the name "Toner Babe" with a kissing emoji added in. Is this because she wants to sell me more high gloss sheet paper? Or toner? And, she lets me know that she has her lunch break at 11:30 and there is a great pub in the same shopping complex that has booths with tall backs. "No one knows who's in the place. Even the servers sometimes forget they have customers," she laughs and winks at me in the same gesture.

Given her exotic look and her obvious interest, it is even easier for me to conclude that I will in fact see her again. I am guessing she pushes the loyalty club membership to get more personal information about customers who draw her interest.

I am not one to consider a lunch rendezvous with every young woman who flirts with me. There is plenty of opportunity when you are a reasonably good-looking former executive interested in such things. Amidst long business trips with colleagues, celebrating a successful meeting, or while commiserating over an unsuccessful meeting, when you indulge in that third Manhattan when you always stop at one at home, things happen.

Driving home, my thoughts turn from Janelle and the next time I might see her, to 20-pound paper with a super gloss finish, and toner cartridges, and finally, to the Subaru driver who flipped me off on the freeway. I return to plotting my revenge scheme.

Once I am home the printer is filled with paper, and the cartridge is replaced. With these tasks accomplished, I turn to a more introspective view of my life. I mentioned before that I took some psychology classes in college. I have friends who believe that people who take psychology classes do so to diagnose themselves. Not a terrible theory at all.

My personal belief is that I have a narcissistic disorder on some spectrum and maybe dissociative indicators as well. Oh, and let's not forget the rage. I have never sought out professional help. Given my personality, it should be obvious why I don't see it as a problem at all. I feel like I thrive just the way I am, my current job search notwithstanding.

I have never done more than a Google search about my self-diagnosis. What I learned is that I am high-functioning, meaning that my disorder actually drives my success in life rather than holds it back, and that there are lots of people who share my disorder. Sure, many of us are in prison for scary violent crimes, but hey, they got caught. "Use your power for good, mostly your own good", says the narcissist in me. And, "never talk about it with anyone" says the dissociative side of me. Instead, I watch my life and events unfold in front of me without engaging or interacting. I view the world as if I am holding a camera and filming it. A younger employee whom I let go, even if he just had his first child, is an emotionally – charged scene, but not one that affects me in any real way.

This is the first time I have ever revealed this about myself. I guess that should be a cathartic event; mostly it makes me feel vulnerable and worried that I will be revealed and it will limit my future success. To protect myself and this information, I immediately create a new password to access my computer and set a reminder for two weeks to change it again. No one may ever know of this secret.

Back to the task at hand, my printer is now cranking out Windows test pages with supreme colors and blacks that leap off the page. Let the productivity begin!

CHAPTER THREE

The next morning. I sit down to update a rough draft of my resume. Before I know it, it is lunch time. The leftovers from dinner last night would be great right about now, so I head to the kitchen for food. We have a rule in our house that eating must be done in the kitchen and dining room area, except for special occasions, such as popcorn for movie night or drinks while working out. Working out, that reminds me that I should establish a workout routine pronto or else I will gain weight and not present well at my soon to be scheduled interviews. How about a bike ride? Leaving now gets me back to the house when the bus lets the girls off. I quickly change into my biking clothes, grab my earphones, and link to the Van Halen station on iHeartradio. I lift my bike down from the hook in the garage.

A few seconds with the air compressor and my tires are topped off and I am pedaling efficiently down the road, heading towards the multi-use trails laid out for miles around me.

My bike, a high-end racing bike assembled for me at a local shop, is light, nimble, and absorbs every bump along the way. The hardest part for me is to remember that I have only 90 minutes to ride and that I have to stop and start heading home seemingly as soon as I start. Under my helmet my wireless sports earphones crank out "Jump", then "Hot for Teacher", then "Right Now", and then "Lights" by Journey.

Wait a minute. Why would iHeartradio play a Journey song if I selected the Van Halen station? If I want Journey it seems like I would select the Journey station. By the way, give me old Van Halen back when David Lee Roth still had a voice over the pseudo-intellectualism from Hagar. Right now, I am wishing it was a DLR VH song. Tomorrow I will create a playlist on my phone and listen to my music instead of letting iHeartradio choose it for me.

By the time I am circle back and my internal monologue continues to complain about Night Ranger being on a Van Halen station, I am struck by a random thought. What am I going to do about that jerk who flipped me off? I have his license plate captured on my phone. Time to teach the Subaru Scumbag a lesson. As my brain begins to formulate a plan, I see the exit path off of the main trail I ride. Sadly, I must get home and hop in the shower before the post-school invasion begins in the house again.

I am back in my office shortly before the home incursion begins with the slam of the door. A heated argument is ongoing about where one sister sat on the bus in relation to the other. One felt slighted because she did not sit next to her while the other refuses to consider doing it as it would destroy her status with a boy who also rides the bus but never looks over at her. My head is spinning trying to keep up with the logic and direction of the discourse. Then I get annoyed because my wife and I constantly correct our daughters about the use of the word "like" for no reason other than as a spacer word before you say something worthwhile. It's like, you know, like, a crutch. I am disheartened to hear them reverting to this unconscious habit when we are not around.

"Girls," I shout. "Please keep the noise down. I'm trying to work in here."

Without a word of apology, the din lessens. At a level that I am not supposed to be able to hear, Mallory smirk-talks to her younger sister, "If he wants it quiet, why doesn't he like close his door?"

"Is it really work when you've been laid off?" Angela responds.

My daughters giggle in a conspiratorial fashion and the heated disagreement of seconds before is past. While comforting to know that unkind words directed at me can result in peace being restored to my fiefdom, my overall reaction is to take note of their impudence.

In general, I listen by choice, ignore much, and respond to only what interests me. In a work setting I am known as thoughtful and introspective. At home, I am accused of being withdrawn and unapproachable. In reality, I don't much care what anyone thinks about me, unless they offend me.

Music begins to blast in the kitchen and just as quickly is muted as wireless ear buds are turned on. I can smell pizza rolls in the toaster oven, and glasses clink as they are removed from the cabinet along with snack plates. I walk over and do in fact close my door.

I really should get started on my job search. I know that, but

I decide to put it off until tomorrow morning when I will have more time to dive in. I need to think about dinner in the remaining short two hours before Jennifer gets home. As I ponder my plan for the remainder of the afternoon, my chair squeaks. I need to replace my office chair or the squeaking is going to drive me mental. I recall seeing several nice-looking chairs at the office supply store. And, of course, several were on sale. A perfect excuse to return and learn more about office chairs with Janelle and maybe explore that flirtatious relationship a bit further.

My fingers are poised over the keyboard. My right hand grasps the mouse. See what's available today on LinkedIn or pursue the license plate? A job site like Indeed, or track down the jerk driver from Wisconsin? Given the time constraints, I feel like I have no choice but to delay the job search for now and instead open a browser while fumbling for the photo gallery button on my phone. I Google the letters and numbers combination from the photo taken earlier in the day.

I get hits of course, but none that are free. Tracking this jerk down is going to cost me. Is it worth $4.95 to learn the name and address of the owner of the offending Subaru? Wait, for $9.95 I can enjoy unlimited searching for the next 30 days. For $8.95 a month, twelve-month minimum, I can have unlimited access for the next year. How many license plates and other various and sundry public records searches will I need to run after today? After much debate and soul searching, and very likely because I clicked the wrong button, I can now run searches for a year. Credit card information supplied, user name and password created, email address input, and a welcome email comes to me, I can hardly wait to begin my stealthy pursuit of the Subaru driver.

If you have ever done searching using one of these paid sites, you know that what is promised in the banner ads and popups rarely makes its way to your screen after the fee is paid. I felt like I was promised ancestry information back to the pilgrims landing on Plymouth Rock, a listing of any and all real estate holdings this chump has owned for the last ten years, and his preferences in clothing. I'm kidding about the last one. He's from Wisconsin – that means he wears flannel shirts, a Packers ball cap, and Wrangler jeans. He feels a need to fit in, after all. I don't need public records searches to tell me that.

I do get the address associated with the license plate, and two other things. First, the name associated with the car is Trevor Peterson. Second, he lives in what appears to be a rural location, on 297th Street. No city in Wisconsin has 297 numbered streets. I input the address into Google Maps. Scrolling around, I learn he lives in what I will politely call an older farmhouse. I then use Google Earth for a satellite view. If I had the choice, the two outbuildings look better built and more stylish. I might live in either of them. Never mind, one of them seems to not have a roof on the west side. We Minnesotans can be cynical and judgmental about our neighbors to the east. When sober, I'm sure they do the same to us.

As I learn more about the real estate transactions in the vicinity of the house in question, and the tax base for several places, I conclude that it would be much cheaper to own property and live in Western Wisconsin. The drawback, of course, is that you would have to live in Western Wisconsin. Over the years I have known several executive types who bought sprawling and spacious spreads across the river in Wisconsin and drove farther to work but gushed about lower taxes and living in the country to raise their family. We Minnesotans would make any number of Wisconsin jokes, or something directed at the overly-rabid and always in denial Packer or Badger fans, and get lots of laughs. The rejoinder would eventually be a reminder of how many Super Bowls the Packers have won, four, and how many the Vikings have won, zero. Losing four is not the same as winning four, I am reminded frequently.

I look at the time and realize I must set aside my public records searching. Sigh. Armed with the precise intel about the 2012 Subaru Outback with tabs due in June for $87, I feel like I am ready to spring into action. One more thing catches my eye. Trevor works at a place called Allied Resources in Oakdale. He must have been on his way to or from work, or on an early lunch break, when I saw him driving to Cub Foods. I know where he lives, and now I know where he works.

Alas, I must begin preparations for dinner. I grilled out beef last night. Maybe pork tonight. Add microwave mashed potatoes and throw frozen peas in the steamer and Jennifer will think I spent the day slaving in the kitchen. I am rapidly becoming a Renaissance man. Especially when I see there is applesauce in the refrigerator.

Jennifer asks two questions as she steps into my office from the garage. The first is how my day of job searching went, and the second is why we are doing the same thing for dinner two nights in a row. "Throwing something on the grill and steaming a vegetable is not making dinner. If you're going to cook, you're going to have to actually do something besides opening packages and heating them in the microwave."

I bet the original Renaissance man did not face this level of scathing criticism. Every other guy who makes dinner is undoubtedly praised for this much effort. We may have to move to Western Wisconsin so I can get appropriate levels of credit for my efforts. There, I am sure, any effort at cooking would be met with unending praise.

Despite the criticism that my cooking is too formulaic, the girls gush over the meal. The applesauce is a huge hit. Angela even mixes her peas into the applesauce and eats her vegetables without being forced to do so. Jennifer raises her eyebrows in surprise at me. Tonight, my cooking earns me a small, wry smile from Jennifer. Conceding, I suspect, that my first few dinners have worked. If you appeal to the fussiest eater, the rest will fall in place.

Lying in bed that night, my thoughts turn inexorably to the Subaru Scumbag. I know where he lives, I know where the offending car probably is going to be both day and night. How do I exact my revenge? A plan begins to coalesce amidst my racing thoughts. Tomorrow I will take action.

The next morning, the kids off to school and the house quiet, I go out to the garage and begin organizing the items I will need for my adventure. I pack them into a small Nike duffel bag and place it in my trunk. Then it's back to the office for what I promise myself will be my most intense job search activity yet. That's not saying much, I admit, but you need at least three days to get things put in place before the heavy lifting can begin. Finding a place to land is a marathon, not a sprint.

The bad news is that I get nothing accomplished as far as my next job is concerned. The good news is that I now know that tomorrow morning I am going to take action against the Subaru Scumbag. Making tweaks to my plan takes me the rest of the afternoon. Plus, I need a few things at the store as long as I am picking up a rotisserie chicken. I freeze the second chicken after wrapping it in plastic and foil to keep it from drying out. Dinner for next week, or perhaps tomorrow depending on my laborious job search process. I also select a chuck roast for the crock pot, and a meat loaf. I look at salmon fillets but decide against it. Best to not set expectations too high too early. Get exotic and they expect exotic.

The chicken goes over well, but I realize I should have focused more on sides while grocery shopping. My wife, ever the food critic, points out that mashed potatoes and corn are both starches, and that a tossed salad with dried cranberries and pecans would be a nice complement.

Still, despite the critique, Jennifer smiles at me, "You could cut up the leftover chicken and we could have chef's salad tomorrow, or I can make chicken salad for sandwiches".

"You seem to be getting used to the lifestyle of having a live-in chef," I smile back.

"I would hardly call what you do being a chef", she smiles back even more broadly. One of the reasons I love my wife is that she is quick-witted and works well within the sarcasm spectrum, even though I am often the object of her barbs.

CHAPTER FOUR

I intend to leave the house right after the bus picks up the girls. Before I leave, however, I decide to crank out one legitimate job submission. Two hours later and it is done. Most employers require that you upload your cover letter and application to their site. The site is frequently beset with glitches, and your attempt to submit either times out or clocks interminably. Then, once it finally uploads properly, the site asks you to, in essence, repeat everything as you type in answer after answer to their rote application questions. I suspect this is part of the weeding out process.

I'm glad to be finally out the door and in the real world again. I need the release. I make my way to a small county park across the street from where Allied Resources is located. I can see the Subaru, parked on the end of a row farthest from the main entrance to the plant. From what I can gather, Allied Resources is in the electronics recycling business, meaning that they mine the metals and other recyclable materials out of things like computers and TVs. Judging from the number of employee cars in the parking lot this must be a pretty lucrative business. There is a loading dock area on the back of the building, and within the first 30 minutes there I see three large trucks drive around back for unloading. Otherwise, there does not appear to be any vehicle traffic in the front parking lot. I notice there is an unmarked entrance about 100 feet from the main entrance where several employees, either alone or in pairs, put a wooden wedge in the door and smoke cigarettes while on break. They are too far away from the Subaru to pose a threat to me.

I step out of my car while popping the latch on the trunk. I am wearing a black Nike ball cap, a black workout shirt, black nylon leggings, and cross trainer shoes. From my duffle bag I grab a seriously sharp knife with a three-inch blade and place the holder in the front zipper pocket of my leggings. I went through a fishing phase not long after we were married. My brand-new knife is about all that remains of that time.

I walk purposefully across the street and to the sidewalk that runs parallel to the building. Several pine trees, the sides facing the street showing burn signs from road salt kicked up from snow plows, are trimmed up about three feet off the ground, but still provide some cover. As I pass the third one, I jump over a slight berm and increase my pace as I head towards the back of the Subaru. I crouch down below the hatchback, and remove the knife. One last glance around and, seeing nothing, I plunge the knife to its hilt on the sidewall and pull it towards me, leaving a six-inch gash in the tire. I crawl to the passenger front tire and repeat. This is fun. I contemplate modifying my plan and getting the other two tires, but I talk myself out of it due to being exposed. I sheath the knife and walk back to my car with as much nonchalance as I can muster. Once in the car, I have to start it up and drive for several minutes as the adrenaline pulses through me. I am beyond exhilarated. I am smacking the steering wheel and whooping all the way to a Holiday station, where I gas up and buy some drinks and snacks. I need to hang around to see the reaction on the face of the Trevor when he leaves work for lunch.

Just about the time I am beginning to regret buying the large water, lamenting a classic rookie surveillance mistake, the main doors to Allied Resources open up and workers begin leaving in clumps for lunch. I recognize Trevor Peterson. He is walking with two other workers, all laughing and smiling at once. Just another day at the recycling factory.

Peterson looks quizzically at his car as he gets within a few feet of the driver door. He calls for his co-workers to come over and take a look. I can see that he is agitated as he strikes the hood of his car and starts looking around to see who did it. He quickly realizes that this is not a work prank. His friends mill around and attempt to calm him. Peterson pulls out his cell phone, presumably to call for a wrecker. No one carries two spares, and tires that are slashed like this cannot be repaired. He is in for an expensive tow to a tire store. Satisfied that my work is done here, I slowly leave the park and join the traffic heading towards home.

I am still more than a little pumped up as I make my way through our neighborhood. I maintain a mental checklist of the things I still need to do. My black stealth clothes need to be removed and placed in the laundry basket for tomorrow's first load. The knife needs to go back in the camping / outdoor bin. The success of the first conquest makes me want to do more. And soon.

CHAPTER FIVE

The next morning, I perfunctorily look at job listings and start to wonder about Trevor Peterson. I cannot decide if he called 911 or the non-emergency number for the local authorities. Does vandalism to a car warrant a personal visit or do they take a report over the phone? Then he called his insurance agent to ask if it makes sense to file a claim for the damage on his automobile policy. I am not an agent, but I would say this amount falls below or near enough to his deductible to not make the claim. Suck it up, Trevor.

As I idly click through job postings that seem to mostly smear lipstick on the pig that is phone customer service jobs or selling life insurance, I come to a significant understanding of what makes me thrive as a human. I sought out revenge on Trevor because he was a jerk to me on the road. Perhaps I overreacted, but I feel good taking a stand for innocent drivers everywhere who are falsely singled out for minor sins on the highway. But I know I did not do this for others – I did it for me. Why don't I feel more of a sense of satisfaction?

The problem, I now realize, is that I need to see the reaction of the person I exact my revenge on much closer than from across the street in a park. That revelation is far more interesting than looking for jobs that turn out to be selling protein powders in kiosks at Costco on evenings and weekends. I need to step up my game to achieve the satisfaction I seek.

Resolutions can be good or bad things depending on if you choose to follow through on them. My resolution that morning is bold but certainly attainable – I want to see the reaction of the people when I hurt them, see it in their eyes.

As I consider my future path in crime, my thoughts turn to actually finding a job. A notice on the right side of my LinkedIn page tells me that Watson United is hiring. The same notice tells me that I have no less than six connections with people at Watson United. I decide that my best bet is Gary Salisbury. Because Gary is listed as a first connection, I am able to email him directly.

I consider LinkedIn to be a Facebook for business people, but with fewer recipe videos and food pictures. When you are working, you build your network of connections without giving it much thought. Occasionally, you get a request that you decline because it is so obviously a fishing expedition. Or, someone who is looking for work reaches out to you and you want to help them out.

Anyway, when you really need to find a job, LinkedIn does offer some tools. I find Gary's contact information in LinkedIn and send him a quick email about seeking opportunities at Watson United. I begin the email with something a tad lame like "I am not sure if you remember me, but we used to work together at …." I want to give him a chance to not reply since I have five other people with whom I can connect.

Gary fires back a response within minutes that he would love to get together and talk about Watson United. I am either quite memorable and likable, or there might be something at Watson United worth pursuing. Many jobs offer referral bonuses to the employee who brings a qualified candidate to the attention of the recruiter. I have done my share of referring over the years without ever getting the bonus, but if I am willing to do it, anyone should be willing to do it as well. I respond to Gary that we can meet for coffee early next week. In my mind, anything earlier shows I have nothing going on and I am willing to meet in 45 minutes all the way across town, and that I am desperate beyond words. I am not there yet and I do not intend to ever get there.

I text Jennifer to let her know that I have a meeting on Tuesday with the someone I used to work with who is now at Watson United. Her reply congratulates me on the opportunity. She ends the sentence with a heart emoji. I have never received a heart emoji in an email from Jennifer. I must be doing something right to achieve emoji status. I resist the urge to continue the emoji war, just thanking her instead. I do not want to overplay my hand at this point.

With Watson United and Gary set up for next week, my thoughts return to Trevor and how I will continue the war I am waging against him, or how I can and probably should move on and let it go. This may shock you, but in these types of situations I have a hard time letting things go. I start to plan out scenarios that involve finding things I could do to him that would allow me to see his reaction. Two ideas begin to compete for my attention in my clearly obsessed brain. The first involves repeating the tire puncturing at his house while I am there to see him react, but maybe get a little closer. Would his reaction upon seeing it satisfy my need to see it in his eyes? Not sure. The second involves an anonymous letter written to his Human Resources department alleging something that would need to be investigated by HR to protect the reputation of the company. Good plan, but how am I able to see it when he gets called in for a meeting with HR?

As I stare at my computer screen and plot my next move, deciding whether to research Watson United or figure out a way to go after Trevor again, I realize I am missing out on the obvious modern way to keep tabs on someone.

Inspired by the revelation, I immediately create a fake Facebook account and start looking for social media information on Trevor. Within minutes I know he is massively angry at the "friends of his ex-girlfriend" who caused several hundred dollars of damage to his car, that he knows who they are, and that if they show up again at his place of work, they are going to get an unpleasant surprise. Now, this is something worth seeing.

The Allied Resources plant just so happens to be right by one of my favorite bike trails in the Twin Cities. I change into my bike riding clothes, hang my bike off the back of my car, and head back towards Oakdale to ride the Gateway Trail. Not sure what I am going to see, and there is really nothing left to do, but I want to see his Subaru in the parking lot. Obsession, which in and of itself can be considered unhealthy, can be offset if it is acted upon during a healthy activity such as exercise. That justification makes sense in my head at least.

One of the keys to finding fulfillment in your life is to do things that are important to you. Bike riding satisfies my need for exercise. Bike riding so that I can learn more about a guy I am obsessing about because he flipped me off on the road a few days ago? This provides fulfillment at a whole new level.

These are the thoughts that guide me as I pedal briskly over the pedestrian bridge near Highway 36 and enter one of the many wooded areas on a paved trail that ends in a park north of Stillwater. It's a 12-mile ride from where I park to where I turn around and come back on the same trail, but it is a ride that is so pretty you don't mind repeating it.

As you ride it, you appreciate the effort it took to oversee a paved multi-purpose trail constructed through expensive residential properties owned by people obviously desiring privacy, bridges built at considerable expense over busy roads, and even rest areas with maps and modest bicycle repair equipment. I will use it gladly, but I would greatly resent giving up part of my backyard for it.

I am not alone in that resentment. I can recall lawsuits and significant legal wrangling between private landowners and a group of people known locally as "bicycle terrorists". The moniker is something I first heard espoused by a local talk radio afternoon drive time host decrying the loss of car lanes and space on busy residential and downtown Minneapolis streets to occasional bicyclists.

I listen to him frequently while stuck in traffic and find myself agreeing with him, while at the same time appreciating all of these accommodations that have been made for the vocal few who ride their bikes. Ever on, windmill-tilting bicycle terrorists, ever on. If Minneapolis is going to be mentioned in the same breath as the most bike-friendly cities in the world, these are the things we need to do. So worth it. Thus far, the increase in bicycle lanes has had little effect on bumper to bumper traffic, but that, it is argued, is because there are not enough bike lanes yet. Build the bike lanes and people will abandon their cars in the street and pedal everywhere.

I smile in an awkward "why is that guy smiling when no one is around?" way as I approach one of the few busy roads for which a bridge for bicycles and pedestrians has not yet been built. I slow down and begin to make eye contact with drivers. There are no cars going south in the single lane. This emboldens me as I have built up speed coming down the incline off of the trail crossing Hadley Avenue. I am going to be able to maintain a good speed even while crossing an uncontrolled intersection. Even though the cars have no trail crossing sign that requires them to stop before they reach the stoplight on Highway 36, many acquiesce to bicyclists and pedestrians and allow them to cross the road safely.

Minnesota has a "Pedestrians Rule" law in place, but even the most ardent pedestrian or cyclist applies some common sense to that rule given the obvious danger to themselves in a situation involving a motor vehicle.

I reward an older gentleman in a gold Buick Riviera with a nod and a wave as he stops to let me cross, even though he has a green light awaiting him at the intersection of Highway 36 and Hadley. Hadley traffic waits forever crossing 36. There is also a second lane for northbound traffic as it connects with highway 36.

I am moving along at a reasonable speed in front of the Buick when out of the corner of my eye I see a large, white SUV barreling down at me from the second northbound lane. The driver, a late thirty-something blonde, is talking on her cell phone and only sees the green light on 36, not the cyclist about to get run over by a 5000+ pound behemoth with leather seats and heated side mirrors. For some reason, in that split second of clarity, I am positive that the Lexus 460 has built-in Bluetooth technology allowing for hands-free and potentially less distracted driving, but this lady is not using it. Instead, she has her iPhone stuck to her ear with her left shoulder, and a fancy water bottle in her right hand. I wonder in that second whether she is steering with her knees, but I see a large diamond ring on her left hand on the steering wheel.

I slam on my brakes and turn my bike south to gain an extra foot of space between my front wheel and the front left quarter panel of the SUV, all the while kicking my shoes out of the clips that attach them to my pedals. I need every inch of the ten inches of space as I feel the Lexus swooshing past me. At such a close distance, it is apparent that while the car appears to be a brilliant white, it has dirt and grime accumulating on the shiny metal. The oblivious driver accelerates to make a light that has already turned red and does not even realize that she nearly ran over someone on a bicycle. Now fully stopped with both feet on the ground, I look and see her accelerating mightily going east on 36 towards North St. Paul.

My eyes catch her license plate as she speeds off amidst a cacophony of car horns. Oh my God, this cannot be happening to me. I nearly got run over by "MUDRNR?" A vanity plate celebrating the fact that she runs in mud? The car behind the Lexus has come to a complete stop well before the intersection, and an undistracted teen driver waves at me apologetically as I pedal to the other side of Hadley. Despite being only two miles into my ride, it seems like a good time for a water break. Trevor is now a distant memory as I turn my revenge-filled mind to 'MUDRNR'. She needs to be taught a lesson on how to drive a car and provide safe and courteous passage for bicyclists and pedestrians.

Once east of Hadley, the trail becomes much safer and more like a paved journey through woods, pastures, and small lakes before eventually ending in Pine Point Park. Such an idyllic area would ordinarily cause a Zen-like calm to overcome me, but my mind is racing. My thoughts begin with the consideration of turning around and tracking down the Lexus on my bicycle to recalling that I have access to my public record searching site. That is what I will do. I will learn all I can about this horrible driver and her oblivious and dangerous ways.

My Billy Joel station plays repeated John Mellencamp songs – I forgot to create a playlist - as I complete my ride, pack up my bicycle, and hurry back to the source of all answers to my pressing issues, my computer. "MUDRNR" needs to learn some road manners.

CHAPTER SIX

Bernadette "Bernie" Bixby adjusted her "Minneapolis PD" baseball cap while staring down at a blue-tinted corpse lying in an undignified but somehow natural state on the shore of the Mississippi River, not far from downtown Minneapolis. It was 3 PM on a Tuesday afternoon in early May. Rising in the wooded and high slopes, above a flat area large enough for sunbathing and soccer but subject to occasional flooding, were the buildings that make up the East Bank of the University of Minnesota campus.

"Why are the arts and architectural buildings always the ugliest ones on campus?" Her partner, Elliott Little, seemed to say exactly what Bixby was thinking.

"If you say they're ugly, you're admitting that you don't get it, and no one wants to show they don'tundertand art," Bixby replied. Little nodded in agreement.

Bixby's first nickname when she was promoted to homicide detective was "Chex", because she was black, female, and a lesbian, and she checked all the appropriate boxes in a minority hire. As is often the case, however, the resentment did not last long as Bixby fit in, worked hard, and, most importantly, she and Little closed cases at an impressive rate.

Bernie Bixby served in Afghanistan as an Army Ranger, then worked as a patrol officer in a nearby suburb of Brooklyn Center for her first two years, then moved to the same job in Minneapolis for three years. She recently passed ten years in law enforcement, the last five as a detective working with the more experienced Little. Bernie was married and had two small children living in a small house in Brooklyn Center. Despite the initial chatter, she had proven to be one of the top young detectives on the force. She and Little were the only detective team comprised of two blacks. It did not matter to them, and slowly all working with them came to agree. They worked hard, they closed cases, and they backed up other members of MPD when needed, and that was what mattered.

Elliott Little defied his parents, both doctors and living in the wealthy suburb of Edina, refusing to join his brother and sister in pursuing a career in medicine. Instead, he spent two years at Normandale Community College getting a law enforcement degree and worked for 12 years as a patrolman for the Minneapolis Police Department before advancing to detective. His first three years working for more experienced partners made him ideal to mentor Bixby when they became partners. Unlike most of his brethren, Detective Little lived within the city limits of Minneapolis, in a nice new condo in the North Loop, a now fully gentrified area just north of downtown. Not that it mattered, since he spent so much time working. Something about being alone in his overpriced but conveniently located two-bedroom condominium with high ceilings and amazing views kept him in the squad room. He preferred to be working. Bixby, a chip on her shoulder about proving she belonged, joined him in the long hours.

Little made a name for himself in one of his first cases when he came to homicide. His partner, Dwight Hartman, was older, more experienced, and just a tad too beaten up by his years in homicide. Hartman deemed a case an accidental death by drowning and pushed Little to agree so that they could file the report and move on to the next one. "There's always," he reminded, "a next one."

The victim, an athletic man in his 30's, was found washed up on the shore of Cedar Lake just west of downtown. Hartman had already dispatched the Crime Scene Unit, and the body had been taken away. "Let's wrap this up and grab breakfast in Uptown. We've got two hours easy before they expect us back." His partner switched his tone between the voice of savvy experience to unmasked exhaustion. Their career arcs were decidedly different.

Little waved him off as he walked along the shore on that brisk morning in June, cold wind blowing across the lake. It was not that he disagreed with his more experienced partner, it was just that he did not feel comfortable wrapping things up before they had even begun. After he walked in the general direction of downtown Minneapolis, he turned back and walked the opposite way. Hartman stood by their car and continuously smoked cigarettes. If it is possible to show impatience and anger while smoking, his partner exhibited all those signs and more. He looked to be napping on his feet, he seemed so bored and ready to have breakfast.

Little decided that morning he needed to move on as well - to another partner. His boss hinted that the partnership would not be ended and Little could not be reassigned without specific details being provided of the need for a change. Elliott Little now felt like the details were apparent.

He was nearly 250 yards from the body when he found something interesting. In an area where the beach was subsumed by overhanging branches, he found two parallel trenches a little wider than a shoe running from the shoreline into the water. Even in the shallow first few feet of the lake he could see slight indentations in the muck below. Armed with that fact, he insisted that the pair drive to the victim's address and see who knew him. When no one answered their knocks, once again Hartman suggested they wrap things up and grab pancakes. He would treat, a very unusual offer.

Little knocked on a neighbor's door instead. A woman, gray hair in a hair net, "The Price is Right" blaring in her apartment behind her, told Little that the victim and his roommate would likely be at work, and gave them the names of their respective employers. She made sure that Little knew that she did not buy for a second that the two were just roommates. "You should see how they dress, like every day is Mardi Gras." Little was not sure what Mardi Gras attire would look like, so he just jotted down in his notebook that the neighbor suggested that they were gay and made no mention of their fashion sense. Hats with bananas, mangoes, and other exotic fruits stacked precariously atop a wide-brimmed straw hat is the vision he conjured up but he did not write it down.

The roommate, who quickly revealed himself to be a jilted lover, broke down during non-confrontational questioning in a small, windowless conference room in a marketing firm located in a nondescript but colorfully decorated office suite four stories above Nicollet Mall. Elliott had a hard time keeping up with his notes as the confession poured out.

While Detective Hartman finished off a short stack of blueberry pancakes and signaled his server for more coffee with his empty mug high in the air, Elliott Little led the suspect to their car in handcuffs. Hartman had to flag down a passing patrol car to get back to the station.

The ersatz roommate and confessed killer detailed getting his soon-to-be former significant other drunk, and encouraging him to take a staggering walk and late-night swim in Cedar Lake. After dragging him in the water and holding him underwater until he died, he carefully left the victim's wallet and keys under a tree just off the shore to make it appear to be an accidental drowning or a suicide. "If only I had remembered to leave a bath towel with his wallet," the confessor said ruefully. "It would have looked more like an accident."

"And maybe not dragged his fully-clothed body into the water and left marks on the shore," Little thought but did not say. Shortly after the suspect was booked, Elliott Little was assigned to the newest homicide detective, Bernadette Bixby.

"Looks like a jumper," Bixby offered while pointing at the woman on the bank with her left foot.

"Oh, Bernie," Elliott replied. "If it only were that easy." While generally regarded as a safe place to live, the twin cities of Minneapolis and St. Paul saw enough homicides each year to keep their homicide departments extremely busy. And, Bixby and Little were thorough, resourceful, and always compassionate in their work. As a result, their close numbers exceeded those of any detective pairing in the department, not that they were keeping score.

"I was just testing your keen observation skills," Bixby responded. "Here is what I see that says 'death by unnatural causes': First, the location of the body is not logical. Remember Dr. Granger, the U professor we spoke with a few months back? She made it clear that the entry point of a body can be predicted with a fair amount of accuracy based on currents and water flow. She told us a jumper would be more likely to end up farther downstream, but a dead body could end up in this area. Speaking of Doctor Granger, did you ever ask her out for coffee like you promised?"

There had been an obvious mutual interest between Little and Granger when they met for a consultation on where to search for a body after witnesses reported seeing a homeless man either jump or be pushed off the Stone Arch Bridge and rescue attempts turned to recovery efforts. Dr. Abigail Granger, with her PhD in hydrology and limnology, gave them her five most likely spots to search. They found the body at the second spot.

"Uh, no, not yet," Little stammered. "Besides, I'm sure she has been very busy. Late spring and early summer are the busiest seasons in Water Resources Sciences."

"Why are we having this conversation again? She's a science nerd working alongside science nerds lucky to live somewhere other than their parents' basement. I am very disappointed, Elliott Theodore Little. In fact, we will march right

COINCIDENTAL EVIDENCE

over to Dr. Granger's office once we are through here and we will speak with her again, and you will get her number and ask her out. If you don't, I will ask her out for you."

Fortunately for Little, a crime scene tech and a uniformed patrol officer walked over to the detectives with updates on what they had found. The crime scene tech, a young but intense-looking blonde named Sarah Broderick, carried a small fanny pack in her gloved hand. "Detectives? Here is what I have found thus far." She held up the pack. "I have not opened this zippered object as of yet. Officer Melrose…" Broderick gestured in the patrolman's direction, "Calls this a 'funny pack' of some sort. I am not familiar with this 'pack' device at all. I'm not sure why it would be deemed funny either."

Melrose cleared his throat, but the detectives could see a twinkle in his eye. Broderick was excellent in investigating the details of a crime scene and following procedures unwaveringly, but she lacked social skills and awareness. "I'm pretty sure I called it a 'fanny pack'."

"Fanny pack. What an unusual name. Probably named after its inventor. I can see it's utility, however."

Melrose smiled again. "Broderick, you wear it on your fanny, that's why it's called a fanny pack. Not too long ago these were all the rage."

"What's a fanny?"

Little interrupted. "So, what's in the fanny pack? Can we open it up and take a look?"

Broderick paused thoughtfully. "There are sufficient witnesses here to allow for the opening of a personal item found within a perimeter measuring no more than 36 inches contiguous to the victim. As we are pursuing identification of the victim, I deem it appropriate that we perform a cursory viewing of the items contained therein, so long as the items are fully cataloged and inventoried in the same sequence as they are removed, and each of us signs off on the Form 1336-43 alphabetically and by reverse rank. Said inspection is for purposes of identifying the victim only. Any other uses will require the completion of Form 1561-19 and require that a search warrant be sought. In fact -"

Clearly, Broderick lived in her parents' basement.

"Good grief, Broderick, open the fanny pack before the sun sets." Bixby loved protocol and numbered forms, but even she had her limits.

Broderick looked sharply at Bixby, briefly pondering whether to chastise her for interrupting, but decided her rank required that she be deferential instead. With a bit of a sigh she began unzipping the pack. She carefully moved items around until she had a visual understanding of the contents. There was no cell phone visible in the pack. Then she handed the pack to Little, who, wearing latex gloves, continued the inspection. One of Broderick's colleagues tapped information into an electronic form on his iPad, documenting the search for an identification of the victim.

Little used his pen to lift a key ring out of the fanny pack and held it high enough for the others to see. "Hmm. Lexus key fob. Melrose, can you see if any parking tickets have been issued for a Lexus? We should be able to get a name and address for the deceased off of the title."

Reaching in to the fanny pack, Bixby removed a second item. All that was left now was lipstick, a brand that Bixby knew she could never afford, and a hair scrunchie. "Or, maybe we could call Citibank and get an address and phone number based on the name on this credit card?" Bixby displayed the credit card in her gloved hand, all the while trying to hide the sense of elation she felt in one-upping her older and more experienced partner.

"Oh, I didn't see that in there. You had a better view. Why don't you take a picture of the front and back of the card with your phone and call the number and get an identification? Unless Ms. Amy J. Nyberg stole the fanny pack or the credit card, I think we know who our unfortunate victim is," Little said.

"I could call in about parking tickets or what information they have for that name," Melrose offered.

"Go ahead and give it a try," Little said. "Since they switched over to the new servers, requests like that have taken forever. Bernie here thinks she can get the information faster calling in on the credit card. Let's see who finds out her address and contact information first."

Bixby took photos with her phone of the front and back, futzing with lighting and distance to make sure she captured the name and numbers on the card, while Melrose called MPD and was immediately placed on hold. The race was on.

"Any guesses as to the cause of death?" Little asked Broderick.

"The coroner's officer will have to perform an autopsy, but, unofficially, I think this is telling," Broderick replied, pointing to two small marks on Nyberg's neck. "I would postulate that these indicate puncture wounds were caused by a very sharp but thin knife."

The three stepped away from Broderick to allow her to continue to investigate the area around where the deceased victim Amy J. Nyberg lay. Bixby and Little walked back to their car. Despite it not being painted or loaded with identifying decals, the blue Impala still screamed 'cop car'. Melrose signaled with his eyes that he would call later when he got through and learned more about the car and any tickets issued.

As Bixby was holding her phone to her ear, trying to convince Citibank to release information about Amy Nyberg without a search warrant or proof of authorized access to the card, she got in the passenger seat. While not illegal, it would not look right if members of the Minneapolis Police Department drove while on their cell phones, all the while advising resident drivers about the laws against distracted driving. Besides, the partners had learned that she was far more productive than Little as a passenger. Elliott tended to focus on improving

Bixby's driving skills, while Bixby could use her time to run searches on a laptop or tablet, sometimes both, and make phone calls, and all with excellent efficiency. And, switching drivers required changing the position of the seat, mirrors, and steering wheel. As a result, Little drove and Bixby worked the technology.

CHAPTER SEVEN

The Limnological Research Center is located on Pillsbury Drive, in the heart of the University of Minnesota campus. While only a short distance away, traffic, one-way streets, and omnipresent construction projects made the drive take far longer than one would expect. Once they arrived, Little walked a few steps ahead of Bixby as they approached the building, smiling at the bureaucratic nightmare his partner had encountered. Bixby was still on the phone with Citibank, on hold, waiting for a supervisor to discuss her options for getting information about a potentially deceased customer. Body language and looks passed between the partners indicated the level of frustration Bixby felt.

Little held the door, sweeping his hand in a grandiose gesture as he invited Bernie to enter the building. Bixby showed her appreciation with her middle finger. Little looked over Bixby's shoulder and admired the fine location where he had finally parked the car, quite illegally. Regardless of status or importance, no one could find parking at or around the U. Little already practiced the argument he would make to a campus cop unfortunate enough to write a parking ticket to a fellow law enforcement officer.

Bixby's voice was beginning to rise, approaching a shrillness Little rarely heard. "Fine, right after we tell her husband she's dead we'll have him call you and authorize our access to the account." There was a pause, and then Bixby continued. "I have a lot of attitude for a woman? Sweetie, you do not want to see or hear me when I have an attitude, believe me." She hung up the phone in obvious disgust and frustration.

"Maybe the car is a better way to get information?" Little laid on the sarcasm and insincerity thickly.

"Yeah. Whatever."

They made their way up the steps to the second-floor office and laboratory where the faculty of the Limnological Research Center housed their equipment. Despite there not being a chemical in sight, and in a room full of only computers, large-format printers, and desks and chairs, an acrid chemical smell pervaded. Two young people, obviously graduate students or teacher assistants, were huddled near a computer screen on one side of the room. Sensing that the visitors were both interlopers as well as law enforcement, their tone became hushed and they moved their heads closer to a monitor that was bigger than most college dorm TVs. The detectives strode across the room towards a woman with her back turned, standing but hunched over, deep in concentration. Bixby recalled her being in exactly the same pose the first time they had requested her assistance on a case. The woman sensed their approach, and slowly turned. A smile lit up her face.

"Well, Detective Elliott Little. So nice to see you again." Dr. Granger stepped away from a machine of unknown purpose but obvious cost and complexity and walked towards the duo, extending her hand to Elliott. "And, you're Detective Baxter, right?"

"It's Bixby, ma'am."

"Of course." Her eyes and body shifted in an obvious fashion to look back at Little. "Elliott, how are you doing?" Bixby, despite her toned body, colorful yet understated professional dress, and self-diagnosed charismatic charm, suddenly felt invisible.

Dr. Abigail Granger was of average height with a body that looked like she watched what she ate and exercised regularly. Her hair was light brown with streaks of lighter color, all pulled back in a too-severe ponytail. She wore glasses that looked as though they could be used to protect her from industrial chemicals, or helped her make a reverse-fashion statement of some sort that said she was so nerdy as to be cool. It would take more than the glasses to make her look cool, Bernie decided without cattiness. Some people just look like science geeks. She was still cute, though, and Bixby could sense a connection between Granger and Elliott.

Bixby had time to think through the possibilities since her presence was being largely ignored. She concluded that any image Dr. Granger projected to others was entirely unintentional. Hers was the pursuit of science and data, little more. This, however, seemed to be changing based on her interest in Elliott Little. A fissure had formed in the seemingly impenetrable wall of her focus on science.

She hung on every word as Elliott explained why they were there. Granger seemed enthralled by Little's presence at first, but then the excitement of being asked to speak on her area of expertise took over.

"Show me where you found the body on my map over here." She gestured to a large monitor hanging on a wall, clicked a few buttons with a mouse, and a map appeared showing the serpentine path of blue signifying the Mississippi River. Within the blue were black lines meant to show, as Bixby remembered from their last visit, varying depths and the directions of the myriad currents that flowed constantly through the mighty river.

"Dr. Granger," Little said, pointing to the spot not far from the building they were in.

"Elliott, remember that I prefer that you call me "Abby." Bixby could swear she heard an emphasis on her name that implied that only Little was allowed to call her by her nickname.

"Sorry. Abby. Of course, I remembered that. Here's where we found the body of Amy Nyberg," he said, pointing to the screen.

It was plain to Bixby that her partner was getting more nervous by the second. She could empathize with him. She was lucky to have met her future wife Francine (Frankie) while they were both in high school and they had been together ever since. While Bixby was on active duty, Frankie went to the

University of Minnesota to get her elementary school teaching certification. When Bernie was honorably discharged, and as she made her way up the ranks in law enforcement, they continued to date. They bought their first house together seven years ago and added two dogs to the family. Two years after that they began the ultimately successful process of adopting a young brother and his sister from war-torn Croatia. Laws legalizing marriage for the committed couple made it official. Esther and Eric proudly spoke of their two moms.

Bixby did not envy her partner having to wade into the dating pool, although both Little and Dr. Granger seemed interested in pursuing a relationship that extended beyond their roles of limnology expert and detective. The question was whether the blockhead Little could be nudged into pursuing it.

Dr. Granger placed a red spot on the screen designating where the body had been found. Using her mouse and punching in numbers on a smaller screen she began moving a second spot upstream.

"Well, I cannot be certain without more testing and field work" she began. Nothing in her voice indicated that the information she would be providing would be anything less than a scientific certainty.

"Oh, Abby, your best guess will save us so much time in locating where the body was put in the river." Bixby had never heard Little sound so obsequious.

Dr. Granger smiled at the compliment before continuing.

"Based on the body being found here," she designated the location where Amy Nyberg had been found, "I would estimate that she entered the water right about here," she pointed to the Stone Arch Bridge. "And," she continued, "I would look right here as the most likely point of entry." She pointed to a spot about a third of the way from the western bank of the river and the bridge. "The body would have likely not made it over the dam intact, but instead was carried down along the slower pooling area until it got picked up by stronger currents right about here." She pointed to a spot about 75 yards past the dam.

An awkward silence began to build. Bixby cleared her throat but somehow Little continued to miss every clue. "So, Doc, let us buy you a coffee. I saw a Caribou not too far away. It's the least we can do for all of your help."

"But I just had coffee on the way over." Elliott had never been as oblivious as he was right now.

"You can just have water," Bixby comforted. Dr. Granger was already walking towards the door. At least she understood what Bixby was trying to do.

Bixby called Melrose, still at the scene at the riverbank, and still trying to get through to track down the name on the credit card, and asked that he and one other patrol officer head over to the Stone Arch Bridge and secure the likely dumping spot and hold it until she and Little finished talking to their expert witness.

At least Little proved capable of being able to walk while in his current tongue-tied and stammering condition. Bixby was enjoying it beyond her dreams. She wanted her partner to be uncomfortable in the current situation forever because it would provide fodder for abuse for years. She could not dispute the obvious connection between the slightly nerdy water current whisperer and Elliott. Being his best friend, though, she had to concede that Elliott desperately needed to make social connections outside of work. He was not a fun person to be around when all he thought and talked about was work.

Little at least revived enough that he held the door open for Dr. Granger, who touched his hand as she walked in, saying, "Oh, thank you. No one ever holds the door for anyone anymore." Elliott smiled nervously but said nothing. Keeping the door open for Bixby, he mouthed the words "Thank you" and they made their way to the counter.

CHAPTER EIGHT

Take a snapshot of every Caribou (or Starbucks) in Minnesota and the same inhabitants appear in each locale. Over by the window, three tables are occupied by intensely overwhelmed young people with large mugs and bottled waters, furiously typing on their Macs. They comprise the 'Hard working for the sake of showing the world how hard they work' substrata of a Caribou crowd.

Interspersed are business people with ear phones plugged into their phones, undoubtedly pretending to be following along on conference calls by nodding occasionally. All are working on their laptops on something entirely different than the topic of the conference call, their phones muted so no one knows where they are currently located. Doing two things at once justifies hanging out in a Caribou during work hours. This is the 'I can hang out at Caribou but still be working while not really working' group.

Two others are seated near the faux-fireplace, fulfilling the 'Relaxing so the world knows how well we relax' requisite. One is reading a recent Sandford 'Prey' hardcover while the other peruses the Star Tribune, City Pages on his lap for later review.

Two young mothers sit at a table with sleeping infants in car seats, regaling each other with how little sleep they get or how their child is crushing the numbers relative to other newborns. One of the moms keeps glancing over at a boy erasing the pithy coffee inspirational sayings off of the black whiteboard, replacing them with mostly random lines and circles. Caring for two children explains the large iced caramel lattes in front of both moms. They personify the 'Anything that gets a new parent out of the house so I can complain and humblebrag about my children' assemblage.

The friendly but hyper counter person took their drink orders. Dr. Granger got them a discount by slowly providing her cell number to access her account while glancing at Little to see if he got the hint. Elliott insisted on paying for all three. He was showing signs of a return to normalcy. Orders fulfilled, they walked over to a table away from the denizens of the coffee shop, fulfilling the 'Conversations so important no one else can be nearby so why hold it in a coffee shop?' element, thus officially completing the cast of a typical coffee shop.

Not wanting to force Elliott to make conversation, as fun as that would be, Bixby asked Dr. Granger how she came to work at the University of Minnesota. They were moments away from the Stone Arch Bridge, and it would take several minutes for the area to be secured by patrol officers and turned over to the crime scene unit.

Taking a drink of her herbal tea with lemon, Abby told them that she was born in Grand Forks, North Dakota. At a young age she was fascinated by the Red River. "It is considered one of only two rivers in the United States that flows north. That is not quite accurate, however, because a river simply flows from higher elevation to lower elevation. I guess when I explained that to my second-grade teacher it was apparent that I had found my passion." Early fascination turned to engineering studies at North Dakota State University, which then led to the successful pursuit of a PhD at the University of Minnesota in Water Resources Science with a focus on rivers and currents. Such degrees tend to result only in careers in academia, and she had been at the University of Minnesota for 10 years as a professor and researcher, and now a leading expert in the field. The implication throughout her review of her life to date was that with such a fascinating subject as river and lake currents to dwell on, there was little time or reason to develop a life away from the pursuit.

Bixby sat back in her chair, sensing that her work as Cupid was almost done. Frankie would be proud of her. Little finally began speaking without prodding. "I spent hours on Lake Harriet in the summers with my brother. My parents had a sail boat and a powerboat for water skiing. We would ride our bikes there and stay until suppertime. And, our house was right across the street from Minnehaha Creek. We would wade in that for hours. I guess I'm a water person, too."

The two chattered on about water quality, currents, lakefront erosion, and several other topics for a feverish few moments that seemed much longer for Bernie. They were sharing a conversation each had thought about and hoped to have for quite some time, and it was finally happening.

"So, Doc, Elliott invited my wife Frankie and me over on Saturday night for dinner. How about you join us and we can continue this fascinating conversation on the currents and the varying seasonal depths of Lake Harriet?" Bernie was finding it difficult to pretend to have any additional interest.

Elliott started to object that he had made no such invitation, but thought better of it. "Seven o'clock work for you, Abby?" He glanced over at Bernie, thanking her again for the assist.

"It does. What can I bring?"

"How about I call you on Friday and let you know? I'm still figuring out what to make."

"You have my number. Call me anytime." Bixby heard a special emphasis on 'anytime'.

After walking Dr. Granger back to her work building, the two retrieved their car. No ticket. As Elliott drove the short distance down Fourth Street toward the Stone Arch Bridge, he seemed deep in thought. Bixby could not tell if he was mad or just thinking about the case. "So, Saturday night, great idea I had spur of the moment, right?"

"What were you thinking?" He slammed the steering wheel in frustration. "I can cook macaroni and cheese in the microwave. How do I make a whole meal for four people?"

"Relax, I already texted Frankie. You and I will throw steaks on the grill while the other ladies do the sides in the kitchen." Due to her more normal schedule, Frankie performed more of the household duties in the Bixby household.

Little sighed in relief. "I forgot that you married well beyond your pay grade. Thanks."

"Hey, no argument there. I just bring the good looks and charm."

Little parked in the circular spot where vehicles stopped to load and unload only and bikers and pedestrians took over. Little placed the blue light on the top of the car to let the world, and Minneapolis Parking Enforcement, know that the car carried some juice and should not be ticketed. They walked on the bridge towards a cluster of police milling around, forcing walkers, joggers, and cyclists away from the west side of the bridge.

The Stone Arch Bridge, built in 1880 to accommodate passenger train traffic, was re-opened to only pedestrian traffic in 1994. Spanning St. Anthony Falls on the Mississippi River, the reduction in available lanes was causing a significant disturbance for people looking to cross the river for exercise, commuting, or sightseeing. There seemed to be just as many pedestrians as there were tourist types stopping along the rails to watch the mighty river roil on its long journey to the Gulf of Mexico.

Sarah Broderick, crime scene specialist and ardent rule-follower, had secured a crime scene as best she could in the midst of foot and bike traffic whizzing by. Tourists were taking photos and videos on their phones of the police presence, already dreaming of the eventual sale to TMZ or some other schlock journalism site.

A man in a high visibility yellow bike jersey, black tights, and wraparound sunglasses under a racing style helmet, veered up to the coagulation of police and sneered, "Hey jerks, get out of my way. Go shoot a black kid." The bike rider managed to laugh at his own joke as he sped away. Bixby had to admit that it was funny, but stifled her laughter.

Little stared down the back of the rapidly disappearing figure on his expensive racing bike. He motioned to the uniformed patrols. "Close off the bridge on both sides. Full barriers on both ends. If they want to give us attitude, they can swim across the river for the duration." Keying their shoulder microphones, the officers barked out the command, wooden barricades appearing at each end of the bridge.

Broderick was of course very strategic in her approach. She had two assistants measure off and create a perimeter for the area she intended to focus on. Within the perimeter they created quadrants. The two of them began covering each inch heading towards the spot designated by Broderick as the center of the area. When they finished a thorough examination of a quadrant, they switched spots so that there were always fresh eyes searching. An orange soccer field cone marked their eventual meeting spot. Broderick concentrated in a small area around the cone. She almost immediately found something, and signaled to the detectives that she wanted to speak with them. She pointed to a spot directly across the bridge where she wanted to confer. She removed her shoe covers and carefully folded them before placing them in a front pocket of her crime scene windbreaker. She zipped the pocket closed to reduce the risk of contamination.

COINCIDENTAL EVIDENCE

"This is, of course, very preliminary, and constitutes mere conjecture on my part." Her attempt to temper her discovery did little to reduce the excitement she showed on her face and in her voice. "There are two almost identical scrape marks with traces of a rubber-like substance on the two rails of the bridge that looks like they will correspond to the markings on the outside of both of the shoes the victim had on her when found. I will have to compare my sample to the shoes, run it through the standard gas chromophotographic protocol, but it looks to me that she went over the bridge exactly where we were told to look."

"And…" Clearly this was the moment Sarah Broderick went to crime forensics school for, and made the student loan payments all worth it. Cue the orchestra and the swelling music. "She did not appear to go over the side of this bridge of her own accord." She nodded approvingly, clearly impressed with the fellow science person Dr. Abigail Granger. Granger, like Broderick, was a woman who knew how difficult it was to be taken seriously in a male-dominated world and to be given so little credit for being so accurate in her predictions.

Hoping for a more enthusiastic response to her initial findings, and looking a bit disappointed, she turned and walked back to the scene. Detectives never appreciated her brilliance.

Before she re-entered the perimeter, Broderick carefully opened the zippered pocket on her windbreaker, removed the light blue shoe covers, and put them back on. From where Little stood, he could see that Broderick had written "right" and "left" using a Sharpie to make sure that each cover went back on over the same shoe. He raised his eyebrow to Bixby, who also saw it and smiled. "That, my friend, is how you secure a crime scene."

"And we now have a confirmed murder investigation on our hands."

Deciding that the Stone Arch Bridge scene was in good hands, the two walked back to their car. As they approached the barriers that had been set up to block access to the bridge, they noticed a gathering of angry cyclists assembled around two younger looking patrol officers making sure the barricades held back traffic on the bridge. The two officers looked at the detectives with pleading in their eyes. Little shook his head to indicate that the barriers should continue to be in place. "If anyone has a complaint, have them take it up with the mayor," he whispered to one of the officers as he walked past. "I hear he bikes to work."

As they stood against their car and watched all that was happening around them, Little returned a missed call back to the department and caught one of their researchers, who had promised to call Little directly rather than going through Officer Melrose. On hold for what promised to be just a few seconds while notes were tracked down, Little winked at his partner. "Dapper is a whiz with computers when they're online."

Dapper came back on the phone after a short hold. Elliott repeated back to Bernie what he was hearing, triumph in his voice. "So, a Leland Nyberg has a white Lexus 460 registered in his name? Same last name as our victim? And she lists this address on her drivers license? Text the address to this number and we'll go pay Mr. Nyberg a visit. Thank you again for doing this for us, Dapper." Looking at Bixby, Little smirked as he closed out the call. "Looks like Officer Melrose reached out to the right person."

"You shouldn't take so much joy in the accomplishments of others."

"Anyway," Little spoke. "We need to go visit a 'Leland Nyberg" in some weird place called Marine on St. Croix and either take a stolen vehicle report, or bring him to the morgue to positively identify our victim." Even though he had done this before many times, the prospect of informing someone of the death of a loved one was never easy.

CHAPTER NINE

Statistics indicate that nearly seven times out of ten the victim knows their killer. The likelihood of the known killer being a romantic partner is very high as well. While Little and Bixby were certainly within their rights and job descriptions to pass along the unpleasant task of a potential death notification to the Washington County Sheriff, or to some other local law enforcement agency for whatever jurisdiction Marine on St. Croix fell within, they knew that the first contact with Leland Nyberg could turn out to be their chance to see a killer in an unguarded moment. Or, to see how well he lied. That was not something experienced homicide detectives offloaded, even if traffic was terrible and the drive covered almost 40 miles.

It was closing in on sunset when the Minneapolis detective duo finally made their way through the traffic fleeing the big cities and found themselves driving along the St. Croix River north of Stillwater. The sun was dropping behind large and stately trees as their car downshifted itself to push up steep inclines and Little had to push the Chevrolet Impala hard as he maneuvered around curves on the way to Marine on St. Croix.

"Did you know that Marine on St. Croix was founded in 1839 and was originally called Marine Mills? There are seven historic sites that have been retained from as early as 1870," Bixby read from her phone. She was awaiting further word from Broderick and her findings at the bridge, plus other inquiries and requests that she had made. The beauty of the landscape was lost on her as she stared at her phone. Her tablet was busy on another angle she was pursuing.

"How about you just get me to the house?" Elliott grumbled. He, too, was lost in thought about the case at hand. This was about as testy as the two ever got with each other.

Little negotiated a narrow turn onto a driveway between two posts constructed from what appeared to be river rocks mortared together in thick white lines. The house number was embossed in a stately granite inlay. Between the post was an ornate metal gate that could be closed for privacy. A small electric motor controlled its movement.

The asphalt driveway curved slightly as it made its way down a steep descent to where it became a full circle in front of a two-story brick structure with huge windows and the largest two front doors the detectives had ever seen.

"Wow," said Bixby. "Buckingham Palace called. They need their doors back."

As she spoke, one of the doors opened as Elliott turned off the ignition. Evidently there were security cameras that advised the owner of approaching visitors and guests.

A man in his late 60's with a full head of too long gray hair parted on the left walked towards the Impala as Little and

Bixby got out of the car. The homeowner did not appear to appreciate the interlopers or their intrusion.

"May I help you?" His tone indicated that he had no interest in helping anyone.

"Are you Leland Nyberg?" Bixby led the questioning because she had a way of disarming people.

A curt nod was the only reply, as if to say "Who else could it be?"

Bixby smiled in an attempt to further disarm Nyberg. "Sir, do you own a white Lexus 460?"

"I do. I don't drive it, however. I drive a Porsche Cayenne." The implication was that a Lexus was not quite good enough for him to drive.

"Sir, do you know where that vehicle is at the present time?"

"Well, it's certainly not here. My wife is out galivanting somewhere. She always is," he said icily. "I just got home from work and realized she did not come home today and she may not have been here last night either."

"Why would you not know if she was home last night either?" Little leaned in imperceptibly, now quite engaged in the discussion, forgetting how stiff he was from driving from the U campus to the stately mansion on the St. Croix River.

"She told me not to wait up for her last night when we talked because she was going to hang out with her gaggle of girlfriends and go running on the Gateway to burn off the Chardonnay and appetizers. She knows I go to bed early when I have meetings first thing in the morning. I got up and figured she was already out the door for another of her workout days."

Bixby and Little looked puzzled.

The coolness dropped slightly. "Look, Amy is my second wife. I ended things with the first Mrs. Nyberg after I met Amy at 3M. She trains for mud runs and obstacle course races as a fulltime replacement for real work. A bunch of crap if you ask me, but that is what she wants to do with her time, so I support it. Mostly by paying off her credit cards each month," he added wryly.

"Sir, we had a report of a Lexus 460 registered in your name abandoned in a parking area not too far from here." Bixby purposely revealed as little information as possible to see if Nyberg would fill in the blanks and reveal that he knew more than he should. In actuality, she had no idea if Oakdale would be considered close to Marine on St. Croix. She made a mental note to look that up later and backfill reality a bit.

"Amy parks near the Gateway Trail and runs towards Pine Point. She's training for a marathon so I think she runs 15 miles a day. Or, she finds a tree along the way and climbs it to get ready for a mudder obstacle course. I can't keep it all straight anymore, and my work keeps me busy enough that I don't really care. Whatever she wants to do for workouts is fine by me."

"The news is worse, I'm afraid. Can we go inside and sit down?" Bixby smiled sadly.

"Look, whatever it is, just tell me. I'd rather not have you in my house if it's all the same with you." Nyberg seemed to be losing patience with the detectives.

"Sir, I'm afraid we found a body on the shore of the Mississippi River down by the University of Minnesota," Bixby began. "And, the body was carrying the Lexus key fob and a credit card with her name on it in a fanny pack."

Leland Nyberg lost his aloofness in the blink of an eye. He looked ten years older and he wavered on his feet. Elliott reached out and steadied him by grabbing his elbow. He nodded at Little appreciatively, for the first time exhibiting some humanity. Elliott helped him over to a set of massive Adirondack chairs and Nyberg sat quietly for a few moments, collecting his thoughts and gathering strength.

Nyberg agreed to join the detectives for the ride back to Minneapolis and the morgue to confirm the identification of the body. As was their custom in these situations, Bixby rode in the back seat with Nyberg to continue to ask seemingly innocuous questions to get more of a sense of Nyberg's potential involvement in his wife's death. Thus far, the looks shared by the partners using the rear-view mirror indicated that Leland Nyberg was looking less and less likely with each answer. Sometimes the percentages do not pay off.

"It sure is pretty out here." Bixby decided it was too quiet in the car.

"I guess so. My first wife insisted we live on the river, buy a big boat, pay way too much to dock it at the best marina in Stillwater, and then let it sit there for entire seasons at a time. Then we just **had** to build a house that was the biggest in the area. When we divorced, she insisted that she wanted the lake house up on Cross Lake, and I got this one. And, a spousal maintenance obligation to keep her in the style that she needed to maintain."

"That had to be hard," Bixby primed the pump.

"Not really. It was time for both of us to move on. She has a boyfriend up on Gull Lake now. She'd remarry except then I wouldn't have to pay her spousal maintenance anymore. She's cheaper this way."

"Amy is your second wife then?"

"Yes. She was a project manager for two of our most successful abrasives launches. One day, near the end of the launch, she called a meeting with me in my office, ordered my secretary to leave and close the door behind her, and announced that we were going to get married right away. Something about not living her best life. I guess it seemed easier at the time to agree than to disagree. She is a very forceful person who frequently gets her way. Then she resigned and announced that she needed to reinvent herself."

"She sounds strong-willed," Bixby agreed.

"What was it like to be married to her?" Little asked from the front seat.

"Well, she started up with all sorts of personal trainers and life coaches and that sort. Most of them are charlatans, but you couldn't tell my wife that. She signed up for every fad, did every new exercise regimen, tried out every health food craze there was, and complained that nothing worked, so she tried something else."

"Didn't you try and stop her?" Bixby inquired.

"No, we had an agreement that she would do her own thing and I would concentrate on work. When I needed her to be my plus one for some executive event, she was there and she looked stunning. She wanted to prove something to every woman at 3M. She didn't care how much they hated her so long as they were jealous of how good she looked in her gown."

Nyberg stared out the window from that point on.

CHAPTER TEN

I did not expect them to find the body so quickly. When I transported her lifeless body across the Stone Arch Bridge in the trailer behind my bicycle, lifted her over my right shoulder and dumped her over the side, I thought it would float downstream and eventually sink to the bottom of the river as part of the natural decomposition process.

Then, several weeks, a few months down the road, maybe a year later, some hapless fisherman would think he snagged a log and drag it up. It is the longest river in North America, so something remaining hidden in it seemed quite reasonable. The time underwater would eliminate any possible evidence that could be gleaned during the autopsy. Take your pick of every crime procedural and there's that inevitable scene where the plucky coroner or medical examiner expresses regret that the body had been underwater too long for any meaningful information to be uncovered. That's what I expected to happen.

Instead, less than 24 hours after she goes in the river she gets found. As I read the story on my computer screen, I have two thoughts. The first is that if I am going to be on my computer looking for work, I need to add a second monitor to increase my desktop space and improve my efficiency in moving from task to task. And, as long as I buy one monitor it makes sense to buy two because they should match in terms of size, aspect ratio, and contrast ratio. Would my current video card be able to sustain two new monitors? Probably not. I might need a new computer as well. I saw computers on sale at the paper and toner super store. I will need to go visit my flirty sales gal soon.

My second thought, however, returns to the news story about the latest homicide in Minneapolis. I know that many criminals mess themselves up after the crime and increase their risk of being caught by going back and doing something ill-advised to cover their tracks. I know I have taken all necessary precautions before and after so second-guessing will be fruitless and potentially result in a life behind bars. Still, it makes a novice murderer wonder…

The story indicates that they have already found the car in Oakdale and are looking for the public's help in figuring out the timeline. Not nearly enough time has passed and the likelihood that someone saw something that could be associated with the murder is high. At least that is what the spokesperson says to encourage the public to call in. That got me thinking, but not in a panicky way, about how I can make sure I am not going to be caught.

Just a few days before, I found the address for the Lexus using my public records all-access pass. I then rode my bicycle on a trail across the highway from the mansion on the St. Croix River listed as the address for the owner of the car. I made it my morning exercise. I took a break and lounged in a comfortable spot underneath several tall pine trees, waiting to see "MUDRNR" hit the road. From what I could see from my verdant vantage point, there did not seem to be any reason to ever leave. Maybe she needed to escape an older spouse who did not understand her. Is he abusive, or maybe just emotionally unavailable? My mind likes to build back stories as it takes in details around it.

Based on the size and location of the house, its tax base, and the finished square footage (thanks public records), I postulate that her husband, Leland, is much older. People her age cannot afford mansions like this unless they inherit it. The architecture and the materials do not seem old enough to be passed down through one family. Plus, the names do not match on the sales documents when Leland took possession ten years ago. Interesting that Amy Nyberg does not appear on the deed now. Second marriage and a leery new husband? Probably a shrewd move on his part to protect himself against someone ostensibly out for his money.

It takes a few more searches to answer the question that has been niggling at me for quite some time. How did someone so relatively young end up without any children and living in a monster house on the St. Croix River? Short of knocking on the door and asking, Google seems to be the best way to find out. I'm not sure why I care to know this about her, but I think I want to further justify my rage.

Running her name, I eventually find a marriage license application and find out that her previously married name was Clifton. Running Amy Clifton through my databases, I find details of her divorce three years earlier. Her marriage dissolution decree granted joint legal custody to both parents and sole physical custody to the father. A father getting sole physical custody is extremely rare unless there is something seriously amiss with the mother in most cases.

That leads me to more searching on the 'seriously amiss' angle. The dissolution decree was based on a Marital Termination Agreement, meaning that the parties settled matters between themselves and asked the court to sign off on their terms, which a judge will do at the conclusion of a very cursory hearing. You hear about divorces that go on for years. This one lasted one week from filing to final decree. No muss, no fuss. So, why would a mother acquiesce on her traditional role as the custodial parent? Go Google, go.

The Stillwater Gazette archive database contained several articles that take me over an hour to sift through. One article features a local woman who re-invented herself as a tri-athlete after a life-altering realization that she devoted too much time to work and not enough time to her children and her marriage. Quoting from her in the story, "I realized that I was doing a disservice to my children and my marriage. I did not like the person I had become at 3M. All I did was tell people what to do and then I would come home from work angry at the world. I yelled at my husband, I yelled at my children, and I yelled at work. I was a horrible person. I didn't even like me anymore."

Another story referenced in the article made her decision even more obvious and understandable. A few months before her dissolution decree became final, a Chevy Equinox containing two child seats crashed into a street light pole on Paris Avenue in Stillwater, not far from the courthouse and the Sheriff's office. Stillwater police found the car abandoned, but easily traced it to Amy and Andrew Clifton.

When they went to the Clifton house, they found Amy Clifton looking "disheveled and frantic" in a bathrobe wrapped around a black turtleneck sweater and tan wool slacks. Her eyes were bloodshot and glazed over. When questioned, Amy Clifton denied driving the vehicle that evening, and claimed her car, usually left in a garage stall, "must have been stolen. If you don't believe me, you can talk with my lawyer." She refused to cooperate further, slamming the door on the police. A witness reported seeing a woman hurrying down the street towards the Clifton home within the last hour. Investigators on the scene concluded that it was not worth getting a warrant signed by a judge to search the Clifton home and question Ms. Clifton further.

Details of the night in question found their way into the possession of a young reporter looking to move up to a bigger newspaper, and she seized the story as her ticket out. Her story suggested that some privileged impaired drivers got special treatment from law enforcement. Amy Clifton declined to comment for the story.

Reader comments in the online versions of the story created an outcry that convicted and punished Amy Clifton as no judge could. She was reviled for driving while impaired, and endangering Stillwater with her behavior. Pictures of the car and its suspected driver appeared on the front page of successive editions under the headline: "Is She Safe to Drive?" No, concluded reader after reader in letters to the editor and comments left after the story. Emboldened by anonymity, readers filled the comments sections asking rhetorical questions like "What if her children had been in the car?" and "How often does a 3M employee drive drunk and not get caught?"

Amy Clifton was eventually charged with reckless driving and leaving the scene of an accident involving property damage. She pled guilty to careless driving, paid fines and restitution, and received a 30-day jail sentence from a judge who knew that she was drunk and put everyone at risk at the time of the accident. The negative publicity fueled by the Gazette stories clearly factored into the harsh sentence.

In the later story, Amy Nyberg called the night driving the car "the lowest point in my life, and the worst decision I ever made." While most people would have been horrified at spending a month behind bars, and she was at first, she instead used that time to "carefully analyze every aspect of the person I was, and "take a careful look at the delta between that person and the person I wanted to be."

After the jail time expired, she returned to work long enough to satisfy the requirements of 3M's policy regarding short term disability claims, gained a commitment from the newly divorced and available Leland Nyberg to fast-track their relationship, and announced to her family her intention to leave them behind and start her life anew without them. She claimed it was in their best interest, but I doubt she ever thought that way once. I am not sure she is capable of thinking of anyone's best interests but her own.

Most moms I know would devote themselves to their children, knowing that is the most important thing any parent can do. Instead, she gave up physical custody of her two children, signed away her interest in their home, and replaced motherhood with intense physical training. She focused on triathlons and the newest crazes in ways to push oneself, including obstacle courses run in the mud. She crawled through deep mud puddles and under low lattices before climbing 20-

foot walls using slippery ropes instead of getting her kids to soccer. From the article I also learn that she does one triathlon of varying length per month, and five or six mud obstacle races a year. I am not sure when the "MUDRNR" vanity plates came to be, probably about the time she had her full driving privileges restored after wiping out the streetlight.

In the ensuing three years, she competes in regional competitions in hopes of earning spots in national events. All she needed at first was a sponsor, and it appeared that Leland Nyberg provided that for her. A cynical view to be sure, but that was the impression I got from the articles. A long feature article contained one sentence saying that her first husband re-married and moved their children to Florida, and she did not object at all. She tried to make herself look good by mentioning that she visited them once when she competed in a triathlon in Winter Haven, satisfying herself that they were doing well in their new home and school.

All photos were of her with her training gear on and working out, not a care in the world outside of competing in her events. Like a phoenix, she had risen from the flames. From drunken mother endangering Stillwater while wrecking her car, she is now the local hero competing nationally in extreme athletic events, someone local girls can look up to and pattern their lives after. Wow, I thought I was self-centered. Narcissism expresses itself in different ways. At least I'm still married with my children living with us.

Nothing I read dissuades me from the conclusion I came to that day on Hadley when she almost ran me over. Living in a world of blissfully ignorant self-involvement has consequences.

M patience pays off about fifteen minutes into my surveillance. This is good timing because I had emptied my water bottle and, not surprisingly, the liquid had to go somewhere. Amy Nyberg's Lexus turns south on Arcola, heading towards Stillwater. No way can I keep up with her even with my high-end equipment. Fortunately, I know with a high degree of certainty where she is going, thanks to the plug she gave to her workout gym in the feature article bragging about her almost daily routines. I continue along Arcola to 95 and descend into Stillwater on the Brown's Creek State Trail.

My car is parked in a lot on the northern end of downtown, right on the St. Croix River. I always appreciate when a governmental entity develops land with prime views in stellar locations and dedicates them to parking lots and green space, with excellent facilities. It is a boon for visitors and encourages shopping at local businesses. I just appreciate clean and free bathrooms. It's hard to cross your legs when you're furiously pedaling a bicycle. After handling my bathroom needs, I walk my bike over to my car. I nod at another couple who also are wrapping up their early morning ride.

With my bike safely attached, I settle in my car with a view of some high-end yoga, Pilates, kick-boxing, and high-energy dancing facility. Amy J. Nyberg starts her day there five days a week.

A personal trainer, dressed in a tight shirt with muscles straining to burst out from under the fabric, joins her outside the facility after about thirty minutes of inside exercising on weights. This appears to be her time for leg work. Based on how she laughs, tosses her head back, and grabs his arm at every opportunity, I would say they do more leg work than just sprinting up the hills near downtown Stillwater. It is surprising to see how people act around each other when they think no one is looking.

After the morning workout, MUDRNR hits the first of several Starbucks for either a coffee drink or some sugary fruit-based slop that is supposed to be good for you. She does that at least three, once four, times while I was surveilling her. I want my ultimate move against her to involve Starbucks just because it is wrong to waste so much money there. I want to act in such a way as to teach car drivers to respect the rights of cyclists, and rebel against over-priced coffee shops, all in one grandiose gesture. Thus far, my planning has not led me to something that will combine both. Focus on the big prize, I remind myself.

Her next stop of the typical day brings her to a swanky shopping mall and a store that caters to women who exercise. Twice on my surveillance days, she walked out of the store with bags, and once she walked in with a bag of returns. On that occasion she left with an even larger bag. On the second day I was doing my stalking / plotting, I saw a mannequin wearing an amazing, color-coordinated outfit with a high-visibility headband matching the swooshes on the sports bra, under a matching mesh sleeveless shirt with matching swooshes on leggings matching half-socks. The shoes had the same colors and swooshes. I suspect she walked in the store and regally pointed to the mannequin and said, "I'll take that." Somewhere on the 3M campus, husband Leland feels a sharp jolt in his wallet. That is the cost of marrying a second, younger, trophy wife with unlimited access to your credit card and expensive taste in exercise clothing, I chide Leland from afar.

Not that she didn't pull off the 'look-at-me-I'm-beautiful-I'm-somebody' ensemble. She is a good-looking woman in great shape. The problem is that she certainly knows it and flaunts it at every opportunity. That conclusion is reflected in her driving, and in how she looks down on people in her interactions. Let me provide a few examples. I jotted down some notes as I looked on with amazement.

Example one of Amy J. Nyberg's me-first character. She buys her protein powders and other elixirs from a health food store in Stillwater. There is free parking along the several storefronts and on the other side of the lot. She has numerous spots available to her that would require some reasonable walking to get to the store. She is, as you recall, a tri-athlete training for national competitions. But instead she pulls in to the handicapped spot directly in front of the store. Most of Minnesota would love to have her "handicap". There is no blue sign hanging on her rearview mirror, and the license plate is not designated to allow parking in this reserved spot. I do not believe laziness and being self-centered rises to the level of disabilities justifying close and convenient parking.

While she is in the store, a retrofitted van pulls slowly up towards the spot, sees that it is not available, and parks several rows back from the stores. An older gentleman gets out, opens the specially designed side doors, and engages a hydraulic ramp to bring his elderly wife in her wheelchair to the ground. It is a slow, painful process to see him move her off the ramp, lock her wheels, and then amble over to the controls to put the ramp back in the car. He has to weave through cars to eventually get to the sidewalk. Then he has to turn the wheelchair backwards and bump his wife up and over the curb. Of course, the only place where the curb is even with the surface of the parking lot is rendered unusable by the monster SUV in its way. I would have offered to assist in some way, but I did not want to blow my cover. I instead stayed in my car and fumed at what her behavior caused.

Example two occurs in the same sequence of events. She is now leaving the store with her powders, vitamins, supplements, and holistic remedies in two bags that she carries easily in one hand. The couple is approaching the store. It is obvious that they are about to enter it. She barrels out of the door but does not hold the door open or offer to help in any way, and looks annoyed as she steps around the lady in the wheelchair on her way to her illegally parked car. The husband, a saint in my eyes, struggles to hold the door open as he wheels his wife in. I consider t-boning the Lexus at an upcoming intersection but can't plot out my escape strategy appropriately.

My non-descript gray Lexus sedan follows her from the health food store on her way towards St. Paul. Her Lexus SUV zips through traffic on Highway 36, up the hill to the newer parts of Stillwater, and then levels off at least 15 miles above the speed limit heading west. My Lexus can certainly can keep up, but I do not want to attract attention to myself given the plans that are coalescing in my brain, so I hang back. I am able to be two or three cars behind her at every stoplight.

While at one of the many interminable stoplights, I pause to reflect. Normal people certainly don't follow an inattentive driver around for days after they are nearly struck while biking. I do. They don't ponder revenge scenarios involving stalking them to learn their routines to find the time and location where they are the most vulnerable. I do. They don't think through how to accomplish a kill and whether to leave the body at the scene or move it to avoid it being found. I do, and I am finalizing my plan.

Mrs. Nyberg careens past 694 and darts across two lanes of traffic to pull into the left turn lane to head south on Hadley. This strikes me as intriguing, as I pull in three cars behind her and wait for the red arrow to turn green. She had been traveling north on Hadley when she had almost hit me days before. Is she returning to the same place?

The light turns and she accelerates quickly through the intersection. The light is already changing to yellow when I make the light and maintain my stealthy pursuit. Highway 36 moves plenty of cars in a given day, and the stop lights take forever, so the time allowed for turns is very short. You had best be paying attention.

I follow along in my best spy way, two cars behind and not trying to encroach. I am sure she has no time to look behind her anyway because she is scant feet behind some poor chump in a Hyundai Elantra, trying to force him to drive faster. She turns off after a few blocks and heads into what appears to be a development of condominiums where a Lexus will definitely not fit in. She pulls in and parks in front of one of the units. Three units in the block are listed for sale, one as a bank-owned foreclosure. Not a great indicator of these properties maintaining their value. Given the slack efforts at maintenance, I can see why people want out.

I park in the street across from the front door and three units down and watch her bound from the car while carrying a gym bag. She takes the steps two at a time to the front door. A man wearing lots of moisture-wicking workout gear meets her at the door. They embrace and she kisses him with passion. They pirouette inside the door and I presume he kicks the door closed behind them. This appears to be another cardio workout getting underway. Work those glutes, sister.

I Google the address of her love nest rendezvous and find that the property is owned by Lance Ball. I also learn that Lance runs a personal, private fitness training business out of the address. I'm pretty sure that violates the covenants of the homeowner's association, but I am not sure to whom I should direct my complaint.

An old guy is walking an old poodle and looking at my car. Feeling like I have spent enough time loitering on a street that sees little to no traffic, I pretend like I am finishing up a call and head back towards Hadley. I park on a service road near the only entrance and wait. I guess, giving Lance the benefit of doubt, that I have about an hour to kill. To pass the time I browse on my favorite office supply store's website and note a few monitors that looked promising. I also look at some computers. Just for the heck of it I text "Toner Babe" and ask her if she knows anything about monitors and computers. Within seconds I learn that she does, especially hard drives, and she adds in an incomprehensible emoji. I am trying to decipher what it means when I see the Nyberg SUV zipping by. I toss my phone on the front seat and start the car to catch up.

As it happens, even impatient drivers get stuck trying to make a left against traffic on busier roads like Highway 36, so I end up pulling up right behind Amy Nyberg. I can see that her hair is now pulled back in a ponytail and looks wet. The services provided by Lance Ball apparently include showering after working out in his private facility. I do not look at her at all, not wanting to make eye contact with her if she should look behind her. I figure that she has the blinders on that create that special obliviousness that defines her life. Her phone is on her ear as she waits for a break in traffic. Again, why not use the integrated Bluetooth and free up your hands?

The traffic signal changes so both vehicles turn on to 36, but I slow down significantly to allow the Lexus to get several car lengths in front of me. I figure if she does not see me in her rearview mirror while stopped, she will not notice me now, but I see no reason to take any chances. Glancing at my clock I see that it is almost exactly the same time as when Nyberg nearly creamed me just a few short days ago. She may be many bad things, but at least she is punctual.

It isn't easy, but I manage to keep up with her speeding along on 36 heading towards North St. Paul. I see her pull in to a bar and grill that looks more like a country club dining area than a place for a beer and shots after a long shift down to the plant. I base this observation on the retail value of the cars in the parking lot, and the understated but classy exterior.

Nyberg jumps out of her car and waits for another SUV, an Acura, to join her. Three other ladies step out of their fancy SUVs and all four cluster together in the parking lot and talk to each other excitedly. Judging by the workout gear on display, this is the meeting of the 'pampered housewives who exercise in fancy clothes' club. I swear I paid less for our first car than what these ladies are wearing while they primp and pose with each other in the parking lot.

They originally are seated on a patio, where I can see a waiter busy bringing white wine several times over the next two hours. I eventually break cover and go inside to use the facilities, but I pick up a takeout menu so as to not make anyone think I went in there just to use the facilities. The group moves inside for another hour, and presumably orders more drinks. Armed with to-go boxes that will probably never be opened before being tossed, the four ladies hug in a fashion that makes sure they do not muss their hair or their makeup and go on their way. The Lexus storms back towards Stillwater on 36, with me following behind.

I call my daughters from the car as I make my way in building traffic. Angela, the younger one, answers. I explain that I am going to an after-work job fair expo, and that I will be getting home later in the evening. I tell her I already called a local pizza place and asked for a delivery to coincide with Jennifer getting home from work. "Already paid for it, even a tip."

"Did you order the alfredo chicken pizza with cheese crust for me?" Angela is very specific in what she will eat in the way of pizza. She is specific about most foods.

"Of course. And pepperoni and sausage with extra cheese for the rest of us. There's enough for you to give the pepperoni a try as well."

"Yuck."

Maybe I will broaden her food horizons another day. "Just go ahead and eat without me, OK?"

Dinner taken care of, and my absence for the evening explained, I continue to follow the Lexus and Amy Nyberg. She appears to be heading back to Stillwater, ostensibly for another workout. I wonder what kind of workout it is going to be this time. I amuse myself with several crisp double entendre workout and sex lines. I have the notebook – I should use them later as part of an open mic night.

The late afternoon workout seems to be a legitimate one, as she pulls into a full-sized athletic spa and club that is part of the Stillwater Community Center. I am able to park in the large parking lot and not feel at all conspicuous.

I want to wait for her to finish, but my bladder again does not cooperate. I feel good that I have been able to match her every workout with a bathroom break.

When I return from the men's room, I go to the front desk and make up a story about my family moving to the area in the near future and ask if I can look around. Wearing my biking gear with an après-ride long sleeve shirt makes me fit in nicely. I carry my water bottle with me for even more effect. I spot Nyberg in a private session, working with a personal trainer. She is shifting a medicine ball from side-to-side while sitting on a ball that builds her core strength. One look at the trainer and I conclude that she is not sleeping with him. He does not look like he sleeps with any of his female clients, not that there's anything wrong with that.

An hour later she emerges in another outfit. I am not keeping score or anything, but she is on her third outfit of the day. This one features longer leggings with pink highlights rather than the bright yellows from earlier, and a short tank top over a yellow sports bra. I know her next stop will be an outdoor distance run as evening approaches. I am glad that this is her last workout of the day because I am exhausted from following her around these last few days. Her exercise regimen is my exercise regimen at this point.

She pulls into a parking lot built for those who use the Gateway Trail. Only two cars remain, and they have expensive bike racks off their backsides. With the sun starting to fall behind the tall trees to the west, soon there will only be two cars left in the lot. Nyberg parks over on the east side and uses the side of her SUV to balance herself as she goes through a rather elaborate stretching regimen to prepare for the run ahead. I must give her credit here – she is remarkably limber. I use the outdoor toilet on the west side. Without making eye contact, I futz with my bicycle and pretend to be adjusting the straps, as though deciding whether to ride. Looking up and down the trail, I am horrified to see that she is walking towards me. I start to remove the bike from the rack in order to avoid making eye contact and avoid suspicion. Is she going to ask me about trail conditions? Where I bought my jersey?

Of course, she just wants to use the john before she runs. I try to look cool and collected as I nod to her. As she approaches, she gives me an appraising look as athletes tend to do, and I suspect she decides that as a mere cyclist I pose no threat to her. There is the slightest acknowledgement of my presence, I imagine a smirk of superiority that I can't see since I am avoiding looking at her. Not wanting to be there when she gets out, I hastily jump on my bike and ride towards Hadley and the setting sun.

I stop several yards down the path and get off my bike and turn back to the lot. I lean down over the bike, as though I heard something in the gear box that warrants a closer look. If she runs toward me, I can remount and easily beat her down the trail, her training as a super athlete notwithstanding. If she heads towards her car, I can follow her into the woods and return to my car and be gone before she finished her run. My breath is catching as I peer through the foliage to see which direction she went.

She jogs slowly to her Lexus and opens the door. She removes her phone and what appears to be some very high-end wireless headphones, probably Bose, and inserts them in her ears. She holds her phone in her right hand as she runs hard down the Gateway Trail to the east.

Breathing a sigh of relief, I return to the car and attach our old bike trailer to my bike. I love it when a plan comes together.

CHAPTER ELEVEN

I know that some murders are committed in the heat of passion, a white-hot rage that consumes a person and as a result they act out. Not to be critical, but how do you expect to get away with something that you do not plan for carefully? I know the punishment for a murder committed in the heat of passion is less than that for a premeditated act, but if you do something without reducing your risk as best you can you shouldn't do it in the first place.

Anyway, dumb people get caught all the time, while smart ones have long and successful runs before someone snitches on them. Keep your secrets secret and you may take them to your grave with you. That's my plan at least. Avoid capture by working the details.

My time observing the movements of Amy Nyberg has helped me piece together my plan to rid the world of a narcissistic and horrible person. I started by taking our old bike trailer out of the attic storage area. It would be tight, but I estimate that I can temporarily store a body in it. Comfort will not be a concern. Back in the day we would haul at least two kids at a time, often with both of them in child seats, so it is surprisingly spacious. Once we had both of them and a cooler in there due to a sudden rainstorm. Good old dad got to pull it back to the van while mom rode ahead faster and stayed relatively dry. The additional weight of the payload was not a problem.

I spent a few rides pulling the trailer empty, to reacquaint myself with what it's like to pull something with my bicycle. There was a two for $8 sale on softener salt so I added 80 pounds to replicate the weight factor. I even broke it down and brought it with me to a few trailheads to get used to storing it in the car, removing it, setting it up, and folding it down again.

I am ready to carry out my plan tonight. Whenever I think maybe I should let things go, I remember her parking illegally in the handicapped spot and ignoring the poor old man struggling to get his wife into the store, and my resolve strengthens.

I did a nice ride earlier down the Gateway Trail, ending at Pine Point Park. It gave me a chance to pick out the optimal spot for the ambush and attack.

What the...? No emotion, no guilt? Are you not human? The notion that this is morally wrong, abhorrent, and of course illegal behavior never crosses my mind. This is just not the way my brain operates. By the time I reach my chosen location for my encounter with Nyberg, I am sure I have thought of and adjusted for all possible scenarios. I have a plan that I am working, I have thought through several possible variations and how I will react. A stone-cold killer stands at the ready under the cover of trees, bicycle and trailer secreted but accessible, lying in wait for his victim. She unknowingly runs about 500 yards east of me, heading west towards her car. Tonight, she will not make it that far.

It is getting very dark as I wait in a low spot near a curve in the trail. I pulled a black long-sleeve shirt over my bright bicycle jersey so I am more inconspicuous in my hiding area. In addition to making me stick out less, it will also serve as way to stanch the blood flow afterward. The less bleeding the less DNA is spread that must be eradicated. Make a plan, work the plan.

Two hundred yards down the trail, I hear something rustling in the woods. Nyberg goes off the trail and does pullups, pushups, and sit-ups before returning to the trail for her final mile west to the parking lot. Where I wait, she will likely slow her pace as a cool-down for the final mile to her car. A very high-end rider on a sleek and fast bike zooms by. He will likely continue east to his home. No one else is on the trail because it is getting to the point where one cannot return to the lot without lights activated to see, not just to be seen.

I can hear her coming down the trail towards me, shoes clapping rhythmically on the asphalt trail. Her breathing is more labored due to the calisthenics. She is running at a marathoner pace to allow her body to recover from her run. Clap, clap, clap. An impressive level of conditioning and training. Regardless of her regimen, she is also at her most vulnerable due to her reduced speed and being in recovery mode. As for me, there is no self-doubt, no stopping to reconsider. Time to act.

I lunge out of the trees low and fast. I can hear Katy Perry blasting through the wireless headphones. As I had surmised earlier, they are expensive Bose sport units. I briefly toy with the idea of taking them with me and replacing my older Beats. Would they just pair with my phone? Probably, like a lost dog bonding with a new owner. Was the yellow-green color too showy? I would have to keep them in my riding drawer in the garage with all of my other biking equipment and only take them out for riding. That would work. Remember to wipe them down thoroughly before using them. Would there be a history of prior pairings in the headphone memory? Can you reset them to factory defaults and clear that out? Stay on task here nascent killer.

My shoulder strikes her in the right hip and the force of the tackle carries both of us off the trail into the softer shoulder consisting of grass and pine needles. My rib cage scrapes over a pine cone, but I am in a zone such that it does not matter. Before she can react, I pull my knife from the sheath attached to the inside of my waist pull string and strike her once in her neck. I remove the blade and pull her left shoulder towards me. I strike again at the base of the neck. Either blow will sever the spinal cord and death comes in a matter of seconds. I return the knife to the sheath after wiping it down on my black shirt. I pull the shirt off and wrap it tightly around her neck to keep bleeding contained in its absorbent cotton. I step on her cell phone. This is the day the music died. I stuff it in my pocket for later disposal.

I pause for a moment to take in all that is happening around me. The crickets are still chirping, other forest noises continue, oblivious to the carnage that has just taken place. I look in the light brown colored sand for wet spots that indicate blood. Nothing. I scan quickly around the perimeter for items that may have fallen out of hands or pockets. Nothing. No scrape marks in the pine needles strewn atop the ground, no suspicious markings on the trees, no broken branches that would indicate a struggle occurred. I can hear my breath begin to modulate as I turn my attention to the next item on my mental checklist, the removal and disposal of the body.

A lifeless body weighing around 125 pounds is not easy to lift and carry, but it is not that hard either. I drape her over my shoulders and lift myself upright, carrying her a few yards to where the bike and trailer are secreted. She is not the only one who has exercised to prepare for this moment in time, I remind myself with a bit of pride. I carefully arrange her in the trailer by curling her inside the passenger area. As I suspected, the trailer is sturdy enough, and large enough, to hold her. I pull on the cover and attach the straps to close off any ability to see into the trailer. I pull my bicycle with its new trailer payload back on the trail, put my helmet on, turn on the headlamp, set it on strobe for maximum visibility, make sure the taillight is strobing as well, and begin pedaling towards the car. Just a safety-conscious rider returning after going a little farther than he anticipated. Happens all the time on a trail as welcoming as the Gateway. You forget that as far as you ride in you have to return that same distance.

As I approach the parking area, I can see my car. Not sure why that calms me, but it does. I can feel my heart rate lower further. Then, however, I catch my breath when I see there is another car in the lot. I had not expected that. How can I transfer the body when there is someone else loading up their bicycle? I start to think about how far I will have to ride farther towards North St. Paul to let that person load up and leave so my car is the only one left in the lot. Then, it dawns on me that the other car in the lot is the Lexus SUV belonging to the person currently occupying my trailer. A sigh of relief and a quick laugh and I am at the side of my car.

Several years ago, Jennifer and I finished off our basement. What I really mean is that we paid people to finish off our basement. I would argue that the guy writing the checks is an integral part of any remodeling project. Without the financing nothing gets done, or started for that matter. Anyway, in order to save a few bucks along the way, we agreed that we would stuff insulation between the studs, and staple the plastic sheathing over it as a moisture barrier. It was a long weekend of work, but we got a sense of accomplishment when we could point out that we had helped out. We also saved money in the process.

When we bought the plastic barrier rolls from the helpful fellow at Menard's, he jokingly said that the plastic sheeting could be as clear as Saran Wrap, or less translucent if you needed to wrap a body. That is what I am thinking about as I move the body from trailer to trunk. I carefully lined the trunk with the plastic earlier in the day, pulled the folds out for more than enough plastic to cover it completely.

The trailer is quickly folded down onto itself and placed on the back seat. The bike takes just a moment to attach to the rack, and within less than two minutes I am starting the car and backing out. I remove the shirt from around the neck, still damp from the blood loss. I place the shirt in a Holiday plastic bag, knot it closed, and stop at a dumpster along the way and toss it in. No loose ends.

Driving along Highway 36, I turn up the radio and carefully follow all traffic laws. This is not the best night to get pulled over for speeding or not signaling a turn. I feel a serenity coming over me as the distance increases. I am exhilarated and I have no regrets, but something is missing for me. I am still pondering that as I pull into my next parking spot so that I can transport the body from my trunk to its final resting spot in the Mississippi River. I am becoming adept at assembling the bike and trailer combo, accomplishing it in the dark of night and seemingly within seconds.

Dropping the body over the railing of the Stone Arch Bridge is quick and easy. The bridge is lit, but in the dark of night the lights create just a circle of brightness below that quickly dissipate as you move away to the areas between the lampposts. Splitting the space between two lamps allows me to work under a level of darkness that leaves me knowing that no one can see me unless they happen upon me on the bridge. That, of course, does not happen. It is too late for exercise freaks and too early for the bar crowd to be on the bridge.

I cut up the plastic sheeting using a box cutter on a side street somewhere south of downtown Minneapolis and make three more short stops on the way to stuff plastic bags filled with plastic into various garbage cans. My route is random and untraceable.

The house is dark and quiet as I creep into the laundry room and place my biking clothes in the washer, starting an express cycle with minimal detergent. I jump in the shower, get cleaned up, and decide to slip into bed this night without my usual bed attire.

Jennifer rolls over to face me as I get settled in under the covers. "You're late tonight. That must have been quite a job fair." I do not have to answer her, as she feels me pressing against her. We kissed long and passionately.

"It was quite a ride indeed." No more words are necessary. And, it is quite a ride indeed.

CHAPTER TWELVE

The drive back from Marine on St. Croix to Minneapolis took close to an hour in traffic. The Hennepin County Medical Examiner's office is located across the street from USBank Stadium, home of the Minnesota Vikings. Not long into the ride, Bixby and Little had communicated, in a telepathic way that only longtime partners in law enforcement can understand, that this was NOG, as in "Not Our Guy". While brusque and a bit arrogant, Nyberg was exhibiting no signs of guilt whatsoever. The two detectives had never ridden with a potential suspect for that long in a car and been wrong about the suspect's involvement in a crime. At this point, they were simply providing transportation for a family member to identify a body. The questions faded as the two of them began thinking about their next moves to advance the case.

It's never easy to watch someone come to grips with the horrible news that their loved one is gone, and, in this case, had been the victim of a violent death. Nyberg did not speak on the return trip. Arranging for a ride back to Marine on St. Croix for him seemed tacky, so the two offered him a ride home. Still dazed and unsure what to do, Nyberg agreed.

"Sir, I know this is uncomfortable, but the sooner we can start talking to people the sooner we can find the person or persons responsible. Do you mind if I ask you some questions about your wife's friends? We need to put together a timeline of her recent activities." Bixby smiled apologetically.

Nyberg waved his hand dismissively. Bixby took this as his agreement. Based on his questions, she assembled a list of four friends with whom Amy spent the most time, and became convinced that they needed to get their hands on her cell phone and its contents immediately. As they saw so frequently, people live their lives through their phones, and it contains incredible amounts of revelatory data. Bernie texted the office and asked that a warrant be drawn up immediately to look at Amy Nyberg's texts and phone records.

The next morning, with Leland Nyberg back at work and his administrative assistant busy making all the necessary arrangements and making the difficult calls notifying friends and relatives of her boss' wife's death, Bixby and Little were seated in a large, picturesque house in Woodbury with Rebekka Sith, Amy Nyberg's best friend. Sith was average in height but very slim. She wore her light brown hair in a pixie style with bangs that came halfway down her forehead.

She asked that the detectives call her "Bekkie", and spelled it out for them. Bixby and Little exchanged a glance that communicated "Exotic Dancer Name" to each other. Unbeknownst to the general public, the homicide department maintained a list of the most unusual names they encountered over the course of their meetings with the public. They reviewed the combined list at their end of the year holiday parties and awarded prizes. Looking up from her notes, fighting back a smile, Bixby asked how Bekkie came to know the victim.

"We first met at the community center gym in Stillwater. Then we both joined the workout center downtown. We were in aerobics classes together, and we decided to train outside the class too because we wanted a better cardiovascular outcome than what the class alone could provide. Not everyone shared our desire to be the best. Being an ultra-athlete can be lonely without someone to work out with and inspire you. We ran, swam, and competed with each other, but never against each other. She was better than me most of the time, but I think I inspired her to go for it."

Little ignored the cliché and pressed on. "Did you do things together besides working out?"

"Yes, of course, that's why we were best friends. We would meet at the gym twice a week for our morning workout, get coffee or smoothies, do another workout focused on our cores, have lunch, go for a bike ride or swim, and then go to the fitness center for more strength and conditioning. Sometimes we even had dinner together. I have a bit of a sweet tooth, so having Amy around kept me on track." For the first time, she faltered. "Who am I going to work out with now?"

"I'm sorry for your loss," was all Bixby could muster as a response. She paused for a moment. "Any ideas why anyone would do this to your best friend?" She emphasized 'best' enough to cause Elliott to raise an eyebrow at her.

"Gosh, not at all. We ultra-athletes are competitive, but we leave it out there and support each other everywhere else. It's about achieving our best selves, not so much competing against someone else."

"What about Leland?"

"Who's Leland?" The best friend label was beginning to fade.

"Her husband. How did she get along with him?"

"Oh, you mean the old guy? I saw him at the finish line a couple of times. I thought it was her dad or uncle or something. She never really talked about him, but if there was anything wrong, she would have confided in me."

Later, in the driveway of the massive house of Bekkie Sith, Bixby looked puzzled. "I don't get it. Where do these people get the money to afford a house like this and then work out all day? I wish I had found a woman like that, one who could support me while I pursued my dream of ultra-fitness and excessive spending."

"Simple, you can marry for love," Little replied. "Or you can marry for money and lifestyle, with little or no regard for love. That's what I'm thinking happened here."

"Man, that's cold. Can't you fall in love with a person who happens to be rich?"

"Every episode of 'Dateline' and '48 Hours' says no, it's not possible," Elliott responded.

Bixby looked over at her partner. "OK, Mr. Cynical, I think this explains why Saturday night is your first date in, what, three years?"

"There may be a connection," Little conceded.

Leaving their discussion of Elliott's cynical view of love behind, they instead drove to their next destination, a Jamba Juice near Radio Drive, also in Woodbury. It was not hard to spot Abby Johnson, their next subject. She was wearing workout clothes that were more expensive than either of their suits, shirts, Elliot's tie, and shoes combined.

From Abby Johnson they learned that she and the victim worked out together once or twice a week, focusing on different aspects of exercise and fitness, went to get coffee and smoothies together, and occasionally drank wine over lunch and dinner with the rest of the "ladies of exercise." The two women shared a passion for extreme road cycling. Abby considered herself to be Amy's best friend, although she was surprised to learn that Amy had two children from her first marriage. "Gosh, she never talked about them at all," was her response to Elliott's question.

In about 30 minutes the two were off to do their third interview. Minnie Kohl lived in a house that suggested she was related to the Kohl's store family. It turned out that she was not, however, but her husband, also her second, was high up at Wells Fargo. She, too, was exquisitely dressed as though coming from or going to a workout, or both. Minnie was the fourth member of the exercise team, and did not know that her best friend used to work at 3M.

Later in the afternoon, sitting in their desk chairs behind two desks pushed together so they faced each other, Bixby and Little compared notes and assessed their situation. Nothing much had been revealed despite their intense focus on the case. Little grabbed a whiteboard on wheels and pulled it over to their desks. He wrote the name "Amy Nyberg" in the top center, and then wrote out the names of those they had spoken to so far. Then they agreed on a snapshot for each of them.

Leland Nyberg – *husband, rich, unlikely suspect, paid the bills and wrote checks but not interested in what she did day to day*

Bekkie Sith – *"Nike", "Best Friend", did not know Leland, mid-morning workouts twice a week, lunch*

Abby Johnson – *"Under Armour", "Best Friend", did not know she had children, lunch, afternoon workout once a week*

Minnie Kohl – *"Adidas", "Best Friend", did not know she worked at 3M before, lunch, shared personal trainer*

Conclusions: *all 'best friends' but not very close, holes in timeline - morning after first workout / before lunch, dinner, after dinner, how did she get to Gateway?*

Bixby took a picture of the whiteboard with her cell phone.

Little stared contemplatively at the board, comparing it to his notes from their interviews that day.

"The first name on the list is the name of the trainer she used every morning. Let's start with the Stillwater gym in the morning and see if we can retrace her steps for the day," Little suggested. They agreed to meet in Roseville first thing in the morning and head to Stillwater together.

The next morning, Elliott Little parked the Impala in a spot two blocks from the exercise spa. As the two detectives approached, they noticed how many expensive SUVs filled the parking spots closer to the spa, which was housed in a converted warehouse. The gym occupied the bottom half of the structure, while the top floors advertised lofts for sale. They walked in to the workout facility, an open area the size of a two basketball courts broken up by large pillars. The pillars were wrapped in foam so that guests could punch them while in the throes of exercise. Above, pipes running the length of the workout area were painted in bright colors. "No way could I afford to be a member here," Little muttered. "And I live in downtown Minneapolis."

"Bless your heart, Elliott, they wouldn't want you as a member," Bixby replied. "They don't cater to men here."

A pleasant but distracted member, trying to keep pace with her fellow exercisers, an exhorting leader, and pulsating Latin music, directed them to a small office area at the back of the workout area. Each group had a canvas curtain in more vibrant colors marking off their exercise space. As they walked back, they encountered three other groups of women similarly engaged but to different kinds of music. The last group featured much older participants dancing elegantly to ballroom music.

"Look, they have men here," Little said, pointing to the couples dancing. "I could handle that class."

"I doubt it," Bixby responded. "You're not much of a dancer."

Once in the small glassed-in office of the owner, Myles Darland, the detectives could still feel the deep bass notes of the music, but it did not overwhelm their attempt to converse. After a few questions, they both noticed that it took him extra seconds before he spoke, as though he had to think about how he would respond. Any pause in answering a question is a clear sign to experienced detectives that prevarication is soon to follow.

"Amy was a regular at my first group workout class in the morning. I call it 'Good Day, Sunshine'," Darland told them.

"After the Beatles song?" Bixby interjected

Darland looked puzzled, not familiar with the reference. Pause before speaking. "Anyway, we have lots of energy in the room, and Amy was always a leader. "

"How long was she in your class?" Little asked.

Long pause, approaching awkward. "Since I opened the gym three years ago. Her success in ultramarathons drew lots of people here. Many other women thought that if they could work out like she did, they could be in great shape, too." Myles had a habit of clearing his throat with a look of nervousness thrown in. He threw off more "tells" with each question and answer.

"What else did you do with her?" Elliott followed up, knowing there was more to his story.

Longer pause, mostly awkward. "I'm not sure I understand what you mean." Darland was beginning to look even more uncomfortable. He was now stammering as well.

"Look, we're trying to establish the timeline for the last day of this woman's life, not judge anyone for their actions." Bixby maintained a tone of skepticism in her every word.

"She was also one of my private clients." He had now taken to blinking frequently.

"What does 'private client' entail?" Bixby asked, enjoying the bracing of a truly bad liar. She raised her left eyebrow as she asked the question.

"Well, she wanted more work on her stamina and hill climbing, so after the morning class I would work with her on the hills behind the gym. She knows, or knew, that you can overtake competitors going uphill better than at any other time during a race." Darland seemed even more tormented.

Instinctively, Bixby and Little knew that silence would be the best response. In a few seconds, it paid off.

"OK, we had an affair last year." As the words came out of his mouth in a torrent, Myles appeared to calm down, as though revealing what was very obvious was a breakthrough towards resolving his internal turmoil.

"And…" Bixby was enjoying the process by which a witness breaks himself down more and more by the second, and with his own words. Best to stay quiet and let it happen.

"We agreed to end it because it was cutting into her prep time for nationals. Once that was over, we each had moved on to other priorities in our lives." He paused, and looked at the two with great seriousness. "Look, my wife cannot find out about this, ever. She's pregnant with our second child. If she finds out, the child support would kill me." He looked at the two pleadingly.

"It will only come up if it is relevant to the investigation of her murder," Little responded, more than a little annoyed that the death of a former client and paramour seemed trivial, and that the pain of his wife finding out about his unfaithfulness was measured more monetarily than emotionally. "What did she do after her two workouts with you in the morning?"

"First, she went to Starbucks. I told her, 'drink coffee or make fruit and protein smoothies at home – so much cheaper and better for you', but she told me she did not have the time and that saving money was not important to her. I got the impression that she was not happy at home, and spending money frivolously was a way to get back at her husband. Larry, I think his name is."

"It's Leland, and we've talked with him at length. From the sounds of it, money was not a problem since she paid you to tell her to run up a hill faster," Elliott smirked.

"There is more technique and training involved in hill work than you realize," Myles responded, looking at Little as though he would surely not understand the intricacies involved with most types of exercise.

"What is your wife's number? We should really talk to her about Amy as well. She must know something that would help -," Bixby interjected. She held her pen poised over her notepad.

"No, no, please don't." Darland pushed back his ball cap, a black one that advertised the name of the club in ornate gold lettering, and ran his fingers through his long dark hair, pushing a stray lock behind his ear. He stared down at the floor.

Bixby had no intention of calling his wife, but wanted to keep him off guard and nervous. Witnesses tend to be more honest when the pressure makes them uncomfortable.

"Ok, we can probably wait on that for now. What did Mrs. Nyberg do after Starbucks?"

"She worked with another trainer later in the morning. He worked on her core strength through a free weight regimen, I believe. I have his number if that would help." Myles had decided that cooperation would be the best tact. And, he ran classes or was in his gym around scores of witnesses all day and into the evening, so he was easily eliminated as a suspect.

Myles walked them through to the front door and the pockets of competing music and the gyrating bodies. He held it open for them as they stepped out into the warming May morning. "This doesn't have to involve my wife, right? I told you everything I know. I promise."

"For now, we will talk to more people and see where that leads us. Our first priority is to find Amy Nyberg's killer, not to reveal that you are not a great husband." Bixby looked hard at Darland. "She probably already knows that. "

"Doesn't your wife deserve better? She's about to become a mother for the second time," Elliott added. Myles Darland looked away, the guilt showing on his face. He nodded shamefully in agreement.

The duo decided to meet next with the weightlifting coach Amy Nyberg also worked out with regularly later in her typical mornings, but before she met her 'besties' for lunch. His gym turned out to be in a twin home in a development full of the same unimaginative cookie cutter architectural design. Many of the places had the dilapidated look of having been turned over numerous times, and of a homeowner's association that did little more than collect a monthly fee and give back the bare minimum in maintenance and upkeep.

Little pulled into a driveway that was almost wide enough to serve the two double stall garage doors separated by a thin column of peeling and fading siding. The one on the right hung crookedly with several deep dents in its cheap aluminum. Looking under the door revealed a garage stall stacked to the ceiling with boxes and clear plastic bins of toys for all ages.

A short time later, seated on a cheap-looking couch in a living room filled with secondhand and mismatched furniture, the detectives spoke with Andre Toffte, strength and conditioning coach, and "extreme exercise" consultant. Toffte sat in a frayed easy chair that was once beige, sipping from a water bottle while constantly flexing his left arm. His arms were barely contained in a 'Gold's Gym' t-shirt that looked older than back when Gold's Gym was still a thing. The lower level of the split entry townhouse was filled with free weights and lifting benches. The unit had a permanent smell of sweat and cheap pine cleaner that was losing the battle on a daily basis.

"Yeah, I was doing the horizontal leg press with her." Toffte spoke with barely concealed pride.

"I don't even know what that means," replied Elliott, a puzzled look on his face.

"I think it means that 'Muscles' here was also sleeping with the deceased," Bixby explained.

"Yeah, but before she was deceased, and I had nothing to do with her getting deceased."

"Thank you for the clarification." Bixby shook her head.

Despite the disgust they felt towards Toffte, it was clear he too had nothing to do with the murder based on his daily schedule that extended until the evening. Although he appeared to be a bit dense, his bookkeeping and appointment calendar was current and well done. They left to make their way to their next stop, the community center. On their way to their car, which was parked next to Toffte's truck, an older gentleman scurried across the street towards them. "Are you the police?"

"Yes, we are." Bixby replied. As she always dressed in a navy or charcoal gray suit with white or light blue blouses underneath, she and Little certainly looked the part.

"Are you here about the illegal operation of a business on homeowner association property? I've called it in several times. All the cars parked on the street, all the people coming and going, it's a clear violation."

"That sounds like a civil matter that you need to take up with your association. This is what, Washington County? We're from Minneapolis."

The attempt to deflect responsibility had the effect of getting the man even more agitated. "The county doesn't care, the Oakdale police sure don't care," he said excitedly. "I provide license plate numbers, descriptions of the cars, everything, and they do nothing. Three years and all they have done is written one warning letter. I bet the homeowner laughed and threw it away."

"I bet he had to sound out the big words in the letter before he threw it away," Little said.

Bernie Bixby jumped in. "Can you email us the plate numbers and car descriptions?"

"I sure can. Anything to get this scofflaw out of here."

The detectives gave him a card, and the gentleman promised to send the information to them the next time his grandson visited. "He's the only one who can run my computer and send emails."

They thanked him and left for Stillwater and their next visit, the community center. In the car, Little asked Bixby to look up 'scofflaw'.

"A person who flouts the law, especially by failing to comply with a law that is difficult to enforce effectively," she read from the Google dictionary.

"That's good to know. Now, can you look up 'flout'?"

Bixby closed her browser in mock disgust. She reached over and touched Little's right hand gently, "Sweetie, you really need to up your game if you're going to hang around a PhD. She's a doctor you know." Elliott looked a little concerned, but said nothing.

"My parents were doctors."

"I do know that, but sometimes brainpower skips a generation."

Once in the community center, a person running the front desk directed them back to the afternoon instructor who did private sessions with Nyberg. He was just coming on duty, and had a few moments to talk with them before his first session of the day.

"Yes, Miss Amy was one of my best clients. She was so dedicated to working out, and so willing to do anything to get stronger and faster. A delight to work with. I can't believe she's gone." Phillip, pronounced 'Phillipe' like the actor Ryan Phillipe, was fighting back tears. "She would come in four or five days a week and push me to push her harder. I've never had anyone so dedicated. I might never again." The battle with tears was lost. Bixby patted Phillip's hand sympathetically, and then hugged her. Breaking the embrace after what seemed like an interminable few seconds, the suddenly uncomfortable homicide detectives mumbled their thanks and made their way to the car.

Bixby was unable to sit still in her seat. "Phillip was the first person who seemed at all affected by Amy Nyberg's murder. We're talking a widowed husband, three self-proclaimed best friends, two men who were sleeping with her, and the only person who shows any real emotion is the personal trainer who had no designs on her outside of training her. This is seriously messed up."

Little agreed. "She must have done a good job of distancing herself from others."

CHAPTER THIRTEEN

The detectives got lost on the 3M campus in Maplewood, their fourth stop of the day. A security guard in a Ford Ranger had to walk up to their car, find out what their business was at 3M, and then have them follow him in the truck to the main building for their obligatory visitor passes. A burly but bored security guard asked them to sit while he called their "host".

"How can anyone find anything in this place?" muttered Little as they waited in uncomfortable chairs in the waiting area. Two women approached, apologized profusely for the delay as they seated the detectives in a small conference room, and promised that someone would be with them shortly. "At least we warrant two people to keep an eye on us," Little noted wryly.

"I guess this is what it feels like to be forced to wait," Bixby noted.

"Now we know why it works. I'd be willing to confess to something to get out of these chairs and this confusing place," Little responded. "I'm not sure I can get us out of here again."

"I read somewhere that corporations purchase uncomfortable chairs for their conference rooms to keep meetings shorter," Bernie responded. "I wonder if that works. Remember when

Brock gives her annual HR sponsored talk about diversity and inclusion?"

"Oh yeah, the one where every year you try to excuse yourself because you're already female, black, and a lesbian? Three minority classifications excuse you from attending?"

"Think sitting in chairs like these would get her to finish on time?"

"No, that's her time to shine. She has way too many examples to discuss with us. Never happen." Little shook his head.

"How about when she told us that we can no longer use 'coarse language' when interacting with the public as a way to decrease the risk of harassment litigation?" Bixby added.

"Oh, you bet I do. Everyone in the room told her to go f-"

The door to the conference room opened and a flustered blonde in a blue blazer and a frazzled but professional look entered. As she stepped in, she apologized profusely for a meeting with a VP that ran late. Dawn Hill continued to tell them how sorry she was as she brought them up the elevator to another rather pedestrian conference room. They settled in their seats and Little led the questioning.

"How did you know Amy Nyberg?"

"We worked together on a project involving a revolutionary new type of sandpaper."

Little and Bixby exchanged a look that communicated "How does anything revolutionize sandpaper?" Rather than ask the question they turned their eyes back to Hill as she continued.

"Amy was a senior project manager here. She made sure products were brought to market on time and on budget. She was very good at her job. At least, some people thought that." She cleared her throat and looked away for a second.

"Why do you say 'some people thought that'?" Bixby pressed.

"Well, she could be demanding, always harping on people to meet their deadlines, accusing them of holding up the project. I guess you could say she rubbed some people the wrong way. "

Bixby concluded that Hill's pun comparing her personality to sandpaper was completely unintentional. "In what way was she abrasive?" Little raised his eyebrows, appreciating the pun being extended.

"I've heard her described as 'condescending' by more than one person who worked with her. One admin refused to work with her and threatened to resign if asked. Apparently, Amy told her an admin's job was to make copies of presentations and to set up the room for a meeting so that a senior project management did not have to waste time. That was not the only time we heard a complaint. There were several people who complained that she was a bully. I have emails she wrote stored in a folder that were quite unprofessional."

"So, did she leave of her own accord? I mean, I've been told I rub people the wrong way, but I figure I'm just a woman trying to make it in a male-dominated world. The thing is, we have a murder victim on our hands. Did someone kill her because she talked down to them at work?" Bixby leaned forward in anticipation of the answer.

"Oh goodness, no, I don't think so. She came to my office and announced that she was leaving, so it was definitely of her own volition. She also told me that it would take at least two additional head count to adequately complete the projects she led." She paused for a moment, as though pondering the notion that a modern corporation would increase head count to replace a departing employee. "When she left we moved her projects over to other project managers and did not replace her."

"Did anyone hold a grudge against her that would extend beyond the workplace?" Little asked.

"No," she said, shaking her head. "I don't think so. But, let's just say we usually hold happy hour celebrations when people leave 3M, just to wish them the best and send them on their way with good thoughts from co-workers. Well, there was a happy hour, but Amy wasn't invited."

"Ouch."

"Exactly. Probably not enough anger for a murder, but you never know I guess…"

The rest of the afternoon was spent meeting with former co-workers. Not one of them called themselves a friend of the victim., either at work or outside of work. The conclusion was that there was angst, but that angst was relieved by Nyberg's departure, and no one carried a grudge. They were just glad she had left the company and they could focus on their projects involving the latest advancements in abrasives.

The next morning, back in their office with desk chairs that felt like they were reclaimed from a 3M remodel, Bernie Bixby filled in more information about their victim and their case. On the board, under Amy Nyberg's name, she wrote "Goodbye Earl."

"What the does 'Goodbye Earl' mean?" Elliott asked.

"You know," Bixby said while poorly attempting to hide her smile and her pride in her upcoming punchline. "Like the Dixie Chicks song. She was the missing person no one really missed at all."

CHAPTER FOURTEEN

The next morning, the girls are off to school, and I am sitting at home in front of my computer. I read stories in both of the local papers, TV news sites, and a few other locations about the murdered ultra-athlete and wife of a 3M executive. Based on what little is being reported, it is looking like the police are stumped. I watch some interviews, one with the guy she met for the midmorning sex workout, and all he can say is that he is "Shocked, man. Just shocked. Not sure what to say." It appears you could ask him what time it is and he would be not sure what to say. He looks good in a tight t-shirt, I have to give him that much.

I continue to look for work, putting together an impressive three cover letters with two variations on my resume. It is clear that I am taking this time off very seriously. I am about to start a fourth application, this one requiring me to take a psychological profile. I am debating whether I am willing to debase myself so much that I will take a psychological profile in order to maybe get an interview for a crappy job. I decide I am willing, but only once. But then fate thankfully intervenes. My computer screen starts to pulsate. I try and answer the remaining questions on this ridiculous profile as quickly as possible, sensing bad things are happening to my laptop. I am almost done answering 'C' to the last few questions, knowing that I will not work for any company that requires applicants to take a psychological profile as part of the initial application process, but mostly because I have failed the test and will likely be on the permanent 'do not hire' list. And then, I am met with the blue screen of death.

I know you've seen this screen. Your state-of-the-art computer reverts to caveman hieroglyphics that give you an incomprehensible message, but you know what's going on. Your computer, "It's dead, Jim." Something to do with a Refmon code or some such thing. My hard drive and processor, or maybe my video card, or maybe something else, or maybe all of the above, is fried beyond repair or reclamation.

Back in the day I could call my tech line at work and some skilled technician would scurry up to my office and futz with my computer for a few minutes, shake his or her head in dismay, and swap out the computer. Instant upgrade and goodbye offending machine, recycle it for parts or maybe sell it off after being 'refurbished'.

Today, on my own, I have no such option. Time to go visit 'Toner Babe'. Just to make sure I will be able to see her when I go to the store, I send her an innocuous text message asking her if she "Still remembers the guy she helped a few weeks ago with toner and paper." The response is affirmative and filled with emojis. Without daughters to provided interpretive services I have to conclude on my own that she does in fact remember me and would be happy to help me with my computer issues. I separate the laptop from the monitor and printer, grab the power cord, and prepare to leave for the office supply store. Before I leave the garage, I text Jennifer and let her know that my computer has died and I am going out to have it looked at.

"Remember our budget," she responds. "Repair if possible."

OK, she makes a good point here. Maybe I have been known to go a little crazy when purchasing electronics. If it plugs in or runs on a battery, I like to buy the best, so her words are based on real life experience. I text back that I will go as cheap as I can, and even repair if possible. I already know that a repair will take days or weeks, and an out of work executive cannot wait that long while his job search languishes.

"Repair if possible," I smirk as I back out of the garage. "Yeah, right." Good thing texting is not accomplished hands-free using telepathy. I am not sure Jennifer would appreciate my mocking internal monologue.

The notion that Toner Babe treats all her repeat customers as she treats me quickly dissipates as she rushes to the sliding door to welcome me. She gives me a quick hug, thanks me for "entrusting your computer to me", and runs off with it to their work area. By the time I join it and her at the counter, the diagnostics have already concluded that the hard drive is shot and needs to be replaced. Despite the obvious benefit to the store if I replace the laptop, her sadness in reporting the news appears genuine. We walk over, her hand on my arm, to see what makes sense for me in replacement laptops.

"You use it for mostly business applications, so no need to consider Apple products," she says confidently. Toner Babe lets me know that touch screens and removeable keyboards and all the other things that make a laptop act more like a tablet add to the expense and are unnecessary since I have a household full of tablets already. I must have either told her our household is filled with tablets or she correctly guessed. Either way, she is good at her job. Based on her recommendations, I select a Dell laptop, mostly because that is what we used at two of my former employers. Nothing fancy – it is a Dell after all - just a basic Windows 10 computer with Office 365 and a decent-sized screen.

Speaking of screens, she asks about my monitors, and is shocked, shocked I tell you, that I get by with only one monitor, as if I may be the dullest person on earth. She insists that I get not one but two new and very large monitors. It gives me the option, if I choose, to use three screens at the same time. Besides, she assures me, I would need to buy an adapter to make the old monitor work with the new laptop, and by the time I get done messing around with it I would want new monitors anyway. And, with her discounts and an almost two-for-one price on the monitors, I am spending about what I expected to spend to replace the laptop in the first place.

Wait, there's more. With the purchase, she assures me breathlessly, she will transfer whatever data she can from the fried hard drive to the new laptop on the spot. I also buy the recommended external drive so my next hard drive failure will not threaten to cost me my files. There is also free Cloud backup as well. How did I get to this point in my life, so far behind the computer times as to be laughable? Laughable, if it were not so sad. I also buy a thumb drive that has about twice the capacity of the original hard drive of the deceased laptop. The world has certainly changed in terms of computers and storage capacity.

We walk up to the checkout area and ring up the purchases. I decline the extra warranties because, she points out, electronics either fail right away or last forever. We take the monitors to my car, and then go back into the store to walk over to the technology nook (her words, not mine) to transfer the data from one hard drive to another. As she sets up the cables and starts to run the software that will accomplish the transfer, she looks at me with full flirtatiousness. "How about I get this started and I meet you at O'Hannihan's? This is going to take about an hour. You can buy me lunch with all the money I saved you." That seems reasonable, since I do not want to watch bytes of data move from one computer to another. "Get a booth by the back. I like privacy," she suggests. Everything she said seems to have a sexual tinge to it, and I am not trying very hard to resist. I text Jennifer to let her know that I had no choice but to replace the laptop. I throw in a sad face emoji at the end so that she understands my emotional state at this tragic technological turn of events. It may have been a poop emoji since I am not really sure what emojis mean. Does one need to have emotions to be able to express them with emojis?

As for Toner Babe, I am not trying to fight this very hard at all. I believe I have already established my narcissistic tendencies. A guy can have fun and still be married and do right by his children. It's not like I'm going to sleep with her or anything like that. At least not over lunch. At least not over saving a few bucks on a computer purchase. I do have some standards after all.

Janelle joins me in a booth away from everyone else in the restaurant about ten minutes after I leave the store. She kisses me on the cheek and gives me a hug before sitting in the booth across from me. "I like these booths the best because the tables are not very wide."

I looked at her quizzically, not having ever given table width much thought. Big enough for the food is the extent of my analysis. "I guess I've never thought about it. It's cozy, I guess."

I nearly choke on my words when I feel her foot rubbing on my leg. "That's why I like these booths," she eyes me knowingly. As I squirm in an attempt to look natural, she is doing very unnatural things to me. I am still feeling self-conscious when we walk out of O'Hannihan's together, her arm entwined in mine.

I give her a ten-minute head start before I walk back in to pick up my new laptop. When I approach, I can see in her eyes that something is different and troubling. "Is there something wrong with the data transfer?" I ask, knowing that is not why she is looking at me like that.

"No, not at all." Her eyes, however, bely her words. Between the restaurant and the store, she has become somehow different, aloof. Is she afraid of me? Something is amiss.

"Hey, I had a great time at lunch. We should do it again," I say breezily, attempting to discern her state of mind. I'm hoping she does not think of this as a one-time deal. For this kind of service, I intend to be a customer for life.

"Oh, I did, too. It's just... Never mind."

I press her for what is wrong. My mind races through scenarios where she calls my wife, turns out to be a clingy stalker type, or suddenly lets me know she needs money for an operation or something. Every movie where casual hookups end badly for the guy. Geez, what was I thinking?

Then it dawns on me. She has seen something on my hard drive. All of the searches about Amy Nyberg, her divorce, her rebirth as the great athlete. Has she put things together and realized that I am a killer? My first attempt at covering my tracks is not going well at all. It appears I have more tracks to cover than I realized.

What do I do? I can't let her get away from me and start making phone calls. I sidle up to her and ask, "So, what time do you get off of work today? Maybe we can go hang out some more and you can teach me how to hook up my new laptop?" I ask this in a very nonchalant way. I, of course, do not need any such help. Plug and play is well within my technological skills.

"I'm done at 4, but I can tell my boss I'm not feeling well and leave as soon as I finish packing up your computer. I've sold enough for the store today."

Maybe she hadn't seen anything after all, but I can't take any chances. I need to be around her to make sure she's not suspicious. And, I can't leave her with any time at all with her phone to call or text someone with her suspicions about me. I need to be at her side constantly.

I take the laptop and leave the store, and then wait in my car for five long minutes that seem like an hour. She talks to some dweeby dude in a red vest, walks out of my sight for less than a minute, and then leaves the store carrying a small backpack. Janelle walks down another row of cars all the way to the end, and then comes back up from behind and joins me. I watch her every step both to and from the car. Laughing conspiratorially at our sneakiness, we are soon on the road.

I am beginning to think that this is not the first time she has done this when she asks me to pull over at a Holiday station. She goes in the store with her small backpack wearing her work polo and tan pants, and comes out in short shorts and a halter. Even her slip-on sandals are gone, replaced by black low-top Converse tennis shoes.

"Where are you taking me?" she asks, giggling. She grabs my arm at every opportunity. My estimation that she is in her late twenties and the age difference between us is not that great starts to change. I realize that she does not have to be a college graduate in order to work at the store, and I start to feel old and creepy. I'm working through a scenario where my daughter Mallory comes home from school with her new friend, Janelle. This has the potential to be 'Jeremy Irons in that 90's movie' creepy.

She must have sensed something because she then tells me she completed a Master's degree two years ago. Not finding a job despite a Master's in Fine Arts, she has been at the store for three years. My quick math makes me think she is in her mid to late twenties after all.

We groove to Van Halen 'Hot for Teacher', (she says "My stepdad loves old music, too" while I realize the lyrics are playing out in reverse), and my mind races to the best end game. If

I wait until dark, her car in the parking lot will draw undue attention to her absence from work and her most recent customers will be first up for scrutiny. Unless she sneaks off of work all the time with customers, I will have lots of explaining to do, and no alibi to rely on.

"So, have you ever hiked in Taylors Falls?" I ask. "The view from the cliffs overlooking the St. Croix River is spectacular."

"No, it sounds awesome, though. How do we get there?"

Based on the distance and the likely duration of the adventure, I convince her that we need to return to the store, pick up her car, and have her follow me there. She agrees to the plan.

"Do you need to text or call someone to let them know what you're doing?" I ask, always wanting to appear thoughtful.

"No, I finally live alone. I used to share an apartment with a co-worker, but she moved home a few months ago when her parents stopped helping with the rent. I got a promotion at work so I can afford the rent by myself. My cat is used to me keeping weird hours, so no worries. I am up for *whatever*." Her emphasis on 'whatever' gives me the tingles. Probably not for the same reason she intended, to be honest.

The loop back to the store parking lot is uneventful. I am able to drive over to Janelle's car without passing another car, and we leave from a more remote exit before getting back on streets with lots of traffic. Shopping centers have parking lots that envision far greater traffic than the stores generate on a weekday afternoon when schools are still in session. Soon two cars are traveling east and north towards Taylors Falls.

My plan is to stage an apparent suicide or accident for Toner Babe involving her jumping or falling off the rocks high above the St. Croix River. Whether intentional or by accident, the area is beset every year with tragedies. Young people who don't swim as well as they think they can get caught in impossibly strong currents, or slip when climbing rocks on a dare. They have no business doing these things, and it all ends the same way. Days or weeks later the bodies are found somewhere downstream. This seems to be the best way to avoid the risk she poses to me.

Parking two cars at the entrance to the park without raising suspicion has my brain working overtime for several miles. I need 24 to 48 hours for memories to fade about my nondescript gray Lexus sedan and a blue subcompact, a Nissan Versa I think, arriving together. I get my plan worked out as I begin the breathtakingly beautiful descent down Highway 8 into Taylors Falls. I make a mental note to return with Jennifer and the girls soon.

Taylors Falls has some of the nicest scenery in Minnesota, short of driving to the North Shore of Lake Superior. Even the most jaded teenager, albeit eventually and without using those exact words, will agree.

Janelle parks the Nissan in a back row away from the entrance to the trailhead, and I pull in a few stalls away. I want to be close but not appear to be part of an obvious pair of vehicles.

COINCIDENTAL EVIDENCE

I quickly join her at the driver's door and offer my arm as a chivalrous gesture. She grasps my elbow, removes her phone from her backpack, and pushes her phone into the impossibly tight rear pocket of her shorts. She did not appear to have used it on the trip here. I am giving thanks to Daisy Duke for her short cut-off jeans fashion look as we walk together towards the trail. It is a bit of an incline, so we need both arms to make our way to the trailhead, even in the paved parking lot.

I am surprisingly winded when we reach the familiar brown sign with the yellow etched letters. We use the reading of the signs and the cautions as a way to catch our breath. "Are we going to swim in the river? I'm not much of a swimmer," she offers.

"Oh, goodness no," I respond playfully. "We're going to be up above the water enjoying the view. See the sign?" I point to the part of the sign that is painted in a thicker yellow and reads 'Danger - No Swimming or Diving'. "We don't have to swim to have fun. Let's start by getting away from all these people," I say, waving to the parking lot that now contains four cars.

She giggles. "You're so funny". She grabs my hand and we start hiking the trail.

We trek along the banks of the St. Croix River, stopping to admire the potholes and other natural sites that are resplendent in the park. Along the way I associate a younger woman and her overly curious chocolate lab jumping around the dangerous potholes back to the cinnamon SUV in the lot. She's too distracted to notice us. Several minutes later we pass an older couple whom I decide belong to the Avalon, as only older people drive Toyota Avalons. This far away from the parking area, we now have the park to ourselves. I also carefully watch across the river on the Wisconsin side for hikers, and look for canoeists and kayakers in the river. "Let's take the River Trail," I suggest.

My confidence is high that we are out past where anyone will be able to see us. And, it is still early enough in the season that there will likely not be many others out today. At least, no one who drove is in the park.

The most popular part of the park is the hiking around the sinkholes, or potholes. It does not extend more than a few hundred yards down the river and from the trailhead. At that point, the park and its trails, mostly rocks with flat surfaces, end. Past the most popular area, however, are unofficial and unmaintained trails over rocks and around scraggly trees that have been used by hikers for years to explore the cliffs and overhangs for the best views of the river flowing rapidly below.

I suggest that we can be alone if we venture past the popular trails. Janelle is a willing participant, although I can sense that she is still troubled about something. Rather than confront me, or risk losing the magic of our beautiful afternoon together, she smiles wanly and begins jumping from rock to rock, turning back to invite me to follow her.

There are lots of rocks to jump to, several winding trails on compacted dirt, and gorgeous views in every direction. Allowing Janelle to set the pace, I notice a rock about the size of the palm of my hand, grab it, and place it in the pocket of my cargo shorts. That makes the right side of the shorts pull down with the weight and exposes the top of my underwear, but this is a minor, and abbreviated, inconvenience.

Janelle stops on a rocky outcrop and turns to me, her arms outstretched. We hug and we kiss for the first, and as it turns out, the last time. I reach down with my right hand, pull the rock from my pocket, raise it quickly, and strike her just above her left eye. I hold her with my left arm so that she cannot dodge the blow and she takes its full force. There is an instant of recognition of the danger, a look of shock in her eyes, followed by terror. I hold her for a few seconds to watch the panic leave her eyes, and then I twist her around and push her with both of my hands as hard as I can into the river below. The rock falls to the ground just below my feet.

As I take a stride towards the edge of the rock, I hear a sickening thud. The body hits a rock formation on the shore of the river, hangs on there long enough for me to start panicking and looking for a way to get down there, and then slips into the river. I pick up the rock with a bloody smudge on it and heave it into the river, never to be seen again. I once again look for anyone in the vicinity who could have seen anything of what had just transpired. Not a soul in sight. I make my way back to the car and soon I am in traffic heading for home. I have new electronics to set up. It's going to be a busy and exciting evening.

CHAPTER FIFTEEN

The investigation into the murder of Amy J. Nyberg had stagnated. The timeline for her last day had been established, but it did little to answer the pressing questions of 'who' killed her and 'why' she was singled out for murder. Detectives Bixby and Little could state with certainty that she left the community center in Stillwater around 7 pm, and bought her last smoothie of the day. The barista remembered her from her previous visits as impatient, unfriendly, and a non-tipper.

From that Starbucks she probably had driven to a parking area associated with the Gateway Trail in Oakdale, parked her car, and begun running and presumably performing other forms of exercise on the trail. No witness had been found or came forward who saw her in the parking lot, and there were no security cameras. She was either killed on or near the Gateway Trail, transported and dropped into the Mississippi River off of the Stone Arch Bridge, and her body was found the next day downstream below the University of Minnesota campus. Many people were questioned but no one was able to provide any additional insight. The best theory the detectives could offer was that the victim was selected at random. No motive for the murder was apparent. Her husband, her friends, her former co-workers, everyone had alibied out.

Murders without motives tend to go unsolved. Late in the afternoon on a Friday, the office deserted, Bixby and Little stared at each other across their shared workspace, trying to plot their next moves. Every turn left them staring at a wall. A blank wall.

"OK, that's it." Little began shutting down his computer and neatly organizing his paperwork back into the files for storage in his locked cabinet. "Monday morning, we start over. We re-interview everyone like it's the first time. We go broader at 3M. We talk to everyone from her exercise classes. We push the guys she was sleeping with harder – they each have a motive. We are missing something. It's out there – we just have to find it."

Bixby nodded her head in agreement. "Hey, more importantly, did you call Doc Granger like you said you would? Frankie wants to make sure we know what she likes to eat."

"Oh, man, I did forget. What should I say?" Little was very nervous, and Bixby had never seen him like this before. He pulled open the middle drawer of his desk and removed a notepad and he grabbed a pen from a re-purposed coffee mug filled with various writing utensils. He looked expectantly at Bixby for pearls of wisdom.

"It's simple. Tell her to show up at your place at 7. No need to bring anything because Frankie and I will take care of everything, Whoa, you're taking notes? How hard can this be? You call her, you tell her your address, she shows up at 7. Make sure to write down that you should shower. May I suggest your wardrobe as well?"

Little looked up from his notepad. "Seven, no need to bring

anything. What if she insists on bringing something? What do I say then?"

"Oh, you're so helpless. No need to bring anything. If you tell her to bring something Frankie will be offended that someone would think that she missed something. You know, Frankie's more excited about this than even you are."

Elliott held his notes in one hand while he pushed the phone icon under Dr. Granger's name on his cell phone. She answered on the first ring. "Hello, Elliott. I thought you had forgotten. I've been distracted too, so much so that I'm afraid I am not giving the flood plains of Zumbrota the attention they deserve."

"I'm sure the flood plains of Zumbrota are in good hands," Little seemed pleased with his drollness. "So, no need for you to bring anything. I've taken care of everything. Does 7 PM work? I'll text you the address so you'll have it on your phone."

Bixby rolled her eyes. If it were true that Elliott would be taking care of everything, they could expect boiled hot dogs, microwave popcorn, and maybe Urban Growler beer as a classy alternative to Old Milwaukee on the menu. Maybe vanilla ice cream for dessert, with chocolate sauce if Elliott went all in. Frankie had insisted that Elliott have nothing whatsoever to do with the event beyond opening the door upon their arrival. "He needs to stay in his swim lane," she told Bernie forcefully. "He will screw this thing up if he does anything to help. Anything at all."

"Are you sure? I live near a Trader Joe's," Abby offered. "I could swing by and grab a jar of an excellent mango salsa and blue corn chips. I had them at a faculty party and they were surprisingly good. Did you know the chips are made with actual blue corn? Blue corn contains anthocyanins, which means less starch and more protein."

"I did not know that. Quite fascinating. But no, I've got things under control. Hang on, Bernie is saying something to me."

"Ask her if she drinks wine," Bixby whispered. Little passed the question along.

"Tell Detective Bixby that in fact I do," responded Abby. "Can I bring a bottle or two?"

"No, I'll take care of it." Little made arrangements to meet her in the lobby and after a few more awkward moments of conversation, he hung up. He excitedly brought Bernie up to speed on the origins of blue corn chips and their health benefits relative to regular corn chips.

Bixby looked alarmed. "Listening to Dr. Science is going to take more beer and wine than I thought, and you're just going to stare at her all night. One's a science nerd and the other is an eighth grader who can't talk around girls."

"Women," Little corrected.

"In your case, neither."

"I disagree," responded Little. "I feel like I made real progress on that call."

"Right, just remember to thank Frankie for doing all the work. And me for setting it up in the first place." With that, Bixby and Little each headed home for a weekend of reflection over what they might have missed in the Nyberg case. They each resolved to make significant progress in the coming week.

On Saturday evening at 6:30, Bernie Bixby and her wife Frankie entered the lobby of the Washington Exchange, a North Loop building where Elliott had lived for the past three years. His decision to buy the condo and move out of his bachelor pad in the Uptown area had been difficult. Bernie and Frankie joined him on weekend showings, and, when they found his current home, would not let him leave until he had put down earnest money and signed the purchase agreement.

Frankie, with frizzy red hair and freckles, looked a bit like Orphan Annie but had a stern and forceful nature when needed, had then steadfastly refused to allow any of his current furnishings to be moved into the new place. She had capitulated in allowing Elliott to at least assist in decorating the condo. Located on the twelfth floor and as a corner unit, it featured large windows with panoramic views of Target Field, where the Minnesota Twins played, the Mississippi River, and most of the skyline of downtown Minneapolis. The wraparound, covered balcony was a bit narrow, about eight feet, really only wide enough for a gas grill, two heavy chairs, and a short glass top table. It offered excellent viewing of both sunrises and sunsets.

Bernie and Frankie were bemused when they saw Dr. Granger already pacing in the lobby. The couple walked over and Bernie introduced her wife. "It did not take as long as I expected to get here, and it was way too early to text Elliott of my arrival," she said by way of explanation. Gesturing towards several plaques on the wall, she said, "I like when a building maintains its heritage and tells the story of how it came to be. This was originally a milling site."

Nodding their heads in agreement, Bixby pulled her keys from her pocket. "We can take you up. I have a fob." Bixby reached over and took a full Trader Joe's canvas sack of groceries from Dr. Granger, avoiding glares from Frankie about her lack of manners over the delay in doing so.

"I couldn't remember which chips and salsa I had at the faculty party, so I bought every one they had," Abby said. She also had two bottles of wine. "Two Buck Chuck. I couldn't resist. I love Trader Joe's." Abigail's enthusiasm made her seem different than the very clinical scientist Bixby saw at the lab.

As they rode up the elevator, Frankie and Dr. Granger discussed grocery stores. Frankie favored Aldi's and Cub Foods because she had a wife and two kids to feed, while the single UofM professor, they concluded, fit in better at Trader Joe's or Whole Foods. "My family wouldn't know organic from a hole in the wall," Frankie said. "Why spend the extra money?"

"I see your point. I, on the other hand, can't see myself eating anything other than certified organic."

"Just to warn you," Frankie advised. "I did not buy organic for the salad or the vegetables."

"That's all right, I grew up in North Dakota. What do I know about organic?" They all laughed.

Elliott Little opened the door, trying in vain to hide his excitement, shyness, and his uncertainty on how to host a dinner party with a woman he was attracted to, and who, by all accounts, felt the same way about him. He was wearing a light blue pinstripe dress shirt with a blazer over what appeared to be pressed jeans and loafers. Much to Bernie's disgust, he was not wearing socks.

"Are we going out on your yacht later, Captain?" Bixby began. Frankie reached out and punched Bernie, not lightly, on her arm, and glared at her as well.

"I just wanted to add some class and decorum." Elliott knew he had erred in his wardrobe choices.

"Probably should have worn socks if you wanted decorum."

Frankie and Abigail, becoming fast friends, rolled their eyes, but did not disagree with Bernie's assessment.

Little excused himself, went to his bedroom, closed the door, and returned wearing a navy-blue polo shirt, cargo shorts, and half socks in his running shoes. "Better?" he asked Bernie.

"Better." The two helped with the groceries in the kitchen, and were shooed out to the balcony with a plate of marinated ribeye steaks and beers in their hands.

"Do they always pick on each other like that?" Abby asked Frankie.

"Of course, that's how those two treat each other. Bernie loves him like the accepting brother she never had growing up." The two said nothing for a few seconds, no doubt pondering what a gay, black female encountered in the military and in law enforcement. Sensing what she was thinking, Frankie added: "Elliott made sure Bernie was treated fairly by everyone in Homicide. For that, I am eternally grateful to him. He's the godfather to both of our children."

"How did you meet Elliott?" Abby asked.

"The two of them were partners for about a week when Bernie brought him over for dinner because Bernie realized that he was a hapless bachelor and would eat Chinese takeout every night if we didn't intervene somehow. Within two weeks they were best friends. My kids adore Elliott. So," Frankie deftly changed the focus of the conversation. "I understand you met Bernie and Elliott when you helped them with a case?"

"Yes, Elliott and Detective Bixby needed some guidance on currents in the Mississippi River, and I thought he was cute. He seems so nervous around me. I'm not sure why, I'm just a boring professor who studies water flow in rivers and lakes."

"He does seem to be enamored with you. Bernie, that's her name by the way, not Detective Bixby, says she had to almost use a cattle prod to get Elliott to talk to you."

"Oh, I noticed. As soon as they're out in the hall, I see him chatting up Bernie like he's been holding everything in. I must confess that I get a little out of sorts when he's around, too. I can't remember the last time I tried so hard to get a man to notice me. Probably high school, or maybe never. More likely never." The two ladies laughed and clinked wine glasses. Frankie refilled both with the Two Buck Chuck white.

Meanwhile, out on the balcony, the two detectives looked thoughtfully out over Minneapolis while sipping their beers. Underneath the cover of the grill, the steaks sizzled. "I think your lady doctor friend spent last night in the lobby. She probably came over right after you called yesterday just to make sure she wouldn't be late," Bernie observed, a smile on her face.

"I noticed she came up with you. You and Frankie were supposed to be here well before her to help me get ready."

"I wish we had been early. We could have avoided the embarrassment of you looking like a pretentious tool."

"Hey, those jeans cost me $150. They came already pressed and ready to amaze. That's what the lady at Macy's told me."

"If I were you, I'd go back and buy a second pair."

"Really?"

"Absolutely. And then I'd throw both pairs away," said Bixby, delivering the punchline of an old joke to someone who had never heard it before.

Little laughed at being set up so well. "Hey, she showed up, so that's a good thing, right?"

"She did. And, I'm guessing that Frankie will give you her all-important seal of approval. They haven't stop yacking since they first laid eyes on each other in the lobby. That works out well for both of us."

"Why is that?"

"We don't have to talk as much."

The rest of the evening went off without a hitch. The food was excellent, the table conversation, as Bixby suggested, was carried primarily by the two other women, and all four attended to cleaning up. Bernie and Frankie exchanged a look when Elliott and Abby sat close together on the couch, initiated by the doctor. Their work, it appeared, was almost done.

It was during the post-dinner conversation that Dr. Granger turned the conversation back to her work again. "As you know, I study rivers and streams and their activities all over the upper Midwest. I saw something in the news yesterday that caught my eye." Realizing that the direction she was about to take the conversation was not in keeping with a casual Saturday evening with friends, Abby stopped herself.

"On second thought, could you two meet me at my lab on Monday morning? I have something interesting I would like to show you." With that said, she would not discuss it further. Little felt a charge because he was guaranteed another chance to spend time with her. Bixby, knowing that the Nyberg case was at a dead end, was hopeful that it would give them a new angle to follow.

The evening came to an end only because the babysitter needed to be brought home. Frankie, Bernie, and Abby all exchanged hugs, and the Bixby couple left to walk to their car. Elliott very chivalrously offered to walk Abby to her car. Once they were apart from Little and Granger, Frankie squeezed Bernie's hand. "If he doesn't marry that girl, I swear I will never speak to him again. She is amazing. You better make sure he doesn't mess this up."

"Hey, Elliott is a great partner and friend," Bernie objected. "But, I do need him to be focused on work and not courting."

Frankie playfully punched her on the arm, and then put her arm around Bernie and squeezed. "No, you need Elliott to have someone who can guide him on the path of life the same way I guide you. Did you see that outfit he was wearing when we first got here? Good Lord."

"He was just trying to impress her. At least he changed once we pointed it out to him."

"He does seem coachable," Frankie agree. "And, I can tell she likes him, too."

"I'm not quite sure why anyone would like him," Bernie said, earning herself another love tap on the shoulder. "But she does, bless her heart."

CHAPTER SIXTEEN

Monday morning in the squad room. Bixby and Little sat across from each other. Little had a smile that looked like it would require surgical intervention to remove. "Saturday night in the parking lot we decided to go for a walk on the Mississippi on Sunday. Did you know that you can tell the depth of the river based on the swirls and eddies? And, back in the 1800's 75% of the Minnesota economy was carried on the Mississippi River and Lake Superior?"

Bernie had never seen Elliott so giddy. Still, "that's interesting," was the best she could muster. As she said it, she was thinking that it was not all that interesting. She let him prattle on for a few more minutes before returning his focus to the case at hand. "How about we head over to the U and see Doc? She said to reach out to her on Monday. Give her a call and see what we can bring her from Caribou." True to her promise to Frankie, she was not going to let Elliott mess this up.

Coffees and a Chai Tea Latte in hand, the two made their way up to the Limnology laboratory to see Dr. Granger. When she saw them enter the lab she leapt up from her desk and did a fast walk / slow run to greet them. Realizing that she was not the only limnologist or limnologist student in the lab, she stopped short of hugging Little and instead smiled warmly at her visitors.

"Oh, Elliott, thank you for the tea. How much do I owe you?"

Bixby waved her off. "Elliott didn't pay for it, but it's on me. Us, really. Frankie sends her regards, and hopes the four of us can get together again real soon. We'll host the next event."

"And, you're kind enough to share your knowledge with us. An overpriced Chai tea is the least we can do," Little added.

"Oh, you are **so** funny, Elliott," she responded, guiding them to her office. Bixby felt as though she might throw up a little in her mouth, but instead she smiled.

Granger closed the door, made sure the blinds obscured all viewing from outside, and gave Elliott a huge hug. "I really loved our walk on the river yesterday. You are such wonderful company."

"Oh, he talks now?," Bixby said, needling his partner. Reading her audience, she decided to leave that topic alone. "So, you had something you wanted to show us?" she said.

"Yes, of course. Our department, well, just me really, tracks reported deaths associated with rivers, streams, and lakes in the area. I saw something on the news about a young woman apparently jumping to her death in the St. Croix River. Her body was found by kayakers near Osceola, but on the Minnesota side near the boat landing. I used our algorithms to plot her point of entry into the water, and based on that I concluded that it was highly unlikely to be intentional on her part."

"Why is that?" asked Little. He leaned forward in his chair, enraptured.

"Let me show you using aerial photography." Granger pulled up something on one of the large screens of her computer and moved the monitor to give them a better view. The equipment in her office seemed as big and powerful as that in the lab area. "Here is where I project that she went in the water," she said, pointing to a rock outcropping.

"That's impressive, Doc, but how can you tell that it's not intentional?" Bixby asked.

"Look down here," she said, pointing to a large, flat rock below the cliff. "See how it sticks out? If someone looked down from on top, they would realize that they would not be able to make the water cleanly and move to another spot."

"OK, but what if she didn't care? Not to sound callous, but dying is dying. Who cares if it is because of a rock, or hitting the water, or drowning?" Bixby felt herself playing devil's advocate perhaps a little too intensely, but Dr. Granger seemed up to the challenge.

"I wondered that myself, so I did some research." She changed to another program, and red dots appeared on the aerial shot of the bank. "What I learned is that when suicides or accidental deaths are plotted along the Minnesota side of the river, no one has ever jumped from that spot. The reason? I can't say for certain, of course, but it is reasonable to conclude that it is because you can't make it to the water if you jump from there."

"So, you think we should go take a look at that spot and see what we can find?"

"Exactly. In fact, my departmental meeting was canceled today due to finals, so if you wouldn't mind, I could tag along and perhaps provide some additional insight."

"That sounds excellent," said Little, his enthusiasm brimming. "There's an old-fashioned drive-in restaurant in Taylors Falls that has the best homemade root beer anywhere. My parents used to take us there on Sunday drives when we behaved. We can stop there for lunch. If it's still there."

"It's a date, then," Dr. Granger replied, choosing her words purposefully. "Let me close out my computer and let my staff know I'm heading out for a field workday."

Because they were taking an official MPD car, Dr. Granger insisted she ride in the back seat so that Elliott could drive and Bixby could continue to operate the myriad of computer power at her disposal. The ride out to Taylors Falls went quickly despite the 50-mile distance. While they rode, Granger asked them questions about their background. Bixby realized she was asking her just to be polite.

"I graduated from Brooklyn Center high school and enlisted in the Army right away. Frankie and I were dating but not seriously. She went to school at the U, but I became a Ranger instead. I did two tours in Afghanistan, and then came home and became a cop. Frankie and I stayed in touch and rekindled things after I returned. We got married when it became legal, and we've adopted two sons. Made my way up to detective and have been working with Elliott here for five years now."

Bixby turned back to smile at Abby. "Hey, and Frankie really enjoyed meeting you on Saturday. She made me promise to tell you that. So, I did. Twice."

"Ah, thank you. Tell Frankie I enjoyed meeting her as well. I hope to see you all again soon." Abby seemed to highlight the word 'soon'.

"Bernie is a highly decorated veteran of foreign conflict, you should know," Little interjected. "Meanwhile, I just defied my parents and didn't go to medical school. Instead, I got my law enforcement Associate of Arts degree at Normandale and joined the Minneapolis Police Department. I've been on the force for 17 years now. I am a little older than Bernie, but the age has made me wiser."

"That's true, at least for now. We both know that with all of my special attributes – race, gender, and sexual orientation, Elliott and most of MPD will be reporting to me at some point. I wonder how that dynamic will play itself out, the alleged wise master reporting to his former underling. I'm asking for a friend."

A hand lightly grasped Bixby's playfully. "You be nice to Elliott. He's a very special guy."

"Yes, ma'am," Bixby responded cheerfully. She found Granger's attempts at protecting him adorable. In fact, everything she said or did about and with Little was adorable. Frankie, her wife officially and unofficially for 10 years, had told her that on their drive home on Saturday night, confirming what Bernie already knew. Frankie's ability to read people was legend. Dr. Abby Granger had been labeled a "Keeper." Bixby was under direct orders to not let Little lose her. If he did, she let her know, both would have to answer to her. This was less than desirable.

As they passed through Lindstrom, Bixby offered to fill up the tank at the busy but clean Kwik-Trip. While she pumped the gas using the MPD card, Granger and Little went inside and bought coffee, water, and snacks. One thing Bernie noticed is that Little now ate healthier. Whereas before he would have bought glazed donuts and a Coke, he now walked out with string cheese, bananas, and water. Like it or not, since she was outside and had no choice in the matter, Bernie Bixby was going to be eating healthier now as well.

"What, no crullers or ?"

"Not sure when I last had a cruller, or any fried food for that matter," Little responded.

"I seem to recall last week. Friday perhaps? The Minute Mart on Lyndale?"

"I don't recall that at all. Did I work Friday?"

"You sure did," Granger joined in. "You called me late in the day to confirm our date on Saturday. You said you were calling from your desk."

"Oh, that's right. I started my new diet on Saturday. No more fried foods for me."

Rather than respond, Bernie bit into a string cheese instead. "We're about 15 minutes out. What's our plan once we arrive?"

"I hope you brought comfortable shoes," Abby responded. "We will have some hiking to do if my reading of the park map is correct."

"Great. I love exercise. Is it possible to run ahead or do I have to hold back and see if Bixby can keep up?" Little gave Bixby a look.

"Funny, last week you said exercise was for fools who didn't have the right cable package," Bixby responded.

"That doesn't sound like me at all. I love to exercise." Elliott sat up straighter behind the wheel, putting his excellent progress on display.

"You also said the best thing about running is that you get to stop at some point."

"I ran just this morning. The river is so peaceful and serene at daybreak," Elliott responded.

"Ok, you two, enough. I can tell by Elliott's BMI that he is not engaged in a sustained exercise regimen," Dr. Granger intervened. "Yet."

"And I can tell by your IQ that he is in way over his head hanging around the likes of you, Doc," Bernie shot back.

"Oh, Bernie. Frankie warned me about your charm and wit."

"He just hasn't managed to show you much of it yet," Elliott said. All three laughed and the banter ended. The scenery had taken their attention away.

Elliott turned off Highway 8 at the bottom of the long descent into Taylors Falls and stopped the vehicle in the park's parking lot. They exited the vehicle and showed their badges to the park attendant, who waved them through.

The trio made their way along the trail, looking for the outcropping from which the doctor postulated the victim had been pushed. Granger, had, of course, downloaded data onto her smart phone and was using longitudinal and latitudinal bearings to pinpoint the location. She guided them off the main, paved trails and onto a makeshift path. After a few more minutes of hiking and pausing to read the GPS app on her phone, she proclaimed that they were at the right spot. "It's right there," she said, pointing to a point high above the St. Croix River.

Little put his arm out in front of her and asked her to stay off the rock while he and Bixby looked things over. After a few moments he motioned for her to join them, as they had seen nothing. "Did it rain here the last few days?

"Let me check my phone. I have an app," Dr. Granger said.

"Of course, you do," Bixby muttered.

"Excuse me?" Granger responded, engrossed by her screen.

"Let us know what you find," Bixby said loud enough for her to hear.

Within seconds, Dr. Granger let them know it had rained, but only briefly, the evening after the incident on the outcropping. "Would a light shower be enough to destroy evidence?" she asked.

"Depends on what type of evidence was here. The only way to tell is to have our evidence team work up the place." Little looked at her and smiled to show his confidence in her theory.

Bixby was staring down at the many rocks below with multiple surfaces above the waterline. "Hey, Elliott, does that look like a blood stain down there?"

Elliott stared intently down at the rock. "It looks like it could be. Any way we can get down there and look more closely?"

Bixby took out her phone, snapped a picture, and then manipulated the photo to get a closer look at the markings. She showed it to Little. Shaking their heads, they realized that it was inconclusive. Bixby studied the rocks and the sheer wall rising high above the water. "It's too steep. No way to climb down there without ropes and expert climbing skills."

"What if you approached it on a boat or kayak?" offered Granger.

"That's a great idea," Little enthused.

"Except we're too close to the dam to be able to navigate the river in anything less than a powerboat. How about we call the Chisago County Sheriff's department?"

A phone conversation with the Chisago County dispatcher was followed by a call to a deputy who happened to be doing water patrol that afternoon on the river. Within minutes, Deputy Kevin Kirby was pulling alongside the rocks below and attempting to communicate with the Minneapolis detectives.

After several failed attempts at communicating through yelling and gestures, Little called to give the dispatcher his cell number, and she passed it along to Deputy Kirby. Soon they were soon able to talk in a near normal voice. "We're wondering if the stain we see on the rock down there next to you might be blood. We don't want to call out a crew without doing our due diligence beforehand."

"Makes sense," Kirby responded. "From what I can see, it sure looks like blood. What I don't know is if the blood is human or from an animal. Deer and raccoons have been known to slip and fall off the cliffs as well."

"We have reason to believe that the body you recovered last week down in Osceola went in the river from this spot. I think we should have a crime scene team check it out."

"We usually call the BCA for our work. Does Minneapolis want to handle it? I can call the sheriff and clear it with him."

"I will call our people and take care of it. Can you provide transport?" Little asked.

"I am scheduled to be in the water until sunset, so unless I get a call, I'm happy to help out. Why don't we meet down at the boat landing in Osceola? I can run you and your crew back up here. That's the easiest departure spot."

Several phone calls later, the last two to confirm the location of the landing on the St. Croix River on the Minnesota side west of Osceola, and the team was assembled. Sarah Broderick and two other technicians joined Bixby on the Sheriff's boat for the ride upriver to the rock outcropping in the park. Elliott volunteered to stay back at the top with Abby Granger and "keep an eye on things." Along the way, the boat passed the large tourist vessel that moored in the same area as the parking lot. Onlookers from the big boat waved to the five in the Sheriff's boat. Three of them awkwardly waved back. Their reason for being in the boat hardly seemed a reason for friendly waving.

Broderick nimbly jumped off the boat as it approached shore, carrying her kit as a backpack. Interestingly, she now was also wearing a fanny pack. She leapt from rock to rock towards the apparent blood stain several yards up the shore. The others waited until Deputy Kirby had secured the boat to the shore and offered his assistance as they stepped off. Bixby inquired of one of the technicians, "How do you keep up with her?"

"We don't."

"Do her heels ever touch the ground when she walks?"

"Not that we've ever seen."

Eventually, with the whole crew near the rock with the stain on it, the area was cordoned off and the technicians went to work. Bixby stayed below with them. Above, Little and Granger sat side by side. Bixby was pretty sure they were holding hands, although discreetly in keeping with the tone of the circumstances. Little appeared to be engrossed in conversation.

It took an hour for the crew to complete their investigation of the scene, and then they all boarded again for the quick ride back to their van. Bixby called Little and agreed to meet them at the local drive in root beer stand in Taylors Falls. Bixby did not believe Elliott when he told him the name of the destination.

"I swear, it's just called 'The Drive In'. Google it. The best homemade root beer around," Little reassured Bixby. "Abby and I will walk down there and meet you. You drive the car to the main road in town and take a left. It'll be on your right about half a mile down. I'll expect all the details you got from Broderick.""

Bernie invited Broderick and her team to join them, but they needed to work the rocky area above the boulder, and they then had a scene waiting for them on Franklin Avenue. "We'll grab something on the way back to Minneapolis."

"Thank you for coming out of Minneapolis to help us out," Bixby said.

"No, thank you for getting us out here," Broderick said. "It reminds me of all the time I spent at my grandparents' cabin."

When Bixby arrived, she found the new couple playing miniature golf on the course at the back of the restaurant, laughing at their atrocious putting. "I'm glad you were able to find a way to deal with the emotional trauma of investigating a homicide," Bixby said derisively.

Little waved back to the first hole. "We bought a round for you too. Grab a putter and a ball and catch up to us."

An extra few minutes of even more horrible putting would help them all unwind, Bixby decided. When they completed their round, the trio walked over to a picnic table under an umbrella and sat down. Within minutes a young server came over and took their order.

"I'm not sure I've ever been to a place like this. It's like time stood still," Little exclaimed. "I remember a drive-in on Lyndale, but it closed years ago."

"I remember the A & W drive in over in New Hope. That's been gone for ten years now," Bixby chimed in.

Noticing a puzzled look on Abby's face, Bernie smiled. "I'm afraid we're dating ourselves, which is how Elliott describes his high school years."

"It's not that," Granger relied. "It's just that I grew up in North Dakota and I have no idea what you're talking about. This place is so neat."

As she spoke, the server returned with their burgers, fries and onion rings, as well as three large frosty mugs of root beer.

They ate for a few moments, relishing the old-fashioned flavor and charm. Putting down his burger, Bixby delivered her report.

"Broderick matched the blood on the boulder to our victim's blood type. She will need to run more tests in the lab, but it looks like Doc was right. Janelle Moreno either jumped or was pushed off the ledge above that boulder."

"Looks like we have another murder on our hands. Let's drop off Abby and talk to the parents on the way back, and work on that first thing tomorrow morning."

CHAPTER SEVENTEEN

Maria Griggs sat on an older but well cared for faded chintz couch with maize flowers on a yellow background in the living room of her rambler in Inver Grove Heights, enveloped in sadness. Her husband, Richard Griggs, not Janelle's father, sat next to her and tried valiantly yet awkwardly to comfort her. Armed with the preliminary report from the Medical Examiner's office, as well as the minimal evidence found in Taylors Falls, the findings showed that Janelle Moreno was a victim of homicide, and not suicide. Of significance was a wound found above the left eye of the victim. It, in and of itself, may not have caused the death, but the coroner concluded that she was unconscious when she struck a boulder below on the shore of the St. Croix river.

"Nothing we can say will bring your daughter back, but we now are investigating her death as a homicide, and we would like your help." Bixby did not like death notification meetings that involved someone who was very unlikely to be a suspect. A grieving mother did not hit her daughter above her left eye and force her into the water. In this particular case, she was too short to have struck the blow. Still, time and repetition had proven that Bernie delivered the news with more compassion and empathy, and therefore she took the lead in most of these situations. When a woman could reach over and touch someone's hand, it conveyed the right message.

"When they told me that she had jumped off the cliff, I knew they were mistaken." Maria had a slight Spanish accent. "She was not suicidal. Janelle had so much to live for. She was just accepted into a PhD program in Texas. When I spoke with her a few days ago, Janelle told me there was a chance she could be promoted to assistant manager at the store, and they would allow her to transfer to a store close to campus in Austin." She stopped for a moment to dab tears with a tissue. "And, she loved her cat. She would never leave her cat uncared for, never. We had to rescue Boots from her apartment." Her husband put his arm around her but she shrugged it off. Now there was a fire in her eyes.

"It was that creepy manager at the store, McGarvey. I bet he did it. He asked her out, she said no, and Janelle told me he kept calling and texting. She finally threatened to file a complaint with the regional office to make him stop calling and texting her."

As she gave them the names of an old boyfriend from college, and her college roommate with sexual identity issues, Little realized that these were not going to be very likely doers. If Janelle was fearful of them in any way, she would not have gone to Taylors Falls with them alone. Broderick and her team had found no indication of any type of struggle atop the cliff, or on the path leading to the location where she went over. No, he concluded in his internal monologue, Janelle Moreno was with someone she knew and thought she could trust. What had happened to her was a surprise attack.

Promises were made to keep Mrs. Griggs informed, phone numbers and email addresses provided, after which the two detectives left the mother and stepfather and made their way to the car. Mr. Griggs had told them that he worked in commercial construction and provided the address of the building where he was working, as well as the names of others in the construction crew. He would be easily eliminated as a suspect.

As they stood next to the Impala, facing each other over the top of the front doors of the car, Little glanced at the house, and then at Bixby. "I guess we should go visit an office supply store. You need any office supplies?"

"No, I take what I need from the office. This manager sounds like a tool, though. I can't wait to meet him and bust his chops." On that, the two were in unison.

There were not many customers in the store when the detectives arrived. A few workers huddled together, and the store had a somber feel as employees still processed the violent loss of a coworker. A nervous young worker who hovered near the combination customer service desk and checkout lanes directed them to a door in the back marked "Employees Only". He suggested that they could walk in despite not being employees only after seeing their badges and learning that they were there because of Janelle. He called back and got his assistant manager, McGarvey, on the office phone to let him know he was about to have visitors.

As they approached the inner sanctum door, a slightly built man with silver-rimmed glasses, thinning brown hair and a weak attempt at facial hair stepped out. It appeared that acne had followed him aggressively out of adolescence and into adulthood. Proactiv Plus would have had no choice but to offer a full refund. His face seemed permanently stuck on the 'before' side.

"Officers? My name is Patrick McGarvey. I'm the acting store manager here."

Bixby listened for, but did not hear, swelling orchestral music to announce McGarvey's status in the store. "We're detectives. I'm Bixby, and this is Detective Little. We are here to ask you some questions about Janelle Moreno."

"Of course." McGarvey held the door open and invited them back to his office. As they walked in, Little noted that it was filled with furnishings and chairs that were nowhere near the top of the line for a store that sold office furniture. Both side chairs made squeaking noises as they sat in them.

"May I ask why you say you're the acting store manager here? My understanding is that you're only an assistant store manager," Elliott began, seeking to get him unsettled from the start. He purposely emphasized 'only'.

McGarvey cleared his throat. "Yes, well, the manager, Ms. Mosher, is out of the country for the next few weeks and I am in charge of the store in her place. Now, this must remain just between us as it may affect team morale," McGarvey leaned in and lowered his voice. "There is a very good chance that she will accept a regional director position in Green Bay. I would then in all likelihood become the manager here."

Bixby and Little nodded agreeably. "Unless that fact impacts the investigation, we can agree not to share that with anyone," Bixby allowed. "What can you tell us about Janelle Moreno?" In her head, she told herself that she would not share that with anyone because no one would care.

McGarvey cleared his throat again. "Janelle was one of my best associates, and we are all in shock around here. Her numbers for accessories sold after initial customer interaction led the store. Third in the state, number 47 nationally. Who would want to hurt her? Always so pleasant and helpful with customers. Very dedicated to the store."

"Our understanding is that you made unwanted advances towards her?" No sense avoiding the hard questions, Elliott decided.

"Detectives, please. Do I look like I would need to make 'unwanted advances' towards anyone?" McGarvey used air quotes to further make his point about how ridiculous Elliott's words sounded. "I'm the current acting manager of the third most successful store in Minnesota based on the customer traffic to gross sales ratio. I know full well that any blemish on my record would likely impact my impending promotion."

Little looked appraisingly at McGarvey and nodded towards Bixby. "Bernie, he wouldn't sexually harass an employee because it might affect his career arc. Isn't that what we were told to expect to hear from harassers? A logical reason why they wouldn't do it?"

"That is correct, Detective Little. He wouldn't kill someone because then he doesn't get to be manager. What were we thinking? It's all so obvious now." Bernie turned his gaze to McGarvey. "Actually, sir, you look exactly like someone who would hit on his employees and not take 'no' for an answer. The poster child, in fact." Bixby despised people who were overly impressed by their status and their ability to lord it over others. "Believe me, I've been dealing with smarmy turds like you my entire life."

McGarvey shifted in his chair and cleared his throat. "Well, actually, not to speak ill of the dead, but the reverse is actually true. Janelle came on to me, actually, and I had to firmly remind her of our corporate policies regarding executive level team members having informal, off-work relationships with non-executives outside of working hours. Actually, I even drafted a memo to that effect and placed it in her confidential personnel file."

Little recalled a training recently where the instructor advised that the more someone uses the word 'actually' the less likely what they say is truthful. "Actually," he said, drawing out the word. "He who writes the memo owns the story. You are not the first scumbag who harasses a woman and then falsifies information to create a fictional paper trail." He glared at the manager, who squirmed a little more in his chair, realizing that what he thought was a brilliant attempt to cover for himself may have been neither very original nor very effective.

Bixby leaned forward, aggression in her tone. "And, that's not what Janelle's family told us. And, because her daughter was on their family plan, her mom signed the waiver to allow us

COINCIDENTAL EVIDENCE

to review her phone calls and texts. Sprint has not provided us that information yet, but when they do, we will be able to see '*actually*' who pursued whom."

"And," Bernie looked threateningly at McGarvey. "What will those phone records tell us? Will they prove you a liar? Is that how you want us to find out the truth about you and Janelle? And, if you lie about something so easy to prove, what else will you lie about? Maybe you took her to Taylors Falls for a romantic rendezvous and she told you to buzz off once and for all? Maybe your feelings were hurt and you lashed out?"

McGarvey cleared his throat again. "Hold on, hold on. Perhaps I pursued her a bit, but she told me she actually had a boyfriend so I stepped aside." When neither detective appeared satisfied, he continued.

"I worked here the day Janelle was killed, actually. I was here from store open to store close. I even had to have my Erbert & Gerbert's delivered that day, that's how busy I was."

"That's easy enough to prove," Little still looked skeptical and hard.

"John, the manager, he delivered my order. The Comet Morehouse on gluten-free bread. They recognize my phone number when I call in. They have the best GF sandwiches around, and they're the only place that delivers. I'm gluten-intolerant you know." McGarvey leaned back as if to suggest that being gluten intolerant proved he was uninvolved in Janelle's death.

"Of course, you are," Bixby was gruff in her response. McGarvey was now confidently adding in too many facts for this to not be the truth.

"You may be gluten-intolerant but you're still an officious little jerk," Little snarled in his best angry voice. "Gluten probably can't stand being around you either." He was enjoying pushing McGarvey around. This was not in character for him, but Bixby felt it was richly deserved.

Little then stood to his full height, glowering down at the temporary store manager. "We're not done with you yet. We need to talk to everyone who knew her in the store, and we need to speak with them immediately." Both detectives now looked angrily at McGarvey.

"Officious" said Bixby, reading from her phone screen as they left McGarvey's office and walked to the worker break room. "Bureaucratic, overbearing, and bossy. Very impressive choice of words. Trying to improve your vocabulary for Doc?"

"You bet I am. She's the smartest person I've ever been around. You told me to improve my vocabulary so I signed up for a word of the day on my phone. I don't want to feel doltish when I'm around her. Doltish means to act or feel like a dolt."

"Yeah, I gathered that."

After spending hours speaking with several co-workers of Janelle Moreno and finding out more about her life both in and out of work, their list of people they needed to talk to grew, but their list of suspects did not. Janelle was well-liked by those she worked with, and by her customers also. It seemed unlikely they would find her killer associated with the store. Although no one particularly cared for McGarvey, no one thought him capable of murder. "Honestly, I think Janelle could beat him up if he tried anything, All of us could. He's just a little twerp," one woman confided.

"We all came to work here to make some money and get discounts on our office supplies," another co-worker said. "Then, three years later you're still here working for a weasel assistant manager and getting yelled at to increase your sales ratios and you wonder where the time has gone. I know Janelle was excited about moving to Austin, but if the right guy came along, she would have given up the PhD in a second. I know that does not sound empowered, but it's the truth. She wanted to quit working and not be alone anymore."

Later, again standing over the doors of the car, the detectives faced each other. "We need to look at her browsing history and see if she met someone online. She sold paper, toner, and computers. Who gets killed over that?" Bixby stepped in to the passenger seat and opened her laptop to check for emails and updates.

Little looked down disgustedly at his notes before he started the car. "Let's go check out her apartment. We got the keys from her mom. We can grab her computer or tablet or whatever she has. It's too bad we can't get phone records as quickly as you told McGarvey we can."

"He folded like a cheap suit though, didn't he?" Bixby beamed with pride. Dominating men who enjoyed dominating women filled her with a special sense of satisfaction.

"It's too bad we can't arrest him for being a pissant. He deserves life for that," Little offered, using another helpful new addition to his vocabulary.

"Or, he could be forced to manage an office supply store for his entire working career," Bixby replied.

"Good point. Karma has a way of getting back at you when you work retail."

"Especially when you're at the executive level," Bernie said.

With that, Elliott started the car and drove off to Janelle Moreno's apartment.

Despite already having been given a key by Janelle's mother, they stopped first and let the manager of the apartment complex know what they were doing. Gaining the cooperation of the people who ran apartment buildings historically had led to good outcomes, especially since they were outside of Minneapolis.

The manager, an older man with gray hair, a mustache, and gray plastic framed glasses, appreciated being advised of their presence and walked them to the right building and directly to Janelle's room. He even offered to open up her storage area. Through the chicken wire enclosure, they could see a bicycle and clear plastic storage bins filled with books and winter clothes. Nothing of interest there.

The manager excused himself after watching them open the door. The unmistakable musk of a cat permeated, although it had been taken out days ago. A plastic container of cat litter in the kitchen provided only a partial explanation. "God, I hate cats," Bixby muttered. "I am so lucky that Frankie loves dogs too. I would have to rethink my relationship status if I ever found out she liked cats." She glared at Elliott. "Is Doc a dog or a cat person? You need to find out now before things get serious between you."

"I will posit that question at my next opportunity," Little responded, pride in his voice.

"You know, a person can go too far in learning new and pretentious-sounding words. Sometimes, the best speakers are the ones who use the simplest word that everyone understands." Elliott nodded in agreement, making a mental note. He was proving to be coachable.

The entire apartment could be seen from the small rug in front of the door. The living room held an uncomfortable chair, with a dark wood end table next to it and angled in a corner, with the kitchen behind it. The rooms were separated by a hip-high divider with a wider faux-wood top extending across about a third of the distance.

Straight ahead was the bathroom, and to the right were two bedrooms, both open doors angled in such a way as to be visible inside. One contained an unmade bed with clothes all over it and on the floor, an iPad near the pillows, while the second room held a cheap computer desk with cluttered bookshelves surrounding it. A short office chair sat askew in front of an Apple iMac computer. When Moreno was in her apartment, they decided, she either lay in bed with her iPad, or sat in front of her computer in her office area.

Bixby wandered through the rest of the apartment, opening the refrigerator, moving clothes around with her foot. She completed her perfunctory tour and joined Little in the office. She paused and read the titles of a bookcase filled with text books, romance novels, and some classic poetry. The apartment did not appear to contain anything useful whatsoever. "There is not a single photograph or any kind of decoration in this place. It must all be on the computer or the iPad. That's what the millennials do you know. You see she doesn't even have a TV? It's all on her iMac. At least she was a reader."

Little was pushing random keys on the small white keyboard while clicking on the mouse. "This is a piece of crap," he said angrily, punching at more keys. "Her mom must have grabbed the computer because all that's left is the keyboard, mouse, and this skinny monitor."

"The monitor is the computer. It's called an iMac. Welcome to the brave new world, Elliott."

"Let's bring this back and let the tech lab figure this out. Stupid thing."

Gathering the iPad, and the monitor that was also apparently the computer, as well as the keyboard, mouse, and power cord, the two left the apartment, locking up as they departed. Loading the equipment in the back seat, Little drove as Bixby started calling the names of friends and customers who had worked with Janelle Moreno. By the time they reached MPD headquarters, she had made calls to all on the list for which she had numbers and eliminated them all as suspects, or even people who were worth following up with later.

"Two murders, nowhere to turn. They appear random and unrelated," said Bixby, ending a call with the last customer to have worked with Janelle. The two sat in the parking garage, pondering their next move. As things stood, there did not appear to be a next move.

CHAPTER EIGHTEEN

When I arrive home, my daughters are in their bedrooms doing whatever social media functions that teenagers need to do by themselves after dinner. My wife is watching TV, some wretched show that disproves the theory that America has any talent whatsoever. I shout greetings and quickly change into my biking gear and head out for a quick ten-mile jaunt, working on speed and quick recovery. Cycling is about pushing yourself and then recovering so that you can do it again. And, in this case, going over the details of what you have done today.

Once on my bike, I start to process what happened. I feel badly that Janelle is gone, but it was necessary. My main thought through this is a sense of emptiness that I feel. Two victims and I do not feel the thrill I expect. Why? What is missing? Am I doing something wrong?

In between miles six and seven, a flat-out sprint on a flat run with an upward slope for the last three tenths of a mile, it dawns on me. I realize what is missing. I have not seen the look of despair and realization of fate in the eyes of my victims, the same look I saw when I let someone know they are losing their jobs. Janelle only showed surprise and confusion before I turned her and pushed her off the rock.

Pushing myself the last few yards, I feel as renewed and

energized as I have felt since I did my last departmental reorganization. Of course, the eyes. I want, need really, to see it in their eyes. I am surprised and a bit disappointed that I have not thought of it before. And, by the way, how about not leaving clues behind so I don't get caught? No more rookie mistakes. I am not a rookie anymore. I am on my way to becoming a serial killer.

A shower, an evening of less sleep and more activity in the bedroom, a very happy wife off to work the next day with a smile on her face, the children on the bus and looking forward to the last few days of school before summer break, and here's me staring at my computer again. The new monitors and the new processor in the laptop are a huge upgrade. I thank my lucky stars that the old laptop gave up the ghost the day before. This new equipment is just the energizer my job search needs.

There has been some dissension in the household about my dinners of late, so I go to the grocery store late in the morning and put together a meal for the ages. I buy a pork tenderloin, scalloped potatoes, frozen peas for the steamer, and dinner rolls. I also buy applesauce in case someone gets testy about the menu items offered. I put the tenderloin in the crock pot, put the rest of the groceries away, and return to my new computer. The renaissance man is back. He can seamlessly handle multiple facets of a complex life without appearing stressed. What a guy. And, while he is at it, he also applies for several jobs. All in a matter of two hours of intense activity.

As often happens in a career reboot (that sounds more palatable) the worst jobs are the ones recruiters are the most likely to contact you about. For instance, within two hours of sending in my information to some lame marketing firm about a marketing position, I get a phone call. Again, my cell number is provided on all my submissions, so I answer no matter what. Today it is a recruiter looking for a self-starter with premium communication skills. Sales experience is preferred, but not necessary, as they will provide extensive training.

Ordinarily, I would dismiss this as beneath me, beneath my children, and beneath my pets, but the young lady is very enthusiastic. The interview is tomorrow afternoon at 1 PM, and it involves a fairly easy drive to an office complex near the Mall of America. I try and think back to my last actual interview. It has been several years. Has the process changed? Have the questions been modified? Will I be smooth and professional? Only one way to find out. And, bonus, there is a bike shop on the way. As a reward for going to the interview I will stop in and look around before getting home for the family.

One would expect office space located within walking distance of the premier shopping experience in Minnesota to be upscale. You would be wrong in this particular case. As I walk into Suite 101, I realize that this is going to be even more laughable than I expected. The waiting area is a square room with six side chairs along one wall. In the middle is a coffee table with old magazines strewn on top. One magazine is pushed off of the stack so that it hides about half of a large gash on the surface of the table. The table must have had a 'Free' sign taped to it. The quality of the overall furnishings, even the alleged art work on the wall, is something less than what you would see in the last hours of a bad garage sale.

Over on one side of the room is a half-wall with several clipboards on it. A handwritten sign asks that each person fill out the questionnaire and wait for their name to be called. I would call this a cattle call interview, but cattle might be offended by the comparison. The kicker to it all is this sign that apologizes for any 'inconvenient'. Tacky furnishings and ambience, grammar and spelling issues, what more must I subject myself to in order to get practice interviewing?

One person, who had been in the room and settled with resume in hand and briefcase open, snaps the briefcase shut, smirks at the sign, removes the filled-out questionnaire from the clipboard, crumples it, shoves it in his pocket, and walks out. There are some levels of self-flagellation to which even the desperately unemployed will not succumb.

Not me. I intend to see this through to the end. Part of me sees a certain dark humor in how tacky this whole operation is, while another part of me wants to be able to report that I am going on interviews and mulling over multiple opportunities.

"Mr. Chandler?" I hear my name called after a solid fifteen-minute wait. You would expect the appointment calendar to re-set itself for the afternoon rush at 1pm, but I guess this place is so busy that they are still dealing with the backlog from the morning. No rest for the tacky. I cheerfully stand and offer my hand to meet my 20-something interviewer.

An hour later, I extricate myself from the office with promises to sign and drop off the paperwork so that I can grab one of the top traffic locations in the Twin Cities area for this weekend. Not wanting to be tacky myself, I find a paper recycling bin in the main lobby and rip up the paperwork and dump it in. I mean, who wouldn't want to schlep boxes of product and flyers to the Costco in Maple Grove, mix up samples of this revolutionary protein powder available in vanilla, chocolate, strawberry, and the newest flavor, pineapple mango, and accost unsuspecting shoppers with free samples of this wretched crap? And, insult to injury, I would have to buy the stock at low, low wholesale prices, and sell it at retail, and split the profit with my supplier.

Given the number of people in the lobby when I leave, I suspect the kiosk will be open for business this weekend and beyond, just not by me. Ever.

Now that I am ready to tackle real job interviews again, having honed my skills with two twenty-somethings who read off scripts, I am renewed in my quest for my next big challenge. I will push out several more cover letters and resumes after I get home. Now that I'm savvier, I will be better able to discern and weed out the bad jobs. My next job will be on my terms. There will be no compromising on the road to my horizon. Soon all the lights will be shining on me. Thank you, rhinestone cowboy. I could not have done it without you.

I hesitate on my way past the bike shop that I had promised myself as an incentive to do this interview. I feel the need to get out of my suit, take it to the cleaners, shower the tackiness mixed with desperation off of my body before it permeates my very soul, and have a beer to calm myself. But, new pedals for my bike will certainly help too. Armed with an expensive new accessory for my bike, having made a promise to return to take a demo ride of the newest models, I head for home and a cleansing. There are some feelings of unwashed that even bicycle equipment cannot purge. And these are not cheap pedals.

Lest you concern yourself about why a guy looking for work is out buying things for his bicycle, and how his spouse will react, fear not. Jennifer and I have an understanding on our workout-related expenditures. I do not comment when she comes home wearing a new outfit or shoes, joins a new gym, signs up for a new class, and she reciprocates when it comes to me and my biking fixation. There is no such agreement, tacit or otherwise, regarding my recent homicidal behavior, but every couple has their secrets. It makes me wonder what hers is.

The next few days are spent looking for work. The fear that I will wind up offering free samples of protein drinks gives me more energy and focus than that miracle product ever could. I am not only cranking out cover letters and resumes matching up exactly to the postings, but I am also sending out emails to former colleagues, friends, and relatives. At this rate I could become a spokesperson for a protein powder that I will never touch, much less sell. It changed my life for the better, and I did not see even one convenient resealable canister.

Responses are now trickling in. Not just the standard "Thank you for applying. We will never consider you for this or any other position at our company, regardless of what the words say in our email" responses, but actual words of encouragement and promises to keep eyes open and to forward opportunities. Sitting in front of my new laptop and reading and re-reading the emails on my new monitors, I started to tear up. Whoa, where is that coming from?

As you probably can guess, I am not an emotional person. It is not in my psychological makeup to express that type of feeling. I wonder if maybe I even have the capability, but I realize that I do have that capability when I see friends take the time to show support and promise to help. I get the feeling that I have this under control.

My confidence takes a jolt later when I got a phone call from Bernadette Bixby, a homicide detective with the Minneapolis Police Department, out of the blue. Given my employment status I answer her call. I ordinarily decline or ignore these and curse the practice of "spoofing" phone numbers by sales people. Now I have to answer it. Such is my fate these days.

I handle the call and the detective quite well, if I may say so myself. Yes, I remember recently visiting that store. Yes, I worked with a sales person. Janelle may have been her name. She was friendly and helpful. No, I just needed paper and toner cartridges, and then I returned to buy a computer and monitors just the other day. Goodness no, she's dead? That's terrible, officer. Detective? Sorry about that. What was I doing that afternoon? Sending out resumes and applying for jobs. Yeah, it's a fulltime job looking for work. I am very optimistic that I will land soon. Yes, if I think of anything else, I will most certainly give you a call. Yes, I have a pen, let me jot down your number. Thank you. Good luck with your investigation. I hope you solve this one. She seemed like a nice young lady. It sure is a tragedy when someone that young dies.

Anyway, back to me at my desk, staring sightlessly into my monitors. Is the perfect crime and its coverup a myth? Were the detectives, armed with today's science, just that good? Breathe. Highly unlikely since I hid my tracks so well. Just a blip. A routine call. I need to relax and think this through. I start with several backdated cover letters and applications to jobs I know I will never get, or want, just to show how busy I was the day that Janelle died. The computer forensics would be able to figure out that my computer was sitting in a box in my car until late in a day when I supposedly showed remarkable productivity. But hey, if it gets to that point the computer will be destroyed, or I will be long gone.

Sending out a resume and cover letters to, among other places, a rival company that also appears to sell protein drinks at Sam's Club, helps me create an electronic paper trail for the day in question. I feel like I can show that I was nowhere near Taylors Falls on the day Janelle Moreno died because I was pumping out resumes and cover letters.

The final days of the school year are approaching. In a schedule that only a school administrator would understand, the girls have four days this week, and then the last day of school is a half-day on Wednesday next week. They each excitedly report that they are watching movies with substitute teachers in two classes already, and their other classes will follow suit next week. They are excited to be in the final days of their academic year. I, by contrast, am not nearly as excited about sharing the house with them during the day. I have grown accustomed to the quiet and the routine I have set for myself. That's right, I tend to be routine oriented.

As I sit in my office plotting out what my days will look like with two teenage girls in the house, the home landline phone rings. My first thought is 'Why do we still have a home phone?', and the second is 'Who would call on that number?' As it turns out, the school district has our home number, and they call to inform me that my daughter Angela is in the office. "Your daughter was removed from class this morning for making derogatory comments to another student regarding their sexual identity."

"What?" is as much as I can muster. Angela is our sweetheart, the one who barely speaks, much less makes derogatory comments regarding sexual identity.

"We are investigating this as a possible suspension or expulsion. As you know, we have a zero-tolerance policy regarding bullying of any kind."

I manage to get the assistant principal, Amanda Dean, to agree to a meeting with Jennifer and me at 3 PM. In the interim, my daughter is going to be sitting in a special "de-escalation" room until we arrive and are permitted to take her home. I am able to exchange texts with her to assure Angie that her mother and I will be there as soon as we can to take care of things. Then, communication is halted because, apparently, cell phones are not allowed in the de-escalation room.

In my head, I envision a room decorated with soft pastel colors and cushioned walls. Do they have one of those two-way mirrors where they can keep an eye on the de-escalating student without her knowing? Is she being recorded without her knowledge?

CHAPTER NINETEEN

Jennifer is furious when I call her and tell her what is going on. "Angie would never bully anyone. She has an older sister who bullies her. She's a victim, Angela's never the aggressor."

"I tried to explain that to Ms. Dean, the assistant principal. She's talking suspension and possible expulsion."

"This is ridiculous. I can't wait to tell her what she can do with her suspension."

We sputter back and forth for a few more exchanges before realizing the futility of it all. We agree to meet at 2:45 in the parking lot and direct our considerable angst at the school and the assistant principal. The principal is too much of a glad-handing milquetoast to be involved in any type of conflict like we are intending to create.

We each arrive on time and still angry. Jennifer tends to be very talkative when angry, and she is chattering incessantly. I have to hold her close and remind her that we do not know what happened, and that we should get the facts straight before we blow up.

"This is bull. We both know it."

"I know it is too, but let's hear what happened first." Finally, she takes a deep breath, several really, and we walk into the school holding hands and head towards the office area. As we get closer, Jennifer squeezes my hand tighter and tighter.

We are soon seated in the uncomfortable wooden side chairs in the office of Assistant Principal Dean. Jennifer is leaning forward in her chair, barely able to contain her anger.

Clearing her throat, Ms. Dean begins. "Before we bring Angela in to join us, let me tell you why we intervened today."

"We would prefer if we could see our daughter. Now." Jennifer emphasizes 'now' with all of her pent-up anger. I would pat her hand in an attempt to calm her down but I see no need or benefit.

Ms. Dean seems taken aback. "Our protocol requires that the student currently under review be kept in a separate location during our first interaction with the parents or guardians. Her safety is our paramount concern."

Jennifer squeezes my hand even harder. I didn't think that was possible. I squeeze back with far less ferocity. "We want to see our daughter immediately or we will call our lawyer." It is my turn to be firm and assertive.

"There is no need to involve a lawyer at this juncture. We are still in the fact-finding stage of our inquiry. In fact, you are not entitled to representation in an intra-school proceeding at any juncture."

I pull my phone out of my dress shirt pocket. "William, do you agree that we do not need an attorney at this juncture?"

OK, I admit it. I stole that idea from Harlan Coben, fiction writer extraordinaire. He frequently has a character with a cell phone call connected to a critical participant in the scene, listening in.

I feel very good about getting William Smithson, lawyer and neighbor, involved. William is a corporate lawyer specializing in foreign commodities trading who has never been inside a courtroom and has only one client, a multinational corporation. But, he went to law school just like the ones who might know what they are supposed to do here, however. In fact, his complete lack of knowledge of protocol just might be a blessing. I switch the phone to speaker and place it on the desk. "William, This is Vice Principal Amanda Dean."

"Ms. Dean? My name is William Smithson, and I am an attorney and friend of the parents, Craig and Jennifer Chandler. If I am understanding the situation correctly, my clients' minor daughter is being held against her will in a secured room? Is that right?"

"Angela is not being held against her will. She is simply being given an opportunity to decompress in a relaxing, stable environment."

"So, she is free to leave the room?"

"Well, no, of course not. Someone would have to let her out."

"Sounds like she's in custody to me. I have recommended that Craig and Jennifer allow me to call a judge and get an injunction requiring their daughter to be released to them immediately. Can I get the spelling of the first and last names of you, the principal, and the superintendent?"

Vice Principal Dean considers her options for a moment, and then picks up her desk phone and whispers to someone to bring Angela Chandler to her office immediately. She gives us a look that says releasing Angela is not by her choice. We do not care.

The door behind us opens, and Angela steps somewhat pensively into the office. Jennifer leaps out of her chair and she and Angela hug. I awkwardly wrap my arms around both of them. Excusing myself, I step out of the office, take my phone off speaker, and thank William for his assistance.

"I am not licensed in the State of Minnesota, I do not know any judges to call, and I am quite sure they wouldn't get involved in this," Smithson said, laughing. "I pulled that stuff straight out of second year Administrative Law. Got an 'A' in the course, but you could probably tell that by my topnotch performance."

"Yes, I think she is fully aware of what you are capable of doing to her and the school." I thank him again and make my way back into the office. Angela and Jennifer are sitting in the side chairs, so I pull one from a small table in the back of the smaller but still nicely decorated office.

Angela has been crying, but now she is angry, showing all kinds of spunk. "Mom, Dad, this is so unfair. I don't even know why I'm here."

"Your daughter used a derogatory term that made the victim uncomfortable about her sexual identity and proclivities. As I said before, we have a zero-tolerance policy when terms of this nature are used." If sense of self-importance and adherence to rules are measures, Ms. Dean will be moving up the administrative ladder quickly.

"Mom, Dad, we were in Biology class watching "Les Misérables" and Hannah North said that Hugh Jackman is gay. Mom, I know you love Hugh Jackman, so I told Hannah she was gay. Next thing I know the substitute teacher sends me to the office and Vice Principal Dean tells me I'm going to be expelled." Angie sniffles.

"That's it? She called Hugh Jackman gay and you called her gay back?" Jennifer is barely hiding her incredulity as she looks pointedly at Dean. "You and Hannah are friends, right? She's been to our house lots of times."

The sniffling pauses. "I'm pretty sure she doesn't even know why I got sent out of the class. She was texting me question marks and worry emojis before they took my phone away."

My reaction is to wonder why, other than it would fill three days of class, a biology class is watching Les Misérables instead of studying biology, but I realize that conversation is nothing when compared to the strangest part of this quite strange event. "And that is why we're here right now and you're talking about expelling my daughter? Maybe I should get Mr. Smithson back on the phone? I wonder if he can still reach out to his judge friends." All lawyers have friends who are judges, I assume.

"Again, nothing has been decided at this point, but yes, the utterance of a derogatory term that makes the victim uncomfortable about sexual preference is considered grounds for expulsion. We also can mete out in-school or out of school suspensions depending on mitigating or aggravating circumstances."

"Is the fact that this is complete and utterly ridiculous a mitigating or an aggravating circumstance?" Jennifer says. It is now my turn to squeeze Jennifer's hand hard to calm her down. Truth, particularly when laced with sarcasm, is not the best tact in these situations. It feels good, but it does not lead to a resolution.

"If the school has a zero-tolerance policy, may I ask about the consequences for Hannah North? She certainly made Hugh Jackman uncomfortable with comments about his sexual preference." I have to tread very carefully here because I fell asleep before the end of the opening scene when subjected to the film in question. I was rudely awakened and banished to anywhere but the room where the movie was playing. Is Hugh Jackman gay? I honestly do not know.

"As Hugh Jackman is not a student or member of the school family, her comments, while unfortunate and ill-advised, are not within the purview of our policy. I will send her parents an email about it tomorrow." She glances at her watch. Sorry, is our daughter being expelled taking longer than you expected? I want to say that, but do not.

"Obviously we disagree with your assessment of this situation," I start, trying to defuse and disarm something that is becoming very serious while at the same time remaining quite ridiculous. "I think my daughter has learned her lesson. How about she apologizes to Hannah, writes a letter of apology to the class, does a paper on a topic pertaining to this issue, and we move past this incident? Maybe she could do a synopsis of Les Misérables as well?"

"You make some good points, Mr. Chandler, and your suggested resolution is within the realm of possibility. However, our zero-tolerance policy at the present time dictates a suspension of some sort or expulsion."

We continue to plead our case, arguing logic, common sense, and even threaten involvement by our attorney again, and Vice Principal Dean finally appears to relent. "I will reflect on it overnight and email you with my decision tomorrow morning." She wants us gone pronto.

As we walk out of the school towards our cars, Jennifer is not buying that we have emerged unscathed. "She's just too passive-aggressive to give us the news to our face. Angie is going to be suspended or expelled. We need to start looking at private schools. How are we going to afford tuition for her? I hear Visitation is over $20,000 a year."

"Before we enroll Angie at Visitation, how about we see what Dean decides? I think we got her thinking the right way at the end. I'm not saying common sense has prevailed, but I am saying there's a chance."

Jennifer scoffs loudly and stomps to her car with Angela, muttering about how she needs to get a second job to afford Angela's new school while I don't even have one job. Our daughter looks back at me, tears in her eyes. She can't believe she is responsible for creating such a mess, and all because she made a flippant comment to a friend. This is a very hard life lesson.

"I'm getting full severance for the rest of the year you know," I remind her loudly. She tosses her right hand back at me dismissively. She burns rubber as she and Angela leave the school parking lot.

CHAPTER TWENTY

I stay behind in the school parking lot, ostensibly to collect my thoughts, but in reality to see where Vice Principal Dean parked and to figure out where she lives. I have little confidence that she will do the right thing either, but I feel like I can do something about it if I have some time to think things over and come up with a plan.

I use my now considerable skills at online research to provide some quick answers while I sit in my car. I find her home address and make one stop on the way. The house features an attached small garage, and that makes my plan come together nicely.

Based on seeing no ring on her finger, and the tiny dimensions of the house, I decide that she lives alone. I make sure of this by casing the house carefully before I confirm that conclusion. I park in a nearby park and go for a leisurely stroll in the general direction of her home. I make sure things are clear, and that there is not a dog in the house waiting to chomp on me. Cutting through her side yard, I am soon at the patio off the kitchen. As I hoped, the sliding glass door was left unlocked. Making sure it is clear, I quickly enter her home. For as neat as her office appears, the home is a bit of a mess. I try not to judge too harshly. She is also a cat person. A gray cat with squiggly whitish stripes purrs and rubs against my leg. It does not change my mind about cats in general, but this one seems friendly enough. Some quick preparations and I am ready for her.

Crouched below the front window with a panoramic view of the street in front of me, I wait for the blue Mazda CX-3 from the school parking lot to appear. I spot it in about five minutes, approaching on the street about half a block away. It confirms my hunch that she is not going to make a decision and send out an email at the end of the day. Thinking about it overnight is code for wanting to leave the school not too long after the visitors depart, especially this late in the school year. I return to the garage.

I crouch behind the garbage can in the garage. It obscures my view of the car entering the garage. The light on the garage door opener does not come on, perhaps because I borrowed a step stool and loosened it. Although it was dingy without the light with the door down, I could see well enough to do what I needed to do by using my phone flashlight app.

Vice Principal Dean stays in her car for an extra few minutes, singing along to, horror of horrors, Barry Manilow. I flash to the thought that "Weekend in New England" will be the last song she will hear in her life. I cannot decide if that is what she deserves or not. Does anyone deserve to have a Barry Manilow song be the last one they hear before dying?

There is not time to fully analyze my feelings about Barry Manilow. This is a debate for the ages that can't be resolved in the three seconds it takes for her to stop singing, turn off the car, open her door, and close the garage door using the remote in her car. I thank her as that makes my next actions so much easier.

You can create a concoction of ingredients, bought from almost any drug store, that, when held over the mouth and nose in a towel, put someone to sleep within seconds. Not wanting to be the subject of a lawsuit, I will not provide further details. Lawyers and all. I'm sure you understand.

Vice Principal Dean goes from shocked to slumped in my arms quickly. I put her back in her car, put my left hand on the brake and press the Power button, starting the car again. I grab a rag from a bucket she uses to wash her car and I stuff it in her exhaust pipe, making sure she looks as natural as possible in her car. I turn up Barry Manilow a tad, and make my exit out the sliding glass door again into the back yard and away from the house. Carbon monoxide will do the rest in fairly short order.

I call Jennifer from the car as I make my way home. "I can bring home dinner. What are you hungry for?"

"I'm not sure anyone will be hungry after this ordeal."

I realize that I need to bump up my despondency and nervous anticipation. No one else knows that I have handled my daughter's potential suspension or expulsion with finality. All done to Barry Manilow crooning about ships that pass in the night. But I sent you away, oh Mandy. Dean. In addition to being more worried about the Vice Principal's decision that I know will never come, I need to limit any further revelations about the extent of my knowledge of Barry Manilow music.

I stop at Carbone's and pick up two pizzas for dinner. Despite the pall of the decision regarding Angela's potential expulsion still hanging over us like a shroud of darkness, everyone holds their own in devouring everything in sight. Angie, who should have been the most concerned of us all, eats the last two pieces. There will be no leftovers this night.

My phone rings the next morning while I am busy working on multiple job applications. Well, two applications, but they're very involved. The caller ID says it is Jennifer.

"Did you hear the news about Vice Principal Amanda Dean?" Her voice makes her seem both surprised and excited.

"No, I've been home working on finding a job. You reminded me yesterday that I don't have one, remember?" I'm still a little bruised from the comment she made yesterday in the parking lot.

"She died. Parents got an email informing them of the news. They're saying she died unexpectedly at home. When she didn't show up at school this morning, someone went to her house and found her. Angie heard someone tell a teacher that she was found in her car in the garage."

"That's terrible news. How is Angie taking it?"

"She seems surprised but OK, I guess. She's not been exposed to people she knows dying."

"Is she still at school?"

"Yes, but of course they're sending the students home shortly."

I soon hear the clatter of my daughters coming home from school. There is no noise in the kitchen. I learn later from Mallory that her sister came home, ate a snack, went to her room, and closed the door. Later in the day, after Jennifer comes home from work, we go to her room to talk to Angela. When we open the door after a tentative knock, we see her on her phone and her tablet. Her reaction is more of annoyance that we are interrupting.

"Honey, do you want to talk about this?" Jennifer asks when Angela looks up from her devices at her concerned parents.

"All I ever saw Vice Principal Dean do was be mean to people, so it sucks that she's dead and all, but I'm fine. Does this mean I have to go back to school tomorrow?" It appears that she has moved on just fine. She will not have to avail herself of the school-supplied counselors currently available, even outside of school hours, to assist with 'processing'. I realize that my youngest daughter and I might share a certain deficit in the human emotion area.

A week later, with school over for the summer, the principal's assistant emails us with the information that the incident had been closed with no further action deemed necessary. Angela will not have to transfer to Visitation after all.

CHAPTER TWENTY-ONE

Detectives Elliott Little and Bernadette Bixby sat in their office chairs, uncertain of their next move. A week had passed and their whiteboard diagrams all ended in dead ends. Bixby suggested they hide the board to avoid hearing the sharp comments from other detectives passing by. The early morning cleaning person innocently offered to erase the board for them. While tempting, Elliott declined the offer. In return, the cleaning person declined the offer to add anything to the diagram.

"Bernie, we need a break here," he said, pointing disgustedly at the board. All it showed was two names at the tops of columns with the names of witnesses with check marks in boxes next to indicate that they had been interviewed. Witnesses interviewed who provided information that then did not lead to anything were also crossed out, leaving no remaining names. In a typical investigation of related homicides, lines, sometimes in red to indicate priority, were drawn between the names with Post-It notes indicating progress and next steps. Here, nothing was circled, no next steps were numbered by priority. No red. If there was a color to indicate icy cold and stagnant it would be plentiful on the board.

"Looks like you two are up against it on this one," commented Lieutenant Everett Daniels, their shift supervisor. He stared at the board, holding a large Speedway insulated coffee cup. He took a sip and apprised the mood of his two best detectives.

"This one is getting to you, I can tell."

"Yeah," Bixby agreed. "We just stare at the board and wonder what to do next. Like maybe the board will start talking and tell us something we missed."

Everett Daniels rose slowly through the ranks of Minneapolis law enforcement, including a brief stint in the Hennepin County Sheriff's department. He settled in as a detective in property crimes and eventually homicide. One afternoon, while providing back-up to nearby uniforms called to a domestic situation in North Minneapolis, a third roommate in the house decided to make a run for it before police discovered that he was wanted on felony drug possession warrants. He snuck out the back door and quietly entered the detached garage.

Seeing a 2012 Prius backing out of the driveway, Daniels jumped behind the car with his gun drawn. The wanted drug felon, realizing his attempt at an escape had been foiled despite the silence of the electric motor, pressed the accelerator and ran into Daniels. Even though it was only a Prius, and even at the minimal speed it was capable of generating, the car hit Daniels on his right leg and knocked him almost clear of the vehicle. The driver side front wheel then ran over the right leg, crushing it. "It hurt like the dickens, but the mileage was excellent" was how Daniels described it later to hospital visitors. Emergency orthopedic surgeries were unable to save the leg below the knee, and Daniels now used a prosthetic lower leg.

After several months of additional surgeries and intense rehabilitation, Daniels found that he did not have a job anymore. MPD administration was forcing permanent disability and medical retirement on him. He refused. "I can still use a computer and run a shift," he told people, including his union representatives. Experienced workers were brought back after heart attacks limited their ability to physically exert themselves, and, he argued, he should not be treated any differently. He and the union fought to allow him to continue his career in some capacity with MPD. Eventually, it made sense to those in power that his mind would be a terrible thing to waste.

He successfully earned the right to sit for and pass the exams necessary to become a supervisor. He then became a shift supervisor of homicide and major crimes detectives. His nickname upon his return and promotion was "Lieutenant Dan", bestowed on him by fans of Forrest Gump. His direct reports liked him because he had more hands-on experience than previous supervisors, and his insight often provided excellent avenues to pursue.

Pulling up a chair, he joined his detectives in their melancholy. "If the killer is the same person, there has to be a connection. You're missing it. Walk me through what you know."

An hour later, Lt. Dan stood and announced that he needed more coffee, and that he had to leave for a budget meeting. "For once," he said, waving his coffee mug at the forlorn board, "a budget meeting seems like it will be more productive than going over and over this case. My advice to you two is to start over. If you talked to someone on the phone, talk to them in person instead. See if they can add something to the story." With that, he left them and walked back to his office.

The two detectives sat and stared at the board, their notes, and their computer screens. "You know, as much as I would like to think that there is something out there that we haven't considered, Lt. Dan is right. We have to start over. Let's start with that weasel assistant manager at the store and go from there," said Little.

"Lt. Dan said we should start with the ones we talked to on the phone and talk to them in person instead," Bixby countered.

"Yeah but working that guy over is way too much fun not to do it again. We need the entertainment for motivation. It's more efficient because we can talk to the co-workers again on the same visit."

"You drive" said Bixby. "I'll run his name and see if he has a criminal record in Minnesota and surrounding states." Anything to not have to stare at the whiteboard that mocked them with its multi-colored diagram of failure.

Patrick McGarvey was as fun as ever to interview but yielded no additional information. Their conclusion was that he existed as a player with the female associates only in his self-aggrandizing dreams. He was little more than what all women in the workplace encounter on a daily basis. The other workers also provided nothing new.

Tracking down all the customers Janelle worked with in the last week of her time at the store took the rest of the day, and still the detectives had nothing to show for it. Their frustration and sense of dread of reporting no progress to the grieving parents mounted. They drove without speaking to their last stop of the day. There were no ideas to bounce off one another to make the drive seem shorter. A drive to the southern suburbs in the late afternoon was slow going made slower by their frustration.

Little stopped the Impala in the driveway of the last subject, who lived in a higher-end but typical suburban home built in the last 15 years. "Who's this guy again?" Elliott asked as he turned off the car.

"The name's Craig Chandler. According to the store receipts he came to the store twice and worked with Janelle both times. I talked to him on the phone a few days after and he said he was sending out resumes and cover letters when Janelle was in Taylors Falls."

"So, another person who has nothing to tell us?"

"Exactly."

Chandler himself opened the door. He was dressed in an untucked green polo shirt, khaki cargo shorts, and flip-flops. "May I help you?" he asked.

"Mr. Chandler," Bixby began. "We spoke a few days ago on the phone."

"Yes, I would have remembered if we spoke face to face." Chandler had an air of superiority about him that both detectives found instantly grating.

"Right. You worked with a young lady named Janelle Moreno recently at her place of employment, and we are talking to the last people who saw her before she was killed," Little added.

Chandler held the storm door open and motioned the detectives to the dining area towards the back of the house. They sat at an oval-shaped table with matching ornate wooden chairs. A glass-enclosed hutch, purposely stressed to look antique, held several pieces of china. There was a granite countertop high enough for decorative leather bar stools near the kitchen area replete with high-end stainless-steel appliances. The officers declined an offer of a drink. Their witness appeared calm, but a little impatient.

As Little spoke, Bixby focused on reading Chandler's demeanor and body language. Eventually, the two detectives would seamlessly switch roles and compare their notes and thoughts later. Their successful close rate for their cases could be traced back to their ability to tag team witnesses and suspects in a way that kept people off guard and unable to know what was coming next.

"I understand," Chandler said again. "As I told you on the phone," Chandler seemed to add extra emphasis on 'phone' to indicate that he was not letting go of the earlier jab he took at Bixby. "She helped me buy toner cartridges and paper, and then a computer and monitors. She was knowledgeable and friendly. What else can I tell you?" He held up his hands with the palms facing skyward as if to express his frustration at having so little to offer.

Little reviewed his notes. "According to co-workers, she commonly would give customers her cell number if they needed anything in the future. Did she do that with you?"

"I think so, let me check my phone." Chandler removed his phone from the front right buttoned pocket of his cargo shorts with practiced ease and began scrolling through his contacts. "Here it is. I can read the number to you if that would help."

"Let me take a look at it, if that's all right." Bixby reached out for the phone. Another test to see if Chandler would balk. He did not.

"You called her 'Toner Babe' in your contacts? Sounds like she was something more than someone you worked with at an office supply store. Care to elaborate?" Bixby raised her eyebrows to show her surprise at what she had seen.

"She took my phone and typed that in herself," Chandler replied, showing annoyance for an instant with a slight amount of defensiveness added.

Little took over the questioning again. "I can assure you that she did not call herself 'Toner Babe' for her other customers. Why would she do that? Sounds like you were more than just a customer." What he said was true, but only because this was the first 'Toner Babe' they had seen. She was 'Printer Babe', 'Laptop Babe', and 'Paper Babe' to other customers, but Little felt confident that Chandler did not know that about their victim. Both detectives now glared at Chandler, looking for a sign of guilt.

"As I said before, she put her information into my phone. I barely even looked at it. Hey," Chandler said, impatience giving way to fulsome earnestness. "She seemed like a nice kid, and she was great to work with at the store. Like I daid, I needed toner, paper, and a then a new laptop and monitors. She helped me out. I feel terrible that she died, but I can't really help you." Chandler shifted in his seat, suggesting that the interview was over.

Little read through the notes he had scrawled on his reporter-style pad. The interview would be over when he and Bixby decided it would be over, and not before. "You said that on the afternoon Janelle died you were applying for jobs. Can you show us what you did that afternoon?"

Chandler looked annoyed again for a second and then stood, confidence returning. "It's all on the computer. Let me show you." With that, he led them down the hall to a bedroom that had been converted into an office.

A laptop with two large screens dominated a desk placed at an angle in the corner of the office. Near it stood an all-in-one printer. Bixby noted that Chandler had better equipment in his home office than they had in the MPD offices. Not fair, but not surprising either. Many things had advanced in the years since the department last upgraded their computer equipment.

Chandler sat in an older office chair with the left armrest cracked. "I was going to buy a chair from Janelle next," he said with a little too much lilt in his voice. "I guess I won't be able to do that now," he finished with a touch of sadness in his tone, as though catching himself.

He pointed to one of his oversized monitors. "Here is the Excel spreadsheet I use to track my applications and submissions. I have a reverse pivot table that automatically reads the time and date from the Word document that I create and tracks it here." He pointed on his spreadsheet to the date and time of four job applications that spanned the afternoon that Janelle left work and never returned. "I can even print it off if you'd like."

Little stared at the screen, a sinking feeling in his stomach. "Yeah, please do." He could see their last best hope disappearing. He locked eyes with Bixby above Chandler's head; they both shared the same thought. 'Where else could they turn?'

"If that is all, gentlemen, I have to get dinner ready before my wife gets home from her job. Now that I'm out of work and on severance, she expects me to run the household. An out of work executive's work is never done," he said ruefully. He stood, letting the detectives know that the interview was concluded. The detectives were out of ways to extend the interview.

Once back in the car, Little slapped the dashboard. "That arrogant SOB. I know he did it. I can feel it in my bones."

"I agree," Bixby replied. "He is too cool, too smooth, and he thinks that we're dazzled by him. The only problem is that we have no proof that he did anything," he said, still fuming. "And he handed us an ironclad alibi."

"A 'reverse pivot table', Elliott said, referring to his notes, "What does that even mean?"

"It means we can't touch the guy," Bixby replied.

Bixby threw the paper holding the dates and times of the job applications on the floor. After a few moments she reached down and placed it in the file. Then she threw the file on the floor. She stared out the window on the ride back to Minneapolis.

CHAPTER TWENTY-TWO

I watch the cop car leave our neighborhood through our dining room window. A nosy neighbor stands in her driveway and watches them leave as well. At some point this evening she will mosey on over (because she is nosy) and inquire about the sedan that looked like an unmarked police car with the two black police officers with suits. I will tell Jennifer both about the visit from the detectives, as well as Gladys. I am not sure her name is Gladys, but she looks like a Gladys to me.

Jennifer's reaction to the visit is as I expect. "That poor girl. Why did they feel like they had to talk to you again?" She motions for the array of seasoning options on the table. My cooking skills are still developing. As a nouveau chef I try not to be insulted when everyone at the table grabs for salt, pepper, Cajun seasoning, and an all-in-one option, and then use them liberally.

"I'm not sure," I say, passing her the sea salt and the pepper. "They told me it was routine to follow up phone interviews with face to face ones in a homicide case. It's really not a big deal because all I did was shop at the store and buy printer paper, toner, and a laptop and monitors, and I happened to get her both times I went there. I feel sorry for the young lady, but they must be hitting a brick wall if they have to drive here and talk to me in person." I feel like I handled my wife's questions as easily and effortlessly as I had the detectives in their cheap dress clothes. She worries me more than they do, and that is not much at all. I turn my attention to the girls.

"So, ladies, how was your day? Do you miss school yet?"

"Not even a little, Dad," Angie says. Mallory, the older one, does not look up from her plate. Her summer job at a local floral shop requires her to work three days a week and Saturdays. Unfortunately for her, the store is an easy bike ride away, or Jennifer can drop her off at a Caribou next door on her way to work and pick her up on her way home. Thus far she has opted to get herself to work on her bicycle. Her sullenness has the potential to sour the dinner table mood.

I clean up after dinner and get dressed for a bike ride. Despite my strong show of self-confidence, I need to think things through and see if there are any holes in my planning. I am worried because I acted impulsively with Janelle, and I feel like the lack of preparation could lead to a clue or clues that can be followed.

I wave at Gladys as I ride past her on my bike. I can tell she wants to ask me about the visitors this afternoon. Sorry to disappoint you Gladys, and your yippy little rat dog too. I see it leaving its feet in barking fervor, but I have no time for either of them. I pedal faster, as though Gladys might be able to pry if she catches up with me. I take no chances.

The first thing I want to think about is the reason for the detectives calling on me well after the phone call that should have eliminated me as a suspect or as someone with any useful knowledge. The detectives claimed they did that as standard procedure. Not knowing what 'standard procedure' is for Minneapolis homicide investigators, I conclude it is a non-issue. If they had anything of significance to work on, they would not be traveling out of their jurisdiction to interview me when the first phone interview had been thorough enough to conclude that it was not necessary to pursue it any further. It is the investigative version of chasing their tails, I decide.

A few miles down the road and a trail and one puzzle is now resolved. The second point to ponder is why Minneapolis is investigating a murder that occurred in Taylors Falls? I'm pretty sure TF is in Chisago County, and that Minneapolis is in Hennepin County. I pause on that thought long enough to downshift a gear and push hard up a hill. I monitor my cycling computer as I do and maintain a good speed on the incline.

Deep analytical thought pushes me even harder. My thighs will feel this workout in the morning. I return to my usual cadence and my analysis of my situation. I also start to think about Lynyrd Skynyrd and decide to save that thoughtful analysis for another day.

Another pressing question: Why didn't I ask them the question about their dubious jurisdiction when they were sitting at our dining room table? She worked in Washington County at the big box office supply store, she lived (I assume) near there and not in Minneapolis. What is the connection? I'm glad I didn't ask because it would show too much interest in the case. I would have no reason to know where she lived. Innocent people, Mr. Chandler, do not dwell on the facts they shouldn't know when they claim they know nothing about the victim.

Back to the bigger and more pressing question. This one should be good for five miles of intense riding. Why are they investigating a seemingly random killing with no ties to Minneapolis? Granted, Minneapolis is not Chicago in terms of homicide rates, but these detectives are not exactly sitting by their police scanners listening for suspicious death calls from other jurisdictions either. No, they have plenty of suspicious deaths to investigate within their own city limits.

There must be a nexus between Janelle's death and the Nyberg killing they are currently investigating. That nexus, I fear, is me, and I wonder how they reached that conclusion and what that means for me. I also wonder if I am mentally spelling nexus correctly, whether I am using it properly, and if the shampoo by the same or similar name is still sold. Oh wait, there's a song "Nexus" by Dan Fogelberg. I briefly dated someone in my early college years (before Jennifer) who called herself a DanFan. She claimed his words and music spoke to her at a level no other singer/songwriter could. That was the last time I spoke to her.

Following along on the thought process I am detailing here should explain why I generally listen to music and attempt to zone out when I ride. Time with your own thoughts can be frustrating when you flit between topics. It keeps your mind feverishly working for over twenty miles of pedaling, but sometimes that is about all it accomplishes for you.

Now, back to the nexus between the cases. Is there an anti-dandruff version? Shampoo and conditioner in one? Come on. Focus. The only real connection between the cases is that both women ended up in a river. One died and was deposited in the river, one died while being pushed into the river, or drowned once there. Despite the seemingly random violent acts of dead women being found in rivers miles and days apart, the investigators were pursuing them as connected cases. Why are they seeing a connection? I will need to explore who or what is responsible for concluding that these cases are really one investigation, seeking one culprit. I am the only person who should know that. And, once I figure that out, what am I going to do about it?

I complete my ride and steer my front wheel at an angle onto my driveway. I now have a plan. First, I am going to discreetly figure out how the connection was made between two seemingly unrelated homicides. Second, I am going to obfuscate matters considerably by taking actions for which no pattern can be found, because they will be done completely at random. I will be unable to discern a pattern because I will purposely avoid any patterns. That should get them chasing their tails, along with whomever or whatever is guiding them in their investigation. Besides, I need to do something with the burning desire to act again.

Over the course of the next week, I accomplish two things. The first is that I have my first legitimate job opportunity to consider. I was contacted by a recruiter on LinkedIn, had a short phone interview with an overly exuberant HR specialist, and will be meeting face to face with a panel that includes a senior vice president hiring manager on Wednesday next week. It seems a local healthcare conglomerate is looking for a vice president level person who can improve sales efficiencies. Of course, the first way to be more efficient as a sales organization is to reduce head count and salary. The second way is to update technologies, which comes at a high price tag. Ostensibly, the need for efficiency is expressed as technology updates, but the reality is they need to bring someone in who can oversee a restructuring of their organization. Reducing costs leads to increased profits with far more certainty than updating servers.

The second thing I accomplish is a head scratching and utterly confounding homicide. It is not at all confusing for me. For me, it is both straightforward and rewarding.

It starts when I drive up to the Coon Rapids area, a north and slightly western suburb of Minneapolis. I return the next evening to commit a "random act of violence against a beloved member of our community," as a local church leader described it later. Towards dusk, an elderly black man is walking alone near empty youth softball fields off the seldom-used parking lot associated with a mini-golf business. The golf course is crowded with teenagers far too busy impressing other teenagers to notice anything police would later find to be helpful. Tennis courts that have not been resurfaced since, I don't know, back when people played tennis, create an excellent cover for a guy with a bike rack and a child trailer.

As the gentleman walks in a dimly lit and lightly traveled trail, I come up behind him and kill him with my knife. I then carry him like a rock salt bag to my trunk, wrap him in in plastic, and drive carefully to a bike trail.

There is a very nice trail through woods, fields, and neighborhoods that stretches from Coon Rapids to Champlin in the west. I put in on the Champlin side with the body in the child trailer attached to my bicycle. I strap on an LED light to my helmet, turn on the headlight and red taillight on my bike, and quickly cover the 12 miles to the Coon Rapids Dam. You would be surprised at the ease with which a bicycle can pull a trailer with 145 pounds in it when the trail does not have many hills. I do not pass anyone on the entire trail from start to finish.

The Coon Rapids dam helps control the flow of the Mississippi River today. It was originally built in 1914 to provide electricity for the surrounding area. It ceased being economically feasible as a source of electricity in 1966, and now serves as a barrier against invasive species flowing down the river towards Minneapolis. A beautiful park now lies on both sides of the river and is quite popular.

For me, I need a quiet place to be able to drop my latest victim into the Mississippi River and create chaos in an ongoing investigation. The Coon Rapids Dam meets my needs.

The expanse of the dam across the Mississippi is impressive. The cement path on top of the dam is widened by cutouts for folks wanting to take a few moments to take in the vista down the river towards Minneapolis, or up the river towards Anoka. Or, as it turns out, to pull to the side and quickly drop a dead person into the river. Because I am the type who likes to finish what he starts, I ride across the entire span of the dam to the Coon Rapids parking area, tour the neighborhood for a bit of the local feel, and then turn around and retrace my steps back to my car. On the trip home, I of course dispose of the plastic and, as always, minimize my risk.

As nothing has been reported that indicates that the "tragic death of a local school administrator" was in any way suspicious, that one does not factor into my thoughts. Thus far, two women have been found in a river and traced back to the Stone Arch Bridge in Minneapolis and Taylors Falls. They were both younger and white. The next body to be discovered in a river will be an older black man from Coon Rapids. Factor that in as you create capture algorithms. I assume there is a capture algorithm at play here, if not now, soon.

Two days later I am reading the local paper online while I prepare for my interview with the healthcare giant. One line in particular catches my eye, and I read it three times, losing my rhythm while memorizing the names of the Chief Medical Officer, an HR Director who also started at Mankato State, and the Senior VP of Sales whom I now cannot remember where she worked last. Killing people and finding work through intensive interviews is hard to keep straight.

Anyway, the article quotes a source who asked not to be identified as saying that "a local expert assisting with the investigation concluded that the body entered the Mississippi River at the Coon Rapids Dam. As a result, forensic technicians are focusing the investigation there."

Unbelievable. The random nature of the victim selection is not even considered. This consultant is starting to get under my skin. As a result, a few hours later I stumble during our introduction when trying to recall the job held by the Chief Product Officer (CPO) before her current position. She did not move to Minnesota from Maryland; she came from South Carolina. Nothing strokes the ego of those you are interviewing with like complete recall of their work and academic background. Nothing, in turn, hurts you more than messing up on a unique detail about the interviewer that is intended to impress. I feel the loss of momentum from that point forward. As I walk to my car, certain that I will not be offered the position. I console myself with the fact that I did not want to work every day in an industry I know nothing about.

In the car, listening to James Taylor as I deconstruct the interview process, I wonder if seeing fire and rain makes me special too. Rather than mock the rather obvious choice in metaphors, I sing along instead. Or is the song replete with analogies? Maybe similes? Like the song, these thoughts are soon in pieces on the ground, and I am planning again. What is my next move? What will you be able to offer in the way of expertise this next time, 'unnamed local expert assisting with the investigation'? Nothing gets you past a disappointing job interview like planning your next adventure. Nothing at all.

We move ahead a few nights and we find our favorite serial killer on the streets of Minneapolis. I am, of course, up to no good, but I am fitting in well. There are others who are also up to something dubious on the streets tonight. In the modern world, one needs to consider the presence and location of security cameras, traffic cameras, and cellphones with cameras. They have become omnipresent, almost. Semi-omnipresent?

Thoughts of the 'Thank You" emails sent to each person I met during my interview a few days ago crossing paths with the rejection email from HR percolate in my head. My conclusion, the one that allows me to maintain a semblance of self-esteem, is that it was an interview done for the sake of proving that interviews were held. The internal candidate for the job had already been selected but could not be offered the job until perfunctory external interviews were completed. This placates me, as does the fact that I get to remain unencumbered by work obligations for the foreseeable future. I should relish the downtime and not fret over my next challenge, says every job search article ever. Free time is wasted on the jobseeker who does not recognize the opportunity to improve and recharge oneself.

Minneapolis is a very large metropolitan area. To help make sense of it all, there are specific neighborhoods that break it down into manageable sizes. Right now, I am in what is considered the LynLake neighborhood, where Lyndale Avenue and Lake Street intersect south of downtown, in the shadow of 35W, the freeway that runs from the Iowa border to Duluth in northwestern Minnesota. Yes, 35W runs north and south, but is called 35W. Any guesses on what directions 35E runs? Pondering these great mysteries only causes me to lose focus, and when your mission requires concentration and swift action, you must purge these distractions.

In my head I have defined my perfect victim. He will be young and white, in contrast to older and black like the deceased gentleman in Coon Rapids. Extra points for skinny jeans and a man bun, just because they are so, so wrong. Despite the hour, approaching midnight on a Thursday evening, the side streets are in motion with walkers, bikers, and cars. I park my car in the lot adjacent to Cub Foods, open 24-hours and thus ideal. To satisfy those who might be angry that I took advantage of the store, I go in and buy chips and salsa for our Mexican-themed dinner Friday. I display my re-useable bag filled with chip bags prominently in the back seat. Tostitos and Doritos are on sale so I do not buy Old Dutch, the local Minnesota company. You cannot appease all of the critics all of the time. Two of the salsas are Old Dutch, however.

While cruising the area streets on my bike with the child bike trailer faithfully in tow, I spot my best target yet. He is short, wearing an unbuttoned flannel shirt over a black vintage rock tee of some sort. His tight black jeans have slits to strategically show how old and worn they might be while still costing way too much, and red Converse high tops. Because of the dark stocking cap worn on an evening with temps still in the upper 60's, I am unable to determine whether he sports a man bun, but I can only assume he does, or has in the recent past. Everything about him shouts 'bonus points' to me.

As he continues south, I see that he is past Lake Street and within another block he will be headed towards a more residential area. Thanks to forward-thinking Minneapolis and a plethora of bike lanes, I am able to pedal behind, abreast, and then ahead of him in what is now a murky darkness due to limited street lighting and houses dark for the night. One swift move allows me to pull onto the sidewalk to block his path.

"Hey, out of my-"

The sentence trails off as I stab him with my knife, twice in a matter of perhaps one second. His lifeless body collapses in my arms as I return the knife to its holder and stuff him in the child carrier. I find his late model iPhone and turn it off. No need to create an electronic GPS trail. Within fifteen seconds the trailer is zipped closed and I am once again on the bike lane and pushing hard. In order to be street legal, I turn on my front light and reach behind me to flick on my blinking red tail light. I am careful to stop at intersections, wait my turn on the one red light I hit, and before long I am on the Midtown

Greenway trail heading towards the lake formerly known as Calhoun. I know, they renamed a lake?

In a fervor of political correctness, Lake Calhoun, named after former Vice President and pro-slavery historical figure John C. Calhoun, became Bde Maka Ska. I want to dump my passenger in there just to make a statement. The world must know of my disapproval of applying current forward- thinking ideology to a person who died in 1850. He was from South Carolina – that is reason enough to not name one of the most popular lakes in Minneapolis after him. This is going to be my strong, albeit unconventional, statement about the renaming of the lake.

Below the parking lot of a beautiful church, serving some strange group of worshippers with orthodox in their name, I roll to a stop. I turn off my lamps and realize that ambient light makes many things visible, making nocturnal rides seem safe without lights. As I stand astride my bicycle, I am distracted by the excited barking of a dog. This is followed by second and third dogs barking, and the angry voice of their human telling them to "shut up, you stupid mutts." My brief reverie is broken by their approach, and I realize that I cannot make the political statement I want to make this night on this lake. I wonder if the dog owner, prodded into walking his dogs when the rest of the city slept, ponders a similar watery fate for any of his three dogs.

The sound places them about 30 yards behind me, with a streetlight providing enough illumination that I will be seen. Time to change the plan. I clip in again and pedal hard for two minutes. I put some distance between my bike with its dangerous payload and the angry nocturnal dog owner.

I take the small feeder trail that leads to Lake Harriet. Traffic is nonexistent on William Berry Parkway as I ride alongside it to Harriet. I start to wonder about whether William Berry Park will need to have its name changed. In a remote area, I stop to consider the spot I identified the evening before when I had put the plan together. I had made it my Plan B. Now it is to become my Plan A. Make the plan, work the plan, even in homicide. Especially in homicide when transporting the victim in your bike trailer.

I complete the loop around Lake Harriet and consider riding back towards the lake that used to be called Calhoun. Surely the path is safe now, unless Shirley decides to go out for an evening stroll. In a slight breach of cycling etiquette, and all of the essential regulations appertaining thereto, I ride in a counterclockwise direction on the bike trail. I also, gasp, decide to ride my bicycle on the pedestrian trail, as it is closer to the water. Those pedestrian types are always walking on the biking trail, oblivious to the world around them, so I consider this to be fair and reasonable this one time.

My thinking is that I like the cover provided by the trees along the shore on the west shoreline. As I approach the spot I have selected, I unclip my feet and pull off the trail and get as close as I can to a thicket of trees along the shore. It is surprising how many trees are in a park that is within a large city. Amidst the cover of lots of foliage, I estimate that the body will not be found for several days. I wade a few feet into the water and push the recently deceased millennial under the surface. My bike shoes are soggy and my socks feel squishy as I return to where I parked, break down the trailer, attach my bike to the car, and drive carefully and well within the speed limit back to our house.

I sleep well that night, despite the surge of excitement racing through me like electricity. Looking over at Jennifer in bed, I consider waking her and burning off some of this excitement, but she looks too peaceful to disturb. I eventually drift off to sleep. The sun is bright when I awake. After years of getting up and plodding off to work, I am getting used to sleeping in.

CHAPTER TWENTY - THREE

The call to Homicide reporting a victim came in just as Bixby and Little were settling in to their desks in the morning. With their computers just coming to life, Lt. Dan walked over to them. "Never mind checking emails, looks like your friend struck again. I'll text you the address."

"Looks like Lake Harriet," Bixby said, reading the address from her phone screen. "Isn't that where you grew up, Elliott?"

"It is indeed. I used to ride my bike down to the lake and sail for hours," Little said, lost in remembrance.

"Yeah, you mention that every time we're near Lake Harriet."

"Are there any lakes in Brooklyn Center? It's mostly just empty retail stores now, right?"

Even Bernie had to smile at that one. "True, it hasn't been the same since Kmart pulled out."

The partners rode without speaking until they reached the bandshell. Four squad cars were parked haphazardly in the lot, all with their lights flashing. An older patrol officer with a gray buzzcut approached their car and spoke to Little through his open window. "The body is onshore not far from the South Beach." As he started to give more precise directions, Elliott waved his hand dismissively.

"I grew up around here. I know where South Beach is."

The officer reached with his left hand to activate the microphone attached to his shirt on his left shoulder. "They're on their way. Driver thinks he's an expert."

Three patrol cars were blocking traffic on Lake Harriet Parkway, directing cars from either direction east on Minnehaha Parkway. As Little approached, one of the cars reversed, pulled abreast of the second car, and Little pulled in the middle of the vehicles. The crime scene vehicle, back doors propped open, was being emptied by two hustling techs in windbreakers with the same MPD crime scene logos repeated on their navy-blue ball caps. They moved with the look of practiced efficiency. Bixby noted that all of them were now wearing fanny packs.

"They dress like movie stars. When did schlepping evidence at a crime scene become so glamorous?" Bixby wondered.

"Right about the time all the TV shows started showing the geeks solving cases while the detectives stood around, watched in awe, and made arrests. Don't get me wrong, they've helped us plenty, but they haven't solved one case in all my years at MPD," Little responded. "Broderick is the best in the business, but there's still a place for us in the investigation of crimes."

"Thank goodness. You're too old to have to find another job. Maybe you could become a house husband for Doc Granger?"

"Hmm," was all Elliott said, as though pondering the prospect, a crooked smile forming on his face.

As they made their way down an embankment, led by another officer, other techs were already busy on the shore. Bixby recognized Sarah Broderick, the tech who had handled the two previous scenes with them. As they approached, they could hear her barking orders at two more techs, letting them know she wanted the scene handled with extreme care. "We can't let the water disturb what we need to do. Remember, IIC. We isolate, identify, and capture," she said. Little and Bixby were confident she would make sure that was accomplished.

"Ms. Broderick," Little began.

"Please stand back, detective," she replied without turning her head. "Due to the potential for natural spoliation I am expanding our sphere of coverage. You will need to keep an appropriate distance."

"We will. Can you give us any preliminary details?" Bixby said.

"Yes, in a moment. We are at a critical stage of scene control," she responded, extending her hand upwards towards them while continuing to direct her coworkers, a gesture indicating she would speak with them when more pressing things had been accomplished to her precise standards. "Again, please keep your distance, detectives."

Little sighed, turned, and walked back several yards, slumping his shoulders as a young child would do when reprimanded. "There was a time when we were in charge of a homicide investigation," Little lamented.

"Was that before you had your first cell phone?" Bixby inquired.

"It was right before I ordered you to go and fetch coffee for us," Elliott responded, pointing in the direction of their car.

Bixby took the hint and returned several minutes later with their two travel mugs filled with Caribou coffee. "I almost went to McDonalds to teach you a lesson about flaunting your authority," she remarked, handing over the mug. Both detectives drank their hot coffee out of large insulated schooners. Appropriate levels of caffeination lead to attention to detail, according to a long-ago squad leader.

Broderick stepped away from the scene thirty minutes later. Despite the voluminous capacity of their mugs, the coffee was almost gone in both, and Bixby was thinking of ways to excuse herself to go to the bathroom. She forgot that as Broderick strode toward them purposefully.

"We are looking at a homicide, but the murder did not occur here," she led confidently. She then provided the basis for that conclusion, the nylon Velcro retro wallet with cash and credit cards, as well as a newer model iPhone powered down in an unsecured pocket. "The victim was also wearing an Apple Watch. Robbery was not a motive," she concluded. "Cause of death appears to be two stab wounds in close proximity on the neck, but I will leave that for the coroner to conclude. From what I see, stab wounds being the most noteworthy indicia, this fits with your other recent water bound victims."

"Any indication of how the body ended up here on the shore?" Bernie asked.

"No sign that we can find," she said, almost apologizing for ordering them away earlier. "That explains the duration of our work here. It is harder to find something that's not there. A negative is a harder conclusion as we postulate that we are missing something that turns out not to be there at all."

Elliott could tell she was bothered by her lack of findings. "That makes sense. The body could have been dropped or placed in the water anywhere on the lake."

Broderick smiled wanly and turned back to the crime scene. It seemed unlikely that she would be able to accept that there was nothing to be found. Little and Bixby started walking towards their car. As they left, Broderick began issuing orders to her crew to redouble their efforts to find something to tell them what had occurred. Crime scene techs were quite accustomed to finding critical pieces of evidence that broke cases wide open. That is why they approached their laborious tasks with such zeal.

"Let's go back to Caribou and figure out our next steps," suggested Bixby, needing a bathroom break more than she needed another refill of coffee.

"How about lunch on Lake Street instead? I know a place that shouldn't be busy this early."

"Anywhere that has a bathroom works for me," Bixby responded.

They arrived just as Burger Jones was opening. Little put down his phone and excused himself, leaving the borderline desperate Bixby to wait a few more minutes. As Little approached the table Bixby got up and announced that she also needed to "wash up for lunch."

When they settled in and placed their drink orders, the two turned their attention to the latest homicide and their next steps. "This guy is taunting us with the randomness of the pattern. He has dumped a body in the Mississippi in two locations, the St. Croix River near Taylor Falls, and now in a Lake Harriet south of downtown."

Little looked up appreciatively as a large burger in a basket heaping with fries approached. For a moment all he could concentrate on was his ritual of eating preparation. Napkin tucked under his chin using his buttoned collar, burger and fries separated so as to not touch, a circular mound of ketchup, also not touching anything else. Bixby had three bites in before Little was ready for his first. "I'm surprised he didn't dump it in Lake Calhoun. That's the more well-known of the lakes, and it gets deeper more quickly," Elliott pointed out before his first authoritative bite.

"It's now called 'Bde Maka Ska'. The mayor sent out the blast email requesting our cooperation in modifying the mindsets of our, and his, constituents," Bixby reminded.

"I think the new name should be pronounced 'Bite Me'. Anyway, I wonder if Doc can work her magic on Lake Harriet and tell us where the body went in the water."

"This is a lake, not a river. I don't think we can use science on this one."

"Oh, you would be surprised what Abby, er, Dr. Granger, can do. Quite surprised, actually."

"That can be our next stop after you finish the three concentric but never touching segments of your lunch." Bixby said, already done eating. She grabbed her phone and stepped away to call in and report progress and proposed next steps to Lt. Dan. Little, meanwhile, the hamburger now fully consumed, was working his way through the fries, each one precisely dunked twice in ketchup between bites. A pickle awaited consumption on a side plate. No part of the lunch would be eaten before its time. Bernie wondered how many of these idiosyncracies had been displayed in front of Abby Granger. "That poor girl has so much to learn," she sighed. "I can only do so much to coach him."

Carrying a hot tea in one hand and his large coffee mug in the other, Elliott could only smile as Dr. Granger welcomed them to her lab. She greeted Bixby in a mechanical fashion before taking the tea from Elliott and giving him a hug. She motioned them to small side chairs by her very neat desk.

"I understand you are looking for some assistance with a body found in Lake Harriet? Too bad it was not discovered on Lake Bde Maka Ska. I have been studying that one since the name change controversy. It's really quite fascinating."

"I find it fascinating as well." Little looked over at Bixby, inviting her to comment. Bernie offered no commentary. Instead, Elliott gazed at Dr. Granger with a now familiar look of enchantment.

"Did you know that Lake BMS – that's what I call it for short – is the largest lake in the City of Minneapolis and at its deepest is 87 feet?"

Elliott leaned forward with rapt interest. "You have got to be kidding me. What else?"

"It covers over 400 acres of area, and is considered the most popular of any lake in Minneapolis."

"What can you tell us about our victim and how he ended up where he did on Lake Harriet?" Bixby figured she could learn fun facts about Lake BMS later.

"Of course. Sorry, I get excited about any body of water. Every lake, river, or stream tells a story. You just need to know where to look to uncover it." Bixby cleared her throat to gently show her impatience. Elliott softly kicked her left foot, letting his partner know that Granger should be allowed to talk uninterrupted.

"Well, no river flows through Lake Harriet, so there is not a natural source of currents in it."

"So, we're screwed? No way to tell where the body went in the water?" Bixby fidgeted in her chair.

Dr. Granger sighed almost imperceptibly, keeping the thought that she was dealing with a hopeless cretin unexpressed. "I wouldn't say that at all. You see, there are natural springs and other ways that water can flow within a lake. For instance, Minnehaha Creek enters the lake on the southeast side. It does not have a corresponding exit point that we can visualize, so that makes it a little more challenging. But we also can look at wind speed and direction at the approximate time that the body would have been introduced into the water. Here, let me show you."

Abby turned her monitor around to face her guests. She almost leaped out of her chair to get to the visitor side of her desk. It was hard to tell if this was because she was so excited about the topic at hand or if she could be next to Little, or both. On the large screen was a color photograph of the lake with lines of depth and other points of geographical interest on the lake superimposed over the image. She removed a Bic pen from a sheath in her shirt pocket to use as a pointer.

"Here is where the body was found," she pointed. "And this is what we know about the lake and the weather conditions last night." Bixby wondered where one found a pocket protector in modern times, especially one that was not overly noticeable and in good shape. She was tempted to ask, but knew it would annoy Elliott. Maybe later.

"Although a lake appears to be fairly tranquil on its surface without the roiling of the wind, in reality the water is in constant motion." She paused for dramatic effect, but there was only an imperceptible reaction. Elliott looked over from the screen and smiled, not sure why she had stopped.

"What I mean by that is there are currents, hot spots, and a constant turning over of the water as the surface heats and cools. This causes anything in the water to move, unless its weight overcomes its buoyancy. That's the difference between a rock sinking to the bottom and a leaf or plastic bottle floating."

"Our victim wasn't particularly heavy, but it seems to me a dead body would act more like a rock than a Diet Coke bottle," Little offered.

"Excellent point, Elliott," Dr. Granger smiled at Little. "The human body has a density that is almost equal to water, .098 percent in fact. That means without doing anything, the body is more likely to float than sink. However, as water fills the lungs and increases the weight of the body, it sinks. What transpired here, I'm guessing, is that the body moved based on the prevailing wind patterns last night, shifts in the water temperature, and this caused the body to float to the location where it was located."

"OK," Bixby sounded a little more interested than she felt, but still leaned forward in her chair. "The body moves because it floats until it sinks because water gets in the lungs, even if he is already dead. How does that help us know where the body went in the water?"

"She's getting to that." Little waved his hand, annoyance in his voice. Dr. Granger smiled at him as a reward. Bernie knew a response would only further delay things.

Granger traced a path along the screen, ending with her pen pointing to a spot. She smiled at Bernie. "In order to understand the conclusion, you must understand the scientific underpinnings."

Bixby sighed internally and awaited the scientific underpinnings talk. She then allowed the vital scientific underpinnings to be established for a few minutes, and then interrupted with a little more impatience than she intended. "So, bottom line, where did the body go in the water, taking into account all of these significant scientific factors?"

Dr. Granger smiled at Bixby. "You do like to get to the bottom line, Detective. So, here's my best supposition as to where the body entered the water." She pointed to a spot on the southwestern shore of the lake.

"That's Beard's Plaisance," said Elliott with enthusiasm. There's a pavilion, picnic areas, and tennis courts. Bixby, remember when we attended a 'National Night Out' there a few years back?" Turning to Dr. Granger, he explained, "The department sends teams of police officers to events all over Minneapolis every year as part of our ongoing community outreach programs."

"That's a good thing for the department to do," Granger said. "It helps humanize law enforcement when you interact with the public in non-emergency situations."

"Yeah, it's great. You should see Bixby have to be nice to our citizenry. You should join us next time. For now, though, anything else you can tell us about the drop location? How certain are you?"

"Oh, I'm quite certain, within a range of plus or minus 25 feet."

"Would you testify to that in court if necessary?" Bixby was jotting down notes as she looked at her.

Dr. Granger blanched at the question. "Well, I guess so. I thought I was just helping point you and Elliott in the right direction by application of scientific principles on an informal basis. I'm not sure our department head would approve of me taking time off of work to testify."

Elliott looked over at his partner. "Bernadette, why don't you call Sarah Broderick and see if she and her team can check out Beard's Plaisance? I'll be with you in a few minutes." When Elliott used her full first name, he was expressing displeasure.

Bixby pulled her phone from his pocket, mumbled her goodbyes and thanks to Dr. Granger, and strode purposefully to the door, cell phone to her ear. She was sensing the discovery of key facts.

As he watched his partner walk out the door, Elliott turned back to Abigail. "I doubt you would ever have to testify," he said reassuringly. "If you did, I would be right there in court with you." They held hands for a moment, just sitting next to each other. Abigail kissed Elliott on the cheek and rose to return to her work.

"The old me would be frightened. This is the new me, however, and I know we could get through it together." She and Elliott hugged as he left her to join Bernie in the hallway.

"Sorry I brought up testifying in court," Bixby began. "I didn't mean to frighten her."

"No worries," Little replied. "She'll do it if she has to, but let's figure out a way to nail this guy so she doesn't have to set foot in a courthouse."

"Deal." The partners exchanged a knuckle bump and as they walked towards their car, Bernie's cell phone chirped. Elliott got behind the wheel as Bixby said a few words to the caller and hung up. She buckled herself in. "Broderick is sending a team to Beard's Plaisance this afternoon. Should we be there to supervise?"

"Yes, but we should talk to the victim's family and friends first, then either split up or both go over there together after that."

"Sounds like a plan."

CHAPTER TWENTY – FOUR

Jarryd Meyer carried full identification on his person. Sheriff Olson in Carver County agreed to notify the parents about the likely death by homicide of their son. Little and Bixby drove instead to a dark brick three-story apartment building near Bryant Square Park. According to his driver's license, this was where Meyer lived. Little parked illegally in front of a hydrant. Even illegal parking spots are rarely available in this part of Minneapolis.

Meyer lived on the third floor of a building that did not have an elevator. They were buzzed in by a roommate, who shrieked "Oh no" when they identified themselves as Minneapolis detectives. The door to 3C was open when they reached the top steps and a young woman, wearing a Pink Floyd 'Dark Side of the Moon' black t-shirt over sliced jeans, waited for them anxiously. This was not going to be a fruitful interview of the statistically most likely suspect in Jarryd Meyer's murder, they concluded without words being passed between them. No one could pretend to show this level of anxiety and concern.

"What's happened to Jarryd?" she asked, a shrill in her voice. "He didn't come home last night after work. He doesn't answer his phone. He like always takes the late shift at that disgusting bar and then walks home afterwards. 'It's too dangerous' I tell him over and over again, but he says it's easier to work later than when it is busy with the after-work crowd. It's like serious, isn't it?"

"I'm afraid it is," Bixby responded. "Can we go inside your apartment and talk?"

Missy Ellenson, the sense of dread palpable in her every move, motioned them inside and led them to a narrow room dominated by a well-built but older tan sectional couch. As she approached it, Bixby thought about the chore it must have been to move it up to a third story apartment with no elevator. Ellenson paced behind them by a large window that overlooked Bryant Square Park. Her anguish seemed to grow by the second. "Is Jarryd all right?" she asked nervously.

"No, I'm afraid he's been killed," Bernie said in her gentlest voice. "I'm so sorry. Were you his girlfriend?"

Missy Ellenson began to sob, her head in her hands, but managed a nod. Bixby allowed her a moment to compose herself.

"Can you tell us where he was and what he was doing last night?"

Missy fought to control her tears and her emotions. Little grabbed tissues from a nearby box and handed them to her. She smiled her appreciation at the gesture and began speaking in a calm but weak voice. Bernie continued to pat her on her wrist. She was finding herself having to do this too much lately.

"He works at this dive bar down on Lyndale and 24th. During the warmer weather he insists on walking home. To avoid traffic, he walks home on either Aldrich or Bryant. I always tell him to ride his bicycle and, like, leave it in the back room at the bar, or call an Uber. He never does because he told me someone would steal his bike, and like Uber would cost him his tip money each night. I told him any place where your bike is not safe is not safe to work either." Having said that, she grew quiet and looked at the detectives pensively.

Little was thinking the murderer had stalked the victim. "We don't know exactly where this happened, but we will start with the bar and work our way towards here. You say he walked each night? Did Mr. Meyer have enemies?"

"No, of course not. I mean, like, maybe my ex-boyfriend, but he lives in Oshkosh now..." her voice trailed off as she pondered the question.

"Why would you mention him? Did things not end well between him and you?"

"Well, there was some overlap between dating him and Jarryd, and when he found out about us, he confronted Jarryd at a bar. The bouncer had to, like, intervene." She paused for a moment, as if thinking through her designation of the ex-boyfriend as a potential suspect. "But that was, like, two years ago now, and last I saw on Facebook he has a serious girlfriend, so probably not him. I think she's pregnant even, like three months along. He, like, moved on just like I did."

"Anyone else? We need to talk to as many people as we can as soon as possible to find the person responsible," Bixby pressed. Time, circumstance, and geography seemed to make the ex-boyfriend angle unlikely.

As she pondered the question, Bixby's phone buzzed and she excused herself and strode over to near the entrance door to the apartment. Little and Ellenson paused to watch her. She spoke in low tones that were not discernible, even in the small apartment, ended the call, and returned to the two on the sectional.

"That was Broderick. She found something on the lakeshore she wants to show us. Now."

The two detectives stood and thanked Missy Ellenson for her assistance, and told her they would be in touch with updates. As Little gave her his card, she instinctively reached out and hugged Bixby. She palmed the card and leaned heavily against the door frame. "I hope you find whoever did this and, like, punish him," she called down the hall after them. As she said this, a door opened and an older woman looked out. When she saw Ellenson and her anguish, she walked immediately towards her to comfort her. They were hugging deeply as the detectives reached the landing for the second floor.

Little glared at a Minneapolis Traffic and Parking Enforcement vehicle that was slowing down as it approached their illegally parked Impala. Bixby waved collegially at the woman behind the wheel while opening her suit coat wide enough to display the detective shield on her belt. The traffic cop paused and looked at the badge, gave them each a look that did not come close to collegiality, and accelerated away.

"She's a bit sanctimonious, wouldn't you say?" Little waved at the back of the parking enforcement vehicle.

"Blocking a hydrant is a towable offense," Bixby replied. "Oh, and, by the way, sanctimonious is a fine word to use there."

"Maybe she'd prefer making death notices instead? That's what makes this job meaningful for me. That, and dropping everything to hear about discoveries from our colleagues in crime scene investigation. What did Broderick find?"

"She wouldn't say. She said we had to see it 'in situ' in order to fully appreciate its significance."

"You know, we're lucky to have her on our side, but I could do without the Latin lessons and the grandstanding sometimes."

"Hey, if she's excited, we're going to be excited, too. Just not in that geeky, crime scene tech kind of way," Bixby pointed out.

CHAPTER TWENTY - FIVE

Within moments they were back on the shores of Lake Harriet. The now familiar crime scene tech van had pulled up to within 20 feet of the shore, right next to a taped off area. The pedestrian trail was closed off with pylons 30 feet on either side of where the technicians were working. Pedestrians hoping to use the trail were being routed above and away from it. They grumbled but still maneuvered to see what was happening down by the shore. Burly patrol officers dissuaded those who lingered too long.

Within the enclosed space, three techs continued their work, combing through the sand and the brush. Broderick stood near the tape, and ducked under it as they approached. The temperature was approaching 85 degrees, but she was still wearing the familiar blue windbreaker and MPD hat. "Detectives, thank you for coming so quickly. I have what I believe will be a significant discovery to show you."

Broderick quickly moved her fanny pack so that the pouch area was in front of her, and unzipped its largest pouch. "In order to maintain appropriate chain of evidence protocols, I keep non-liquid gathered evidence here in my personal, portable storage unit."

Broderick removed a large plastic freezer Ziploc bag containing a water bottle. "We discovered this 17.8 feet from the spot where the physical evidence indicates that the body breached the water."

The blue hard plastic water bottle had a Minnesota Twins logo on it, with a flip lid over the soft tubular opening. With the bottle still in the bag, Broderick pointed to the flip lid. "That orifice will most likely contain DNA, and if the DNA is in our system, we will have a match within 24 hours." Noticing the raised eyebrows and the shared looks of excitement, Broderick looked at Little and Bixby, excitement in her eyes. "I know this case is the highest priority. I will go back to the lab and run the test myself if necessary."

Little and Bixby looked at each other. For the first time they seemed to have caught a break in the case.

CHAPTER TWENTY - SIX

Imagine my surprise waking up three mornings after my latest caper and learning that I was arrested the previous afternoon. Here I am, lounging in my pajama shorts and a well-worn Twins T-shirt with the number 29 and "Carew" on the back, looking at my new monster monitors, and an article in the online version of the Star Tribune announces 'Arrest Likely in Lake Harriet Homicide'. Below the main headline, in smaller font, 'Suspect has History of Violent Sexual Assault Crimes'. The first paragraph speculates that the police have finally solved the "Water Killer" case. Am I OK with being known as the "Water Killer"?

Reading the first few paragraphs, I learn that one Michael Jeffrey Green was convicted of forcible sexual assault "involving a fellow student at Augsburg College after a night of drinking". He claimed the sex was consensual, she claimed it was not, and the morning after she called campus security to report him. Testimony about bruising and bleeding led to a jury conviction and a three-year stint in the St. Cloud Reformatory. Green then escalates, according to the theory, to an alleged homicide five years later on a male victim instead of a female. The reporter indicates no connection between the Augsburg case and the recent homicide, hinting that somehow revenge will prove to be a motive.

As I read the article, I can see the holes in the logic, and I can sense desperation on the part of the Minneapolis detectives. While I feel like I handled my interaction with detectives Little and Bixby quite well, I know that Little was giving me 'the look' as they left my house. That look indicated that they found me to be a 'person of interest' in Janelle's death, but with nothing tangible, all they could do is glare at me and hope I confess.

I note with interest the facts revealed about this Michael Jeffrey Green and his sordid past, and how the authorities placed him at the scene with a water bottle found within feet of the entry point to the lake. The MPD spokesperson indicated that Mr. Green initially denied any involvement in the murder of Jarryd Meyer, and then insisted on having an attorney present. "He asserts," the spokesperson spoke, "that he has no idea how his drinking bottle ended up in the brush by the lake."

Ooh, ooh, Mr. Kotter, I can answer that one. I saw the bottle on the ground near a bench and tossed it near where I put the body in the water. My fingerprints were not on it because I had my biking gloves on the whole time, being a cyclist and all. I figured it would create a swirl if and when the dumping spot was ever uncovered. Nailed it. Bonus points because the bottle belonged to a convicted sex felon and not a teenage girl. Had the bottle been pink or purple and not blue I might have left it in the grass by the bench.

Reading on in the article, I learn that the detectives once again consulted with University of Minnesota Limnology Department member Dr. Abigail Granger, who guided them to the location of the body drop. I Google the 'University of Minnesota Limnology Department' and learn that it contains about six people, depending on how you count unpaid interns and graduate assistants. It's a mini-department at best. Even a micro-department. If I ever meet a person who claims to work in the Limnology Department at the U, I will most definitely push back. Pithy comments will ensue.

As I study the online Curriculum Vitae of Dr. Abigail Granger, I conclude that placing a body in a river poses no challenge for her. If I am going to beat her, I need to up my game. In one view, I should no longer dump bodies in water, but I feel like that is something of a signature move on my part. To not do so would disappoint and indicate that I have conceded defeat. My one landlocked kill, the unfortunate vice principal, has been ruled a suicide with no further investigation. That particular one needs to stay out of the discussion because it could be traced back to me under the theory that the death of a vice principal of the school where the suspect's daughter attended would be far too coincidental to not warrant deeper inquiry. Every TV show or movie ever tells you that there are no coincidences.

Great news on the professional front. I met with Gary Salisbury at Watson United meeting a few months ago, and it took until now for them to move. Turns out Watson United is looking to restructure over the next several years, and the executive team is not sure how to handle it, but they do know for sure that they do not want to sully their hands with the actual implementation of their restructuring. In corporate terms, they need a Vice President of Corporate Strategy. In real terms, they need a hatchet man.

A meeting with Gary is followed several weeks later with an informal meeting with someone in HR. Everything handled offsite, informally, and in the strictest confidence, as when word spreads of a hire of this nature, employees start to panic.

Instead of doing their jobs, they spend the extra money for the LinkedIn Premium package, and they update their resumes during office hours. Not good for company productivity and morale.

I met with the Senior Vice President of some weird department after work hours one Thursday afternoon and she offered me the job. The start date will be in mid-October, after the Q3 results have been reported and the shareholders will need to be assuaged regarding the slow organic growth of their corporation. By the time the year-end results are reported, it is assumed, the reductions I have implemented will once again assure a profitable year, reflected mostly for the executives in their bonuses.

My salary will be higher than at my previous company, my control and responsibilities will be commensurate, and I will even have my own dedicated administrative assistant. When I balk at the later start date, she offers an immediate signing bonus the equivalent to what I would make if I started with Watson United the following Monday. Reserved close-in parking is added quickly and I agree to join up. Had there been an executive washroom I could have negotiated a gold pass. Gary's insight about what to ask for and what to accept as counter-offers proves invaluable.

Because I am not returning to my former employer, they are obligated to continue my severance payments through the end of the year. For the first time since I was let go in May, Jennifer finally relaxes. Things are going to be fine for the Chandler family after all. I live in the rarified air of those who double-dip. I will draw income from two separate companies at the same time. The taxes are out of whack, but it is going to feel great to continue to stick it to the old boss while getting paid by the new boss.

Jennifer wants to use the extra income to enhance our college funds, and my investment guy agrees. We also decide to add a porch to the house. We find a contractor ready to pull the permit and get started right away because, as always, cash is king. It means that my final five weeks of freedom at the house will be severely impacted by the flurry of activity.

While I am loosely supervising the construction from my home office, I am also going to check off items on my list of fun things to do while unemployed. That means long bike rides, bingeing TV shows, and thwarting Dr. Abigail Granger.

All in all, it has been an uneventful summer. As soon as I announce I am returning to work Mallory's car persuasion begins anew. What we are learning as parents is that a third car is the best way to get out of giving rides to your children. With school starting again, Angela will need rides to tennis. A third car allows Mallory to drive her. This is the lever we needed to make the purchase. That, and being flush with cash for the remainder of the year.

As for me, I decide for the last five weeks that I will double my daily mileage. What that really means is I will ride the same route twice, begin exploring new routes that take me on new trails to new adventures. Packing up the bicycle and traveling gets boring in the first week so I return to riding from the house and take side jaunts off the usual trail, or I just reverse directions and try not to notice the repetitiveness.

We have a consistent crew of four guys working on the house. In the morning, the contractor walks me through his plans for the day and updates me on the progress. It seems like we are going great, although we are new to the whole construction game and have little with which to compare. Despite the late start, it looks like they will be done before I start my new job. Things are moving along smoothly.

That all changes about two weeks into the project. I leave the house mid-morning and return around two hours later. Summer is transitioning into fall in Minnesota. Many consider fall weather to be the best the state has to offer, with sunny skies and reduced humidity during the day, and a crisp feel to everything throughout. I consider extending my morning ride for a third revolution around the route, but realize it would be the third revolution seeing the same things again, so instead I ride home. Listening to a Bruce Springsteen and the E Street Band concert from 1975 can only distract you for so long from the reality that you are repeating your route.

I use the keypad to open the garage, hang my bike up on its hooks, and finish off my second water bottle while recovering on my camping rocker chair in the garage. As 'Thunder Road' ends in a crescendo and is drowned out by thunderous applause (my pet peeve about live recordings from back in the day), I pause the music on my phone. As I do so, my wireless headphones announce that its battery is low. It is time to charge them. I turn off my headphones, and walk in the house. My charger for the wireless headphones sits in in my office. I walk into my office and see one of the workers sitting at my computer. His boots make tread impressions on the carpet. At least they're clean.

"Excuse me," I say, anger obvious in my voice. We have approved worker bathroom breaks, although a porta-potty has been set up in the back yard, AC breaks when the heat and oppressive humidity necessitate it, coming inside for more water, and keeping lunches stored in the refrigerator in the kitchen, but we never agreed to a worker looking up porn or whatever he is doing on my computer. "What do you think you're doing?"

"Sorry, dude," he says, swiveling in the office chair and standing quickly. "I had to check my email real quick. My phone gets like zero service this far from downtown."

First of all, who cares about his service and need to check email? Second, I can bike to downtown and back, so spare me the sob story about the distance. I stare at him. "We made it clear that the office and the rest of the house are off-limits. You are allowed in the kitchen, the dining room, and the bathroom off the kitchen. That's it."

"I'm expecting an email from someone. It's important, dude."

"So is our privacy. Look," I say, realizing that this is going nowhere. "Not again, OK? You remind the others where all of you can go in the house and it ends right here and now. I won't tell your boss."

The worker nods agreement, and claps me on the shoulder with a convivial "Thanks, dude" and hustles back to the rest of the crew. He pushes his way through the hanging plastic temporary door that does a surprisingly good job of keeping the hot air and dust outside. I can see and hear him tell the crew to stay out of the off-limits areas of the house. Two of the crew shoot back that he is the only one who didn't abide by that because they already know better.

Once he is working again, I close the door to the office and sit down in front of the computer. What had I been doing on the computer before my ride? I remember researching bodies of water around the Twin Cities, reading articles in the Star Tribune and Pioneer Press about the body found in Lake Harriet and an arrest being made, and looking at Watson United as I prepare to 'right-size' that organization before the end of the year. Not to mention that I have shortcuts built in to my Chrome home page view, saved passwords to expedite accessing my investment accounts, and that glance I got from the worker as he attempted to breezily walk by me and return to the work. Did I see fear in his eyes? Like he understood who I really am and what I have done? This is developing into a risk I cannot afford.

As my brain calculates and recalibrates and works feverishly to resolve the current challenge, it comes up with a plan. The first component is to prevent him from saying anything to the other three workers. If I make it so loud that they cannot communicate with each other, that risk should be mitigated. Glancing at the rear yard I see that the lawn is in need of mowing. Not really, but the cacophony of a lawn mower will prevent the kind of conversation where secrets are revealed about a homeowner who might be that killer they've been reading and hearing about.

Not to toot my own horn, but my actions over the last few

months have drawn the attention of our various competing media outlets. And, another of my acts remains buried in secrecy. The family of the vice principal wanted to avoid shame being brought to their family, so nothing appeared in any local news outlet beyond "Local School Vice Principal Dies Unexpectedly in Home" over a short three paragraph article with no details provided.

As I fire up the self-propelled lawn mower and put on my noise-suppression headphones, I start to think about all of the great serial killers and even mass murderers of our time. Many of their acts are revealed and discussed at length with a certain amount of fascination, but how many more killings are out there that were perhaps practice runs or a different technique was deployed?

The work crew wraps up work every day at five. The owner / contractor arrives from his other job sites and reviews with his crew what has been accomplished and what the next day looks like with the owner if available. One of the guys, not my next victim, drives separately and he takes off in his truck. If something is needed during the day, he is the runner – heading to Menard's or Home Depot, or making a coffee or snack run. Definitely the role fulfilled by the newest member of the team, maybe the nephew of the contractor working this summer job that hasn't ended yet because he is not going off to college or trade school.

My guy and the remaining crew climb in with the boss and the four head out to their morning meeting spot, which happens to be the large parking lot of the Kwik-Trip a few miles away. I know this because I happened on them one day last week when I rode there for milk and bananas and saw them unload from separate vehicles and pile into one. Since tonight is pot roast night with vegetables and potatoes already cooking away, I am able to leave right after they do. I text Jenny, jump in my car, and follow them to Kwik-Trip. Since I know where they're going, I hold way back to avoid drawing any suspicion.

The contractor's truck stops by a line of pickups and older cars, and my guy pops out of the passenger door with the others and jumps in an older blue Chevrolet sedan. I take a picture of the license plate to run later in my public records database, and I follow behind at a reasonable distance. I'm not too worried about losing him since I can get his home address from the database. Once out of the parking lot and on the street, he moves with the rest of the cars in the midst of what is rush hour for the side streets. That means longer delays at stop lights and controlled intersections. He does not drive aggressively so keeping up with him from several cars behind is easy enough.

He lives in an older neighborhood in Burnsville that has more multi-family housing options. That sounds better than saying it's where the trailer parks and Section VIII housing can be found. I hate to sound less than politically correct in my description, but these are streets filled with older twin homes with faded vinyl siding, large circles of dead grass where kiddie pools once helped kids through the heat of summer, bigger dogs on chains either bored or barking, and lots of cars a few vital pieces short of running again. All this and short shared driveways leading to dilapidated garages.

I quickly realize that my Lexus will not fit in well in this neighborhood, so I drive slowly past a few places, pretending to be looking at house numbers and acting as though I am just a little lost. I settle on a spot outside the main entrance that serves as the border to a park that spreads out at least three city blocks, but with a view to the Chevy in a driveway in front of one of the twin homes. I open all my windows, pull out my phone, and settle in to wait for my opportunity to silence this despicable computer snoop. I note that the housing area is within walking distance of fast food, non-franchise restaurants and cafes, at least two bars, and a liquor store. I like my chances of seeing my guy at some point in the next two hours. I just hope he does not have a dog, as that would complicate things for me. I'm not sure what I would or can do to a dog. I'm not a monster.

The sun is starting to set and darkness is beginning to take over when he emerges from the neighborhood and starts walking towards the cluster of businesses. I have my money on the liquor store, and it turns out I am right. Pay up, sucker. He carries an 18-can box of Schlitz and a narrow paper bag containing, going out on a limb here, not a nice Chardonnay. I wait until he is walking along the park border on the sidewalk and pull the car on the same side of the street but several yards in front of him. My windows are now up. I push the trunk open button, jump out of the car, and approach rapidly. It is at the point of the evening, I believe the word here is 'gloaming', where you can see forms and shapes but not faces. My headlights obscure his view as well.

"Excuse me, my dog ran off again. Did you see a chocolate lab heading in your direction, or in the park anywhere? He usually heads towards the park when he gets loose." In my experience, any animal lover is instantly at ease and distracted when there is a dog potentially in peril. His eyes naturally are drawn away from me and towards the direction of the park where my lost dog is supposedly cavorting.

"No, but –," he begins to say, his eyes not looking at me. I see in his eyes an instant of recognition, when he realizes that his suspicions from earlier in the day are spot on. I can only hope that relaxing and drinking after work has consumed his time, and he has not contacted anyone about me. His phone will tell me that story soon enough.

Those are his last words. We are right alongside my car by then and I take my knife out of the holder and I strike twice, quickly and fatally. The beer and the bottle land on the grass area between the sidewalk and the curb. I place the beer and liquor on my front seat, and slip his phone in my pocket. I push him in the trunk, close the lid, and off I drive. All accomplished in a matter of seconds. Several miles away I pull into a Target parking lot and turn off the car.

Lifting his phone off the front seat, I see that no password is necessary to access the phone, and it has plenty of battery life. I turn it off. I will later dump the beer and the bottle on a bus bench and make someone's evening. A little while after that I will stop and dump the plastic sheeting that protects my trunk in a random dumpster behind a building that is poorly lit and has no security cameras.

Due to the reactive nature of the killing, I have to be a little less strategic than I want in dumping the body. When found, due to what has now been termed 'a signature puncture wound pattern', the murder will be attributed to me almost immediately.

Obeying every traffic law possible, I follow the river heading north and east. I feel that pang of vulnerability of transporting a body in my car. While stopped at a light, I look up a hill and see the building where I had an interview earlier in the summer. It makes me think for a moment about whether I would continue this homicidal hobby of mine after I start working again. The light turns green as I decide to adopt a wait and see approach. Maybe working again will satisfy the 'urge to purge' so to speak. Maybe, and this is my conclusion, it will distract me for a time, and then the need will return. The intoxicating nature of seeing the look in the eye of the almost dead, their realization that I have caused that is going to be hard to replace. I doubt any new job, regardless of how sweeping the reductions in work force are, can match that feeling.

I make turns, double backs, go under bridges and over bridges, drive on freeways, highways, and side roads that sometimes flood, all the while knowing exactly where I am going, but at the same time making it impossible to follow me. Biking in the Twin Cities has prepared me well for the task of pulling up to a deserted boat landing on the Mississippi River, pushing the construction worker's lifeless form into the water, and watching the body get caught in the currents and float away in the glow of lights of the city across the river. I check for anything I dropped or that fell out of the car, find nothing, and slowly drive back to 35E.

I'm not sure what compels me to do this, but I see a 24-hour Walgreen's open on an upcoming street corner, while the CVS across the way is closed. I signal my left turn and pull in. This won't take but a second. I walk in purposefully to where the disposable cell phones are located. I pay cash for the cheapest one they have with the smallest amounts of data and talk time available, and decline the proffered receipt. I resist the offer to punch in my number to get loyalty points.

Once in the car and in a lighted area of the parking lot, I call the Minneapolis Police Department. I follow through the dizzyingly difficult prompts, pressing 1, then 6, maybe 7, back to 3, and finally hit 0 as my last hope of getting a live person, and engage the voice modulator app I just downloaded seconds before.

A recorded message from Detective Elliott Little invites me to leave a message, so I do. I let him know that even their great river whisperer will not be able to know where all the bodies will be found.

I'm not sure why I feel like I have to taunt them, but this doctor lady they use is getting on my nerves. They will not be able to catch me, and giving them a taunt delivered on an untraceable burner phone is not much of an additional risk. The call made and the message delivered, I throw the phone out the window on 35e and continue home.

Jennifer barely stirs as I slip into bed beside her. The more I do this, the easier it gets to return to the normalcy of domesticated life after the deed is done.

My last thought before I fell asleep is how much longer the remodeling project will take now that the crew is going to be down a man. Don't snoop on the homeowner's computer and you never have to find out, I conclude to no one.

Our contractor shows up late and frazzled the next morning, although he tries not to let it show. "We had a miscommunication at our meeting point this morning," he began. "One of my workers called in sick last minute," he lies. "I will shift someone from another site over later this morning and that will keep us on our timeline."

I nod and smile, lamenting with my look the state of the labor force these days. One of the reasons we hired this contractor, other than his open schedule and willingness to start immediately of course, was his honest assessment of the difficulty he faces finding and keeping reliable help. He pointed out and talked up the relative longevity of his crew.

Despite being down a worker for most of the day, the crew seems productive. While they are doing that, I am feverishly uploading everything I can to a secure Cloud-based storage site. My hard drive is squeaky clean when I am done. I set my browser to delete sites as soon as I close the tab, my search history is deleted, and anything I want to keep I upload. Working on my phone takes me even longer. I realize that I have not been creating a digital bread crumb trail; it is a freaking superhighway that will lead me to a lifetime spent in a correctional facility.

On a positive note, my searching and scrolling through the phone I pulled from the pocket of my latest victim proves to be clean. He had not gone online and run any searches about the case that evening, he had made and received no phone calls, and his text messages were of a sexual nature directed and responded to by Mariela. Meeting Friday night at a dance club for dancing and "?!!?" is not going to happen. Later, and at three different garbage bins in three different parks, three pieces of the phone are tossed.

CHAPTER TWENTY - SEVEN

Sarah Broderick kept her promise about getting the DNA results quickly from the water bottle retrieved from near where Jarryd Meyer's body was dragged into Lake Harriet. She excitedly called Bixby as Bernie slipped on her shoulder holster and removed her gun from the gun safe in the bedroom closet. She held the phone to her ear with her left shoulder as she secured the strap over the handle.

"I found a conclusive match to a Michael Jeffrey Green, and records show that Mr. Green lives in South Minneapolis, within a close proximity to the crime scene."

Bernie left their bedroom and pulled the door closed behind her. Frankie and the kids needed to sleep before heading off to school.

"Wow, that's a fast turnaround, Sarah," Bixby said.

"There's more," Broderick continued, walking a line between excitement and scientific impartiality. "The reason Michael Jeffrey Green is in the database is that he is a convicted sex offender." She told Bernie that she had already emailed everything to the two detectives.

Bixby thanked her for the phone call, feeling the excitement of a solid lead building inside of her. She drove towards downtown using a mixture of side streets and interstate 94. She called Elliott on the way with the news. Little joined her in the excitement, promising to be at his desk when Bixby arrived. Bernie thought she heard someone moving around in the background at Little's condo, but did not inquire. The case was moving on its own for the first time since it started. The two detectives had an opportunity to be proactive rather than reacting to the acts of the killer. For once, the game was afoot.

Detective Little fulfilled his promise to beat Bixby to the office. He was listening to a phone message on his desk phone, and looking perturbed, while at the same time scrolling through his emails at a vigorous pace. Bixby sat down. The two nodded at each other as their usual morning greeting. Bixby logged in and soon she too was scrolling through the emailed information from Broderick.

"Bernie, before you get settled in, you've got to hear this message," Elliott said, offering the headset to Bixby. Bernie walked around the desk and stood next to her partner.

"This call was left on my voicemail. Our automated system transferred the call in from the main number." Each detective frequently had to work their way through voicemails left on their extensions that were meant for other departments, despite callers being admonished to listen carefully to the options as they had recently changed. The improper recipient then had to transfer the message internally to the proper recipient, or, worse and more likely, delete the message with the knowledge that if it was important enough the caller would try again.

Bixby listened to the message, her face showing a range of emotions over its 37-second duration.

"This is a message for the detectives investigating the 'Water Killer' case," it began. The voice sounded like it came from a pre-teen girl, very high-pitched and wavering. "I just wanted to let you know that oops, I did it again last night." The caller giggled. "I don't think your little friend from the U will be able to figure out where the body went in the water this time. Send along my best to her, OK? Tootles." The call ended with more giggling.

Before she spoke, Bixby clicked, scrolled, and read on her phone with ferocity in her eyes. She held up the screen towards Elliott. "There are eight free voice changing apps in the store, so no help there."

"What about the message? Why is he taunting us?"

"I'm not sure, but we better catch him in a hurry because he appears to be escalating and devolving all at once. And fast."

Elliott agreed. "The shelf life of a killer is not long, especially when the time between kills shortens."

"Let's forward that to Broderick and see what she can find off of that, but let's not lose focus on the prize here, Elliott. We have a suspect in the Jarryd Meyer Lake Harriet case."

They returned to their respective chairs, turned their focus to the computer monitor, and continued to carefully read through the email with attachments from Broderick. The DNA reported a match to the 28-year old white male with 98% certainty.

Both of them knew a DNA match is helpful, but corroboration makes it sing. Little focused on Green's criminal record while Bixby looked for his current address and other information available through enhanced access to public record databases available to law enforcement. Little found the name of Green's probation officer and emailed her, and then left a message on her office voice mail. Her 'Out of Office' auto-reply on email indicated that she would be unable to respond to emails for most of the day, but left her cell number for emergency contact.

"Yeah, this is an emergency" muttered Little as he dialed the number. Bixby looked up as his partner spoke, but realized he was talking out loud, but not to anyone in particular. It was his usual tendency to exhort additional speed and helpful information from his phone or computer by talking to it. To date, it had not worked, but that did not dissuade Elliott from continuing the practice.

Bixby sent a search result to her phone and stood. "Let's go grab this guy at his house. He lives about six blocks from Lake Harriet." Little nodded in appreciation at the proximity to where the murder victim was found, and quickly followed her to their car. The proximity to the location of the body put a bow on the DNA results.

Michael Jeffrey Green had not been dealt many breaks in his life. A promising baseball career at Hutchinson High School ended with chronic shoulder pain and eventual surgical intervention. A felony sexual assault conviction with extended prison time ended his time at Augsburg College and any hope for a college degree.

The parolee worked in an enclosed metal pit below a seemingly endless stream of cars, trucks, and SUVs at a quick oil change shop in Richfield. He was not allowed to ever interact with any customers above the pit. Instead, he loosened oil filters and filter covers, emptied oil pans, and tightened drain plugs all day, every day he worked. As a result, he had no chance for advancement, and every application for new jobs inquired about felony convictions. If he lied, a background check would reveal the deceit, and he would be denied the job. And even he did not want to work for a place that would hire felons without a background check.

He rented a small former carriage house in the Lynnhurst neighborhood, near Humboldt. Green lived alone and worked out feverishly when he was not changing the oil in car after car. As soon as he got home from work, he changed into his workout clothes and either jogged or rode a high-end training bike around the many lakes in Minneapolis and St. Paul. On his most aggressive weeknight rides, with lots of daylight, he would ride upwards of 30 miles around lakes and along both sides of the Mississippi River. He would take hydration breaks and watch pickup games of volleyball at courts on Lake Harriet. He passed on invitations to join because his shoulder continued to bother him all these years after high school.

While watching volleyball one gorgeous evening, he put his water bottle down next to the bench he sat on, climbed back on his bike, and did not realize the bottle was gone until he got home and pulled his bike into his living room. He never knew how costly a mistake he made until he heard loud and insistent knocking on his door that morning. Without even looking at the door, Michael Jeffrey Green knew it was the police. People who never get a break learn to expect this.

Green opened the door and saw two angry looking detectives. "Can I help you?" he asked.

"Are you Michael Jeffrey Green?" asked Bernie Bixby, wearing her most severe frown.

"Yes."

"Mind if we come in and ask you some questions?" Little spoke in a tone that suggested the question had already been answered affirmatively, and took an aggressive first step inside. It was understood amongst the parties that convicted sex offenders on probation did not have a right to refuse a member of law enforcement any request under almost any circumstance.

"Sure, I guess so. Come in," he said sarcastically to the back of Little's shaved head. Green stepped aside and held the wooden door open for Bixby. As he closed the door, Green looked across the street and saw the ubiquitous nosy neighbor watching his place from her living room bay window. He wondered if she ever missed a thing that might cast one of her neighbors in a negative light. And, he wondered, how long it would be before she started gossiping about it to everyone she saw? She would likely be the first to speak up when they canvassed the neighborhood, providing all sorts of background information about their new suspect.

Little touched him on the shoulder and asked him if he was carrying a weapon. Before he could respond, he turned him towards a wall and patted him down. Grabbing him just above his left elbow, he then guided Green towards the only chair in the room and joined Bixby on a threadbare couch. As is typical of a bachelor's place, a large TV and two small end tables completed the furniture in the living room. Two bicycles, a road bike and one with fat tires, were leaned against a half-wall behind the couch that separated the living area from a small kitchen area that held a table and two unmatched vinyl and metal chairs. Except for the TV and the bicycles, the place was filled with furnishings a local donation center might reject as below standard for repurposing to the needy.

"What's this about?", Green asked. "I haven't done anything wrong."

Ignoring the question, Elliott Little pulled a business card from his shirt pocket and read Miranda warnings to their prime suspect. Green acknowledged that he understood them and that he would voluntarily answer questions.

"Sir," Bixby began. "Where were you two nights ago?"

"Well, I worked, I rode my bike home, I ate a quick dinner, and I went for a bike ride. Why do you ask?"

Bernie ignored the question. "What was the route of your bike ride?"

"I can show you. It's on my computer." Green started to stand up.

Little immediately rose and pushed Green back in his chair. "Do not get up unless we tell you to, is that understood?"

"Yeah, sorry. It's just that I have an app that tracks my route and my mileage. My laptop is in the second bedroom," he said, gesturing down the hall.

Little looked towards Bixby and then back to Green. "You can show us that later. How about for now you just tell us where you rode?"

"OK, sorry." Green used his most obsequious tone. Over the years, he had learned that it was best to apologize for everything when talking to law enforcement. "Tuesdays I generally do the lakes, Greenway to the Mississippi River, across to the U, and then down the Parkway to Raspberry Island and over the river again on Cedar. About 32 miles total."

"Did you make any stops along the way?" Bixby was beginning to think their number one suspect had probably biked through stop signs and exceeded posted speed limits on bike trails, but not killed anyone.

"I stop twice for water. There's a cool lookout under the pedestrian bridge in St. Paul, and on Lake Harriet. Tuesday is volleyball night at Plaisance and I usually stop and watch and finish my last water bottle."

Bixby leaned forward. "So, you admit that you were in Beard's Plaisance Park on Tuesday night?"

"I guess. They're pretty good volleyball players. It's fun to watch."

"Did you talk to anyone while you were there?"

"No, I just sat on the bench, drank my water, and relaxed. By that time, I'm a sweaty mess. I'm not sure anyone would want to talk to me. What's this about?"

"Sir, a water bottle with your DNA on it was found in the bushes near Lake Harriet where a body was placed in the water. What time were you there?" Bixby glared at Green, even as she knew she was hearing the truth.

Green slapped his thigh. "That's where I left it. When I got back here on Tuesday, I realized I had lost one of my water bottles." He stopped to consider his situation for a moment. "Wait a minute, you think I killed some random person and dumped their body in Lake Harriet and then was dumb enough to leave my water bottle behind? That's ridiculous."

"Who can vouch for you Tuesday?"

"Like I said, I just stopped there, got off my bike, sat on the bench, and drank my water while watching people play volleyball. There were people all around when I was there."

Bixby stood. "Sir, we are going to need you to come down to the station and continue this interview."

"Why? I've told you everything I know. I think I want that lawyer now."

"That might be a good idea. Stand please."

When Green stood, Little once again turned him around to face the wall. This time, he grabbed a wrist and soon had him handcuffed.

"Is this really necessary? Is it because I asked for a lawyer?"

"It's for your own protection, sir," Little responded.

"Yeah, right."

As he was placed in the back of the car, Green made eye contact with the neighbor across the street, then continued with his eyes facing downward and with a dejected shuffling motion. The neighbor, now standing in her driveway, shot him a most disapproving look.

CHAPTER TWENTY-EIGHT

Little drove while Bixby rode in the back seat with their suspect. Green stared out the window and looked insolent. Expecting that she would get nothing out of the suspect during the brief time in the car, Bixby instead called Lt. Daniels and inquired about a search warrant for Green's phone, laptop, car, and house. Daniels agreed to get the paperwork started. Knowing that his house was about to be turned inside out might get Green to reveal more.

"Murphy's on desk duty after his knee replacement. I'll put him on it."

"That might be the most he's ever accomplished," Bixby responded, forgetting that a suspect shared the back seat with her.

"I'll let him know you send your regards."

Someone had leaked news of the suspect in the serial killer case to Channel 4. If Channel 4 had someone with a cameraman in tow lurking by the law enforcement entrance to the police department in downtown Minneapolis, something must be up. Soon Channel 5, 9, and 11 reporters and camera people followed suit. A couple more freelancers made for a gaggle when Little pulled up to the door. Bixby leapt out, strode quickly behind the car, and opened the other passenger door. Michael Jeffrey Green, accused and detained but not yet officially charged, began his "Perp Walk" as the cameras captured it all.

Questions shouted over the top of each reporter were met with averted eyes from Green. Bixby demanded that room be made for the two to get through. She badged the electronic pad, awaited the click, and hurried Green through the door. Little would park the car and meet them inside. They could have just as easily used the parking ramp entrance, but wanted the additional pressure of the gathered reporters to help in breaking Green. Lt. Dan had made the call to a reporter contact always in search of a scoop.

Bixby placed the suspect in a locked interrogation room, offered water or coffee, and then left him in the locked room to get him a bottled water. The standard protocol in interrogation was to leave the suspect in a locked room, by himself, with the temperature set high to literally sweat the truth out. Discomfort is an excellent technique in breaking suspects. Bixby found Little seated at Lt. Daniels' desk.

"Good work, detectives," Daniels began when they were all seated. "This must be very satisfying to be able to close this case. Congratulations. How about drinks on me after work?"

Daniels looked in their eyes for the excitement of having closed out a major case with an arrest based on their solid police work. As with any department these days, any good news helped deflect attention from mounting social unrest about negative police interactions with the public.

"I don't know," Bernie began. "It seems a little off to me."

"How so?" The look of confidence was fading from the lieutenant's visage as well.

Elliott leaned forward. "In my eyes, a felon is a felon, and a guy with a sexual assault conviction from college against a woman can certainly take the next step and become a serial killer."

"I'm not disagreeing with that," Bixby said. "But if the computer says he was there a little before eight o'clock, taking a water break right where and when he said he did, how does he kill someone and drag them to into the water in front of all those people and then ride off on his bike? And, why does he leave his water bottle behind?"

"As soon as the search warrant is signed by the judge, walk Green's phone to the lab, search the house, get his computer back to the lab techs, and find people who saw him on his bike ride." Daniels started to rise.

"Can we get the lab working on what we locate right away?" Bixby asked, knowing the answer but wanting to keep her supervisor engaged as well.

"Absolutely," Daniels replied. "As soon as we finish here, I'll call down and set things up. The tech van will meet you at Green's house. I don't think I need to remind you that this case has everybody talking. This 'Water Killer' guy needs to be taken down and right now." He would also leak a scoop to his friendly reporter at the Star Tribune as an unnamed source familiar with the investigation.

A few blocks out, Bixby's phone beeped. Murphy had shepherded the search warrant through to a judge's signature, Bernie reported. "The judge approved the house, garage, and car. She also signed off on any and all electronics, including, but not limited to, computers, cell phones, and storage devices. Heck, even the GPS in his car. Man, Murphy is thorough," Bixby said.

"It helps to get a judge cooperating because it's an election year," Little responded. Although most Hennepin County judges ran unopposed, they frequently worried that an unexpected challenger would file and claim the incumbent was "soft on crime". No judge wanted that label, preferring "firm, but fair" on their re-election yard signs planted in the yards of friends and neighbors.

Sarah Broderick and her team backed into the driveway just as Little parked the Impala on the curb in front of the house. As she stepped out, Bixby could see movement in the window across the street. Police presence at Green's house would be the talk of the neighborhood for the next several days. The recipient of the attention seldom could explain it away, regardless of the outcome or how quickly it was revealed to be a mistake.

There was a bustle of activity almost immediately. One tech started with the car in the garage, while Broderick and two others began bagging things in the house.

"Can we see what's on the laptop before you take it to the lab?" Bixby inquired.

Broderick, holding the laptop in a large, plastic bag, frowned for a moment, then reconsidered. "So long as you use your gloves we can at least see if it is password protected. Did you know that the vast majority of personal use laptops are either not password protected or use the word 'password' as the password? 'Qwerty' is the next most likely password." She shook her head disapprovingly. Finished expressing her concerns over data breaches caused by laziness or careless disregard, she removed the laptop from the unsealed bag and opened it, offering it to Bixby.

Bixby moved her gloved fingers over the mouse pad and the screen came to life, reconnecting to the home wireless signal. The background showed a biker, sporting a space-age style helmet, a sponsored multi-colored jersey, spandex biking shorts, and clipped biking shoes straining to pedal faster, lithe muscles bulging. Michael Jeffrey Green: long-distance cyclist and serial killer? It seemed incongruous at best. It probably had happened at some point in history, but the likelihood was not great.

One of the icons on the desktop was "Map My Ride", a popular app for cyclists tracking their rides using the GPS functions on their phone. Bixby opened it up and the most recent workouts were displayed. Scrolling down to the date of the murder, she clicked on the route and angled the computer so Little could see it. "Rats," was all Little said. He shook his head in disappointment.

"Yeah, rats indeed. It says here he went for a bike ride that covered over 30 miles, stopped right at the time he said he stopped for water at the park, and then, what, returned later with the victim and dumped him in the lake? This is reasonable doubt with a bow on it." Little's face showed the disappointment.

"It gets worse," said Bixby, scrolling through the workout history. "These are the dates of the other murders." She gestured at various workout maps marking time, distance, and average speed per mile. "He has rides that correspond to three of them, showing he was nowhere near where the body was dumped."

Little shook his head again. Bixby closed out of the tracking application, pushed the screen down, and handed the laptop to Broderick, who immediately placed it in the evidence bag and sealed it. "He is not our guy, unless Broderick finds us a miracle."

The two detectives stayed at the house for a few more minutes before heading back to the interrogation room. The feeling of elation that they had found their man was a distant memory as they rode along, each deep within their own thoughts.

Later in the day, with no fanfare, an unknowing Uber driver gave former Water Killer suspect Michael Jeffrey Green a $7.50 ride back to his house. The passenger stared wordlessly out the window and gave only an average rating. Once inside his home, he sat on a couch and again stared out a window. His laptop was gone, his phone had only been returned after his assigned attorney threatened to call the judge who signed the search warrant.

Looking around the house he could see the mess that had been created by the techs rummaging through everything. Drawers remained open, their contents strewn on the floor and on every available surface. Even the refrigerator had been emptied. He knew a bike ride would clear his head and help put this nightmare of a day behind him, but instead he sat and stared at nothing until it was dark out. He hoped tomorrow would be a better day. Hope was about all a convicted sex offender had, and right now it was running in short supply.

CHAPTER TWENTY - NINE

The anger and frustration felt by the former best suspect in the 'Water Killer' case was shared throughout the Minneapolis Police Department, particularly in its homicide detective squad. A community awareness and public information officer suggested a tersely worded statement be released advising that a 'person of interest' had been brought in for questioning, but no charges were filed as of yet, and the case was still considered active and ongoing. This of course was code for "We arrested the wrong guy and we don't know what else we can do."

The next morning, Little and Bixby stared at their respective computer screens, occasionally tapping on their keyboards to give the impression that they were being productive. The reality was that they had nowhere to turn now that their top suspect had been conclusively cleared of any involvement in any of the murders.

After allowing for enough time for appropriate wallowing and self-pity, Elliott Little stood and demanded that the partners embark on a mid-morning walk-about. "Let's go" was all he said. Bixby strode alongside Little wordlessly until they were no longer in the detective cluster of desks and cubicles. The two had a walking route that involved internal stairwells, loops through other floors, the skyway connection to the Government Center, and, if necessary, all the way to USBank stadium. Today looked like it would result in a record number of steps.

Other than a few greetings extended to people they recognized, not much was said. The purpose of the walk-about was to clear their heads and, eventually, formulate next moves. The degree of the complexity of the situation dictated the number of steps needed before ideas were proffered. They were approaching 2000 steps when their phones buzzed and chimed in unison.

Lt. Dan had texted them the same message: "Where are u? Body found in Miss."

"Holy crap," Little exclaimed. "This is the one he called about." In their excitement over a possible killer, they had forgotten about the taunting phone call from the morning before. The walk changed in focus to instead getting back to their desks and to their car as quickly as possible.

An unfamiliar crew of patrol officers and crime scene techs scurried around an area abutting the Mississippi River below and just east of the 35E bridge in Mendota Heights. Several vehicles clogged the ramped driveway that led to the entrance to the St. Paul Pool and Yacht Club, most with lights strobing and flashing. Valet parking attendants stood around with nothing to do but sulk. One smoked a cigarette, something that would be forbidden if any members needed parking services on any ordinary day. No members or their guests dared drive up to the club as it had become the launching point to an active crime scene on the Mississippi River just behind the building.

Flashing their badges got the Minneapolis detectives through the club and down to the sand boat landing area below the covered patio. Every window of the dining area was filled with members and employees straining to see what was happening. A large boat was lashed to the member-only dock. The 'Miss Adventure' contained four boaters who now only cared about seeing what was happening onshore. It promised to be far more interesting than languidly cruising the river or pulling a tuber in the sketchy water.

A man and a woman walked up to the yellow tape that impeded anyone from walking on the sandy area. From their attire and their demeanor, the Minneapolis detectives could see they were their St. Paul counterparts. The St. Paul detectives walked towards the two Minneapolis detectives, sharing tight nods. Detectives recognize their own.

"You the Minneapolis detectives?" asked the woman unnecessarily. Her badge hung on a lanyard around her neck. Her dark hair was pulled back in a ponytail. She wore a gray pantsuit over a cream-colored blouse. Detective Lopez looked like she could work at any company in the Twin Cities, so long as the company allowed her to wear sensible, camouflage rubber-soled hiking boots. Her partner, McGraw, wearing a dark brown pinstriped mess of polyester and sheen, stood next to her and did little to hide his disdain for the interlopers from across the river. While unstated, there existed a clear parochial tension between the two largest police squads in Minnesota.

"Yes, we are. I'm Elliott Little, and this is Bernadette Bixby." The four exchanged handshakes. An awkward silence ensued, neither side knowing who should start and what should be said.

Lopez filled the void. "Our LT reached out to your LT because we're seeing similarities with the wound pattern and water disposal methodology of your cases and this one. Nothing that we can confirm, but in the spirit of cooperation we felt it prudent to involve you from the start." Lopez seemed to have at least accepted the company line since she delivered it with a modicum of sincerity.

McGraw scowled. "It's just what we need, getting big-footed by Minneapolis cops. Lopez and I can close cases just like you can, except faster and with a better conviction rate." He paused for a beat, still glowering.

"We have no intention of 'big-footing' you," Bixby responded. "That's for the Feds, isn't it?"

Before McGraw could respond and continue to complain, Lopez raised her hand. "Folks, like it or not, we're in this together. How about we figure out what happened and decide bragging rights later?"

The situation calmed enough that the yellow tape was raised and all of the detectives walked single file on a marked path through the sand to where a grouping of techs moved around hurriedly. "Here is where a member seated for early lunch looked out and saw the body. She thought it was a log until she saw the red letters on his shirt," Lopez gestured as she spoke.

As they approached, they could see a possibly Hispanic male in his late 20's with dark hair and the blue, translucent look of death. "Any identification on the body?" asked Bixby.

"A wallet with a debit card and a driver's license issued to a George Rodriguez led us to believe that we had a solid identification. You Minneapolis types are free to verify if you would like," responded McGraw, showing begrudging cooperation. He took a large plastic bag from a tray on a plastic cart used to collect evidence before it was packed and stored for transport to the lab.

"That seems pretty solid," Bixby allowed. She wanted to add a choice word in addition, but remembered that they had been admonished to get along. "Our LT wants us to defer to you and Ramsey County on the crime scene and wherever that leads you. We can exchange our numbers and email addresses and agree to meet what, maybe tomorrow at 9 AM for coffee? We should have a better idea of what next steps look like. In the meantime, what can we do to help you right now?" Bixby looked at Lopez, letting her know life was hard enough for women in law enforcement without the pettiness the four were exhibiting towards each other.

Lopez agreed, and they went about the ritual of exchanging vitals. She texted her contact information to Bixby and Little and they reciprocated. McGraw declined receiving or sending text messages and instead pretended to type in numbers and letters on his phone as he was fed them by the Minneapolis detectives. Even as they spoke, they knew it was a sham. This conclusion was confirmed by the flourish he exhibited when he turned off the phone, acting as though he had captured important information.

"How about you two work on the victim's background?" Lopez offered. "Perhaps you can answer the question of why he ended up dead in the Mississippi River."

"We can do that. Also, how about if we take on identifying where he went in the water? We have worked with someone on previous Water Killer cases and she is pretty good about identifying the drop spot." Little hoped his personal interest in involving Dr. Granger did not show.

Even McGraw nodded his head in agreement. "We get first crack at the drop location since it will be upriver from here," he said, pointing in the general direction of downtown St. Paul.

"As soon as we know something, we will call you and Lopez," Bixby promised.

As it involved seeing Abigail Granger, the duo elected to travel to the U first and visit her office. Bixby called Lt. Dan from the Bluetooth in the car and briefed him on the accord they had reached with the St. Paul detectives. "That is about as good as we can get in cooperation with St. Paul," Daniels said. "Heck, that is about all that we would do if they tried to involve themselves in a Minneapolis case," he continued. "We might not even do that much. But..." he paused for an extra beat. "The chief says we need to reach out and help when we can. Speaking of help, how about if I put Murphy on the victim and see what he can find out for you fellows?"

"Tell him if he finds something interesting the IPA is on us next time we go out," Little responded. "He's a beer connoisseur, so that should motivate him."

"That would be helpful if he can get things started for us. You know Lt. Dan, if Murphy keeps this up, he might become a halfway decent detective one day," Bixby tossed in helpfully.

"Man, he must be exhausted having to work for the first time in his career," Little agreed.

"I'll let him know how much you appreciate his efforts."

Once the call ended, Little paused for a moment. "Is this the body that anonymous caller promised us?"

"I bet it is," Bixby agreed. "Let me call Broderick and see if they found anything helpful with the message on your voice mail." She quickly dialed the crime scene tech. After a short conversation she hung up again, shaking her head. Nothing.

"Think Doc can figure out where the body went into the Mississippi?" Bernie asked. "The floodwaters haven't receded since spring."

"I know she can," Elliott replied confidently.

After parking their car illegally near the Physics and Nanotechnology Building, the two made their way to the Limnology lab. Dr. Granger met them at the door. Little had called ahead with the details of their quest. The excitement was evident in her eyes, some of which could be attributed to Little being present, but mostly because of what she had found. They were barely able to keep up with her as she bolted towards her desk and computer screens.

"Here is where the body was found over by the St. Paul Pool and Yacht club," she began, pointing to the screen. "What makes this fascinating is that the currents are constantly in flux due to rains and flooding."

"Fascinating may not be the word I would use to describe it," Bixby remarked. Little glared at her, letting her know that Abby had the floor. Bixby decided to wait until the end before speaking. Best to smile and nod as she laid out the science that led to her conclusion, she had learned.

Minutes later, the discussions of confluences and water temperature and turbidity ended with a triumphant pointing at the map. "My best guess is that the body was placed in the water right here. My deviation of plus or minus 3.6 meters fits in this situation." Granger looked at the detectives with a gleam in her eye. This had been her most challenging work, for reasons they would never be able nor care to comprehend.

Little promised to call her later in the day and figure out their dinner plans, and they left Dr. Granger at her desk, triumphantly staring at her monitors. Although there was no ticket on the car, they could see a parking officer closing in. They departed before being accosted.

The boat ramp for the Lilydale / Harriet Island Regional Park sees steady use but always lacked any real amenities. Silt and algae covered the long, narrow, rectangular cement blocks that gave trailer and truck tires purchase when backed into the river. A dilapidated wooden dock looked like it had not been maintained in years, and as though it had endured many floods and more than a few collisions with drunk drivers, either on boats fighting the current, or in trucks, backing the trailer in and scraping up against it. One porta-potty and an overflowing trash receptacle completed the amenities offered. Now it was closed off while Ramsey County crime scene techs looked for anything that might show that a dead body had been placed in the water there.

True to their word, Bixby called the St. Paul detectives, Lopez and McGraw as soon as Granger identified the drop spot. She called McGraw's number first, but it turned out to be a wrong number. Their conclusion was that it was either on purpose or an indication of a man uncomfortable with technology. "I think he is more uncomfortable working with us than he is with his phone," Little observed. Bixby nodded her head in agreement and called Lopez. She answered on the first ring and said they would beat their Minneapolis counterparts there by fifteen minutes, and they did.

They exchanged handshakes and greetings again. The hostility from the first meeting was abated, as though a test had been given and passed by the advising of the drop location.

"Anything so far?" Bixby inquired.

"Not yet, they're still scoping things out and figuring out how wide to search," Lopez replied. "They like to be very thorough and make sure they do not miss anything, just like your people, I'm sure."

The Minneapolis detectives agreed, and a collegial conversation ensued amongst the four about how crime scene techs and their laboratory-bound counterparts now considered themselves the keys to effective crime investigation. There were even a few laughs, laughs that died away as the team lead approached. Little noticed she did not have a fanny pack. If she proved to be helpful, he decided he would reciprocate with a helpful suggestion about accessorizing while investigating crime scenes.

"Detectives? Sorry to interrupt, but one of our techs found something interesting. I wanted to show it to the two of you," she said, looking pointedly at Lopez and McGraw.

"You can show these two as well," Lopez responded. "It's likely their killer we're after." After a moment to cover their shoes with blue slip covers, words of caution that they stay in her vicinity at all times, the five made their way towards the edge of the river.

"You see this shoeprint?" asked the tech, pointing to a well-defined mark in a muddy area about two feet from the shoreline. It was surrounded by short weeds and some very hardy grass trying to grow in unfriendly soil. The back of the print was closest to the water, as though its maker was standing with their back turned to the river. The four nodded.

"We think this belongs to the person responsible for dragging the body into the water." She showed them scrape and scuff marks, some of which had been obliterated, although not entirely, in the weeds surrounding the print. She then walked them over to another shoe print on the opposite side of the concrete boat ramp landing.

"This is, we are certain, the same shoe pattern, but also heading away from the water. The reason we think it is the exit path and not the entrance is the depth of the impression. Quite simply," she said, suggesting in her tone that putting it 'quite simply' was the only way the four in her audience would ever understand what she was saying, "the depth of the impression is shallower, suggesting no weight was being transported other than the weight of the shoe owner, and there are additional impressions in the weeded area alongside the ramp with no attempt being made to hide or obscure them."

"The good news is that we can get a solid impression of the tread of the shoe. The bad news is that I can already tell that it is a Nike shoe owned by thousands of people with size ten feet."

Little and Bixby thanked the Ramsey County crime scene techs and started to say their goodbyes to Lopez and McGraw. As they did so, Bixby's phone buzzed and rang softly in the outside pocket of her blazer. She excused herself and stepped away to take the call. It was Murphy, the sidelined detective on desk duty while recovering from knee replacement surgery.

"I found out some things about your victim, George Rodriguez." Bixby thought she could detect some boredom in Murphy's voice. Being relegated to desk duty was hard on any law enforcement member used to being on the streets or being able to function in any capacity away from his desk.

"What ya got?"

"Your vic lives, or lived, in Burnsville. He's single, and rents a townhouse, drives a 2012 Chevrolet Cruze, and files his taxes on time. Usually gets a refund. He also gets laid off for a few months every year, then goes back to work for a company called Tri-State Construction out of Eagan. I can give you the number for his employer if you would like it."

Bixby was taking notes as she listened to the details about Rodriguez. She was almost caught up to Murphy when Murphy asked if she wanted the number. "Yeah, go ahead. I'm writing down notes to share with Elliott." She jotted down the number. As she did, she could see Little approaching with his two new friends. Lopez and McGraw waved and walked to their car. Little climbed in behind the wheel and Bixby joined him.

When the details about George Rodriguez had been shared with Little, they agreed that calling the boss would be the next step, as the work day was coming to an end, and Rodriguez's rental property, assuming he lived alone, could wait until after.

"Derek Manley speaking," the man answered the call from Bixby. Little listened in as best he could while driving in heavy but moving southbound traffic on 35E in Mendota. Their intended destination was the address listed as the primary business address for Tri-State off Cliff Road in Eagan.

"Mr. Manley? My name is Bernadette Bixby. I am a detective for the Minneapolis Police Department. I am calling in regards to someone listed as an employee of Tri-State, a George Rodriguez. Are you familiar with him?"

"Yeah, ex-employee is more like it. I told him if he missed one more day this summer he was done. I can't afford to spend my days trying to find temporary help when someone decides to take a sick day and never bothers -."

"Mr. Manley, let me stop you there. It appears that your employee was the victim of a homicide. My partner and I would like to meet with you and ask some questions, right away if possible."

"Oh geez, I'm sorry," Manley stammered. "Of course, I had no idea. God, yeah, anything to help. I'm on my way to a job site right now. Can we meet there?"

Bixby and Little navigated their way to the address Manley provided. As they exited from 35E, Little asked Bixby to read the address to him again. When he did, Little slammed his hand on the steering wheel, saying: "Son of a – ."

"What?" Bixby looked concerned.

"That's the address for Chandler, that smug jerk we met earlier this summer. I'll bet coffee for a week on it."

Bixby paged through her notebook, scanning prior notes from interviews and work on the Water Killer case. Finding the pages that held the notes from their interview with Craig Chandler, she whistled softly in confirmation. The addresses were exactly the same.

As they pulled on to the street where Chandler lived, they were passed by a silver Lexus with a bicycle attached to a rack off its trailer hitch. It moved quickly in the opposite direction. The driver, in his thirties with an intense look on his face and wearing stylish sunglasses, seemed to be trying way too hard to avoid eye contact. The car sped off away from the house they were driving towards. Ahead they saw the Tri-State truck that in all likelihood belonged to the owner Manley, as well as one other older Ford truck. The two looked at each other as they rolled to a stop in front of the job site. Rodriguez had been working at the home of Craig Chandler, the man they had questioned recently about the Janelle Moreno case and concluded that he was a suspect with no way to prove it.

"Partner, do you believe in coincidences?" Bixby asked.

HAROLD (MERNIE) BUDDE

"No, I do not."

CHAPTER THIRTY – CHANDLER – 4:46 PM

The sky was still dark this morning when I rose upright in bed. The adrenaline rush that follows a conquest is replaced by a massive fear hammering through my body. I have screwed up terribly. The victim, whatever his name, George I guess, will be easily traced back to our house and the remodeling project. Why did I have to taunt the lady water whisperer? No more sleep tonight.

Yeah, I most certainly recognize the detective's car as I drive away from our house.

I get out of bed, pull on my casual shorts, meaning I would never be seen in public with them, and a Kirby Puckett t-shirt. Nothing but the best Twins players for this guy. I start pondering if they allow Twins shirts in prison. Probably not, as it would differentiate me from others in the population, and most prisoners are Cubs or Yankees fans, or, even worse, Packers fans, thus leading to fights in the exercise area. I have no proof of this, just an instinct.

Door closed, sitting in front of my computer, I start randomly running searches on Google. Is a mathematically improbable event enough probable cause for a search warrant? No, said a

Washington state court of appeals. It's a point of law.

That's a relief, especially if I'm in Washington state and not here in Minnesota. Not a great search history for a multiple murder suspect, so I clear my search history and lock my computer. I will have to work this one out without relying on a YouTube video or a Redditt blog entry. Deep breath, I can do this. During my last exchange with the Minneapolis detectives, both of whom looked like they could chew and spit out nails, especially the lady cop, I had played it too cocky. I was smug and it showed. Now that they really did have something on me, albeit insufficient from a legal standpoint, I have three choices. The first is to be confident and let them know that they cannot break me when they reach out to me.

The second choice is to stonewall them. Let them know that I will not answer any questions without my lawyer present. They in turn will respond that if I have nothing to hide my cooperation is the best option. Only guilty people refuse to cooperate is the implied or direct message. My ego tells me that I can manipulate and taunt them and hide behind the law and remain safe from them. Common sense and logic say to tell them to consult with my attorney. How much of a thrill do I get obfuscating and toying with law enforcement? Can it come close to, or even supplant, the act of murder itself? And, is that the type of arrogance that historically trips up killers? Which leads to my third option, going on the offensive.

I leave the house and bike to a remote trail access and begin the real ride. I need time to think. Overall, the decision to kill George Rodriguez because he looked at my computer was turning out to be a bad one. Impetuous and an overreaction for sure. I now have to deal with the consequences of the increased scrutiny of the two Minneapolis homicide detectives. Dumb.

I am not a high-end computer nerd, but I know the basics. I need to do some things immediately to erase my tracks on the computer. I consider how to best accomplish the task. If I completely erase my hard drive, I am sending a signal of my guilt as strong or stronger as if I did nothing and left everything on the drive. I need to strike a balance between a normal interest in the Water Killer murders and proof positive that I am in fact the Water Killer. I Google some things on my phone during a rest break and formulate a plan. I am going to act as though my hard drive has been compromised and destroy it, after first copying over the documents and applications I need onto an external drive and up to the Cloud. I'm probably going to need a new phone as well.

It is surprising how small a high capacity internal hard drive is these days. They are about the size of a Pop Tart, and the thickness of half a deck of cards. They hold the equivalent of the Smithsonian in data. Not really, but they hold lots of data.

The kid at Best Buy, obviously very impressed that I rode my bike to the store, is excited to show me how easy it will be to run an auxiliary cable between the existing drive to the new drive that is plugged into a temporary slot on my motherboard. The kid is the reason Best Buy survives when other brick and mortar stores cannot – geeky kids who can explain stuff while they show you how the stuff works. Even more effective than a YouTube video. Believe me, I ran some searches to see if I could do it myself. I hope I don't get hired by Best Buy to enact a reduction in force mandate. Their store people are too valuable.

I ride my bike home, brimming with a sense of accomplishment that I can now pull the board out of the shell and transfer data from one drive to another. It takes me twice as long as the kid said it would take, but even so I am wrapped up by early afternoon, and the old hard drive is broken into several pieces and in my riding backpack for disposal in three different public garbage and recycle receptacles in well-trafficked areas. Wearing biking gloves with fingers and a full riding bandana under my helmet may look unusual, but I know I am not going to be leaving any fingerprints or hair strands as a result.

The thing that keeps popping in my brain, even while my fingers race over the keyboard and mouse, is what I am going to do to get one by Dr. Abigail Granger? How is the Water Killer going to continue on his murderous rampage if this geeky science nerd keeps tracking every corpse to its dumping spot? At some point I will screw up and leave something behind that will be traceable to me. From what I can see, it can be explained to be a strange coincidence that I had interactions with two of the victims. But even coincidental evidence can mount to a level of criminal culpability when combined with just one piece of real, hard evidence.

The normal reaction at this point would be to vow to stop killing people and dumping their bodies in various lakes and rivers across the Twin Cities. I've got a new job coming up with lots of departments to restructure, and people to downsize. That should keep me busy and distracted. Or, maybe, instead I become the "Deep in the Woods Killer". Or, maybe the "Abandoned Commercial Property Killer". The problem with these options is, of course, that normal people with normal thoughts tend not to be serial killers. We find far too much

COINCIDENTAL EVIDENCE

thrill in the kill. Let's face it – we're wired differently. No, I am up for the challenge of the water whisperer. The Water Killer versus the Water Whisperer. I can outwit her.

There comes a moment of clarity when I am just finishing the data dump to my external drive, and the last of the incriminating bytes are excised from my hard drive. What if I kill the one person who seems to know what I am doing and where I am doing it? All of my hatred suddenly comes into focus, directed towards the one person who eventually will lead to my downfall unless she is somehow stopped.

Hello, Dr. Granger, we haven't met, but I'm the guy you've been helping your detective friends track down. Big fan at the beginning, but not so much now. That overly exuberant reporter who leaked your name did you no favors. We need to talk. Oh, gosh, no, now is the perfect time. You'll feel a poke for just a second, and then you'll go to sleep. Here, let me help you into the child carrier. It seems small, but you're in good shape. I'm sure you'll fit just fine. It won't be a long ride. Not for you at least.

This is the plan that I have come up with as I mount my bicycle on my trailer hitch bike rack and head down my driveway later in the day. As I make my way up the street that leads to my house, I see an obvious government issue sedan turn and head towards my house. I avoid eye contact and drive a little faster. They will lose interest in waiting over the course of three plus hours before anyone is back at the house. I am sure they will return tomorrow, and by then it will be too late. I will have dealt with my lingering problem and they will once again have no proof that I did anything more than go for a bike ride that same evening. Just a coincidence really.

No one is left at the house today besides the workers. The contractor was angry when his fourth worker did not show up today, and came to the house twice during the day to help out. The family is gone because Jennifer has a late-night happy hour for a departing colleague, a full dinner with drinks planned. Mallory is out of town for a JV soccer match, and Angela is studying at her friend's house after tennis practice until evening when the rest of the family is home. Mallory will drive home in our newest car, a later model Ford Escape we begrudgingly bought to accommodate her practice schedule. The bus with the JV and varsity returns very late from their matches in Northfield.

I am applying common sense as a brake to make sure I am being prudent. Desperation is not a good look for someone attempting to avoid detection. In the back of my mind I am thankful that I created a stash of documents, credit cards, identification cards, and lots of cash that I secreted over the years in the garage until recently when I moved them to another location. I also carry an emergency escape kit with me everywhere I go. If I need to disappear, I am able to do so with everything I need for at least four months. My concern is that I will need to rely on that sooner than I expected.

CHAPTER THIRTY – ONE –
BIXBY AND LITTLE - 4:47 PM

Derek Manley paced on the covered front porch of the Chandler house. Little and Bixby approached cautiously. "Is the homeowner here?" Little asked, his hand reaching towards his holstered Glock reflexively, unsure of why Manley was so agitated.

"No, he left with his bike on his car. I have never understood why you need to drive somewhere to go for a bike ride," Manley replied.

Bixby and Little exchanged a knowing look. The car with the bicycle on the bike rack they just passed was Craig Chandler. A coincidentally timed bike ride just as they approached. How coincidental. "Tell us about George Rodriguez," Little began.

"He worked for me for the four years. He started as an unskilled laborer, showed some gumption and ambition, and this summer was his first as a team lead. A very reliable employee until the last two months."

"What has been going on the last two months?" Bixby inquired.

"Missing work, showing up late, the usual stuff that I see before I have to replace a guy. I thought he was either doing a side hustle project or talking to another construction company, and looking to jump ship. Then one of his team members told me he was having girlfriend issues. It's usually one of those three things."

"What kind of girlfriend issues?"

"I'm not sure. Let me ask the guy I heard it from." Manley called over to the crew, who were cleaning up after another long day of work, and one of them walked over. A pall had set over all of them, as they silently processed the loss of their coworker. Manley introduced Arias to the detectives. He looked particularly crestfallen.

"George is the dude who gave me my first job," he told them. Arias was of average height and build, wearing a red bandana on his head. He had a diamond stud earring in his left ear. He spoke deliberately, the sorrow showing on his face. "This is the first job here where I got paid with real checks, not just cash, with money taken out and everything. I could provide health insurance for my family and not have to go to the county for everything anymore. We all have him to thank for getting us hired here," he said, waving to the crew that continued to clean up industriously. One got the impression that this level of effort was not just because the boss was on the job site.

"You told your boss that Mr. Rodriguez was having some troubles recently. What can you tell us about that?" Bixby asked.

"It started when his ex-girlfriend met a new guy, and wanted to move his daughter to Wisconsin so the boyfriend could be closer to his parents," Arias began. "George spent weekends and nights after work with his daughter, and the thought of losing her was killing him." He paused, realizing it was a poor choice of words.

"He hired a lawyer and tried to get a judge to force her to stay here in Minnesota so he could keep seeing his daughter. He kept missing work because he had to go to court, meet his attorney, had to go to some meditation sessions and try to work it out – "

"You mean mediation?" Little interrupted.

"Go on," said Bixby, glaring at Little, as if to suggest Elliott answer questions in Spanish to test his grasp of and fluency of a second language.

"Yeah, mediation." Arias held his gaze at Little for a second longer than one would expect, a small frown on his face. He was thinking the same thing as Bernie.

"Anything unusual happen recently?"

"Well, he went to court about three weeks ago and the judge was supposed to release her decision this week. George was checking his phone every break to see if it came through, but his phone kept losing its signal here at the job site, so he went in and used the owner's computer to check his email."

"No one is supposed to go in the house. We make that clear on every jobsite. It drives the owners crazy," Manley added in protectively.

Arias nodded his head in agreement that he and the rest of the crew understood the rule and followed it. "We all know the rule - George just felt like he had no choice but to break it."

"How did Mr. Chandler respond to George using his computer?" Bixby asked.

"Well the owner caught him and we could hear he was pretty upset with him through the plastic wall. No words, just loud talking. And then George came outside and told us no one was allowed to go inside the house except to cool off or get water. But he had to know about his kid and the judge's decision, you know?"

The detectives shared the thought between themselves that Rodriguez had seen something on Chandler's computer that led to his demise, but neither spoke. Another piece of the puzzle fit together. They needed to look at Chandler's computer right away before he could delete files or destroy his hard drives.

The Tri-State workers wrapped up for the day, and two trucks, one with Manley driving, left. Little and Bixby sat in their car in front of the house and waited for Chandler, or anyone from the family, to return. While they waited, they called Lt. Daniels and made their pitch for a search warrant for Craig Chandler and all his personal property, including electronics.

"So, wait a minute. You're telling me this Chandler guy you spoke with earlier this summer had a heated conversation with the latest victim the day he died, but no words were specifically heard, but we think it was about the victim improperly using the computer in the house that he shares with three other people, but we're not sure, and today we find him dead in the river. Also, today, when you go to talk to him, he leaves in his car for a bike ride and is not around for you to interview. And when you interviewed him before you didn't really like him but couldn't pin anything on him. Does that sum it up?"

"He's probably the only person in Minnesota who had a conversation with two of the victims within days of when they died," Little pointed out. He could tell they were not winning over Lt. Dan with their string of coincidences argument.

"Oh, and I just remembered," Bernie chimed in. "I got an email from this old guy that confirms that a silver Lexus that is the same model as Chandler's was seen in the neighborhood where one of the people who was sleeping with Amy Nyberg lived. The license plate almost matched, the old guy must have transposed the numbers when he wrote it down."

Little looked sharply at his partner. "When were you going to tell me about this?"

"Sorry," Bixby replied. "I got the email when we were pursuing Michael Green and had Dapper run the plate, but it came back wrong so I dropped it." Little looked vexed, but did not speak.

"Bernie and Elliott, you know I've gone to bat for you lots of times when you've had borderline evidence, and I get the judge to sign off on a search warrant. But you've never presented me a case built solely on coincidental evidence. It's just not going to fly. We need more, especially after the cluster-you-know-what we just had with Green. We can't afford to be wrong twice in such a high-profile case."

Their attempts to state their side more convincingly seemed soft and unpersuasive even to Bixby and Little. They didn't have it and they knew it.

"Let's call it a night, and go at everything hard tomorrow morning," Little suggested. In the car heading back to Minneapolis his phone buzzed to indicate that he had a text message. Elliott pulled the phone from his shirt pocket and handed it to Bixby. Bernie read out loud the text message from Abbie Granger suggesting a bike ride and dinner. On behalf of her partner, she replied with a "Yes, where and when to meet?" Otherwise, Elliott drove quietly, deep in thought. What were they missing and how could they catch Chandler when all they had were too many coincidences?

CHAPTER THIRTY – TWO – ABIGAIL GRANGER – 5:14 PM

Dr. Abigail Granger dated another scientist type at the U for a year not long after she joined the Limnology department. He worked in organic chemistry, seeking his PhD after earning his Master's degree at Indiana University. The relationship faltered when he was offered a fellowship at Purdue University and she halfheartedly agreed to attempt a long-distance relationship using FaceTime and texting selfies. He met a fellow chemistry student not long after arriving in West Lafayette, and Abbie was more than a little relieved. Yes, she no longer felt any chemistry with the chemist.

Elliott Little told her that he had not had a serious girlfriend since his days at Normandale Community College, and even that one was not very serious. At least the girlfriend did not consider it to be very serious, as evidenced one night at a party when she found her latest boyfriend while Elliott watched numbly. There were any number of reasons, he explained, why he remained single into his thirties. One reason was that he was laser-focused on a high-intensity, high-risk, all-consuming job in law enforcement. Another was that he was an introvert, a bit socially awkward, and guarded when meeting people. The people he did meet were either criminals or suspects, or had their lives indelibly marked by horrible crimes. It can skew one's world view, Abby was sure.

After the awkward meetings at the Limnology lab with Elliott and Bixby, and the first dinner that was made very much less awkward by Bernie and Frankie, the two started seeing each other as a couple. What once was awkward became as natural as lifelong friends meeting over coffee. They started with walks along the Mississippi River in downtown Minneapolis, began riding bikes to lunches and dinners in hip North Loop eateries, grew to alternating nights at each other's places, and were now discussing the bad economics of maintaining two separate residences.

The Twin Cities real estate market placed a premium on being near downtown. As Granger rented and Little owned, the decision was made that when her lease expired in October she would move in with Little. The best part of it all was that neither felt any trepidation whatsoever.

For his part, Elliott ceded control completely to a better sense of style. As more and more of her stuff moved to the condo on the twelfth floor, Abby now spent less time at her place. The final move-out date in October was going to be only ceremonial rather than exhausting.

Elliott worked what was purported to be the day shift for MPD. According to the schedule, he should be done each day at 4 PM, but he and Bernie Bixby rarely wrapped before five, and often much later. They each felt that if they were doing their jobs properly, they would not be in the office when their shifts ended. Let the case and the investigation dictate the hours, the pace, and where their day ended. So, to have Bixby texting on Little's phone with Abby just after 5 pm on a weeknight was unusual.

Dr. Granger took advantage of the warmer weather and rode her bike to work most days in the summer and fall. She would pack clothes and necessities in her backpack, or in the panniers on her bicycle. She had rain gear if the weather turned inhospitable. Faculty members had access to showers and lockers at the nearby university recreation and wellness center. Many left their sweaty riding clothes hanging on hooks in the locker room for the ride home later in the day.

To avoid theft, she carried her bicycle up the stairs to her office and left it leaning against an empty desk, sharing the edges of the desk with others who were also convinced of the joys of riding. Granger rarely left the lab until after others wrapped up for the day, preferring an hour of quiet.

These days, she and Elliott called or texted when they would be able to meet for dinner or an evening workout. As the days grew shorter, their time for exercise without headlamps, rear lighting, and warm reflective gear decreased as well. Granger texted Elliott and suggested they meet for a bike ride and a late dinner of takeout. While he was not overweight by any calculation, Elliott had benefited from all of the exercise falling in love had brought him. He made better choices for food. He could now stomach kale. This alone marked a significant shift in his diet and taste.

Elliott was able to respond right away through Bixby with the question of where they should meet. He would need to return to his condo, change clothes, and grab his bicycle. It was unusual that he could respond since he did not spend his days poring over topographical charts and staring at computer screens with a phone sitting on his desk. Abbie replied with a suggestion they meet at Bohemian Flats on the Mississippi River at 6:30 pm. She would have time to ride several miles before meeting Elliott.

While he was improving as a cycling partner, she still needed the extra time and miles of riding to tire herself out before traveling at the more leisurely pace that was the best that Elliott could maintain. Even though she did not consider herself to be a strong rider, Elliott was still emerging as a distance cyclist.

Abby shut off her monitors, closed the lid on her laptop, and placed it in her backpack. She turned off the lights in the office, and carried her bike to street level. She rode it over to the recreation center, locked it, and changed back into her full riding gear. Soon she was cutting through campus towards East River Parkway, heading towards the Mississippi River.

It took a few minutes of riding before the damp coolness and grossness of a sweaty jersey and bike shorts became comfortable again. Cold Play kept her mind off of the effort she was exerting while she exercised to prepare for her exercise session and dinner date with Elliott.

CHAPTER THIRTY - THREE – BIXBY AND LITTLE – 5:19 PM

Bereft of evidence but wanting to show the world that they had found their killer, Bixby and Little spent the time in the car slowly making their way back to downtown in a heated and intense discussion, looking for something, anything, that would get them a search warrant to execute on the home and the electronics of Craig Chandler. Nothing came to light despite their thorough review of their notes, the case files, and another step-through of all the witness statements. They even called Sarah Broderick, who offered the services of her electronic forensics guy to run some preliminary searches to see what he could find legally on Chandler and his family. His quick-fire conclusion was that nothing he or his family did on social media gave any indication of his dark, murderous side.

They considered a trap or some other form of subterfuge, but could not come up with anything. Maybe if they switched cars and reconnoitered in Elliott's Ford Explorer on the end of the block leading to the Chandler home? They could leave their police car back in Minneapolis in hopes of appearing less conspicuous. The hope was that Chandler would slip up in some way and they could swoop in and catch him in the act of something nefarious. Even if it was just mildly nefarious it might give them enough of an opening for a search warrant where nothing at all existed.

"How about tomorrow we roust him and see if he will come with us voluntarily to the station? Maybe we could finesse a confession, or, if not that, enough to get a warrant signed," Little suggested.

"Yeah, like maybe we force him to prove his whereabouts and he has to rely on the GPS or his 'Map My Ride' app like Green did. Once we see it, we can maybe get a look at all of his rides over the summer," Bixby agreed, more excitement in her voice than she had shown in the last few days. As soon as the words were out of Bernie's mouth, she was on the phone with the electronics forensics guy, asking him to look for any rides that Chandler posted on 'Map My Ride' that he shared with the public. Shaking her head in disappointment, Bixby thanked the technician for the effort. "Dapper says he doesn't make any of his routes or rides public. He's been a member since 2011 though."

They rode back towards Minneapolis, stuck in construction traffic, without speaking. They knew what Lt. Dan would tell them upon their return, and they could not help but agree. Refusal to cooperate is an indication of guilt, but once again not enough to support a search warrant being issued.

"Sometimes I detest the 4th Amendment," Little grumped, referring to the constitutional prohibition against unreasonable search and seizure.

"Especially when there is no way around it," Bixby agreed.

CHAPTER THIRTY – FOUR -
CHANDLER – 5:21 PM

I am riding my bike with my trusty trailer behind me around the University of Minnesota campus, waiting for Dr. Granger leave her office. Unconsciously, I reach up and pat the waterproof pouch I carry in the zippered pocket just above my heart. In it is the storage disk and everything else I need in order to create my new identity. As I am doing that, I see her leave her office with a bike on her right shoulder. This is going to be easier than I expected.

CHAPTER THIRTY – FIVE – GRANGER – 5:38 PM

After texting her suggested dinner plans to Elliott, Abby Granger cruised along at three quarter speed, enjoying the tranquility of a quiet University of Minnesota campus. Although many riders, joggers, and walkers were also out and about, she prided herself on avoiding the busier trails and streets and exploring. It is what made the ride more enjoyable for her – the discovery of something she had not seen before, or not seen from a new, unrushed perspective. Most folks went right to the Dinkytown Greenway and crossed over the river on the converted railway bridge, and that was precisely why she avoided that route. There were construction projects on campus for her to track progress on, unexpected views of her beloved Mississippi River to be had, and most of all, less congestion on the roads and trails.

Even on her bicycle, Abby Granger appreciated being able to avoid social interaction when possible. Since she got off Church Street and began cutting through campus, she had only seen one other rider, and he was taking his child for a ride in a trailer. The trailer had the clear plastic windows shaded from the inside, preventing the child from seeing the view. Seeing that made her think about having a child or children herself one day, and whether she or Elliott would pull the trailer with their child onboard, likely sleeping or enjoying the view. Probably she would have to do it so that Elliott could keep up, she decided.

Any trailer she owned, she promised herself, would have more clear plastic so that their child could enjoy the scenery. They would fuss undoubtedly because they could not see what was happening around them. No trailer she owned would be closed off to the view. Life is about the experiences. Did they need plastic on the sides at all? Could they enjoy the rush of the air so long as it was not too chilly?

The cyclist with the trailer announced his intention to pass on the left. Impressed with his ability to push at such a speed while pulling a trailer with a child on board, Granger moved almost imperceptibly to the right to allow unimpeded passing. "Great night for a ride," she called as he passed. She only saw a brief side-view of a yellow helmet, a slender man with racer sunglasses, and then his back. The rider lifted his hand in response. Those intent on speed or maintaining time did not speak, preferring to save their breath for increased efficiency while riding.

"Good for him," Abby thought. Some just appreciated that they were out for a ride on their bicycle, or enjoyed what was going on around them to see. She was definitely in that category.

The cyclist with his trailer quickly increased the distance between them. He even stood and pedaled harder on a straightaway. That was some intensity. Granger wondered if she could keep up with him if she wanted to push herself. Probably not, she concluded, owing to her wider, more comfortable tires, and the extra weight she carried in clothing, laptop, and other work commuter essentials. Her bike was built to withstand the bumps and potholes of urban riding over all surfaces, while his bike was designed for road racing and paved trails only.

Checking her speed on her cyclometer made her realize that she was pushing harder than average in a subconscious effort to keep up. This, she smiled to herself, was similar to what Elliott had to do in almost every athletic endeavor they shared. She could out-pedal, outrun, out-walk, out-climb, out-everything him because she was in better shape. He would never admit it so she took more frequent water breaks to allow him to recover. She found his dogged effort to always try to keep up without complaint endearing, another sign that their relationship was becoming more and more serious with each passing day.

As she rode along, she recalled a co-worker who recounted his recent trip to Greece, and how his partner insisted that every day feature a minimum ten-mile hike up nearby mountains. He only managed to survive the exercise with the promise of bottles of wine at the top. "Every day I wrote my obituary in my head. On the really bad days I wrote his obituary."

Her thoughts shifted from her co-worker and his travails on Greek mountain trails to the passing cyclist pulled over on the side of the trail ahead. It looked like a mechanical issue. Her thoughts turned to concern that an extended delay could make for an uncomfortable situation for the child in the trailer, even in the cooler air. Lately she had noticed a strong maternal instinct stirring inside of her. Where had that come from?

One advantage of carrying so much cargo when riding is that

including a repair kit with tools and tubes is both possible and prudent. This would not be the first time Abby Granger had been able to offer assistance to a fellow stranded cyclist. The rider had the sheepish look of someone who had toppled from the peaks of braggartly athleticism to the depths of mechanical woes. She slowed to a stop and dismounted her bicycle. "You blow a tire?" she asked.

The rider, kneeling by his bike, stood. "No," was all he said.

CHAPTER THIRTY – SIX – CHANDLER – 5:43 PM

On one of my errands before beginning my ride on this beautiful early fall evening is assembling the ingredients for the contents of my syringes. It involves two stops, Walgreens first, followed by Fleet Farm. When prepared in the appropriate proportions, large animal painkillers can be used to tranquilize and immobilize humans. No need for prescriptions. You just need some reasonable math skills as they pertain to proportions to be able to determine appropriate dosages for humans.

Despite vehicle traffic making for slow riding near downtown, bike lanes and dedicated bridges get me to where I can watch Dr. Granger, the water nerd, ride through campus. She will be vulnerable on the mostly deserted bike trails around campus in these last few days before fall semester starts at the U.

I stay a comfortable distance behind her as she meanders through the campus before hitting a river trail that seems to have been forgotten or ignored by other cyclists and pedestrians. I realize that I have to act now.

A stranded cyclist always draws the attention of a fellow cyclist. It is one of those unwritten rules. I know that when I speed past the good doctor and then pull over and kneel down to look at my bike that she will be compelled to stop and see if she can assist. She looks like the type who will even have all the tools. I reach back to the pouches on my jersey and briefly palm the syringe. No good deed of a Good Samaritan cyclist goes unpunished today.

I pass her on a paved trail that runs behind a warehouse on one side, with the river bank on the other. It is as desolate a spot on an urban trail as you are going to find. Believe me, I have done my due diligence over my months of biking. No security cameras, no views from the top floors of apartments or other buildings. And, no one else seems to be using the trail besides Dr. Granger and me.

As I expect, she pulls over about three feet in front of my bike and uses the edge of the asphalt to provide a solid surface for her kickstand.

I put on my best hapless cyclist look as Granger approaches. "You blow a tire?" she asks.

"No," I respond. For some reason, I think she might keep going if it was as simple as a tube change, because any serious cyclist can fix a flat tire with little assistance. Some other unknown mechanical issue requires that all important second set of eyes that only she can provide right now.

I use my right hand to point in the general direction of my gears. Instinctively, her eyes follow my hand towards the ground and my seemingly disabled bicycle. I take one step towards her and grab her around her shoulder with my left hand, pinning her right arm in the process, and clutching her tightly. I bite off the cap to the syringe, and, before her left arm can react, I inject her in the neck.

I hold her for a count of three before she slumps. Not sure if that is because my math is inaccurate and she received a dosage more appropriate for a Holstein cow, or if that is just how fast it works, but she is out for the count at three. I put the cover back on the syringe and place it in the middle pouch on the back of my riding jersey.

I check around me to make sure that there is no one in sight, and there is not. I carefully place her in my trailer, cover her with a dark blanket, zip the cover closed, and turn my attention to her bicycle. There are some short bushes along the trail between the mowed area alongside the asphalt and the fence of the warehouse. It is not dense enough to completely conceal the bike, but it will only be found if someone is looking for it. I throw a few random dead leaves and grass on it for good measure. As I remount and push ahead towards the bridge a cyclist approaches from the opposite direction. I nod succinctly as we pass.

CHAPTER THIRTY – SEVEN - BIXBY AND LITTLE – 5:46 PM

As Little drove back towards Minneapolis, traffic finally moving again, Bixby read out loud the latest text message from Abigail Granger, suggesting the couple meet at the Bohemian Flats on the Mississippi River near downtown on the Minneapolis side. As was her wont these days, she ended the message with a heart emoji.

"Yes," Bixby texted for Elliott in response. "How many miles?" And, to Elliott she asked, "Should I include a heart emoji back? Too late, I already did." She closed out of the text app. She waited for a moment to see if Little would react. He did not.

"Things are getting pretty serious between you and the good doctor," Bixby observed.

"Yeah, and I suppose you want me to give you the credit for setting us up again," Little responded.

"Not all of it. The wife deserves some."

"Does she like it when you call her 'the wife'?"

"Not if I want to stay married to her."

"Abby should have responded to my text by now," Little said.

Bixby looked over disgustedly at his partner. "Why don't I just call her?"

"I guess, it's just that she texts me the route and the mileage so I know what to prepare for."

"She can't tell you the route over the phone?"

"I suppose." Little shrugged and motioned for Bixby to hit the 'Call' button on his phone. The Bluetooth connection put the call over the speakers in the car. Bixby could hear the ringtone Granger played for those who waited for her to pick up the phone, "She Blinded Me with Science". The call went to voicemail.

"Hi, honey," Little began, feeling a little foolish talking to the phone with Bixby next to him. "Just calling to see what the route is for our ride tonight. I'm really looking forward to it. Um, love you." As he said it, Elliott looked over to see Bixby roll her eyes as if disgusted, but smiling at the same time. The public display of affection was acceptable. The phony enthusiasm for the bike ride triggered the eye roll. Bixby knew Little looked forward to nightly exercise the way other people looked forward to stubbing their toe.

More silence ensued, but Bixby could tell her partner was deep in thought, running scenarios in his head about why Abigail Granger had not picked up or texted. Being both highly scientific and logical, she was habitual and routine oriented.

"You know her routes when she rides her bike, right?" Bixby asked. "Why don't we drive by the U and make sure she didn't break down? She always takes the same route, right?" Little nodded his affirmance. "Let's start at her office and go from there." Let it not be said that Bernie Bixby did not support her partner and best friend.

The parking spots on Pillsbury Drive were finally available. Little pulled in and jumped out of the car, leaving the driver side door open. Once at the entrance, he covered the sides of his face in order to see through the tinted glass. He returned a moment later and got back in the car. Bixby thought it best not to point out that even if he had been able to see inside the building, he would not have been able to see the bicycle stored inside the upstairs office and laboratory. She could sense that Little was concerned, and perhaps with good reason.

Once he was in the car again, Bixby instructed Elliott to follow her anticipated route as closely as possible. Bernie tried calling her cell phone for at least the fourth time. The tinny sound of Thomas Dolby once again could be heard, but no one answered.

"Would she stop for coffee on the way home?" Bixby offered helpfully.

"No, she drinks only decaffeinated Earl Grey in the afternoon, and then only after grant meetings with the department head. They tire her out."

"Maybe she needed water?"

"She fills her bottles at the Recreation Center using the filtration unit. She never leaves for a ride without her water bottles filled and secured in the racks."

While not helpful in terms of information, keeping Elliott talking about Abby's hydration routine seemed to have the desired effect of distracting him from his growing alarm and causing him to maintain his focus. He drove the route she would normally take to cross the river to their agreed upon meeting location on the western bank of the Mississippi River.

A bicycle has much more flexibility in where it can be ridden, so the detectives had to stop twice on campus so that Bernie could jump out and fast-walk to make sure they covered Granger's route. During their rides together that traversed the campus, Abby would point out to Elliott what her route was when she rode along the Mississippi River, and when she rode to his place, now almost exclusively referred to as "our place". She avoided busy streets and intersections, never rode on sidewalks intended only for pedestrians, and made sure she was on East River Parkway as soon as she could get there because she considered the views amazing yet underappreciated by fellow walkers, joggers, and cyclists.

Bixby cut through the commons area near Northrop Auditorium on foot while Little crossed the river on Washington Avenue and reversed direction to get on the parkway off of Delaware. They met at Arlington and East River Parkway and rode silently. There was no need to confirm that they had seen nothing.

"She always says she prefers to take the Northern Pacific Bridge," Little pointed out the left fork of the parkway. Bixby reached her hand outside the passenger window and placed the magnetic blue strobe light on the top of the car. Elliott drove slowly towards the bridge and trail. The car straddled the pedestrian and bicycle path as it moved along. Each detective kept their eyes on their side of the car, looking for something, anything.

"Stop," Bixby commanded, pointing towards overgrown brush and vegetation on the side of the trail. "There's a bike in the weeds." She jumped out of the car.

Little joined his partner as they stared down at an unlocked black bike with pink handle wraps and panniers on either side of the rear wheel. He knew it was her bike. It had been abandoned in the bushes unlocked, both water bottles intact. Even the electronics were still attached. Her cell phone lay next to the bike saddle on the ground. It looked like it had been stepped on. No rider would ever do this unless they were forced to leave the bike behind unwillingly. Bixby put her hand on Little's shoulder. "Oh my God" was all she could say.

Little pulled off the trail, backed up, and returned to the street again. Bixby reported the potential kidnaping using the car radio, and requested that all law enforcement personnel be on the lookout for Dr. Granger. She described her riding gear as well as her hair and eye color. Two squad cars and Sarah Broderick and team soon arrived at the site of the found bicycle. They stood outside the car, their gazes affixed to the point where the bicycle lay in the weeds, trying to find something else, or perhaps hoping that Dr. Granger would magically reappear.

"If the bike was dumped here, it makes sense that whoever took her is either on foot or also on a bicycle," Little said. "Maybe in a car, but I don't think so." He continued to stare down the trail.

"Why?" Bixby knew the answer, but wanted Elliott to talk through the scenarios to distract him from the crushing feeling of a loved one in peril as he stood by and felt helpless.

"The bike is too far from the street," he said, pointing up the trail at least two hundred feet away. "He would have had to have contained Abby, put her somewhere out of sight, and then rode or pushed the bike all the way to the bushes and hid it. It just doesn't make sense."

"Or," Bixby agreed, "He meets her there on foot, immobilizes her, dumps her bike, and has to carry her all the way to the street to his waiting car. Way too exposed and too far to carry anyone."

"There's only two people we know who ride bikes all the time involved in this case, Michael Jeffrey Green and Craig Chandler. My money is on Craig Chandler."

"I agree. Why don't we call each of them and see who answers?"

While Little called Lt. Daniels and gave him an update on what was happening and what he and Bixby were doing about it, Bernie reviewed her notes and found Green's number. She dialed and Green answered on the second ring.

"Hello?"

"Mr. Green, Bernadette Bixby from the – "

"I know who you are. What do you people think I did this time?"

"Look, I don't have time for your attitude. We have a woman who's been kidnaped. Where are you right now?"

"I'm packing my house up. My landlord evicted me after I got arrested. I don't fit the type of person she wants in her prop –"

Bixby clicked off the call. "He's not our guy. That leaves Chandler or Doc was abducted by a random stranger. That seems a bit too coincidental to me."

Chandler's phone went to voice mail right away, indicating

that he was on a call or that he had turned it off. "I bet he turned it off so we can't trace it with GPS. It will take forever to get the provider to assist us." Bixby wanted to do something, but could not decide what to suggest.

Little slapped the top of the car. "Let's go to his house and see if he's there. You know he isn't."

"But we decided he won't talk to us unless he has an attorney present."

"Yeah, but I bet he didn't tell that to his wife and kids."

Bixby nodded grimly and sat in the passenger seat. Little quickly accelerated down the streets to the on ramp to 35W south. "I'm going to hit the siren. We don't have much time."

CHAPTER THIRTY-EIGHT – CHANDLER – 6:09 PM

My final act before spiriting away the good doctor is to step on her phone. Not sure if you have ever done this intentionally, but it feels really good to destroy a phone. Grind it like a fiend. There will be no fancy GPS tracking going on here. I resist the urge to step on my phone also, just turning it off instead.

According to my research on the dark web, my concoction should keep my passenger out for roughly two hours. My plan for her requires that she be at least conscious when I exact my revenge on her.

Based not so much on the time of the sunset but more bike and pedestrian traffic when it grows dark, I need to keep moving for another almost two hours, or until around 8 pm. Too early and people are still moving around, even on a week night. I have another dosage ready for Dr. Granger in the event she stirs too early to suit my needs. If I am forced to inject her again, I will have to ride around for even longer. This may seem like a long time riding a bicycle pulling over 120 pounds of weight behind me. First of all, thank you for your concern. Secondly, I have been riding for hours and hours this summer for a reason. The reason is that I knew at some point I would need to be able to pull off a ride like this, and I have been preparing for it. This is my marathon.

Yeah, it's a haul, but the adrenaline of my capture pushes me along as I meander down the Greenway trail towards St. Louis Park, reversing on the Cedar Lake trail back towards downtown, riding the river up and down, first on the Minneapolis side, and then on the St. Paul side. The pedaling and the time lets me think about what I am going to do next. While the idea of kidnaping Granger was impetuous and not well-planned out in the beginning, once it is in motion, I am able to hone in on any weaknesses and correct them as I ride. Ill-conceived and reckless becomes well-planned and ultimately will prove to be successful as a result.

The sun is starting to set as I ride through neighborhoods in Minneapolis. I thank the memory of Martin Olav Sabo for the wonderful pedestrian and biking bridge over Highway 55 that allows those on the Greenway Trail to go all the way to the Mississippi River. I follow the river south down to Ford Parkway before crossing the river and going north again on Mississippi River Boulevard. My cyclometer silently records each tenth of a mile as I approach my longest and most satisfying ride of the year.

My original plan was to drop the pesky doctor off of the Ford Parkway Bridge if traffic permits. It does not. I consider Lake Street and two other parks with water along the way, but I do not like the feel of any of them. Then, in a moment of supreme clarity, I arrive at the perfect dénouement. Her meddling involvement began on the Stone Arch Bridge. That is where it should end. With renewed vigor, I make my way to the famous Stone Arch Bridge.

CHAPTER THIRTY – NINE - BIXBY AND LITTLE – 6:43 PM

An aggressive Little pushed the car to its limits, veering off of Cedar Avenue and pushing it harder as it made its way to the Chandler residence. "Nine minutes out," announced Bixby. "Screw the traffic lights – let's blow through everything we can." Little nodded in agreement, his face screwed up in resolute concentration.

Bernie Bixby had been busy on her phone, her tablet, and on the radio advising all who were on the streets to be on the lookout for anyone or anything suspicious riding or associated with a bicycle, particularly those pulling trailers. When pressed for more specific information, Bixby replied that the rider was likely carrying another person with him in the trailer, and provided a basic description of the rider. As she said it, she realized that she was describing any number of riders with trailers on the streets and trails of the Twin Cities. Without colors and trailer type she was asking for a miracle.

Elliott turned off the lights and the siren as he approached the Chandler neighborhood. They were within two blocks of the house now. He parked the car in the driveway and the two jumped out of the car and strode quickly to the front door. As his right arm rose to knock forcefully on the door, it opened and Jennifer Chandler met them. She did not look happy.

"May I help you?"

"Good evening Mrs. Chandler. My name is Elliott Little, and this is my partner Bernadette Bixby. We are homicide detectives from Minneapolis."

Jennifer Chandler bristled, wondering how they would know her name. "I'm not sure how I can help you. We live here in Apple Valley. I work in Bloomington. I rarely go to Minneapo-"

"Ma'am, let me stop you there. This has nothing to do with you. We are looking for information about your husband Craig, his bicycle, and a bicycle trailer."

"Craig? Why do you need to talk to him again? He's not even here right now."

"We figured as much," Bixby said, taking over the questioning. "He is a strong person of interest in a series of murders we'e investigating."

"That's even more ridiculous," Jennifer Chandler snapped. "He's a senior level executive at major corporations. He's not a killer. I'm going to call our lawyer." She started to back away from the door and the intruding detectives, giving herself room to swing the front door closed.

"Ma'am, you are not under arrest so there is no need for an

attorney. What we need right now from you is a description of your husband's bicycle, and what kind of bike trailer he uses." As he spoke, Elliott stepped over the threshold and entered the house. Jennifer backed up a few steps, surprised by Little's aggression.

"I'm not sure that's any of your business. This is completely ludicrous. I'm definitely going to call our lawyer."

Elliott Little slammed his fist on the frame of the front door, lifting himself to his full six feet three inches of height. He glared at Jennifer Chandler. "There is no time for an attorney. Tell us right now about the bicycle and the trailer."

Mrs. Chandler jumped back, startled at the sound of a fist hitting her door frame. She glared at him. A moment of hostility and anger hung in the air. Little clenched and unclenched his fists in frustration at the delay. "Fine," she said, the tension easing for a second. "Let me ask my daughter. She knows more about all of Craig's bike stuff than me." She stepped back from the door and called for her daughter.

Angela Chandler had been watching TV with her mother in the living room, and she approached the front door tentatively. Little and Bixby now stepped in the foyer uninvited. Bixby lowered her face to be on the level of the twelve-year old girl. The tone of the conversation softened as Bernie expertly maneuvered between hostility and amiability. "What kind of bike and trailer does your dad ride?"

Angela looked quickly at her mother for support. Jennifer

Chandler nodded grimly in the affirmative.

"It's a road bike. Speciali-"

"What color?" Bixby interrupted, now rising again.

"Well, I guess its black, maybe dark gray. I'm not really sure. I think he buys new ones and never tells anyone."

"What about the trailer? What color is that?" Bixby pressed, leaning down again to Angela. Jennifer Chandler was now forced to step back until she was against the steps leading to the top floor, and she did so unwillingly, still unhappy with the intrusion.

Angela looked confused. "The trailer? We haven't used that since I was little."

Jennifer Chandler looked coldly at the detectives. "See, I told you this was a big mistake. We probably don't even have the trailer anymore. We bought it for our first child and she's driving a car now."

"Where is the trailer?" Little demanded, returning the cold look. If there was a protocol requiring pleasant interactions with citizens, he was in clear violation.

"He stores it up above the garage," Jennifer said, pointing in the general direction of the people door to the garage to their right and her left. "But it hasn't been used in years."

Bixby and Little sprang into action, pulling open the door to the garage and jumping the concrete step. Bixby turned on the lights in the darkened three-stall garage. Jennifer Chandler pushed a button and the larger of the two garage doors opened, providing some additional natural light. Little pulled down on a cord with a handle on it and the retractable steps to the attic came down with several squeaks and groans of rusty springs and metal supports. He clambered up the wooden steps, which shifted with his weight. A white string hung below a light bulb, and Elliott pulled it on. With his upper torso in the hole and hidden to those below, they watched as he reached into a pocket and pulled out his cell phone. He used it as a flashlight to further illuminate the storage area above the garage.

"There's no bike trailer up here" he yelled, although it was muffled by the drywall and insulation. He used his phone camera to document that the bike trailer was not there. He pulled the string and shut off the light, and climbed back down the steps.

A horrified look passed over Jennifer Chandler's eyes, as she realized that perhaps the outlandish accusations had some truth to them. Could what they were saying about her husband be true? She turned from resistance to a more thoughtful look, as though piecing together the events of the last several months in a new light.

Still glaring menacingly, Little demanded: "What does the bike trailer look like?"

Bixby looked at the young girl, reestablishing their earlier connection. "Sweetie, we really need to know about that trailer. What can you tell us?"

"It's orange and lime green" Angela responded. "But it's super old and faded."

"I'm sure my husband sold it on Craigslist, or maybe traded it for more bike equipment. He does that all the time." Jennifer Chandler now sounded less than confident in her statements defending her husband.

"No, Mom. Remember when Dad took it out this spring and cleaned it up? He said it was good as new once he replaced the tubes in the tires. He even put new plastic in the windows."

Little and Bixby shouted their thanks as they ran through the open garage door to their car. Jennifer and Angela could hear the car starting up seconds later. Tires squealed as the car took off. Mother and daughter looked at each other with alarm in their eyes, and silently hugged. Jennifer Chandler had the feeling that her family's world was coming apart and would never be the same again.

It did not seem possible that Little could drive faster back towards Minneapolis, but he did. Bixby updated her previously sketchy information on the rider, his bike, and color of the trailer. Unsure of where they were going but knowing they needed to get there fast, Elliott pressed hard and furiously onward. All they needed was a destination.

CHAPTER FORTY – ELVIN MCCORMACK – 7:04 PM

Elvin McCormack was finally showing signs of doing something with his life. After high school, he took law enforcement classes with decidedly average grades, and then applied online to every police department he could. His mother suggested, forcefully, that he should take his resumé and walk in to the stations where he wanted to work and hand his resume over to the person in charge. "They appreciate candidates who show initiative like that." As it turned out, they did not. His parents encouraged him to apply to cities in outstate Minnesota. Elvin told his parents that he had done so, but in reality, he could not see himself living in Albert Lea or Roseau, not that they would have hired him anyway.

No departments were interested, despite the widespread talk of police forces desperate for new faces. Two years passed, and Elvin lamented his fate while indulging in two of his favorite pastimes. The first was competing in online video games using high-end electronics located in his parents' basement. This kept him sprawled in front of a monitor for sometimes up to 20 hours a day. The second indulgence was snacking. Empty or partially eaten bags of Old Dutch potato chips, sour cream and onion predominantly, littered the basement floor. McCormack considered adult diapers as a way to avoid interruptions while engrossed in gaming. He also liked not having to pay for anything while living at his parents.

Finally, his parents decided that it was time to stop enabling their son as he wasted his life away. His mother came home from work one day with an application that she helped Elvin fill out. His father bought him a basic hybrid bicycle and a helmet, and soon Elvin was a bike patrol volunteer on trails and greenways throughout Minneapolis and surrounding suburbs. This transitioned into a weekend auxiliary supervisory role.

Elvin now rode with a radio transmitter clipped to his waist and a microphone attached to the collar of his patrol organization issued jersey. He even had a badge and the authority to give verbal warnings and even issue citations for illegal activity on the trails. True, a citation was really just a written warning with no fines or any other real repercussions, but the educational aspect of the interaction was considered valuable in teaching trail users how to best share the trails with others, and, most importantly, the cars on the roads the riders crossed.

An interview with the Minneapolis Parks and Recreation department as an enforcement officer was scheduled next week. With actual income in the offing, Elvin's parents were beginning to dream of a life without their less rotund but still overweight son claiming squatter's rights to their entire lower level. "We're keeping that monster TV," his father insisted. "It's nicer than either of ours upstairs."

Earlier in the evening, Elvin's radio buzzed and squawked while he was riding his now decal adorned bicycle near Minnehaha Falls, advising that all (both) units be on the lookout for a suspicious looking man riding a bicycle and pulling a trailer with someone, a potential kidnap victim, inside it. When he looked up after hearing the BOLO, Elvin saw three such riders, none of whom looked particularly suspicious, just ordinary, tired people lugging a trailer behind them. He used his keen sense of observation to note that each trailer contained at least one child, and none of the children looked like they were being held against their will.

When the second call came in with more specific detail, Elvin knew he had seen that bike and trailer. In retrospect, the man had looked a bit suspicious, but Elvin knew from his extensive training on that weekend several weeks ago that sometimes your mind sees things it wants to see. Nevertheless, he set off in the direction where he had last seen the rider and hoped he could catch up to him again. Elvin's voice cracked with excitement when he radioed his report in to headquarters and Commander Jette.

Commander Jette was also a volunteer rider, but since he was recovering from recent shoulder surgery in his apartment near Powderhorn Park, he manned his police scanner and directed his staff of three rotating volunteer riders. Neither he nor Elvin could believe that Elvin was in pursuit of the actual suspect. The third volunteer had carried her bike up to her apartment an hour ago but still listened for calls in the event backup was required. This was a dedicated and unpaid staff who all were willing to ignore the time clock.

Either keen sleuthing and deduction, or just blind luck, or perhaps a combination thereof, put Elvin McCormack on East River Parkway about 125 yards behind the bike and trailer in question. Although it violated the rules of biking, Elvin thought it wise to extinguish his front light as darkness settled in. He did, however, keep his red rear light on, just without the strobe feature, not wanting to attract undue attention. He breathlessly gave updates to Commander Jette, who in turn informed the dispatcher at the downtown precinct of MPD, who in turn kept Bixby current on her cell phone.

"He's turning on to the Stone Arch Bridge" informed McCormack.

"Roger that" replied Commander Jette.

"He's stopping. He's getting off his bike. He's opening the trailer flap. Oh my God, there's a woman in the back."

"What's her condition?" Jette asked.

"She's dead. No, wait, she's alive. Never mind, she's definitely alive. For sure. Yup, totally alive."

"Ranger McCormack, you're babbling, son. Get a grip."

"Sorry, sir. Oh my gosh. He's going to throw her over the edge. I'm going to intervene. Wait, he's not throwing her off the bridge, he's just leaning her against the cement rails. Someone has to stop him though. What do I do?"

"Take deep breaths, Ranger McCormack, you're hyperventilating." Commander Jette's little brigade of volunteers was finally going to get the recognition and increased funding they so richly deserved.

With that, radio communication ceased because Elvin accidentally knocked the transmitter off of his waist and stepped on it while dismounting his bike. He had been told to place the transmitter in one of the three pouches on the back of the jersey provided by the club, but he liked it being visible to riders he stopped. It added to the air of authority he wanted to establish, as if to tell them that he could call in for backup if he encountered any resistance whatsoever.

Jette barked out McCormack's name but got no response. He reported to the Minneapolis police dispatcher that communication had been interrupted, and that the suspect and one of his best rangers were on the bridge together, the implication being that a volunteer brigade of bike trail monitors was better at locating a dangerous suspect than all of the Minneapolis police force combined. It was the ultimate moment of glory for the unselected but eager to please.

The dispatcher, not at all interested in adding to the grandeur of a bike ranger, calmly passed along to Bixby that they needed to get to the Stone Arch Bridge as their suspect was with a woman and things looked grim. The dispatcher did not pass along that Ranger McCormack was on the scene. She did not share the commander's confidence in his best volunteer bicycle ranger. Instead, she wondered how they were able to patch into a supposedly secure police line.

CHAPTER FORTY – ONE – CHANDLER – 8:13 PM

It is completely dark and pedestrian and biking traffic has finally dropped off. The Stone Arch Bridge is virtually deserted. It will be like that until closer to midnight, when the party people decide not to use Lyft or Uber and either walk or pedal home. The time is now to make my statement. I turn onto the Stone Arch Bridge and begin to ride towards downtown Minneapolis. Behind me, in the trailer, I can hear some rustling. My human cargo is beginning to stir. I have to either complete my task or keep her incapacitated for two more hours. I am not sure what the cumulative effect of multiple doses of my concoction would entail, so it is time. I ride to the spot where I threw Amy Nyberg into the river and I get off my bike. As before, there is a spot between the circles of light that is quite dark and I can do what I need to do without attracting undue attention.

The doctor of water currents (seriously, water currents?) remains limp as I lift her from the trailer. Her breathing is still shallow and fast, but I can feel that she is coming out of her drug-induced haze. I lean her against the brown metal rails and turn back to the trailer to close the flap so I can ride off as soon as she is in the water.

"Sir, I am going to need you to step away from that lady." The voice behind me sounds weak and quavering.

I look back and see this dweeby kid in a garish biking jersey that reads "Minneapolis Trail Patrol" on the chest. The fabric seems stretched beyond its limits.

"You don't understand," I smile at this bike trail patrol dork. "My girlfriend had too much to drink and I think she is going to throw up." As I say this, I feel in my riding jersey and close my hand on the handle of my knife. I was going to use it on Granger, but if I need to, I will use it on him too. I am confident that I can get the drop on him if needed. He is nothing more than an aggravation.

"Uh, I don't think so. I've been following you and she was in your trailer. I saw you take her out just now."

"That's right. We had to leave her bike back at the bar. She passed out. It's not the first time," I say, a touch of sadness in my voice. My hand tightens around the knife handle. The guy seems too dense to convince of much of anything. Maybe if I offer him some Cheetos he will go away. Instead I offer a 'trust me' smile and open my left hand with the palm showing as a sign of my innocence. Perhaps I could try the 'things we do for our girlfriends' bridge-builder, but I doubt it would resonate with him. He doesn't look to be familiar with having a girlfriend.

Skippy still seems unswayed by my persuasion. "Sir, I think you should step away from the lady while I call the police." He reaches behind himself for what I assume is his cell phone in one of the three back pockets of his jersey.

I wrap my left arm around Dr. Granger's neck. I pull her up to her feet. She is still limp and unable to stand on her own. I pull out the knife and place its blade up to her neck, I glare at the junior cop wannabe. "Don't touch the phone or she gets hurt. Understand? And then I come after you."

From somewhere to my left I hear someone yell: "Drop it or I'll shoot." I am not inclined to drop anything at this point.

CHAPTER FORTY – TWO –
BIXBY AND LITTLE – 8:16 PM

Lights were flashing but the siren was turned off as Little drove maniacally towards the Stone Arch Bridge entrance on Portland and West River Parkway. He flew up 35W, exiting on Washington, and heading west on Washington to Portland. Bernie leaned forward against the shoulder strap, willing them to get there faster. Little squealed to a stop in the parking lot and they both jumped from the car and dashed down the pedestrian bridge. No words were spoken as they sprinted down the bridge to where Abby Granger was being held.

Everything they heard from the dispatcher told them that there was little to be hopeful about with a bike trail patrol volunteer as the closest person to the doctor and her captor. If words had been passed, it was likely that Little would have assured Bixby that he would shoot Chandler first and take any and all consequences that came their way, while fully exonerating Bixby. Abby's safety was paramount to him. The usual constraints placed upon him by the law were going to be subverted this time, and he felt totally justified in doing it.

As they approached at their maddeningly slow fastest sprint, they could see three people at a point just about a third of the way down the bridge. Even in the dark, the volunteer ranger bike jersey stood out in ridiculous luminescence. Both detectives drew their guns as they saw Craig Chandler with this left arm wrapped tightly around Abigail Granger, the bike ranger standing nervously nearby.

"Drop it or I'll shoot," yelled Little as the two came to a stop ten feet from Chandler and Granger. They could see that Chandler held a knife with a narrow blade against Abby's neck, and that she was groggy and unconscious.

"Stay back" warned Chandler. "I'll cut her if you take another step."

"Whoa, no need to hurt anyone here. We can figure this out," said Bixby. She talked calmly as Little lined up his shot. Bixby went through an exaggerated show of returning her gun to its holster, and then showed the palms of both of her hands to Chandler. She gestured for Elvin to step away from the two of them, and then tried to move him a few more feet away with her eyes. Elvin nervously stepped to the side a few feet, but not any farther from Chandler and Granger. If he could run away, he most certainly would have, but fear kept him locked in his spot. This forced Chandler to move his head from side to side to see all three of them.

Chandler's eyes darted back and forth amongst the three now fanned out around him. "Let's not kid ourselves. The only way this ends without the doctor getting hurt is if you step down and let me ride off in your car with the doctor. Him," he gestured at Elvin with his knife. "Him, you can keep him. Otherwise, she gets hurt, probably killed, and at that point I don't care what happens."

As Chandler spoke, Little stared at both the captor and Abby Granger. At first, she seemed listless and almost lifeless. Then, as the conversation went on, she opened her eyes furtively and looked at Elliott. Wordlessly she was alerting him that she was more alert than she was letting on, and that she was willing and able to assist him in taking out Chandler.

"We can't let you leave here with Dr. Granger, and letting you take her in our car is not going to work either. But that doesn't mean you can't help yourself out by letting her go," Bixby intoned. In the background, still a mile away at least, a Minnesota State Patrol helicopter could be heard approaching, its searchlight already brightening streets and buildings as it approached.

"That's not gonna happen. You," he glared at Elvin but did not remove the knife from Abby's neck. "Get over by the other two. I want to be able to see all of you at once."

McCormack looked over at the detectives for affirmation and they nodded. He tried to comply, but his feet refused to move. He stared helplessly at Chandler and the detectives. He was rethinking his decision to pursue a career in law enforcement, even one where he did not carry a gun and patrolled city and county parks looking for litterers, expired bicycle licenses, and those who rode the wrong way on paved trails. Even that seemed terrifying right about now.

One of the many new activities that Elliott Little and Abigail Granger shared, at her insistence, was self-defense training and boxing. Little did not need the training so much as he needed the cardiovascular workout, but Abby had learned several very practical tactics for just this moment in time. Bixby, sensing a play at hand, decided to keep Chandler talking and possibly distracted while her partner set in motion a plan telepathically communicated with Granger.

"How about I switch places with Dr. Granger? She's done nothing wrong, she's just someone who was able to answer some questions we had. Your issue is entirely with us." Bixby held her hands up higher, as though surrendering.

"No, my issue is with her, and you two." Chandler stared at the two detectives, hatred glowing in his cold, impenetrable glare.

Distracted ever so slightly, Abby did a silent and almost imperceptible signal to Little. As she blinked and nodded, he raised his gun. Granger lifted her shoe and slammed it on top of Chandler's left foot. Although they were not full biking shoes, they had very hard bottoms to minimize the energy lost when she pedaled.

Chandler grunted in pain and loosened his grip on her. Abby ducked to her right and elbowed him with gusto in his rib cage with her left elbow. Her training had paid off in significant dividends. His right arm dropped down protectively as he gasped in pain from the double strike he had just received.

Little wasted no time when he saw Abby shift away from Chandler's center mass. Still, wanting to be supremely careful as he pulled the trigger, he struck Chandler in the left shoulder, farthest away from where Granger had been just microseconds before.

Reddish mist flew from the bullet entry point, and Chandler pivoted away from Little as though stepping aside to allow the passage of an imaginary person. In the next seconds his body crashed against the metal fencing and made a dull noise as he struck the railings with great force and momentum. Rather than sink to the ground, however, he remained suspended against the guardrails of the bridge barrier.

Feeling that Chandler temporarily posed no additional threat, Little kept his pistol raised but moved to hold Abby, keeping both of them a safe distance from Chandler. Abby was unsteady on her feet but quite willing to hit Chandler again if given an opportunity. Bixby moved to her right as Little passed in front of her, pulling her gun out as she shifted and pointing it at Chandler. No additional shots were fired.

Although he appeared stunned and unsure what had just happened, Chandler started to rise to his full height again and looked at Bixby as she slowly approached, her gun pointing at his chest. Chandler gave a weak smile of defiance, but instead of surrendering, he lunged at Elvin. He buried the blade of his knife in McCormack's right thigh, completely to the hilt. Bernie looked over at McCormack, and her gun dropped slightly.

Sensing that he had created the distraction he needed, Chandler quickly darted to the side of the bridge, placed his right hand on the top railing, pulled his body upward to the top of the rail, and jumped over it and down to the river below.

Little and Abby Granger rushed to the rail, and pulled together in a deep and wordless hug. Bixby went down on her knees beside Elvin McCormack. No words were spoken for several seconds. Bixby pulled a narrow belt from her suit pants and wrapped it tightly around Elvin's upper thigh, all the while telling him to relax because help was on its way. She kept looking away at the railing, trying to see what was happening in the water.

Elliott pulled out a small but powerful LED flashlight and aimed it at the roiling surface of the river. 30 yards downstream he thought he saw or heard the sound of something breaking the surface of the water and aimed the flashlight beam at it, but neither he nor Granger saw anything that would confirm it. No other signs could be seen for the next several minutes as the two gazed down the river.

"No way someone survives a fall like that after being shot in the shoulder," Little stated with more uncertainly than confidence.

"Actually, there is about a 13 percent chance of survival in a fall of 27 feet with the present currents and water volume per second," responded Dr. Granger. "Remember that it was an average summer in terms of rainfall, and it has not rained in the last 72 hours."

"Of course, she knows that," Bixby noted from behind the couple, pressing her hand against Elvin's wound to stanch the bleeding.

The sound of approaching sirens and flashing lights came quickly. The four could both hear and feel the vibration of approaching police and emergency personnel. The searchlight of the helicopter bathed the bridge deck in stark white light. Elliott waved to the light operator to redirect down the river, but to no avail. The trio remained bathed in the unforgiving searchlight beam while the body of Craig Chandler, the Water Killer, disappeared downstream.

CHAPTER FORTY – THREE – CHANDLER – 8:24 PM

This seems like the right time to mention that I was an all-state diver in high school. Sure, I ride my bicycle more than any other form of exercise these days, but swimming and diving is like riding a bike. You never forget how to do it.

CHAPTER FORTY - FOUR

Elliott Little sat on an uncomfortable bench outside a courtroom in the Hennepin County Government Center in downtown Minneapolis. Beside him sat his partner, Bernadette Bixby. The two of them were waiting to be called into the courtroom by either a bailiff or the judge's clerk. Little was scheduled to appear at 2 PM in front of Judge Brooks, but the judge was running late due to an evidentiary issue involving additional testimony from Sarah Broderick that required the courtroom to be cleared. An elevator pinged and Dr. Abigail Granger stepped out. As she approached the detectives stood. She hugged Bernie and thanked her for coming.

"The law requires my appearance, but under the circumstances I would have been here no matter what," Bernie replied.

Elliott hugged Abby and they kissed. "Are you nervous?" he asked as their embrace lingered.

"Yes, a little," she responded.

"Is this your first time?" Bernie asked.

"Oh, gosh no, I've been nervous before, Bernie. Defending my thesis was quite nerve-wracking." As was typical of Abigail Granger, you could not tell if she was making a horrible pun or being completely serious. Bernie decided she didn't care either way. She was adorable.

"At this point we just sit out here and wait for the judge to call us in," Bixby said.

The two weeks since the events on the Stone Arch Bridge had been hectic. The trio had answered questions and sat in the back of separate squad cars overnight, and then the detectives joined in the search for Craig Chandler's body. Abby was offered a trip to the emergency room for a thorough examination, but she declined, instead expressing a desire to assist with the likely location of the dead body. Elvin McCormack was rushed to the local trauma emergency room where the staff, expert in treating knife wounds, stabilized him. He was released the next morning to his parents' care. The wound, while deep, had not caused significant damage.

It took longer for Dr. Granger to be transported back to her laboratory than it took for her to pinpoint the likely spot that a lifeless body would be found washed up on shore. She was hurried to that location, Elliott still at her side. It was 100 yards downstream from where Chandler's first victim, Amy J. Nyberg, had been found. The difference, she explained, had to do with nocturnal variances and seasonal fluctuations in the velocity of the current.

Regardless of why that spot was the right one, no body was found, but there was no evidence that Chandler had emerged from the water alive either. Sarah Broderick and her team headed up searches up and down the shores of the Mississippi River, along with various local water search and rescue teams on land and in boats, but no one found either a body or any evidence of Chandler walking away from his fall into the river.

The investigation remained open, but the general consensus was that Chandler had perished that night due to the gunshot wound to his shoulder, the fall, or from drowning, or from a combination of the three. Speculation was that his body had been caught under a submerged log or some other underwater trap that might release the body in the next week, or perhaps never. One never knows when the Mississippi River will give up its dead.

For the Chandler family, the onslaught of every type of media created chaos around their house. Daylight had not broken the next morning and local TV station vans with large antennae on top, SUVs, and cars with decals were parked in front of the Chandler home. With crawler headlines saying "Suspected Serial Killer Thought Deceased" scrolling along the bottom of TV screens across the state of Minnesota, four morning broadcasts went live to their reporters in the driveway and in front of the house. It seemed they expected the dripping wet and tired serial killer Craig Chandler to emerge between houses and attempt to let himself in using the garage door keypad.

Jennifer Chandler disconnected her landline phone and called in sick to work using her cell. Friends and family texted and called out of concern or curiosity. Local police were indifferent when called upon to assist with traffic control. The family of a suspected serial killer does not get exemplary service from law enforcement.

Evidence was collected and pieced together now that the perpetrator had been identified. Amy J. Nyberg, Bixby and Little decided, either met Chandler while biking, or when Chandler and his company had dealings with 3M. A careful perusal and comparison of Outlook calendars did not show a mutual meeting, but there had to be some reason why he had chosen her as a victim. They just hadn't found it yet.

The afternoon after the Stone Arch confrontation, Little and Bixby went to the home of Maria Griggs and confirmed to her that her daughter had been the victim of a serial killer. Not wanting to besmirch the memory of Janelle Moreno, they did not reveal their evidence of the too cozy lunch between Chandler and Moreno, or his credit card receipt for lunch and drinks for two. Instead, they told the mother, slumped over with tears running down her cheeks, that they met when she sold him paper, toner, and computer equipment. "Janelle was always so helpful to everyone," her mother sniffed.

Because they refused to believe in coincidences, a post-burial autopsy was performed on Vice Principal Amanda Dean. Her apparent suicide was changed to a likely homicide due to suspicious levels of chemicals that would suppress breathing and heart rate.

Although no evidence was found that categorically connected Chandler to the murders in Coon Rapids and Lake Harriet, the stab patterns provided sufficient proof to conclude that he was responsible, and the cases were closed. The murder of George Rodriguez was easily explained because he had used Chandler's computer without permission. Bixby and Little visited the families of the other victims as well, all the

COINCIDENTAL EVIDENCE

while wondering if providing details about the serial killer helped the families deal with their grief and loss, made things worse, or did not matter at all.

The detectives received an email from the Chief of Police, copying Lieutenant Daniels, that they would be honored in an upcoming ceremony for their "unflagging efforts in solving the well-publicized 'Water Killer' case, and taking a serial killer off the streets. The duo wished wished they could confirm that Craig Chandler was in fact off the streets.

One afternoon, several days after Stone Arch, Little and Bixby sat in a Caribou drinking coffee. "What we may never know, partner, is the 'why'. Most of these deaths look to be purely random acts, a serial killer out looking for his next victim and that person is there at precisely the wrong moment," Bixby postulated.

"I agree," said Elliott. "The best we can tell people is that their loved ones did nothing to deserve what happened to them. They were in the wrong place at the wrong time and they paid the ultimate price for it. Not much solace in that, I'm afraid. Solace means comfort you know."

"Then why not just say comfort?"

The duo sat quietly for a few moments, each thinking about the case that was winding down and on hold until authorities either discovered the corpse of Craig Chandler, or he was arrested somewhere on something as innocuous as a traffic violation and the homicide warrants for his arrest were revealed. Hennepin County initiated grand jury hearings that resulted in in-abstentia multiple first and second-degree homicide indictments being issued after a closed-door proceeding.

The courtroom door opened and two attorneys and one angry looking defendant stalked out of the courtroom. The Assistant County Attorney smiled apologetically, as if to indicate that she was the reason the hearing went long. A few minutes later, the judge's clerk stepped into the hall. "The judge is ready for you, Detective Little. Is everyone here?"

As she said that, the elevator opened and Frankie Bixby rushed out. "Sorry I'm late. I couldn't find a parking spot anywhere. I had to park over by the stadium and run here in my heels." Her face was flushed from the effort. Looking at Abigail Granger, Frankie extended her arms and hugged her. "You look radiant." Granger blushed at the compliment.

"Yes, she does. Your timing is excellent. We just got called in by Judge Brooks," Bernie said, kissing her wife on the cheek as they embraced.

Sarah Broderick was sitting in the spectator area, her testimony complete, tapping notes into her iPad. "You mind if I stay here and witness the event?" she asked. Little nodded and smiled. She had certainly played a part in bringing the two of them together.

Judge Brooks was one of the few Hennepin County judges whom Bixby and Little liked appearing of front of, at least most of the time. He possessed a quick wit, and decided criminal cases fairly. The detectives did not always agree with his decisions, but they always understood the basis for them. And, they had played golf with him at a law enforcement fundraiser for a cancer-stricken patrol officer and found him to be more than tolerable, almost nice even. This is high praise for a judge from homicide detectives.

The courtroom was now dark, with most of the fluorescent bulbs turned off. Desk lamps remained on, and the remaining lights created a more hospitable and warmer atmosphere than usually found in a courtroom. Judge Brooks was leaning against the defense table without his black robe on, and with his white shirt sleeves rolled up to his elbows. His trademark bright red bow tie was tight and precise on his collar. He stood and shook hands with the four people who entered the courtroom. "Thank you, Elliott, for asking me to preside over these proceedings. I am honored and happy to oblige."

Elliott and Abigail had decided that they did not want to wait any longer to get married. Eschewing a long engagement and a formal wedding, they opted instead for a civil ceremony just weeks after the Stone Arch Bridge incident and with Elliot's judge acquaintance presiding. Later, they would host a large reception for family and friends. Today, they decided, was going to be about just them and their two best friends. And Sarah Broderick. "Life contains too many variables to predict accurately," Abby noted.

And with that, their lives together began in a civil matrimonial proceeding, before the watchful eyes of Bernadette and Francis "Frankie" Bixby. Sarah Broderick would report back to her team that the ceremony was expeditious but heartfelt. She carefully documented the scene with an array of photographs, both posed and informal. She wisely resisted collecting physical evidence.

CHAPTER FORTY – FIVE - THREE YEARS LATER

"Mr. Carroll, your four o'clock is here." Wait a second here, I feel like when this story started my last name was Chandler, and I lived in Minnesota. But now, I am in Phoenix and my administrative assistant, Candice, has my next appointment waiting uncomfortably in an alcove outside of my office. He can wait, as I am going to be delivering bad news to him about his limited future with Ellison Pharmaceuticals, headquartered here in Arizona. Let's back up three years, to that night on the Stone Arch Bridge when I got shot in the shoulder and jumped over the bridge railing and landed in the Mississippi. Ouch, in a word.

My high school dive coach would not have been very pleased with my entry into the river, but with my shoulder setting off pain bombs and the overall shock to my system, I feel like I did pretty well. I must have submerged twenty or more feet, but somewhere along the way down towards the murky bottom my instincts took over and I kicked towards the surface. Within seconds I realized that I would be better off staying underwater and allowing the swift current to carry me away from the scene of the crime. I base this on the risk of being shot at, the lights that will illuminate me in the water, and that I cannot use my arms to swim. So, holding my breath and kicking, I travel downstream and away from the bridge and certain capture. When I finally do come up for air, I force myself down immediately and kick as hard as I can.

When I pass the dam, I realize that I am no longer at risk of being shot, and any search and rescue efforts will be too slow to catch me. My shoulder is on fire, but the water temperature and flow are helpful in stanching the bleeding and reducing the swelling. I wonder what risk of infection I face being in the turbid waters of the Mississippi. I turn over on my back and try to formulate a plan, all the while ignoring the pain as best I can. My trusty waterproof pouch is about to become critical.

My hours and many miles of cycling on the banks of either side of the Mississippi River gave me time to run various escape scenarios involving me being in or near the river. I need a spot where I can unobtrusively emerge from the water, and then find clothes and transportation, all the while avoiding being recognized. I exit the river below Marshall Avenue, mostly because my teeth are chattering. I may be in shock due to the gunshot wound. I clamber up the bank. On this night, luck is on my side.

As it is late in the season and well after dark, I walk, dripping water and sloughing off mud, up to the parking lot of an old money golf club, located right on the banks of the river. The valet parking became self-serve when the attendants went off duty. I have my choice of transportation based on the fobs hanging on the hooks on the wooden platform under the overhang at the entrance. I choose a Mercedes fob, press the unlock button as I approach the parking area, and a black SUV blinks its lights at me. I suspect the general manager of the country club is now regretting his cost-saving procedure for self-serve after-hours valet parking. That was too easy. He probably works in Texas now.

The seat warmer, set on high, keeps the shivering to a minimum as I make my way up and down the neighborhood streets around the University of St. Thomas, looking for clothes to grab. I find a maroon University of Minnesota hooded sweatshirt hanging over the railing of a front porch, gray sweat pants left to dry at another house, and a ball cap on a bus stop bench, and my transformation from wet cyclist to unremarkable white dude in ballcap is complete.

The shoulder hurts like nothing I have ever felt before, so I am groaning in agony with each bump the Mercedes goes over. The problem is that a medical facility has a duty to report gunshot wounds, and I most certainly qualify. Plus, I am sure police bulletins have been issued about me as well. I am able to buy some basic wound supplies at a Walgreens without raising suspicion, my teeth gritting as I fake a friendly smile to a bored clerk. His only concern is whether I provide my phone number to associate the purchase to my loyalty account. I do not. I slather on the generic Bacitracin and wrap gauze around the wound. The bullet hit my left shoulder and needs medical attention, far more than I can provide.

I don't have his phone number because my phone is long gone, but I can find the house of a former doctor I know from years ago when we met at college. Dr. Wagoner (is he still allowed to be called that?) lost his medical license due to drug addiction and some very bad decisions made in the pursuit of highs, but he can still provide medical services for cash without the need to report, and with complete discretion. It's a win-win scenario, he can't report me because I can't report him.

He's not thrilled to see me after Fallon or Kimmel has already started, but the hundred dollar bills I peel off mollifies him pretty quickly. Fifteen minutes later I have an appropriate dressing on my shoulder, supplies for when I need to change it, and instructions on how to administer prescription strength antibiotic cream samples he secreted before being banished from his practice. I also learn that I am very lucky that the bullet did not do more serious damage, missing critical spots by a fraction of an inch.

He assures me that the pain will subside in the two or three days. He offers to put me in touch with guys who can sell me something to "take the edge off" of most anything, but I decline. I tell him the pain will keep me alert and focused. He is disappointed that I do not want to buy pain pills and share them with him. The good former doctor has not exorcised all of his demons just yet.

I have one more errand to run before I leave the Twin Cities behind. My contingency plan, which I worked out when I first started acting out on my new hobby, includes a backpack filled with cash in denominations too small to draw attention to but plentiful, a passport, multiple credit cards built around my new identity, a social security card, and a driver's license. I spent thousands of dollars to substantiate the existence of one Craig Carroll, born in Moline, Illinois, and now ready to start his new life somewhere, anywhere, other than Minnesota.

Over the course of the last several months I have been adding to the backpack, securing it in a waterproof plastic bag, wrapping it in a black garbage bag, and hiding it under a pile of rocks located in a city park well away from any amenities. Included in the backpack is a case containing gold-rimmed glasses with no correction in the lens. I put them on. Psychologically, I feel as though the transformation is now complete.

I park the 'borrowed' car at a Wal-Mart parking lot, finally removing my cycling gloves and stuffing them in the backpack. I pay cash for some basic toiletries and a full change of clothes. I walk across the street to a large truck stop convenience store. This is considered an oasis for over the road truckers, with showers and sleeping areas for drivers. I purchase a shower pass and, feeling refreshed but still sore, I put on my new clothes. I manage to keep the dressing reasonably dry while still cleaning up elsewhere. The old clothes are stuffed in the Wal-Mart bag and tossed in an outside dumpster.

I negotiate a ride with someone heading to Omaha as he refills his coffee thermos in the all-night cafe. Soon I am dozing off in the passenger seat heading down interstate 35, my backpack at my feet. Three rides later and I am anonymously in Arizona. At one of the stops I buy a pre-paid smart phone and read all about the intense search and rescue underway for Craig Chandler. Is he alive or dead? In many ways he is dead, but in one very important way he lives on.

I also use my cell phone to find a marginally furnished room for rent for a month at a time that accepts cash and asks few questions. I have credit cards but I want to use them judiciously at first. I use Craigslist and buy an older Accord in good mechanical condition.

It takes two weeks for me to get aligned with a recruiter who, for a substantial fee, will vouch for my background with an employer so that they do not do their own due diligence checks. "I golf with the guy twice a week, and he owes me big-time," he explains. He further advises that the higher up in a company the opening exists, the more inclined they are to accept the word of a well-respected recruiter with a good track history.

Three new suits, three face-to-face interviews, only one of which is perfunctory, and Craig Carroll, he of the fresh make-believe background, is the new Vice President of Business Development and Strategic Enterprises at Ellison Pharmaceuticals. My salary and bonus potential are significantly higher than what I would have received at Watson United, the job I did not take due to my disappearance and some rather alarming news stories about me. My recruiter, now knee deep in the conspiracy, pushes them at the end for a significant upfront housing allowance and reserved parking. While his morals are iffy, his negotiating skills are superb. The two might be connected.

My first day on the job is probably the most nerve-wracking I have ever experienced. All new Ellison employees, even executives, are required to provide their driver's license, birth certificate, and social security card. The driver's license was not a big deal, as I had turned in my old one from Illinois and received the new Arizona license the same day a few weeks ago. That was a relief. But, would my other phony documents work? I only half-listened to the exuberant HR gal as she excitedly recited factoids about Ellison history and its impact on the Phoenix community and Arizona as a whole.

When my documents are returned at the first break with no questions asked, I am so relieved that I agree to a voluntary charitable giving deduction from each paycheck and a DNA sample as a way to reduce my monthly health insurance premium by ten percent a month. Who doesn't want to pay less for health insurance these days? My healing shoulder has been creaking lately so I know I will be seeing a doctor soon about that. A hunting trip with college buddies, lots of beer, and a wrestling match gone wrong will be my explanation of the wound. "We won't allow guns in the lodge next year," is what I intend to say. Men dressed in expensive suits get away with fact-deficient explanations all the time.

After opening a bank account with a series of deposits, and stacking up my remaining cash in a safety deposit box, I buy a house in Paradise Valley. I guess that qualifies as money laundering. My rise within Ellison is fairly steep, as I am now a Senior Vice President. My bonuses are ridiculous based on our introduction of a new drug regimen that reduces the medications necessary after a kidney replacement. Ridiculous.

I create bogus social media accounts to creep on my now ex-wife and kids. Jennifer seems happy with Richie, a pig farmer who practices estate planning law on the side, or vice versa. My daughters are doing well also. I am glad they have moved on without me. I do not really miss them that much because I am so engaged in my new life.

Here at Ellison, I am still the one who handles all reduction in force appointments. For what I get paid, I am happy to do it. Everyone else abhors them, I love them. Line them up and I will set them free. I am excited about all of the careers I have ended today. Excited, but I am doubting that it will enough to keep me from introducing Phoenix to the desert version of the Water Killer.

I am lost in my reverie, amazed but always appreciative of my good fortune, when my desk phone buzzes. Candice, my admin, informs me that a Paradise Valley detective is here to discuss some thefts that have been occurring in my neighborhood. My girlfriend had called in to report that her BMW had been broken into a few weeks ago, I am impressed with the personal visit on something so minor, since all she lost were designer sunglasses and the car had scratches on the driver side door. I ask her to send him in.

"OK," she says. "I'll send them, I mean, him, in."

CHAPTER FORTY-SIX

Sarah Broderick introduced a new procedure for the Minneapolis Police Department a few months after the incident on the Stone Arch Bridge. It involved collecting DNA from every crime scene possible, and running it through databases across the country. Any case that her department worked on where DNA evidence was collected was uploaded to a database and website that ran the samples against those collected by other law enforcement agencies across the world to help solve cold cases.

Due to the volume of the samples and her team's limitations on time and resources, it took her almost six months to upload the DNA sample collected off of a water bottle left on the bicycle ridden by Craig Chandler, and abandoned on the Stone Arch Bridge on the night Chandler presumably died in the Mississippi River.

Her expectation, if she had any, was that his DNA would link him to unsolved abductions or homicides in other jurisdictions, allowing them to be closed out and the affected families notified of the likely perpetrator. No matches were ever found, despite the addition of new samples daily across several states. Two years passed by and other case wins justified the ongoing practice.

While attending a family function one Sunday afternoon, Broderick heard a heartwarming story about her adopted cousin finding his birth mother back in New York using a consumer genealogy site. While driving home later that afternoon, she wondered if law enforcement had any restrictions against uploading DNA collected at crime scenes to consumer genealogy sites as well. Her research the next morning indicated that it was acceptable, so long as the original sample was collected legally. While it would mean a significant amount of menial and repetitive work, she added that to her checklist of things to do while at her desk as other tests were running.

It was a rainy Tuesday afternoon when she got a most curious result. She double-checked the protocol on her end, and emailed the tester at the other end in Palo Alto, who confirmed the validity of his findings. Excitedly, she called Bernie Bixby, who answered on the first ring. Bixby had submitted something for testing that morning, and was surprised at the quick turnaround.

"You got something on Beckel?" Bernie asked. Every request made of the crime scene lab included begging that it be placed at the head of the line, but it never seemed to happen. Bernie figured she had caught a break and her request for a rush job had finally been accommodated.

"No, Beckel is still in line to be processed. I doubt it will be available before tomorrow afternoon. But what I do have is very interesting. I think you will want to have Detective Little hear this as well."

CHAPTER FORTY-SEVEN

Ken Golden worked as a detective in robbery and property crimes for the Paradise Valley Police Department. He started his career in law enforcement in Portland, but moved to Arizona so his wife could find relief from her allergies. Other than the unrelenting heat of Phoenix summers, he liked his job and his life, looking forward to retiring in the next five years, sooner if the city offered enticements. He liked where they lived so much that he did not anticipate leaving their paid-for house upon retirement. The pool, the cabana that slept four, and a nearby golf course made their house a desirable destination for the rest of the family for several months of the year.

An email awaited him that morning as he sipped his coffee and got settled in for the day. It had been forwarded to him by his supervisor, who had received it originally from the chief. The email started its journey back in Minnesota, written by Lieutenant Everett Daniels, requesting local assistance with the arrest of a person suspected of multiple homicides. As a courtesy, since the suspect lived in Paradise Valley, local law enforcement was made aware of the situation, and asked to assist. A reciprocal courtesy would be extended at some point when requested. Golden was asked to meet two Minneapolis detectives, Elliott Little and Bernie Bixby, at the Phoenix Sky Harbor International Airport when they landed at 1:43 PM on a Southwest Airlines flight.

Cops always recognize cops, so deciding which disembarking

passengers were Detectives Little and Bixby was easy. Golden was initially surprised that both detectives were black, and that one was female, but their attentive and always active eyes gave them away as law enforcement. Little and Bixby had no problem identifying their local counterpart either with his square jaw and graying hair worn in a tight crewcut.

In Golden's car heading towards the Paradise Valley office, Bixby, sitting in the front seat, gave the background for their visit and their assignment. Her soliloquy took almost half an hour.

"Wait a minute," Golden said, turning his head for a second towards Elliott in the back seat. "You're telling me this Chandler guy grabbed one of your expert witnesses but you shot him, and then he jumped over the bridge railing and into the Mississippi River, you thought he was dead, but his DNA showed up because he gave a sample for his new employer here in Phoenix like three years ago?"

"That is exactly it," Elliott Little leaned forward from the back seat. "We thought he drowned and his body never came up out of the river, and then one of our tech people hits pay dirt on some random DNA site. Turns out, it's becoming a thing, finding killers and fugitives based on DNA searches."

"And," Bixby jumped in. "If Elliott could shoot straight, the guy would have been dead before he hit the water. Someone should teach that man how to use a gun."

"That lady doctor sounds like she's pretty smart," Golden

asked, ignoring Bixby's comment. "It's a good thing you two saved her."

"Well, she married Elliott right after the rescue. They're expecting their second child in another six weeks or so." Bernie smiled. "And, they're going to name the child Bixby. That's my last name you know."

"I think we agreed to name our next dog after you. But, you and Frankie are going to be the godparents again," Little said. "That's quite an honor."

Once at the station, the three met in a small conference room and made their plans for the arrest of Craig Chandler, AKA Craig Carroll. Golden noted that there had been several reports of vandalism and thefts out of cars left in driveways and carports in Paradise Valley. In fact, he found a report from the Carroll home, phoned in by a Lora Towns, presumably Carroll's girlfriend. "We could call and ask to see Carroll this afternoon, and you two could tag along and pop him."

"Would he believe that a detective would want a face-to-face meeting on a car break-in report? We would never do that in Minneapolis," Bixby asked.

"He lives in a house worth north of a million bucks. He probably expects a face-to-face. Besides, how does he know whether we do personal visits on vandalism and car break-in cases?" Golden replied. The visiting detectives nodded their heads in agreement, impressed with the logic and the simplicity of the plan.

COINCIDENTAL EVIDENCE

The trio arrived shortly before 4 PM, and settled in chairs outside the closed door of Craig Carroll, each wearing visitor tags. A nervous-looking gentleman moved over to make room for the three new visitors.

As an extension of the original courtesy, the head of Ellison Pharmaceuticals, a former homicide detective himself from Dallas, was made aware and offered his staff as needed. "It would appear we have a flaw in our hiring protocols," he concluded. "Once you get him out of here, I'll reach out to our HR department and let them know they hired a serial killer. That should create quite a stir."

Golden asked Candice, the friendly and competent admin to Craig Carroll, to tell Mr. Carroll that he was the only one waiting to see him. "It's a surprise," he winked at her.

She buzzed Carroll to let him know his appointment was outside his door. "OK," she said. "I'll send them, I mean, him, in." Candice looked at the three detectives in alarm, mouthing an apology. The three of them leapt out of their seats and moved quickly towards the door.

Golden maneuvered the handle downward and pushed the door open, stepping to the side to allow Bixby and Little to enter. Carroll looked over from his computer screen, surprise showing in his eyes as three people entered instead of one. He looked at the large windows on two walls of his corner office, but realized that he could not jump through them, and that he was on the highest floor. Then, a look of resignation settled in. He rose, adjusted his suit pants, put his hands together and lifted them in front of his body, realizing that the game had finally been lost.

EPILOGUE

Craig Chandler waived extradition when a young Maricopa County prosecutor informed his hastily retained defense attorney that if Chandler stayed in the state of Arizona the death penalty would be considered strongly, as Chandler advanced his conspiracy to commit murder while living in the state. He was transported back to Minnesota in handcuffs and leg shackles on a Southwest Airlines direct flight. He sat between Little and Bixby, a blanket covering his lap and the handcuffs. An air marshal sat directly behind them. Chandler made no attempt to escape, and enjoyed priority boarding and deplaning.

On his second court appearance, Craig Chandler surprised the court and changed his plea to guilty. At his third court appearance, the judge sentenced him to five consecutive life sentences with no chance of parole. Chandler was transported to Bayport and the maximum-security prison, where he remains today. He is allowed one hour of outside exercise per day, but prefers lifting weights and doing calisthenics in his solitary cell. He is protected from harm by a cadre of beefy inmates of multiple ethnicities based on his help in writing their prisoner appellate briefs.

He earned the right to unlimited computer time to write his

memoir, working title "Reflections - The True Story of the Water Killer", by assisting the warden in establishing a rolling furlough policy that delayed staff reductions. He then coached the warden on how to handle reduction in force meetings. Chandler is considering a digital self-publishing arrangement, with movie rights to be negotiated separately. He wonders if Jake Gyllenhaal has the emotional range necessary to portray him. Having him record the audiobook would be a good test.

Jennifer Chandler accomplished a dissolution of marriage in-abstentia in Faribault County. She had her last name restored to Sales, and petitioned the court to have her daughters' names changed as well. Mallory, the oldest daughter, graduated from Blue Earth High School and is attending college at a private liberal arts college in Vermont, where no one has ever heard of the Water Killer, or Craig Chandler. Angela is a sophomore at Blue Earth. She also intends to leave the state for college. Jennifer works at a coffee shop in Blue Earth. She is dating a lawyer with whom she graduated from high school who chose to stay in his hometown. She has thus far resisted the offer to move in with him at his hog farm.

Elvin McCormack nailed his interview with the Minneapolis Parks and Recreation enforcement supervisor based on his story about how he was instrumental in the capture of the infamous Water Killer. His right thigh was still wrapped and he walked with an exaggerated limp into her office. The supervisor hired Elvin and assigned him to three city parks in and around Lake Nokomis once he recovered. He has not yet encountered a hostage situation, but now has the ability to give real citations with actual dollar fines to bike riding miscreants.

Sarah Broderick was promoted to a supervisory position in the crime scene and laboratory department, a long overdue advancement. She insists on spending as much time in the field as she can, and has hired a technician who specializes in submitting DNA samples across the world. While nothing as notorious as the Water Killer case has been solved, the successes justify continuing the effort.

Dr. Abigail Granger–Little and her husband, Elliott, recently welcomed their second child Magdalena, into their lives. She and the family are doing well. Discussions are underway to sell their condominium with the amazing views and move to a house, perhaps in Northeast Minneapolis. Colleagues and friends were surprised that Abby takes the full allotment of six months off before returning to work. She continues to surprise her colleagues by leaving work at the same time they do, and availing herself of the relaxed rules regarding working from home on Fridays, or taking meetings via Zoom from her home office, children nearby. Photographs of the Little family are displayed all over both of their work areas.

Bernadette Bixby and her wife Frankie are indeed the doting godparents to the children. Bernie is only slightly kidding when she castigates Elliott for not naming either of his children after his best friend and longtime partner. Elliott did keep his promise, however, and named their dog, an energetic labradoodle, Bixby. Bernie was only slightly appeased by the gesture.

The End

ACKNOWLEDGEMENTS

This is a work of fiction. The characters in this book are all creations of my imagination. Speaking of which, I want to be clear that I do **not** have a dark side. Craig Chandler is not my alter ego, nor does he mirror me in any way. I simply heard lots of stories from friends and colleagues who lost their jobs over the years, and from that an idea formed for a main character who has a very dark side indeed.

I first started writing this novel in 2013, not long after being laid off after almost 20 years at the same company. It started out, in all honesty, as a revenge project, and waned during the first year as the need to find my next work opportunity became more pressing. In 2017, I realized how much I enjoyed and missed writing. I took up this novel again, working nights, weekends, and discovered that I am very creative and energetic around 4 AM each morning.

As early drafts were underway, I used my longtime friend Patrick McCormack as my reviewer and muse. His encouragement and sage advice kept me going. While Elvin McCormack shares Patrick's last name, they are not related. Patrick told me I needed to bulk up the climactic bridge scene, so I that's what I did. What better way to show my appreciation?

Patrick and several others of the "Austin Crowd" get together on Tuesday nights to golf, poorly. Their names, or adaptations thereof, were used in this book. Reestablishing the connection with all of them is a high point of every week. I am honored and privileged to call all them my friends. I have learned that you don't get away with much when you hang around people who have known you since fourth grade.

I took advantage of several hours together in a car traveling from Chicago to our home in Minnesota to read a draft to my daughters, Amy and Amanda. Their insight and suggestions were invaluable. Amy helped edit later versions of the book, and Amanda helped with cover designs and all things marketing. Sorry that two of the victims share your names. They are, in my defense, very popular names.

Thank you to two very special women, my mother Jaqueline (OJ), and my wife Jodi. From my mother I received the gift of a lifelong love of reading. Even in the final stages of Alzheimer's, she still worked her daily crosswords and read what my Dad calls "Grown up Hardy Boy books." I know she will get a chance to read what I have done because Amazon Prime delivers everywhere. Jodi indulged me as I spent countless hours in front of the computer, writing and editing, editing and writing. Sorry I could not watch all of those YouTube videos about restoring Air Streams, Big Foot, volcanoes, and the making of the Star Wars movies with you. Thank you and love always.

Finally, if you are reading this, chances are you finished reading my novel. Please leave a review and let other potential readers know your thoughts. If you have questions or comments, or just want to send me an email to see if I will respond, use: **HMBudde2012@gmail.com**. Stay in touch.

Also, stay up to date by following me on my author page: https://www.amazon.com/-/e/B082842CV5

Mernie Budde, December, 2019